Cimarron Rose

James Lee Burke

Cimarron Rose

WHEELER
PUBLISHING, INC.
ROCKLAND, MA

★ AN AMERICAN COMPANY ★

1515 7090

Published in Large Print by arrangement with
Hyperion in the United States and Canada.

Wheeler Large Print Book Series.

Set in 16 pt Plantin.

Library of Congress Cataloging-in-Publication Data

Burke, James Lee, 1936–
    Cimarron rose / James Lee Burke.
        p. (large print) cm.(Wheeler large print book series)
    ISBN 1-56895-527-8 (hardcover)
    1. Trials (Murder)—Texas—Fiction. 2. Teenage boys—Texas—Fiction.
3. Texas—Fiction. 4. Large type books.
I. Title. II. Series
[PS3552.U723C56 1998]
813'.54—dc21
                                                                        97-43874
                                                                            CIP

To my mother,
Mrs. James L. Burke, Sr.,

and my aunt and uncle,
Mr. and Mrs. James Brown Benbow

Cimarron Rose

CHAPTER

I

My great-grandfather was Sam Morgan
Holland, a drover who trailed cows up the
Chisholm from San Antonio to Kansas. Most
of his life Great-grandpa Sam fought whiskey
and Indians and cow thieves and with some
regularity watched gully washers or dry
lightning spook his herds over half of Oklahoma
Territory.

Whether it was because of busthead whiskey
or just the bad luck to have lost everything he
ever worked for, he railed at God and the
human race for years and shot five or six men
in gun duels. Then one morning, cold sober,
he hung his chaps and clothes and Navy Colt
revolvers on a tree and was baptized by immer-
sion in the Guadalupe River. But Great-
grandpa Sam found no peace. He sat each
Sunday on the mourners' bench at the front
of the congregation in a mud-chinked Baptist
church, filled with an unrelieved misery he
couldn't explain. One month later he decided
to ride to San Antonio and kill his desire for
whiskey in the only way he knew, and that was
to drink until he murdered all the warring voices
inside his head.

On the trail he met a hollow-eyed preacher
whose face had been branded with red-hot
horseshoes by Comanches north of the Cimarron. The preacher made Sam kneel with him
in a brush arbor, then unexpectedly grasped

1

Sam's head in his hands and ordained him. Without speaking again he propped his Bible against Sam's rolled slicker and disappeared over a hill into a dust cloud and left no tracks on the other side.

For the rest of his life, Great-grandpa Sam preached out of the saddle in the same cow camps his herds had trampled into shredded canvas and splintered wagon boards when he was a drover.

His son, Hackberry, who was also known in our family as Grandpa Big Bud, was a Texas Ranger who chased Pancho Villa into Old Mexico. As a young lawman he locked John Wesley Hardin in the county jail and was still wearing a badge decades later when he stuffed Clyde Barrow headfirst down a trash can in a part of Dallas once known as "The Bog."

But Grandpa Big Bud always made sure you knew he was not at Arcadia, Louisiana, when Bonnie Parker and Clyde were trapped inside their car by Texas Rangers and sawed apart with Browning automatic rifles and Thompson .45 submachine guns.

"You don't figure they had it coming?" I once asked him.

"People forget they wasn't much more than kids. You cain't take a kid down without shooting him a hundred times, you're a piss-poor Ranger in my view," he said.

My grandfather and his father were both violent men. Their eyes were possessed of a peculiar unfocused light that soldiers call the thousand-yard stare, and the ghosts of the men

2

they had killed visited them in their sleep and stood in attendance by their deathbeds. When I was a young police officer in Houston, I swore their legacy would never be mine.

But if there are drunkards in your family, the chances are you will drink from the same cup as they. The war that can flare in your breast with each dawn doesn't always have to come from a charcoal-lined barrel.

I lived alone in a three-story late-Victorian house built of purple brick, twenty miles from the little town of Deaf Smith, the county seat. The house had a second-story veranda and a wide, screened-in gallery, the woodwork painted a gleaming white. The front and back yards were enclosed by poplar trees and myrtle bushes and the flower beds planted with red and yellow roses.

I made sun tea in big jars on the gallery, grilled steaks for friends under the chinaberry tree in the backyard, and sometimes cane-fished with a bunch of Mexican children in the two-acre tank, or lake, at the back of my farm. But at night my footsteps rang off the oak and mahogany woodwork inside my house like stones dropped down an empty well.

The ghosts of my ancestors did not visit me. The ghost of another man did. His name was L.Q. Navarro. In life he was the most handsome man I ever knew, with jet black hair and wide shoulders and skin as brown and smooth as newly dyed leather. When he

3

appeared to me he wore the clothes he had died in, a dark pinstriped suit and dusty boots, a floppy gray Stetson, a white shirt that glowed like electrified snow. His hand-tooled gunbelt and holstered revolver hung on his thigh like a silly afterthought. Through the top buttonhole of his shirt he had inserted the stem of a scarlet rose.

Sometimes he disappeared into sunlight, his form breaking into millions of golden particles. At other times I did pro bono work on hopeless defenses, and my spectral visitor declared a temporary amnesty and waited patiently each night by himself among the mesquite trees and blackjack oaks on a distant hillside.

The phone rang at 10 A.M. on a Sunday morning in April.

"They got my boy in the jailhouse. I want him out," the voice said.

"Is that you, Vernon?"

"No, it's the nigger in the woodpile."

Vernon Smothers, the worst business mistake in my life. He farmed seventy acres of my land on shares, and I had reached a point where I was almost willing to pay him not to come to work.

"What's he charged with?" I asked.

I could hear Vernon chewing on something—a piece of hard candy, perhaps. I could almost see the knotted thoughts in his eyes as he looked for the trap he always found in other people's words.

"Vernon?"

"He was drunk again. Down by the river."

"Call a bondsman."

"They made up some lies…They're saying he raped a girl down there."

"Where's the girl?"

"At the hospital. She ain't conscious so she cain't say who done it. That means they ain't got no case. Ain't that right?"

"I want a promise from you…If I get him out, don't you dare put your hand on him."

"How about you just mind your own god-damn business, then?" he said, and hung up.

The county courthouse was built of sandstone, surrounded by a high-banked green lawn and live-oak trees whose tops touched the third story. The jailer was named Harley Sweet and his mouth always hung partly open while you spoke, as though he were patiently trying to understand your train of thought. But he was not an understanding man. When he was a deputy sheriff, many black and Mexican men in his custody never reached the jail. Nor thereafter did they stay on the same sidewalk as he when they saw him coming in their direction.

"You want to see Lucas Smothers, do you? We feed at twelve-thirty. Better come back after then," he said. He slapped a fly on his desk with a horse quirt. He looked at me, slack-jawed, his eyes indolent, waiting God knows for what.

"If that's the way you want it, Harley. But

5

from this moment on, he'd better not be questioned unless I'm present."

"You're representing him?"

"That's correct."

He got up from his desk, opened a door with a frosted glass window in it, and went inside an adjoining office. He came back with a handful of Polaroid pictures and dropped them on his desk.

"Check out the artwork. That's what she looked like when he got finished with her. She had semen in her vagina and he had it inside his britches. She had skin under her finger-nails and he has scratches on his body. I cain't imagine what the lab will say. You can really pick your cases, Billy Bob," he said.

"Where was she?"

"Thirty yards from where he was passed out." He started to drink out of his coffee cup, then set it back down. His silver snap-button cowboy shirt shimmered with light. "Oh hell, you want to spend your Sunday morning with a kid cain't tell the difference between shit and bean dip, I'll call upstairs. You know where the elevator's at."

When other boys in high school played base-ball or ran track, Lucas Smothers played the guitar. Then the mandolin, banjo, and Dobro. He hung in black nightclubs, went to camp meetings just for the music, and ran away from home to hear Bill Monroe in Wichita, Kansas. He could tell you almost any detail

6

about the careers of country musicians whose names belonged to a working-class era in America's musical history that had disappeared with five-cent Wurlitzer jukeboxes—Hank and Lefty, Kitty Wells, Bob Wills, the Light Crust Dough Boys, Rose Maddox, Patsy Montana, Moon Mullican, Texas Ruby.

His hands were a miracle to watch on a stringed instrument. But in his father's eyes, they, like Lucas himself, were not good for anything of value.

When he was sixteen Vernon caught him playing triple-neck steel in a beer joint in Lampasas and beat him so unmercifully with a razor strop in the front yard that a passing truck driver climbed out of his cab and pinned Vernon's arms to his sides until the boy could run next door.

Lucas sat shirtless in blue jeans and a pair of scuffed cowboy boots on the edge of a bunk in a narrow cell layered with jailhouse graffiti. His face was gray with hangover and fear, his reddish blond hair spongy with sweat. His snap-button western shirt lay at his feet. It had blue-and-white checks in it, and white cloth in the shoulders with tiny gold trumpets stitched in it. He had paid forty dollars for the shirt when he had first joined the band at Shorty's.

"How you feel?" I asked, after the turnkey locked the solid iron door behind me.

"Not too good." His wrists were thick, his wide hands cupped on top of his knees. "They tell you about the girl...I mean, like how's she doing?"

7

"She's in bad shape, Lucas. What happened?"

"I don't know. We left Shorty's, you know, that joint on the river. We was kind of making out in my truck...I remember taking off my britches, then I don't remember nothing else."

I sat down next to him on the bunk. It was made of cast iron and suspended from the wall by chains. A thin mattress covered with brown and yellow stains fit inside the rectangular rim. I picked up his hands in mine and turned them over, then pressed my thumb along his finger joints, all the time watching for a flinch in his face.

"A lady's going to come here this afternoon to photograph your hands. In the meantime don't you do anything to bruise them," I said. "Who's the girl?"

"Her name's Roseanne. That's all she told me. She come in with a mess of other people. They run off and left her and then her and me got to knocking back shots. I wouldn't rape nobody, Mr. Holland. I wouldn't beat up a girl, either," he said.

"How do you know?"

"Sir?"

"You don't remember what you did, Lucas...Look at me. Don't sign anything, don't answer any of their questions, don't make a statement, no matter what they promise you. You with me?"

"My father got you to come down here?"

"Not exactly."

His blue eyes lingered on mine. They were bloodshot and full of pain, but I could see them trying to reach inside my mind.

"You need a friend. We all do at one time or another," I said.

"I ain't smart but I ain't stupid, either, Mr. Holland. I know about you and my mother. I don't study on it. It ain't no big deal to me."

I stood up from the bunk and looked out the window. Down the street people were coming out of a brick church with a white steeple, and seeds from cottonwood trees were blowing in the wind and I could smell chicken frying in the back of a restaurant.

"You want me to represent you?" I said.

"Yes, sir, I'd sure appreciate it."

He stared emptily at the floor and didn't look up again.

I stopped at Harley's office downstairs.

"I'll be back for his arraignment," I said.

"Why'd he have to beat the shit out of her?"

"He didn't."

"I guess he didn't top her, either. She probably artificially inseminated herself."

"Why don't you shut up, Harley?"

He rubbed his chin with the ball of his thumb, a smile at the corner of his mouth, his eyes wandering indolently over my face.

Outside, as I got into my Avalon, I saw him crossing the courthouse lawn toward me, the sunlight through the trees freckling on his face. I closed my car door and waited. He leaned one arm on the roof, a dark loop of sweat under his armpit, and smiled down at me, his words gathering in his mouth.

"You sure know how to stick it up a fellow's snout, Billy Bob. I'll surely give you that, yessir. But at least I ain't killed my best friend and I don't know anybody else who has. Have a good day," he said.

CHAPTER

2

Lucas's arraignment was at eleven Monday morning. At 8 A.M. I met a sheriff's deputy at the courthouse and rode with her in her cruiser to the spot on the river where Lucas and the girl from Shorty's had been found.

The deputy's name was Mary Beth Sweeney. She wore a tan uniform, with a lead-colored stripe down the side of each trouser leg, and a campaign hat that slanted over her brow. Her face was powdered with pale brown freckles and her dark brown hair hung in curls to her shoulders. She was new to the department and seemed to have little interest in either me or her assignment.

"Were you a law officer somewhere else?" I asked.

"CID in the army."

"You didn't want to work for the feds after you got out?" I said.

She raised her eyebrows and didn't answer. We passed Shorty's, a ramshackle club built on pilings over the water, then pulled into an old picnic area that had gone to seed among a grove of pine trees. Yellow crime scene tape was stretched in the shape of a broken octagon around the tree trunks.

"You responded to the 911?" I said.

"I was the second unit to arrive."

"I see."

I got out of the cruiser and stepped under the yellow tape. But she didn't follow me.

"Where was the girl?" I said.

"Down there in those bushes by the water."

"Undressed?"

"Her clothes were strewn around the ground."

"On the ground by her?" I said.

"That's right."

The soil in the clearing was damp and shady, and tire tracks were stenciled across the pine needles that had fallen from the trees.

"And Lucas was in his truck, passed out? About here?" I said.

"Yes, sir."

"You don't have to call me 'sir.'"

I walked down to the riverbank. The water was green and deep, and cottonwood seeds swirled in eddies on top of the current.

"You know, I never heard of a rapist being arrested because he was too drunk to flee the crime scene," I said.

But the deputy didn't answer me. The ground among the bushes was crisscrossed with

11

dozens of footprints. I walked back to where Lucas's truck had been parked. Mary Beth Sweeney still stood outside the crime scene tape, her hands in her back pockets. Her arms looked strong, her stomach flat under her breasts. Her black gunbelt was polished and glinted with tiny lights.

"This is quite a puzzle," I said.

"The sheriff just told me to give you the tour, Mr. Holland."

She put on a pair of dark green aviator's sunglasses and looked at the river.

"Did Lucas attack her in his truck, then pass out? Or did he attack her in the brush and walk back to his truck, have a few more drinks and then pass out?" I said. "You don't have an opinion?"

"I'll drive you back to your car if you're ready," she said.

"Why not?" I said.

We drove through rolling fields that were thick with bluebonnets and buttercups, then crossed a rusted iron bridge over the river. The river's bottom was soap rock, and deep in the current you could see the gray, moss-covered tops of boulders and the shadows they made in the current.

"You're pleading your man innocent?" she said.

"You bet...You think I'm firing in the well?"

"I just wondered," she said, and didn't speak again until we pulled into the shade of the live oaks that surrounded the courthouse.

I walked to my car, then turned unexpectedly and caught her watching me, her sunglasses hanging from her fingers.

I stopped the prosecutor outside his office just before Lucas's arraignment. The corridor was empty, and our voices echoed off the old marble floor and high wood ceiling.

"You're not going to jam us up on the bail, are you, Marvin?" I said.

"Don't expect any slack on this one, Billy Bob," he replied.

He wore a bowtie and seersucker suit, and his face looked at me with the quiet moral certitude of an ax blade.

"You don't have a rape case. You're not going to make assault and battery without a weapon, either," I said.

"Oh?"

"Lucas doesn't have a bruise on him."

"You see the medical report on her genitalia? Or maybe that's just Lucas's idea of rough sex...You want to talk about weapons? How about if he beat her face on the side of the truck?"

"You have evidence of that?"

"It poured down Saturday night. The whole crime scene was washed clean."

"Pretty convenient, Marvin."

"No, pretty sickening. And the charge isn't assault and battery. Where have you been this morning?"

I stared into the righteous light in his eyes and knew, with a sinking of the heart, what was coming next.

"She died an hour ago. The doc says it was probably a brain hemorrhage. You want to plea out, give me a call. He's not going to do the big sleep, but I guarantee you he'll get to be an expert at picking state cotton," he said.

Because Lucas was being arraigned on a Monday morning, he was brought to court on the same wrist chain as the collection of DWIs, wife beaters, and barroom brawlers who had been in the drunk tank over the weekend. Each Monday morning they would ride down to the first floor in an elevator that resembled a packed zoo cage and, in stumbling peckerwood or black or Mexican accents, offer their explanations for the mercurial behavior that seemed to affect their lives like a windstorm blowing arbitrarily through a deserted house.

Normally the weekend miscreants waved at their friends in the courtroom or punched one another in the ribs and snickered while one of their members tried to talk his bail down. But not today. When they sat in the row of chairs at the front of the court and the bailiff unlocked their wrists and dropped the chain to the wood floor, they rounded their shoulders and looked at their shoes or moved a chair space away from Lucas, as though eye contact or proximity to him would stain them with a level of guilt that was not theirs.

I stood next to him when it was his turn to rise and face the court. His father had brought him a clean white shirt and flowered tie and pair of starched khakis, but he was unshaved and his wavy hair was uncut and wet and combed straight back on his collar, so that he looked like a 1950s hood rather an uneducated rural kid whose father had belittled him since he was a child.

Marvin, the prosecutor, asked that Lucas's bail be set at $200,000.

I heard Lucas's breath catch in his throat. I touched the back of his wrist with mine.

"Your Honor, my client is just nineteen and has very little in the way of resources. He has no felony arrests of any kind. He's lived his whole life in this county. The bail request is not only unreasonable, it's deliberately punitive. The real problem is, Marvin doesn't have a case and he knows it."

The judge's glasses were orbs of light and the lines in his face seemed gathered around his mouth like crinkles in papier-mâché. "'Punitive' is it? Tell that to the family of the dead girl. I also love your first-name familiarity. There is nothing I find more heartwarming than to feel I'm involved in a court proceeding that might be conducted by Lum and Abner. Bail is set at one-hundred-fifty-thousand dollars. Count yourself fortunate, counselor," he said, and clicked his gavel on a small wood block.

On the way out of the courtroom Vernon Smothers's gnarled hand clenched on my forearm. His gray eyes were jittering with anger.

"Everything you touch turns to shit, Billy Bob," he said.

"Go home, Vernon," I replied.

"I don't want my boy locked up with low-rent nigras. Get him in a special cell or something."

"Don't go home. Find a wastebasket and stand in it, Vernon," I said.

I rode up in the elevator with Lucas and a deputy. Lucas's lower body was draped in a clinking net of waist and leg chains. The deputy slid back the wire-mesh door on the elevator, then used a key to unlock a second, barred door that swung out onto the third floor. We walked under a row of electric lights with wire baskets over the bulbs, our footsteps echoing off the sandstone walls, past a series of cells with solid iron doors and food slits, past the tank where the drunks were kept, toward three barred cells that faced back into the corridor. Lucas's cheeks and throat were pooled with color, as though they had been burned with dry ice.

"This is where we keep the superstars," the deputy said. He started to unlock Lucas's wrists in front of the middle cell. A hand and arm came out of the bars to the right and undulated in the air like a serpent.

"You got fresh meat for us, boss man?" the half-naked man in the cell said. His eyes looked maniacal, the structure of his head as though it had been broken in a machinist's vise. His arms were too short for his thick torso, and his chest and pot stomach were white from lack of sunlight and covered with green and red tattoos.

The deputy slipped his baton from the ring on his belt and whanged it off the bars an inch from the tattooed man's hand.

"You stick it out there again, I'll break it," he said.

"Come on, keep my Jell-O tonight and put that sweet thing in here with me," the man said, his palms wrapped around the bars now, his eyes dancing with malevolence six inches from mine. His body exuded a raw, damp odor like sewer gas.

After the deputy had unlocked Lucas's wrists from the manacles, I saw the fingers on both his hands start to tremble.

"Give me a minute," I said to the deputy.

"No problem. But I'm going to lock you inside so nobody don't grab one of your parts. You think the smart-ass here on the right's bad? They ain't thought up a name for that 'un on the other side."

I went into the cell with Lucas and watched the deputy turn the key on us and walk back down the corridor and sit at a small table and take his lunch out of a paper bag.

"I don't care if I cain't remember anything or not, I didn't hurt that girl. I liked her. She always come in there with college kids, but she didn't put on like she was special," he said.

"Which college kids?" I said.

He sat down on the bunk. A blowfly buzzed over the seatless toilet behind him. Lucas's eyes started to film.

"People she went to school with, I guess. Are they gonna electrocute me, Mr. Holland?" he said.

"Texas doesn't have the electric chair anymore. But, no, you won't be tried for capital murder. Just give me some time. We'll get you out of this."

"How?"

I didn't have an answer for him.

On the way out, I heard the man with the misshaped head and white pot stomach laughing in a high, whinnying voice, mimicking the conversation he'd heard in Lucas's cell: "They gonna 'lectrocute me? They gonna 'lectrocute me?...Hey, you punk, the black boys gonna take you into the bridal suite and teach you how to pull a train."

He held his chin and loins close against the bars and made a wet, chugging sound like a locomotive.

I went home and fixed lunch in the kitchen. The silence of the house seemed to ring and pop in my ears. I opened all the downstairs windows and pulled back the curtains and felt the wind flow through the hallway and puff open the back screen. The morning paper lay folded on an oak table in front of the hallway mirror. A full-length photo of Lucas in handcuffs

18

stared up at me. He didn't have my eyes, I thought. They were obviously his mother's. But the hair, the cut of the jaw, the six-foot-one frame...None of those belonged to Vernon Smothers.

I went back into the kitchen and tried to finish the fried pork chop sandwich I'd fixed.

His mother and I had gone to high school together. Both her parents had been road musicians who worked oil field honky-tonks from Texas City to Casper, Wyoming. When she was sixteen she met and married Vernon Smothers, who was ten years older than she. When she was nineteen she found me in Houston and asked for money so she could leave him.

I offered her half of my ancient rented house in the Heights.

Two weeks later a fellow Houston police officer called Vernon and told him I was living with his wife. He came for her at night when I was not home, in the middle of a hurricane that tore the pecan tree out of my front yard. I never saw her again.

A month after Lucas was born she was electrocuted trying to fix the well pump that Vernon had repaired with adhesive tape from the medicine cabinet.

I wrapped my unfinished sandwich in wax paper and put it in the icebox. When I turned around, L.Q. Navarro was leaning against the back doorjamb, his arms folded across his chest. His Stetson was the color of ash, his eyes as lustrous as obsidian.

"How's it hangin', L.Q.?" I said.

"This weather's a pistol. It don't get any better."

"You're not going to try to mess me up today, are you?"

"I wouldn't dream of it, Billy Bob."

He slipped the scarlet rose from the top buttonhole of his shirt and rolled it by the stem between his fingers. Where the rose had been was a hole that glowed with a bloodred light, like a votive candle burning inside red glass.

"It was an accident," I said.

"That's what I keep telling you. Get rid of this for me, will you?" He drew the rose across my palm. My fingers constricted as though the tendons had been severed by a barber's razor.

Ten minutes later I heard an automobile in front. I opened the door and looked down the flagstone walk that dissected the wall of poplars at the foot of the lawn, and saw the sheriff's deputy named Mary Beth Sweeney getting out of her cruiser. She fixed her campaign hat so that the leather cord drew tight against the back of her head, pushed her shirt down inside her gunbelt with her fingers, and walked toward me. She had a walk that my father would have referred to as a "fine carriage," her shoulders erect, her chin lifted, her long legs slightly accentuating the movement of her hips.

"How you doin'?" I said.

"You going to use a PI in discovery?"

"Probably...You want to come inside?"

"Out here is good. At the river, night before last? The scene investigator picked up a vinyl bag—load of beer cans. They're not in the evidence locker."

"Why are you telling me this?"

"That kid's going down on a bad bounce. I'm not buying into it."

"You can lose your job for this."

"Look, you know all these things. The victim's teeth were broken. Your man didn't have any cuts on his hands. There was no weapon. When we cuffed him, he was too drunk to stand up."

"Criminal Investigation Division, huh?" I said.

"What about it?"

"Doing grunt work in a place like this... You must like the mild summers. In July we fry eggs on the sidewalks."

"Use what I've told you, Mr. Holland, or wear it in your hat," she said.

She walked back to her cruiser, her attention already focused on a cardinal perched atop a rose trellis, her hat tipped forward on her curly head like a Marine Corps DI's.

CHAPTER

3

Before she became a private investigator, Temple Carrol had been a corrections officer at Angola penitentiary over in Louisiana, a patrolwoman with the Dallas police department, and a deputy sheriff in Fort Bend County. She lived with her invalid father only a mile down the road from me, and every morning, just at sunrise, she would jog past my house in her T-shirt and sweatpants, her chestnut hair piled on her head, the baby fat winking on her hips. She never broke her pace, never did less than five miles, and never stopped at intersections. Temple Carrol believed in straight lines.

Tuesday morning she tapped on the glass to my office door and then came inside without waiting. She wore a pair of sandals and blue jeans and a brown cotton shirt stitched with flowers. She sat on the corner of my desk and pointed her finger at me.

"What did that deputy tell you?" she asked.

"They bagged a whole load of beer cans and whiskey bottles at the crime scene," I answered.

"Try five cans and a couple of wine bottles. The cans all have Lucas's or the dead girl's prints on them. The bottles are probably twenty years old."

"What have you got on the girl?"

"Raised by an aunt...Long welfare history...In high school she was known as a real piece of work...Went to a community college for a while and dropped out...Worked at a church store, got fired from Wal-Mart for stealing...Get this, though. Three people at Shorty's say she came there by herself, not with a bunch of college kids. Not good news for Lucas."

"Maybe she met them there."

"Maybe...There's another problem, too, Billy Bob. You'd better get that boy out of jail."

"What's going on?"

"Harley Sweet."

She widened her eyes and held them on my face.

I rode up to the third floor of the courthouse with a turnkey. The heat had risen in the building and the stone walls were speckled with condensation.

"I'd like to talk to Lucas in an interview room," I said.

"Sorry, Billy Bob. Harley says he stays in lockdown...By the way, don't worry about that 'un on the left. He's got a lot more Christian perspective today."

The man in the cell to the left was dressed only in a pair of paper-thin Jockey undershorts. His sparse hair was the color of Mercurochrome, pasted in oily strains across his head. His skin had the unblemished smoothness of latex stretched over stone, and his left eye was smaller than the other, like a dime-size blue marble pushed deep into clay.

"What's your name, buddy?" I said to him, while the turnkey opened Lucas's cell.

"Garland T. Moon," he answered, his eyes brightening with challenge.

"They treating you all right?"

He got up from the bunk, his stomach cording with muscle, and stood close to the bars.

His breath was sweet, like prunes that have fermented in a jar. "I like it here. I wouldn't trade it for a half dozen Californias. It don't impress me out there."

"Ask him what happened inside that family's house in Santa Monica. If you got the stomach to hear it," the turnkey said.

The man who called himself Garland T. Moon smiled into my face and ran his tongue along his bottom lip. His tongue was red and thick as a biscuit.

The turnkey locked me in Lucas's cell. I sat down next to Lucas on his bunk.

"My PI says you've seen something that might get you in trouble," I said.

Lucas pointed over his shoulder with his thumb. "The guy in there," he said, his voice lowered. "Harley was telling him last night Texas won't send him back to California because California don't like to give people the death penalty. He was telling the guy what it's like to die by injection, how the guy's muscles are going to turn to cement so his lungs cain't go up and down, how he'll suffocate way down inside himself while everybody watches.

"Harley was almost back to the elevator and the guy says, 'One...one...one Fannin Street.' It made Harley go crazy. He got three other guys up here and they went in the guy's cell and chained him up and drug him down to the shower, then Harley went back to a locker and got a cattle prod. Mr. Holland, the guy's eyes was rolled in his head and his britches was

24

around his knees when they drug him back..."

"Listen to me, Lucas. As long as you're in here, you didn't see any of this," I said.

"I cain't take it. The guy in the other cell, Jimmy Cole, he told me this morning what he done to a little boy in Georgia."

He started to cry, unashamedly, his arms stiff on his knees, his eyes squinted shut, the tears streaming down his cheeks.

The sheriff kept his office behind the courthouse in the squat, one-story yellow sandstone building that had been the original county jail in the 1870s. He was six and a half feet tall and weighed over three hundred pounds, ate five meals a day, chain-smoked cigars, kept a spittoon by his desk, and hung framed pictures on the ancient log walls of every man his department had helped the state of Texas execute.

With no more than a fourth grade education, he had managed to remain sheriff for twenty-seven years.

He spun a poker chip on his desk blotter while I talked. The brow of his granite head was furrowed, his massive upper arms red with sunburn.

"Evidence disappearing? No, sir, not in this department. Where'd you hear this?" His eyes, which were flat and gray, lifted into mine.

"It happens, sheriff. Things get misplaced sometimes."

"My response to you is simple. The sono-

25

fabitch told you it is a goddamn liar. But—"
He picked up a pencil stub in his huge hand and started writing on a legal pad. "I'll make a note to myself and get back to you. How's that?"

"I want my client moved."

"Why's that?"

"Harley Sweet makes nighttime visits to some of the cells. I don't want my client involved as a witness in any other kind of court proceeding."

He leaned back in his swivel chair, the ends of the pencil stub crimped in the fingers of each hand.

"You telling me Harley's abusing a prisoner?" he asked.

"In my view, he's a sick man."

He looked at me hard for a moment, then burst out laughing. "Hell, he's got to do something, son. I cain't have the whole goddamn county on welfare."

"I'll see you, sheriff."

"Don't get your tallywhacker out of joint. I'll move the boy and I'll talk to Harley. Go get laid or develop a sense of humor. I swear you depress the hell out of me every time you come in here."

That evening my investigator, Temple Carrol, and I drove out to Shorty's on the river. The parking lot was filled with rusted gas-guzzlers, customized hot rods like kids built in the 1950s, chopped-down motorcycles, gleaming new convertibles, vans with bubble windows, and pickup trucks scrolled with chrome.

The interior was deafening. From the screen porches and elevated bandstand to the dance floor and the long, railed bar, the faces of the patrons were rippled with neon, their voices hoarse with their own conversation, their eyes lighted like people who had survived a highway catastrophe and knew they were eternal. When people went to Shorty's, they went to score—booze, barbecue, homegrown reefer, crystal meth, a stomp-ass brawl out in the trees, or the horizontal bop in the backseat—and they came from every background to do it: ranchers, sawmill workers, oil field roughnecks, business-men, ex-cons, dope mules, college kids, blue-collar housewives dumping their husbands, pipeliners, hillbilly musicians, pool hustlers, steroid freaks with butchwax in their hair, and biker girls in black leather whose purple makeup bloomed like a death wish on their cheeks.

But the revelers were two nights' distance from the rape and murder of a girl in an aban-doned picnic ground down the road, and their unfocused smiles never left their faces at the mention of her name.

Temple and I finally gave it up and walked back outside into the coolness of the evening. Far in the distance, the green land seemed to cup and flow off the earth's edge into an arroyo lighted by the sun's last dying spark.

"Billy Bob, if anybody could help out, it'd be the guys in the band," she said.

27

"So?"

"They turn to stone." She averted her eyes. "The girl came here alone. She left with Lucas. They were both drunk. We're going to have to go at it from another angle."

"He's a gentle boy, Temple. He didn't do this."

"You know what a state psychologist is going to say on the stand? About a boy who was controlled and abused all his life by a father like Vernon Smothers?"

An elderly black man with a thin white mustache and a stub of pipe between his teeth was spearing trash amidst the chopped-down motorcycles with a stick that had a nail on the end. He pulled each piece of trash off the nail and stuck it in a cloth bag that hung from his shoulder.

"I'll buy you a Mexican dinner," I said to Temple.

"I think I'll just go home and take a shower. I feel like somebody rubbed nicotine in my hair."

I backed the Avalon around and started to pull out of the parking lot. I saw her eyes watching the black man, a tooth working on the corner of her lip.

"You didn't interview him?" I said.

"No, he wasn't here before."

I stopped the car, and we both got out and walked over to him. He kept at his work and paid little attention to us. Temple held out a photo she had gotten from the dead girl's high school.

"Have you seen this girl before, sir?" she asked.

He took the photo from her and looked at it briefly, then handed it back.

"Yeah, I seen her. She the one killed up the road," he said.

"Did you know her?" I asked.

"No, I didn't know her. But I seen her, all right."

"When?" I asked.

"Night she got killed. She come here in a cab. Some boys was fixing to leave, then they seen her and axed her to go off with them. She had her own mind about it, though."

"Sir?" I said.

"She hit this one boy right 'cross the face, *whap*. He stood there, holding his jaw, just like he had a toothache. Then she give him the finger while she was walking back inside. Didn't even bother to turn around when she done it, just held it up in the air for him to see."

"Who was the boy?" I said.

"Ain't seen him befo'. Ain't sure I'd know him again." His eyes drifted off my face.

"Yeah, you would," Temple said.

"Why didn't you tell this to someone?" I said.

"They come to a place like this more than once, it's for a reason. The wrong one, too. What I say ain't gonna change that."

"What kind of car did this boy have?" Temple said.

"What reason I got to watch his car?"

"Who was he with?" Temple said.

"I ain't seen them befo'."

29

"Give me your name," she said. She wrote it down, then stuck a business card in his hand. "You just became a witness in a murder trial. Stay in touch. Work on your memory, too. I know you can do it."

I followed the two-lane county road along the river, past a cornfield that was green and dented with wind under the moon.

"That's kind of a tough statement to make to an old fellow," I said.

"I don't like people who're cutesy about a raped and murdered girl," Temple said.

After I had dropped her off, I made a call to the jail and then drove to the house of Marvin Pomroy, the prosecutor. He lived in a white gingerbread house, shaded by live oaks, in the old affluent district of Deaf Smith. His St. Augustine grass was wet with soak hoses and iridescent in the glare of the flood lamps that lit and shadowed his property.

His wife answered the door and invited me in, but I thanked her and asked if Marvin could simply step outside a minute. He still had a dinner napkin in his hand when he came out on the gallery.

"I've got a problem with some missing evidence," I said.

"See the sheriff."

"You're an honest man, Marvin. Don't jerk me around."

"Same response. You shouldn't try to do business on my gallery."

"Somebody's sandbagging the investigation and setting up my client."

He reached behind him and closed the front door. His well-shaped head and steel-rimmed glasses and neatly combed short hair were covered with the yellow glow of the bug light overhead.

"You listen, goddamn it, that kid's got dirty written all over him. You get out of my face with this bullshit," he said.

"I asked the sheriff to move him today. It didn't happen."

"That's not my problem. You know what is? A guy who could have been dredged up out of the Abyss, Garland T. Moon. He murdered a whole family in California, he tied them up in a basement and killed them one by one with a knife, but his attorney has already gotten most of the evidence suppressed because the cops seized it with a bad warrant. If I don't make the case on that old woman he killed here, he'll be back on the street, in *our* midst, ready to do it again...Listen, I could get Lucas on capital murder. But I choose not to do so. Do you hear what I'm saying, Billy Bob?"

"No."

He shook his head, a sad, private thought in his eyes.

"Don't look at me like that," I said.

"You were an assistant U.S. attorney. Why'd you blow it?"

"Go to hell, Marvin."

"Come in and eat," he said.

"No."

"Good night to you, then," he said.

I walked across the grass to my car. The yard seemed filled with shadows that leaped and broke apart and reformed themselves in the wind. I looked back over my shoulder through the front windows of Marvin's house. He and his wife and children were seated at the dining room table, a chandelier dripping with light above their heads, their faces animated with their own company as they passed bowls of food back and forth to one another.

CHAPTER

4

I woke before sunrise and fried eggs and ham in the kitchen and ate them out of the skillet with bread and a cup of coffee on the back porch. The dawn was gray and misty, the air so cool and soft that I could hear sound from a long way off—a bass flopping in the tank, the creak of the windmill shifting directions, a cowbell clanging on my neighbor's gate.

L.Q. Navarro was stretched out on the perforated, white-painted iron lawn bench under the chinaberry tree, his Stetson tilted sideways on his head, his cheek resting on one hand.

I tried to ignore him.

But when I closed my eyes he and I were on horseback again in a reed-choked muddy bottom across the border in Coahuila, our eyes stinging with sweat in the darkness, our noses and mouths filled with insects. Then the fusillade exploded all around us, from behind sandhills and scrub brush and mesquite and gutted car bodies, the muzzle flashes blooming in the dark, our horses caving under us as though they had been eviscerated.

But L.Q.'s mare labored to her feet again, a hole in her rib cage squirting blood like a broken pipe, and began galloping in terror up an arroyo, flailing her head against the collapsed reins. Then I saw L.Q.'s boot and roweled Mexican spur tangled in the stirrup and his body bouncing across the rocks, his arms folded over his head as the mare's iron shoes sliced the suitcoat off his shoulders.

My right arm felt dead, useless at my side, the upper bone snapped in two by a round that had struck it like a sharp, solitary blow from a cold chisel. I stood erect and fired and fired, until my nine-millimeter locked empty, then I dropped it to the ground and began firing my .357 Magnum, not taking aim, the air crisscrossed with ricochets and toppling rounds that made a *whirring* sound past the ear or *pinged* out into the darkness like a broken spring.

Then I heard our attackers begin moving through the brush, the sand slicks, from behind the rusted car bodies, through the blackened greasewood and tangles of wire fence. I heard the man behind me before I saw him, his boots digging hopelessly for purchase into the soil as he slid down the arroyo. I turned just as his weight propelled him toward the bottom of the arroyo, the starlight glinting on the barrel of his rifle, and I pointed my revolver straight in front of me and squeezed off the last round in the cylinder, the hammer ratcheting back and slamming down on the cartridge before I recognized the thin, silvery tinkle of L.Q.'s Mexican spurs.

I pushed away the frying pan and coffee cup and wiped my mouth on a paper napkin.

"Why'd you pick up that damn rifle?" I said.

He adjusted his cheek on his palm and tipped back his hat. *"I dropped my piece. What was I supposed to shoot at them with, spitballs?"*

"They all made it back into the mountains. We lost you for nothing."

"I wouldn't say that. I busted off my pocketknife in the guy I took the rifle from. It's that same dude we liked to smoked a couple of other times. I expect he took his next leak with one kidney."

"You were sure a fine lawman, L.Q."

He cut his head and grinned and stuck a long grass stem in his mouth.

I heard a car out front, then the doorbell ring.

"Come around back!" I shouted through the kitchen.

The deputy named Mary Beth Sweeney walked around the corner of the house, the sun like a soft yellow balloon at her back. L.Q. was standing under the chinaberry tree now, looking at her curiously. She walked right through

34

him. His silhouette broke apart in a burst of gold needles.

I pushed open the back screen for her.

"How about a cup of coffee?" I said.

She stepped inside and took off her campaign hat. She pushed a curl off her forehead.

"This won't take long," she said.

"Excuse me?"

"You jammed me up with the sheriff."

"About the missing evidence?" I said.

"You violated a confidence, Mr. Holland."

"I didn't," I said.

"Yeah? I think it's Bubba and Bubba lighting each other's cigars."

"Who are you?" I said.

She fitted her hat on her head and let the screen slam behind her.

I followed her to her cruiser.

"You're wrong about this," I said.

I watched her cruiser spin gravel onto the county road and disappear over a rise between two pastures filled with red Angus.

My law office was above the old bank on the corner of the town square. From my window I could see the iron tethering rings that bled rust out of the old elevated sidewalks, the hardware and feed stores that had gone broke, the tiny neon-scrolled Rialto theater that still showed first-run movies, the yellow tip of a Spanish-American War artillery piece under the live oaks on the courthouse lawn, the

35

Roman-numeraled clock perched atop the third floor, where Lucas Smothers waited in a cell with a sociopath behind the wall on each side of him.

I sat at my desk with a cup of coffee and stared at the glass case on the wall where I had mounted Great-grandpa Sam's Navy Colt .36 caliber revolvers and his octagon-barrel Winchester '73 lever-action rifle on a field of blue felt. I picked up the telephone and punched in the sheriff's office extension.

"My client hasn't been moved," I said.

"Talk to Harley."

"Harley's a sadistic moron."

"You're starting to try my patience, Billy Bob."

"Tell your scene investigator I'm going to fry his ass."

"The missing beer cans or whatever?"

"That's right."

"What would they prove, that a lot of people get drunk and diddle each other in that picnic ground?...Go to a head doctor while you still got time, son. I'm worried about you."

I drove out to the clapboard, tin-roofed home of the victim, Roseanne Hazlitt. The aunt was a frail, wizened woman who snapped the screen latch in place as I stepped up on her tiny gallery. Behind her, the television set was tuned to a talk show on which people shouted and jeered at one another. An ironing board on a short stand was elevated in front

36

of the couch. Through the screen I smelled an odor on her like camphor and dried flowers and sweat baked into her clothes by the heat of her work.

"You asking me to hep set that boy loose?" she said.

"No, ma'am. I just wondered if Roseanne had other friends she might have met sometimes at Shorty's."

"Like who?"

"Like one she had reason to slap the daylights out of."

"She never hurt nobody in her life. It was them hurt her."

"May I come in?"

"No."

"Who's *them,* Ms. Hazlitt?"

"Any of them that gets the scent of it, like a bunch of dogs sniffing around a brooder house. Now, you get off my gallery, and you tell that Smothers boy he might fool y'all, he don't fool me."

"You know Lucas?"

I drove back to Deaf Smith, parked my Avalon by the office, and walked across the street to the courthouse. I opened Harley Sweet's door without knocking.

"I want to see Lucas in private, in an interview room, and I don't want anybody disturbing me while I talk to him," I said.

"I wouldn't have it no other way, Billy Bob." He leaned back in his swivel chair, his

37

jaw resting on his fingers, a shadow of a smile on his mouth.

Upstairs, inside the jail, the turnkey unlocked Lucas's cell. The man with the misshaped head and pot stomach in the cell to the right, whose name was Jimmy Cole, walked up and down, tapping his fists one on top of the other, oblivious to our presence. The man on the left, Garland T. Moon, sat naked on his bunk. He had been exercising, and he wiped the sweat off his stomach with a towel and grinned at me. His shrunken, receded left eye glistened with a rheumy, mirthful light.

The turnkey walked Lucas and me down a short hallway to a small windowless room, with a wood table and two wood chairs and a urine-streaked grated drain in the concrete floor.

Lucas sat down, one hand clenched on his wrist. He watched my face, then licked his lips.

"What's wrong, Mr. Holland?"

"You led me to believe you didn't know Roseanne Hazlitt outside of Shorty's."

"I didn't know her real good, that's all."

"You're lying."

"I drove her home a couple of times after Shorty's closed. We didn't go out reg'lar or nothing."

"No, all you did was get in her pants."

He swallowed dryly. There were discolorations in his cheeks, like small pieces of melting ice.

"You want to spend the rest of your life in Huntsville? You keep lying to me, and Marvin Pomroy is going to grind you into sausage...What are you hiding, Lucas?"

He stared fixedly at his hands, but his eyes seemed to be looking over a cliff into a canyon that had no bottom.

"She said she might be pregnant."

"She wanted you to marry her?" I asked.

"No, sir. She said she was gonna fix some guy good. She said, 'I'm gonna show him up for what he is. People around here gonna be real surprised. I bet I can get my story on TV and make this whole town look like two cents.'"

"Why didn't you tell me this?"

"'Cause maybe that baby's mine. Maybe y'all would think I had reason to kill her 'cause I didn't want it." He breathed through his nose and dug at a callus with his thumbnail, a hard light in his eyes.

"I've seen the autopsy, Lucas. She wasn't pregnant."

"Then why—"

"She was probably late."

He dropped his hands in his lap, his face empty, like someone whose head is filled with white noise.

"I got to get away from them two back at the cells," he said.

"Don't pay attention to them."

"They talk in the dark when nobody else ain't around...Last night Garland told Jimmy Cole, that's the one with the tattoos all over him, Garland says to him, 'Damn if that old woman didn't put me in mind of my mother. She was trussed up like a little bird behind the counter there, peeping up at me, scared to death, I declare she looked so pitiful she made me hurt. So I walked back to her and said, "Lady, a good woman like you ain't deserving of the evil a man like me brings into the world," and I put both my hands on her face and she wet her panties and died right there.'

"Mr. Holland, they laughed so hard I had to wrap the mattress around my head to keep the sound out...Mr. Holland?"

Ten minutes later I tapped on the frosted glass of Marvin Pomroy's office door.

"How bad you want to zip up the package on Garland T. Moon?" I said.

"What have you got?" Marvin said.

"Lucas can put a nail gun in Moon's mouth."

Marvin made an indifferent face. "So go on and tell me," he said.

"What's on the table?"

"It's not a seller's market, Billy Bob. I've got a witness who saw Moon go into the store."

"Forget your witness. I've got the confession."

"You want to plea out?"

"Nope."

"If it's what you say, maybe his bail can get cut in half...Maybe we can go south one bump on the charge."

"Manslaughter, no rape."

"Manslaughter, sexual battery."

"Not good enough."

Marvin scratched the back of his head.

"If it goes to sentencing, I won't object to an argument for his youth and lack of criminal history," he said.

He listened quietly while I repeated the story just told me by Lucas Smothers, his red suspenders notched into his shoulders. He removed his steel-rimmed glasses and polished them with a Kleenex.

"She suffocated. She didn't die of fright," he said.

"He says he put his hands on her face. Same thing. Did she wet her underwear?"

"Yep."

"You got him, then," I said.

"Maybe."

"Nice doing business with you, Marvin." At the door I turned around. "You set this up, didn't you?" I said.

"Me? I'm just not that smart, Billy Bob. But I appreciate your thinking so."

That evening I worked late in my office. It was Easter break, when college kids came home to Deaf Smith and re-created their high school rituals as though indicating to the classes behind them they would never completely relinquish the joys of their youth. My windows were open and I could see the pale luminous face of the clock on the courthouse roof and the oaks ruffling in the wind and the kids dragging Main from the rich neighborhoods out east all the way to the dirt side streets of the Mexican and black district on the far end of town.

The sun was almost down and the square seemed filled with a soft blue glow, the air scented with flowers and the distant smell of watermelons in the fields. Down below, the procession of customized cars and pickups and vans snaked around the square, the lacquered paint jobs like glazed red and orange and purple candy, the deep-throated Hollywood mufflers rumbling off the pavement, the exposed chromed engines rippling with light. A beer can tinkled on a sidewalk; a stoned-out girl stood on the leather backseat of a convertible, undulating in a skin-tight white dress that she had pulled above her nylons.

Lucas's bail hearing was scheduled for nine in the morning. For no reason I could quite explain I picked up the phone and called the jail.

Harley Sweet answered the phone.

"You make sure that boy's all right tonight," I said.

"Say again?"

"Bad things happen to people in your jail, Harley. They'd better not happen to my client."

"Your client is a pissant I wouldn't take time to spit on if he was burning...You liberals kill me, Billy Bob. You want to come over here and feed Jimmy Cole and Garland T. Moon, see they got toilet paper and showers and ain't nobody infringing on their rights?...I didn't think so."

He hung up.

Neither Harley nor I could guess how much our lives would change because of that night's events.

CHAPTER

5

At 12:01 A.M. the turnkey stopped by Harley Sweet's office and signed off his shift.

"I caught Jimmy Cole eating a bar of soap," he said.

"We better get a new cook," Harley said.

"I wouldn't let that boy get into the hospital, Harley. He's planning something."

"You haven't had more trouble with Garland T. Moon, have you?"

"No, sir."

"See there, it just needs Bible study."

At around 3 A.M. a Mexican in the drunk tank heard the cables on the elevator working, then the wire-mesh door rattling open and a key turning in the barred second door. Harley Sweet walked down the row of cells past the drunk tank with a paper bag rolled in his right hand, his leather-soled boots echoing off the concrete floor, a bleached straw cowboy hat cocked on his head.

The Mexican in the drunk tank, who was surrounded by men sleeping on the floor, pressed his face against the bars and tried to see farther down the corridor but could not.

A key turned in another cell door and Harley's voice said, "Turn around and lean against the wall. Your face sure don't brighten my work. Your mama must have beat on it with an ugly stick."

The Mexican in the drunk tank heard scuffling, intense and prolonged, with no words spoken, like that of men who know the cost of a wasted movement or an exhalation of breath. Then there was a single, abrupt gasp, a body collapsing on the floor, followed by a series of blows, which began with a whistling sound, like a baton ripping through the air, then the *thunk* of wood against muscle and bone, and more blows, one after another, until the Mexican pressed his palms against his ears and crouched in the back of the drunk tank and hid from the sound.

Five minutes passed, then the cell door at the end of the corridor clanged shut again and a figure dressed like Harley walked past the bars of the drunk tank, the straw hat held to the side of his face. The wire-mesh door on the elevator clattered into the jamb, and the walls hummed with the reverberations of the elevator's motor as the cage dropped to the first floor.

A few kids who were still dragging Main said they saw a figure in boots and a white straw hat emerge from the side door of the courthouse and walk across the darkened lawn to Harley's truck, tap on his shirt pocket as though the package of cigarettes he discovered there were a nice surprise, light one, and drive away.

44

The turnkey who came on duty at 6 A.M. rode up to the third floor of the courthouse and saw nothing out of the ordinary. At 7 A.M. the trusties brought up the food carts loaded with aluminum containers of grits, fried ham, white bread, and black coffee. The men in the drunk tank were fed first, then Lucas Smothers, who had been moved into an isolation cell by the showers. A trusty stopped his food cart in front of Jimmy Cole's cell and tapped a wood serving spoon against the bars.

"Fixing to tote it back, Jimmy Cole...Hey, boy, you want to eat, you better roll it out."

The trusty looked more closely at the man in the bunk, who was dressed in jailhouse whites, and at the striped pillow pressed down on his face with one arm, and at the thin coppery glint buried in the folds of his throat. The trusty whirled and shouted down the corridor at the turnkey: "Inmate out on the ground, boss-man!"

"What the hell you talking about? That's him right yonder," the turnkey said, pointing through the bars. Then the turnkey saw the chipped, black baton on the floor under the bunk and the lower part of the face under the pillow. "Oh Lord have mercy," he said, and unlocked and flung back the door and then gingerly pulled the pillow loose from the arm folded across it, like a person who cannot watch the next frames of film about to flash on a movie screen.

The copper wire had been unwrapped from the head of a broom, twisted into a hang-

45

man's noose, dropped over Harley Sweet's neck, and then razored into the flesh. Later, the medical examiner would report that the blows with the baton had been delivered while Harley Sweet strangled to death on his knees.

Garland T. Moon wolfed his breakfast and talked the trusty into filling his tin plate again with grits and the ham fat from the bottom of the serving container. Then he leaped up and grabbed the lip of a steel crossbeam at the top of his cell with his fingertips and did chin-ups in his Jockey undershorts, the veins and sinew in his body erupting across his skin like nests of twigs.

"Hey, bossman, don't Mr. Sweet's mother live at 111 Fannin Street?...I'd put a guard on her if I was y'all. You got Jimmy Cole out on the ground, there ain't no telling what might happen," he said. He dropped flat-footed from the steel crossbeam and giggled uncontrollably.

The courtroom was almost empty when Lucas Smothers appeared before the judge and had his bail reduced from $150,000 to $75,000. His father, Vernon, was supposed to appear in court with a bondsman. He didn't. I put up my property for the bond, then waited on the front steps of the courthouse for Lucas to be processed out of the jail.

Vernon Smothers parked his pickup by the curb and cut across the lawn toward me. He wore a pair of dark blue overalls that were wet at the knees.

"Where were you, Vernon?" I asked.

"Putting in pepper plants. I didn't watch the time. That little snip of a bondsman didn't call me back, either. What happened in there?"

"I went his bond."

"I ain't asked for that."

"It's no big thing."

His eyes looked out at the glare of sunlight on the walk, the traffic in the square, the old men who sat on benches by the Spanish-American War artillery piece. The olive skin of his narrow face twitched as though someone were touching it with the tip of a feather.

"Them that's got money use it to put their shame on others. That's the way it's always worked around here. I won't abide it, though," he said.

"Vernon, don't hurt your boy again."

"Seems like the calf's mine only when it's time for you to lecture, Billy Bob."

I walked away from him, through the doors of the courthouse and down a hallway whose woodwork seemed infused with the dull amber glow of its own past. Marvin Pomroy came out of his office and almost collided into me. His face was bloodless, as though it had been slapped.

"What's wrong?" I said.

"We messed up. Moon and Jimmy Cole did time together at Sugarland," he answered.

"You're not communicating, Marvin."

"The witness...The customer who saw Moon go into the store where he killed the old woman...Somebody sliced her back screen

47

and stabbed her to death with a screwdriver this morning...Harley's truck was found in a pond a half mile away."

I saw Lucas Smothers walk down the circular stairs in the center of the courthouse, a possessions bag in his hand.

"We've got no physical evidence to put Moon in that store," Marvin said.

I stared into his face and the knowledge there that I didn't want to accept.

"That crazy sonofabitch is going to get out, Billy Bob."

"Lucas's deposition—" I began.

"It won't hold up by itself."

"Does Moon know that Lucas..." I could feel the pinpoints of sweat breaking on my forehead.

"You already know the answer to that...I'm sorry. We thought we had this guy halfway to the boneyard," Marvin said.

Lucas walked toward us, his face uncertain in front of Marvin.

"How y'all doin'? Is my dad outside?" he said.

I sat alone in my office with the blinds down and tried to think. I kept seeing the grin on the face of Garland T. Moon, the latex skin, the liquid blue eye; I could almost smell the breath that was like fermented prunes. I pulled open the blinds and let the sunlight flood into the room.

The secretary buzzed me on the intercom.

"Mr. Vanzandt and his son are here to see you, Billy Bob," she said.

Jack Vanzandt, the college baseball star who'd fought in Vietnam and had come home decorated and had made a fortune in the Mexican oil business, then had lost it and made another fortune in computers. He'd called yesterday, or was it the day before? Yes, about his son, the one who had been expelled from Texas A&M.

"Bad day for a talk?" Jack said.

"Sorry. It's been a peculiar morning," I said.

Jack still lifted weights and worked out regularly on a speed bag and played polo at a club in Dallas. He was well mannered and intelligent and made little of his war record. Few found any reason not to like him.

His son was another matter. His blond, youthful face always seemed slightly flushed, overheated, his gaze turned inward on thoughts that swam like threadworms in his green eyes.

"Darl had a fistfight with a Mexican kid. We'd like to just shake hands and forget it. But it looks like the family found out we have a little money," Jack said.

"What about it, Darl?" I asked.

"At the American Legion game. Kid scratched all over my hood with a nail. I asked him why he did it. He said because of the cheer we were yelling in the stands. So I told him it was a free country, people can say anything they want 'cause that's why we got a First Amendment. Wets don't like it, they can swim back home."

"What cheer?" I asked.

49

"'Two-bits, four-bits, six-bits, a peso, all good pepper bellies stand up and say so.'" His eyes smiled at nothing. He rubbed the thick ball of muscle along his forearm.

I looked at his father.

"The Mexican boy had to have his jaws wired together," Jack said.

I took a yellow legal pad and a ballpoint pen out of my drawer and pushed them across my desk toward Darl.

"I'd like you to write down what happened for me. Just like you're writing a school essay," I said.

"I just told you what happened," he said.

"Darl has dyslexia," Jack said.

"I see," I said. "I tell you what, I'll get back with y'all this afternoon. I'm sorry I'm a little distant this morning."

Darl Vanzandt played with the high school ring on his finger, his cheeks glowing with peach fuzz. His eyes seemed amused at a private thought. Then he looked me straight in the face and said, "My father says Lucas Smothers is your woods colt."

"Go to the car, son," Jack said.

After Darl was gone, his father extended his hand.

"I apologize. Darl has serious emotional problems. His mother...It's called fetal alcohol syndrome. He's not always accountable for the things he says and does," Jack said.

"Don't worry about it," I said.

"I really appreciate your helping us, Billy Bob."

50

He squeezed my hand a second time. His grip was encompassing, long lasting, the skin moist and warm. After he was gone and I was seated again behind my desk, I found myself unconsciously rubbing my hand on the knee of my trousers.

Why, I thought.

There was a cut, an indentation, newly scabbed, the size of a tooth, on the ring finger of Darl Vanzandt.

No, I told myself, you're letting it get away from you.

That night, as an electrical storm raged outside, L.Q. Navarro stood in the middle of my living room, his ash-colored Stetson tipped back on his head, and said, *"You were as good a lawman as me, bud. When they're poor and got no power, like Lucas and the dead girl, and other people get involved with what happens to them, you know it's a whole sight bigger than what they want you to think."*

"Why'd you go and die on me, L.Q.?"

He twirled his hat on his index finger, and an instant later, through the window, I saw his silhouette illuminated by a bolt of lightning on a distant hill.

CHAPTER

6

The next day, after work, I dug night crawlers and cane-fished with a little mixed-blood

Mexican boy in the tank on the back of my property. His name was Pete, and he had blue eyes and pale streaks the color of weathered wood in his hair, which grew like a soft brush on his head. He grinned all the time and talked with an Anglo twang and was probably the smartest little boy I ever knew.

"That was the Chisholm Trail out yonder?" he asked.

"Part of it. There're wagon tracks still baked in the hardpan."

He chewed his gum and studied on the implications.

"What's it good for?" he asked.

"Not much of anything, I guess."

He grinned and chewed his gum furiously and skipped a stone across the water.

"Black people say you spit on your hook, you always catch fish. You believe that?" he said.

"Could be."

"How come you don't marry Temple Carrol?"

"You have too many thoughts for a boy your age."

"She sure spends a lot of time jogging past your house."

"Why do you have Temple Carrol on the brain this evening, Pete?"

"'Cause there she comes now."

I looked over my shoulder and saw Temple's car drive past my garage and barn and chicken run and windmill, then follow the dirt track out to the levee that circled the tank. Pete thought that was hilarious.

Temple got out of her car and walked up the slope of the levee. Her face looked cool and pink in the twilight.

"He's out," she said.

"Moon?"

"None other."

"Excuse us, Pete."

I leaned my cane pole in the fork of a red-bud tree, and we walked down the levee. The late red sun looked like molten metal through the willows on the far bank.

"He was at your office," she said.

"*What?*"

"Sitting on your steps for maybe an hour. In a blue serge suit and a Hawaiian shirt that's like an assault on the eyeballs. I told him your office was closed. He just sat there, cleaning his fingernails."

"Don't mess with him, Temple. Next time call the cops."

"What do you think I did? A half hour later, this new deputy, Mary Beth Sweeney, shows up. I told her I was glad somebody from the sheriff's department could finally make the trip from across the street. Get this, nobody sent her. She just happened to be driving by. She told him to hoof it."

Temple forked two fingers into the side pocket of her blue jeans.

"He left you a note," she said.

It was written in pencil, on the inside of a flattened cigarette wrapper.

Mr. Holland, I find it damn inconsiderate you

53

dont post your office hours. Call me at the Green Parrot Motel to talk this thing out.
    Garland T. Moon

We were back at her car now. She opened the driver's door and reached across the seat and picked up a revolver. It was an ancient .38—40 double-action, the metal as dull as an old nickel with holster wear.

"Keep this. You can add it to your historical collection," she said.

"Nope."

"I got a friend in Austin to run Moon on the computer. Corrections thinks he did two snitches in Sugarland."

"Thanks for coming by, Temple."

She lowered the revolver, which she held sideways in her palm.

"Where's it end?" she said.

"Excuse me?"

"You gave up your badge, then your career as a prosecutor with the Justice Department..." She shook her head. "Because you think an accidental death takes away your right to judge people who are evil?"

"Pete and I are fixing to fry up some fish. You're welcome to join us."

"You make me so mad I want to hit you," she said.

Later that evening, I called the sheriff at his home.

54

"My PI made a 911 on Garland Moon," I said.

"So?"

"Nobody was dispatched."

"What's the man done?" he asked.

"He was in your custody. You let him out. I don't want him on my doorstep."

"You think I want this lunatic on the street?"

"To tell you the truth, I'm not sure, sheriff."

"You're a natural-born pain in the ass, Billy Bob. Don't be calling my house again."

After I hung up, I called a friend in the sheriff's department and got the address of Mary Beth Sweeney. She lived in a new two-story apartment complex with a swimming pool just outside of town. It was 9 P.M. when I walked up the brick pathway at the entrance, and the underwater lights in the pool were turned on and pine needles and a glaze of suntan lotion floated on the surface. The lawn was empty, the portable barbecue pits left on the flagstones feathering with smoke.

I climbed to the second landing and rang her doorbell. My right hand opened and closed at my side and I felt warm inside my coat and wished I had left it in the Avalon.

Her face had a meaningless expression when she opened the door.

"Sorry to bother you at home. But I heard Garland Moon was at my office," I said.

"Yes, is there something I can tell you?"

"Maybe. If I'm not bothering you."

I waited.

"Come in," she said.

Her small living room was furnished with rattan chairs and a couch and a round glass table. A yellow counter with three stools divided the kitchen from the living room. She was barefoot and wore jeans and a white and burnt orange University of Texas Longhorn T-shirt. A copy of *The New Yorker* was splayed open on the glass tabletop and a pair of horn-rimmed glasses lay next to it.

"You just happened by and saw Moon outside my office?" I said.

"What's this about, Mr. Holland?"

"I think I'm developing an ongoing problem with the sheriff's office. I think it's because of Lucas Smothers."

She hadn't asked me to sit down. She placed one hand against the counter and pushed her feet into a pair of white moccasins as though she were about to go somewhere. Her eyes were violet colored, unfocused, caught somewhere between two thoughts.

"You shouldn't come here," she said.

"I wonder how I should read that. Is there hidden meaning there? I always have trouble with encoded speech."

"If you don't like rudeness, you shouldn't keep forcing the issue, Mr. Holland."

"My name is Billy Bob."

"I know who you are." Then I saw the color flare behind her freckles, not from anger but

as if she had made an admission she should-
n't.

"You like Mexican food?" I asked.

"Good night." She put her hand on the
doorknob and turned it.

"Tomorrow night? I appreciate what you've
done for me."

She opened the door and I started outside.
I was only inches away from her now and I could
smell the perfume behind her ears and hear
her breathing and see the rise and fall of her
breasts. A tiny gold chain and cross hung
around her neck.

"Moon won't come at you head-on. He'll
use Jimmy Cole," she said.

I felt my mouth part as I stared into her eyes.

It was sunrise the next morning when I pulled
into the dirt drive of Vernon Smothers's two-
bedroom white frame house, with a mimosa
in the front yard, a sprinkler spinning in a sickly
fashion by the wood steps, a partially collapsed garage in back, and every available
foot of surrounding property under cultiva-
tion.

I walked along the edge of a bean field to
an irrigation ditch where Lucas stood up to
his knees in the water, raking dead vegetation
out of the bottom and piling it on the bank.

"What are you doing?" I said.

"My dad uses it in the compost heap."

"He's not one to waste."

"You don't like him much, do you?" he

said. His face and denim shirt were spotted with mud, his arms knotted with muscle as he lifted a rake-load of dripping weeds to the edge of the ditch.

"Garland Moon's out. I want you to be careful," I said.

"Last night a Mexican in the poolroom offered me five hundred dollars to drive a load of lumber down to Piedras Negras."

"What are you doing in the poolroom?"

"Just messin' around."

"Yeah, they only sell soda pop in there, too. Why's this Mexican so generous to you?"

"He's got a furniture factory down there. He cain't drive long distances 'cause he's got kidney trouble or something. He said I might get on reg'lar."

"You leave this county, Lucas, you go back to jail and you stay there."

"You ain't got to get mad about it. I was just telling you what the guy said."

"You thought anymore about college for next fall?"

"I was just never any good at schoolwork, Mr. Holland."

"Will you call me Billy Bob?"

"My dad don't allow it."

I walked back to my car. The sun was yellow and pale with mist behind Vernon Smothers's house. He stood on his porch in work boots and cut-off GI fatigues and a sleeveless denim shirt that was washed as thin as Kleenex.

"You out here about Moon?" he asked.

"He's been known to nurse a grievance," I answered.

"He puts a foot on my land, I'll blow it off."

"You'll end up doing his time, then."

"I busted my oil pan on your back road yesterday. You'll owe me about seventy-five dollars for the weld job," he said, and went back inside his house and let the screen slam behind him.

Just before lunchtime, my secretary buzzed the intercom.

"There's a man here who won't give his name, Billy Bob," she said.

"Does he have on a blue serge suit?"

"Yes."

"I'll be right out."

I opened my door. Garland T. Moon sat in a chair, a hunting magazine folded back to ads that showed mail-order guns and knives for sale. He wore shiny tan boots that were made from plastic, and a canary yellow shirt printed with redbirds, with the collar flattened outside his suit coat.

"Come in," I said.

My secretary looked at me, trying to read my face.

"I'm going to take my lunch hour a little late today," she said.

"Why don't you go now, Kate? Bring me an order of enchiladas and a root beer. You want something, Garland?"

His lips were as red as a clown's when he smiled, his head slightly tilted, as though the question were full of tangled wire.

He walked past me without answering. I could smell an odor like lye soap and sweat on his body. I closed the door, turned the key in the lock, and put the key in my watch pocket.

"What are you doing?" he said.

I sat behind my desk, smiled up at him, my eyes not quite focusing on him. I scratched the back of my hand.

"I asked you what you're doing," he said.

"I think you're a lucky man. I think you ought to get out of town."

"Why'd you lock the door?"

"I don't like to be disturbed."

One side of his face seemed to wrinkle, his small blue eye watering, as though irritated by smoke. He was seated now, his thighs and hard buttocks flexed against the plastic bottom of the chair.

"I want to hire you. To file a suit. They took a cattle prod to me. They put it all over my private parts," he said.

"My client's deposition has no meaning for you now. You're home free on murder beefs in two states. I wouldn't complicate my life at this point."

"That little bitch they planted in the cell, what's his name, Lucas Smothers, he told y'all a mess of lies. I never had no such conversation with Jimmy Cole. I been jailing too long to do something like that."

I looked at the backs of my fingers on top of the desk blotter. I could hear the minute hand on my wall clock click into the noon position. Outside the window, the oak trees were a deep green against the yellow sandstone of the courthouse.

"Don't misjudge your opponent, sir," I said.

"I know all about you. But you don't know the first thing about me. Me and my twin brother was in a place where they switched your legs raw just because you spilled your food on the floor. You ain't gonna find that on a rap sheet. When he was nine years old they pushed epilepsy pills down his throat till he choked to death. You doubt my word, you go look in the Waco Baptist Cemetery."

"You're a sick man."

"There's some that has said that. It never put no rocks in my shoe, though."

I got up from my chair and walked to the door and turned the key in the lock.

"Get out," I said.

He remained motionless in the chair, his face looking away from me, the back of his neck flaming with color. He mumbled something.

"What?" I said.

He didn't repeat it. When he walked past me, his eyes were fixed straight ahead, a single line of sweat glistening on the side of his face like an empty blood vein.

CHAPTER

7

At sunrise Sunday morning I put on my pinstriped beige suit and a short-sleeve white shirt and a pair of oxblood Tony Lamas, walked down to the barn and lifted my saddle off a sawhorse in the tack room and threw it on the back of my Morgan. The breeze blew through the doors on each end of the barn and the air was cool and smelled of wildflowers, fish spawning, oats and molasses balls, green horse dung, hay that had turned yellow in the corners, and well water spilling over the lip of the corrugated windmill tank.

L.Q. Navarro sat on top of a stall, the heels of his boots hooked onto a plank, his body slatted with sunlight.

"You should have taken that .38—40 that gal tried to give you," he said.

"It's Sunday, L.Q. Take a day off."

"It's them kind of days the shitbags crawl out of the storm sewers. Tell me it wasn't fun busting caps on them dope mules down in Coahuila."

"Adios, bud," I said, and flicked my heels into the Morgan's ribs and thudded across the soft carpet of desiccated horse manure in the lot.

I crossed the creek at the back of my property and rode through a stand of pines, then up an incline that was humped with blackberry bushes into Pete's backyard. He waited for me on the porch, dressed in a pair of pressed jeans and a starched print shirt and freshly shined brown shoes. I reached my arm down and pulled him up behind the cantle.

The Morgan's hooves clattered on the flattened beer cans in the yard.

"Was you really baptized in the river?" he said.

"Sure."

"I never heard of a river-baptized person converting to a Catholic."

"Somebody's got to keep y'all honest."

He was quiet a long time, rocking against me with the horse's steps.

"Does it bother you when people say you're crazy, Billy Bob?"

"Most of the human race is, Pete."

"I knew you was gonna say that."

We came out of the pines into the backside of a rural Mexican neighborhood with fenceless dirt yards and abandoned privies and alleys blown with litter and bloodred hibiscus growing out of rusted car shells.

This area was part of what was known as the West End, a place where cedar cutters and field-workers and "bohunks," people who were of mixed German and Mexican blood, had always lived. It was exactly twenty miles down the same road that led into the East End, where Deaf Smith's country club set, and there were many of them, had bought and refurbished Victorian homes that were as big as steamboats when spot market oil was forty dollars a barrel.

It was cool inside the small stucco church, and electric fans oscillated on the walls by the Stations of the Cross, and the votive lights in front of a statue of Christ's mother rang with color each time the breeze from the fan passed over the burning wax. The people in the pews were almost all elderly, their hands sheathed in callus, the skin around their eyes wrinkled, as though they had been staring into the sun for a lifetime.

After Mass Pete and I rode my Morgan up the street, then cut through a grove of cedars and an empty filling station that had been built in 1945 and went inside a clapboard café and ate breakfasts of pork chops, biscuits, milk gravy, scrambled eggs, grits, sliced tomatoes, and coffee.

"What's a crystal meth lab?" Pete asked.

"A place where people make narcotics. Why?"

"My mother said to stay away from some men that's in the neighborhood."

"Oh?"

He looked out the window at a dog tied on a rope in the bed of a pickup. He chewed on the corner of his thumbnail. The light had gone out of his eyes.

"You shouldn't tie a dog in the back of a truck. If he falls out, he'll get drug to death. He won't have no chance at all," he said.

"Who are these men, Pete?"

"People my daddy knew once." His face was empty, his gaze still focused outside the window. "My mother made up that story about him getting killed in the army. He just gone off one day and never come home."

"Maybe you shouldn't study on it."

"It don't bother me. If people don't want you, they ain't worth fretting on. That's the way I see it."

Then he grinned again, as though the world's capacity to injure had no power over him.

Jack Vanzandt lived in a large white-columned home built of old brick and Spanish iron-work salvaged from a plantation in Louisiana. The lawn comprised eight acres and sloped upward from the street through shade trees to the wide, breezy front porch of the house, the four-car garage with servants' quarters on top, two clay tennis courts, a screened-in pool stippled with sunlight, a stucco guest cottage, a satellite television dish that was the size of a barn door.

His first wife had died in a traffic accident on a bridge over the Pecos River gorge. The second wife, Emma, came from Shreveport, where her mother and father had run a fundamentalist church, then had become moderately wealthy by starting up a mail-order wedding cake business. Emma's approach to civic and charitable work seemed to be governed by the same entrepreneurial spirit. She ran on high-octane energy that made her eyes flash and her hands move abruptly when she became impatient with the way someone else did his work, until she simply took over it. Like her husband, Jack, she was always polite, and her high cheekbones and long Indian-black hair were lovely to look at. But you always felt you wanted her as a friend, never as an adversary.

"How are you, Billy Bob?" she said, rising from her work in a rose bed, pulling off a cotton glove and extending her hand.

"Sorry to bother y'all on a Sunday, Emma," I said.

"We always love to see you. Did you bring your tennis racquet?"

"No, I'm afraid I have to chop cotton today. Is Jack around?"

"You're going to take his picture?" she said, her eyes dropping to the Polaroid camera in my hand.

"Not really," I said, and smiled.

Jack came out on the front porch, a frosted highball glass wrapped with a napkin and a rubber band in his hand.

"Can you handle a gin and tonic?" he said.

"I just need a minute or two, then I'll be gone," I said.

He watched my face, then said, "Walk out here with me and I'll show you part of an Indian work mound Emma dug up."

We strolled through the trees toward a white gazebo. Pine needles and rose petals had been scattered on the grass by a windstorm during the night.

"My PI had to do some checking on Darl's record," I said. I kept my eyes straight ahead on the piled dirt and sacks of pasteurized

66

fertilizer and potted hydrangeas by the edge of a freshly spaded flower bed.

Jack cleared his throat slightly. "Why's that?" he said.

"You don't want to find out later the other side is waiting for you with a baseball bat. Darl has four arrests involving violence of some kind...Am I correct, he beat up a waitress in a bar?"

Jack squatted by the mound of black dirt and picked up some pottery shards and rubbed them clean between his fingers. There was a thin, round place in the center of his gold hair.

"He shouldn't have been there. But she wasn't a waitress. She was a prostitute, and she and her pimp tried to roll him when they thought he was passed out," he said.

"I'd like to take a Polaroid of Darl."

"I'm a little unclear as to where this is going."

"The kid who might take you for seven figures should at least be able to identify your son in a photo lineup."

"Wait here. I'll get him."

Five minutes later the two of them came out of the back of the house together. Even though it was almost noon, Darl's face looked thick with sleep. He raked his hair downward with a comb, then gazed at the lint that floated out in the sunlight.

"What's that spick say?" he asked.

"Darl...," his father began.

"That you blindsided him and kicked him on the ground," I said.

67

"How about my car? I was supposed to enter it in the fifties show in Dallas. What right's he got to ruin my paint job?"

"That's a mean cut on your ring finger," I said.

"It collided with a flying object. That guy's mouth."

"Two weeks ago?"

"Yeah, his tooth broke off in my hand. I'm lucky I didn't have to get rabies shots."

"Look up a little bit," I said, and popped the flash on the Polaroid.

Darl's eyes stared back at me with the angry vacuity of an animal who believes it has been trapped in a box.

"I'm going back to the house," he said.

"Thank Mr. Holland for the help he's giving us, son," Jack said.

"He's doing this for free? Get a life," Darl said. Thick-bodied, sullen, his face unwashed, he walked through the shade, his hand caressing the peach fuzz along his jawbone.

Jack turned away, his fists knotted on his hips, his forearms corded with veins.

That afternoon Temple Carrol found me back by the windmill, hoeing out my vegetable garden. The sky behind her was purple and yellow with rain clouds, the air already heavy with the smell of ozone.

"My sister-in-law works at the video store. This tape was in the night drop box this morning," she said.

I stopped work and leaned on my hoe. The blades of the windmill were ginning rapidly overhead.

"Somebody must have dropped it in by mistake. You'd better take a look," she said.

We went through the back of the house to the library and plugged the cassette into the VCR.

At first the handheld camera swung wildly through trees illuminated by headlights, rock music blaring on the audio, then the camera steadied, as though it were aimed across a car hood, and we saw kids climbing out of convertibles, throwing ropes of beer on each other, passing joints, kissing each other hard on the mouth for the camera's benefit, their features as white as milk.

Then we saw her in an alcove of trees, in Clorox-faded jeans and a maroon T-shirt with a luminous horse head on it, a long-neck beer in one hand, a joint in the other, dancing to the music as though there were no one else present on earth.

"Roseanne Hazlitt," I said.

"Wait till you see what a small-town girl can do with the right audience," Temple said.

Her auburn hair was partially pinned up in swirls on her head, but one long strand curled around her neck like a snake. She let the beer bottle, then the joint, drop from her fingers into the weeds, and began to sway her hips, her eyes closed, her profile turned to the camera. She pulled her T-shirt over her head, her hair collapsing on her shoulders, arched her shoulders back so that the tops of her breasts almost burst out of her bra, unsnapped her jeans and stepped out of them, then twined her hands in the air and rotated her hips, ran her fingers over her panties and thighs, grasped the back of her neck and widened her legs and opened her mouth in feigned orgasm and pushed her hair over her head so that it cascaded down her face while her tongue made a red circle inside her lips.

The screen turned to snow.

"How about the look on those boys watching her?" Temple said.

"You recognize any of them?" I asked.

"Three or four. Jocks with yesterday's ice cream for brains. How do kids get that screwed up?"

I looked at my watch. It had started to rain outside and the hills were aura-ed with a cold green light like the tarnish on brass. "I'll buy you a barbecue dinner at Shorty's," I said, and dropped the Polaroid photo of Darl Vanzandt in front of her.

We sat on the screen porch and ate plates of cole slaw and refried beans and chicken that had been cooked on a mesquite fire. The river that flowed under the pilings of the club was dented with raindrops, the trees along the bank smoky with mist. Downstream, some boys were swinging out over the water on a rubber tire tied to a rope, cannonballing into the current.

I heard beer cans clattering outside the screen.

"He's an old-timer, Temple. Let's try to keep him in a better mood this time," I said.

"I'll just watch. Maybe I can learn how it's done," she said.

We went out the side door to a woodshed with a tarp that was extended out from the roof on slanted poles. The elderly black man we had interviewed earlier in the week was heaving two vinyl sacks of cans into the shed. When he saw us, he took his stub of a pipe out of his shirt pocket and pared the charcoal out of the bowl with a penknife.

"My memory ain't no better than it was the other day. Must be age. Or maybe I don't take to rudeness," he said. He pointed the stem of his pipe at Temple.

"I get the notion you don't like working here," I said.

"The job's fine. What a lot of people do here ain't."

I held the Polaroid of Darl Vanzandt in front of him. He dipped his pipe in a leather tobacco pouch and pressed the tobacco down into the bowl with the ball of his thumb.

"Is that the boy Roseanne Hazlitt slapped?" I said.

He struck a wood match and cupped it over his pipe, puffing smoke out into the rain. He tossed the match into a puddle and watched it go out.

"You a church man?" I said.

"My wife and me belong to a church in

71

town. If that's what you're axing."

"That girl didn't deserve to die the way she did," I said.

He tapped his fingernail on the Polaroid.

"That ain't the one she slapped," he said. His eyes lingered for a moment on mine, then looked out into the rain.

"But he was in the crowd?" I asked.

"A boy like that don't have no use for anybody else 'cause he don't have no use for himself. What other kind of place he gonna go to? Come back tonight, he'll be here, insulting people, yelling on the dance flo', getting sick out in the weeds. He ain't hard to find."

"Was he here the night she was attacked?" I said.

"Why you giving me this truck? You know the one question y'all ain't axed me? Who'd that po' girl leave with? It was Lucas Smothers. *That's* what I seen." He pointed to the corner of his eye. "Y'all always think you find the right nigger, you gonna get the answer you want."

In the car, I felt Temple's eyes on the side of my face. She rubbed me on the arm with the back of her finger.

"Lucas didn't do it, Billy Bob," she said.

On the way home, by chance and accident, Temple and I witnessed a peculiar event, one that would only add to the questions for which I had no answer.

It had stopped raining, but the sky was

sealed with clouds that were as black as gun cotton and mist floated off the river and clung to the sides of the low hills along the two-lane road. A quarter mile ahead of us, a flatbed truck with a welding machine mounted behind the cab veered back and forth across the yellow stripe. A sheriff's cruiser that had been parked under an overpass, the trunk up to hide the emergency flasher on the roof, pulled the truck to the side of the road and two uniformed deputies got out, slipping their batons into the rings on their belts.

It should have been an easy roadside DWI arrest. It wasn't. The driver of the truck, his khakis and white T-shirt streaked with grease, his face dilated and red with alcohol, fell from the cab into the road, his hard hat rolling away like a tiddledywink. He got to his feet, his ankles spread wide for balance, and started swinging, his first blow snapping a deputy's jaw back against his shoulder.

The other deputy whipped his baton across the tendon behind the truck driver's knee and crumpled him to the asphalt.

It should have been over. It wasn't. We had passed the truck now, and the two deputies were into their own program.

"Uh-oh," Temple said.

They lifted the drunk man by each arm and dragged him on his knees to the far side of the truck. Then we saw the humped silhouettes by the back tire and the balled fists and the batons rising and falling, like men trading off hammer strokes on a tent post.

I touched the brake, pulled to the shoulder, and began backing up in the weeds.

From under the overpass a second cruiser came hard down the road, its blue, white, and red emergency flasher on, water blowing in a vortex behind it. The driver cut to the shoulder, hit the high beams, and the airplane lights burned into the faces of the two deputies and the bloodied man huddled at their knees.

The driver of the second cruiser got out and stood just behind the glare that blinded the two deputies, a portable radio in her left hand, the other on the butt of her holstered nine-millimeter.

"Y'all got a problem here?" Mary Beth Sweeney said.

That night I fell asleep as an electrical storm moved across the drenched hills and disappeared in the west, filling the clouds with flickers of light like burning candles in a Mexican church that smelled of incense and stone and water.

Or like cartridges exploding in the chambers of L.Q. Navarro's blue-black, ivory-handled, custom-made .45 revolver.

It's night in the dream, and L.Q and I are across the river in Mexico, where we have no authority and quarter comes only with dawn. We're dismounted, and our horses keep spooking away from the two dead drug transporters who lie in a muddy slough, their mouths and eyes frozen open with disbelief.

L.Q. pulls a pack of playing cards embla-zoned with the badge of the Texas Rangers from the side pocket of his suit coat, unsnaps two cards from under the rubber band, and flicks them at the corpses.

I pull their guns apart and fling the pieces in different directions.

"The tar is still up in one of them houses. You take the left side and don't silhouette on the hill," L.Q. says.

"Burn the field and the tar will go with it, L.Q.," I say.

"Wind's out of the south. I'd sure hate to lose a race with a grass fire," he says.

The houses are spread out along a low ridge, roofless, made of dried mud, their win-dows like empty eye sockets. My horse is belly deep in a field of yellow grass, and he skit-ters each time the withered husk of a poppy jitters on the stem.

The rifle fire erupts from the windows simultaneously all across the ridge. My horse rears under my thighs, and I feel myself plum-meting backward into darkness, into a crush of yellow grass while tracer rounds float into the sky.

But it's they who set fire to the field, who watch it spread behind a thirty-knot wind that feeds cold air like pure oxygen into the flames. I feel my left foot squish inside my boot, feel my knee collapsing as I try to run uphill and realize that this is the place where all my roads come together, now, in this moment, that the end I never foresaw will be inside an envelope of flame, just as if I had been tied to a medieval stake.

Then I see L.Q. bent low on his mare, pouring it on through the grass, his Stetson low over his eyes, his coat flapping back from his gunbelt, his right hand extended like a rodeo pickup rider's.

I lock my forearm in his, palm against tendon, and swing up on his horse's rump, then feel the surge of muscle and power between my legs as we thunder over the top of a ridge, my arms around L.Q.'s waist, my boot splaying blood into the darkness, my face buried in his manly smell.

Then, as in a dream, I hear the horse's hooves splash through water and clop on stone and L.Q. holler out, "Why, goodness gracious, it's Texas already, bud!"

CHAPTER

8

At five-thirty Monday morning I went to Deaf Smith's sole health club, located a block off the town square in what used to be a five-and-dime store, where I worked out three times a week. I lifted in the weight room, then exercised on the benches and Nautilus machines and was headed for the steam room when I saw Mary Beth Sweeney on a Stair-Master machine, by herself, at the end of a blind hallway. Her cotton sports bra was peppered with sweat, her face flushed and heated with her movement on the machine. Her curly hair stuck in strands to her cheeks.

"Good morning," I said.

"How do you do, Mr. Holland?" she said.

"Nobody calls me 'Mr. Holland.'...Never mind...That was impressive last night. That guy in the welding truck owes you one."

"*You* stopped, didn't you?"

"Can you go to a picture show tonight?" I asked.

"Why do you keep bothering me?"

"You're a handsome woman."

"You've got some damn nerve."

I bounced the tip of my towel on the base of the StairMaster.

"Adios," I said.

A half hour later I walked outside into the blue coolness of the morning, the mimosa trees planted in the sidewalks ruffling in the shadow of the buildings. Mary Beth Sweeney, dressed in her uniform, was about to get into her car. She heard me behind her, threw her canvas gym bag on the passenger's seat, and turned to face me.

"You strike me as an admirable person. I apologize for my overture, however. I won't bother you again," I said, and left her standing there.

I walked down the street toward my car. I paused in front of the pawnshop window and looked at the display spread out on a piece of green velvet: brass knuckles, stiletto gut-rippers, barber's razors, slapjacks, handcuffs, derringers, a .38 Special with notches filed in the grips, a 1911 model U.S. Army .45, and a blue-black ivory-handled revolver that could have been a replica of L.Q. Navarro's.

I felt a presence on my back, like someone brushing a piece of ice between my shoulder blades. I turned around and saw Garland T. Moon watching me from the door of a bar, licking down the seam of a hand-rolled cigarette. He wore a cream-colored suit with no shirt and black prison-issue work shoes, the archless, flat-soled kind with leather thongs and hook eyelets.

I walked back to the door of the bar.

"Early for the slop chute, isn't it?" I said.

"I don't drink. Never have."

"You following me?"

He lit the cigarette, propped one foot against the wall, inhaled the smoke and burning glue into his lungs. He cast away the paper match in the wind.

"Not even in my darkest thoughts, sir," he said.

I headed back up the street. The three-hundred-pound black woman who owned the pawnshop was just opening up. She saw my eyes glance at her window display.

"Time to put some boom-boom in yo' bam-bam, baby," she said. She winked and tapped her ring on the glass. "I ain't talking about me, honey. But I 'preciate the thought anyway."

At noon I carried a ham sandwich and a glass of milk out on my back porch. Beyond the barn I saw Pete sitting on the levee that surrounded the tank.

He heard me walking toward him, but he never turned around.

"Why aren't you in school, bud?" I asked.

"Stayed home, that's why," he said, looking out at the water.

Then I saw the discolored lump and skinned place by his eye.

"Who did that to you?" I asked.

"Man my mother brung home last night." He picked at his fingers and flung a rock into the tank. Then he flung another one.

I sat down next to him.

"Is your mom okay?" I asked.

"She ain't got up yet. She won't be right the rest of the day."

"Where could I find this fellow?" I said.

We went into the barn and I strapped on L.Q.'s roweled spurs and saddled my Morgan. I pulled a heavy coil of rodeo polyrope off a wood peg and hung it on the pommel. It was five-eighths of an inch in diameter and had an elongated eye cinched at the tip with fine wire.

"What are we doing, Billy Bob?" Pete said.

"The man who owned these Mexican spurs, he used to tell me, 'Sometimes you've got to set people's perspective straight.'"

I put my arm down and pulled him up on the Morgan's rump.

"What's 'perspective' mean?" Pete said.

We rode through the back of my farm, crossed the creek and went up the slope through the pines. The ground was moist and netted with sunlight under the Morgan's shoes, and ahead I could see the stucco church where Pete and I went to Mass and the deserted filling station on the corner and up the dirt street an unpainted plank-walled tavern with a shingle-roof porch and boxes of petunias in the windows.

I stopped the Morgan by the side window.

"You see him?" I asked.

"That's him yonder, by the pool table. The one eating chili beans out of a paper plate."

"I want you to go on back to the café and wait for me."

"Maybe you oughtn't to do this, Billy Bob. My eye don't hurt now."

"Did you eat lunch yet?"

"He's got a frog sticker in his right-hand pocket. I seen it when he..."

"When he what?"

"Hung up his britches on my mother's bedpost."

I put five dollars in Pete's hand. "Better get you a hamburger steak and one of those peach ice cream sundaes. I'll be along in a minute."

Pete slid off the Morgan's rump and walked down the street toward the café, looking back over his shoulder at me, the lump by his eye as red as a boil.

I took the polyrope off the pommel, unfastened the pig string that held the coil in place, worked the length of the rope through my palms and ran the bottom end through the eye at the tip. Then I double-folded the rope along half the loop, picked up the slack off the ground, and rode my Morgan up on the porch and through the doorway, ducking down on his withers to get under the jamb.

The inside of the tavern was well lighted and paneled with lacquered yellow pine, and neon Lone Star and Pearl beer signs and an enormous Texas flag were hung over the bar.

"I hope you brung your own dustpan and whisk broom," the bartender said.

I rode the Morgan between a cluster of tables and chairs and across a small dance floor toward the pool table. The man eating from a paper plate looked at me, smiling, a spoonful of chili halfway to his mouth. He wore a neatly barbered blond beard and a shark tooth necklace and a blue leather vest and black jeans and silver boots sheathed with metal plates.

I whipped the loop three times over my head and flung it at the man with the blond beard. It slapped down on him hard and caught him under one arm and across the top of the torso. He tried to rise from the chair and free himself, but I wound the rope tightly around the pommel, brought my left

spur into the Morgan's side, and catapulted
the blond man off his feet and dragged him car-
oming through tables and bar stools and
splintering chairs, into an oak post and the legs
of a pinball machine and the side of the juke-
box, tearing a huge plastic divot out of the casing. Then I ducked my head under the
doorjamb, and the Morgan clopped across
the porch and into the road, and I gave him
the spurs again.

I dragged the blond man skittering through
the parking lot, across layers of flattened beer
cans and bottle caps embedded in the dirt. His
clothes were gray with dust now, his face
barked and bleeding, both of his hands gripped
on the rope as he tried to pull himself free of
the pressure that bound his chest.

I reined in the Morgan and turned him in
a slow circle while the blond man rose to his
feet.

"Tell me why this is happening to you," I
said.

"Wha—" he began.

"You turn around and you tell all these
people how you hurt a child," I said.

He wiped the blood off his nose with the flat
of his hand.

"His mama told me there was a fellow liked
to put his head up her dress," he said.

I got down from the saddle and hooked
him in the nose, then grabbed his neck and the
back of his shirt and drove his head into the
corner of the porch post.

The skin split in a scarlet star at the crown

of his skull. When he went down, I couldn't stop. I saw my boot and spur rake across his face, then I tried to kick him again and felt myself topple backward off balance.

Pete was hanging on my arm, the five-dollar bill crushed in his palm, his eyes hollow with fear as though he were looking at a stranger.

"Stop, Billy Bob! Please don't do it no more!" he said, his voice sobbing in the peal of sirens that came from two directions.

CHAPTER

9

I sat in the enclosed gloom of the sheriff's office, across from his desk and the leviathan silhouette of his body against the back window. The deputy who had arrested me leaned against the log wall, his face covered in shadow. The sheriff took his cigar out of his mouth and leaned over the spittoon by the corner of his desk and spit.

"You turned that fellow into a human pinball. What's the matter with you?" he said.

"It's time to charge me or cut me loose, sheriff," I said.

"Just keep your britches on. You don't think I got enough drunk nigras and white trash in my jail without having to worry about the goddamn lawyers?...Ah, there's the man right now. Cain't you beat up somebody without starting an international incident?" he said.

83

The door opened, and a dark-skinned man in a tropical hat with a green plastic window built into the brim and a tan suit that had no creases entered the room. He removed his hat and shook the sheriff's hand, then the uniformed deputy's and mine. He was a little older than I, in his midforties, perhaps, his jawline fleshy, his thin mustache like the romantic affectation of a 1930s leading man.

"Felix Ringo, a Mexican drug agent?" I repeated.

"Yeah, you know that name, man? Is gringo. My ancestor, he was a famous American outlaw," he said.

"Johnny Ringo?" I said.

"Yeah, that was his name. He got into it with guys like, the guy there in Arizona, was always wearing a black suit in the movies, yeah, that guy Wyatt Earp."

"Felix is jalapeño and shit on toast south of the Rio Grande. You fucked up his bust, Billy Bob," the sheriff said.

"Oh?" I said.

"The guy you drug up and down, man, I been following him six months. He's gonna be gone now," the Mexican said.

"Maybe you should have taken him down six months ago. He hurt a little boy this morning."

"Yeah, man, but maybe you don't see the big picture. We take one guy down, we roll him over, then we take another guy down. See, patience is, how you call it, the virtue here."

"The guy I pulled out of that bar isn't the

Medellín Cartel North. What is this stuff, sheriff?" I said.

The sheriff rolled his cigar in the center of his mouth and looked at the Mexican drug agent.

"Billy Bob used to be a Texas Ranger, so he looks down on the ordinary pissant work most of us have to do," he said.

"That's a bad fucking attitude, man," Felix Ringo said.

"Get out your fingerprint pad or I'm gone, sheriff," I said.

He dropped his cigar hissing into the spittoon.

"There's the door. Don't mistake my gesture. Stay the hell out of what don't concern you," he said.

Felix Ringo followed me outside. The light was hard and bright on the stone buildings in the square, the trees a violent green against the sky. I could see Mary Beth Sweeney outside her cruiser, writing on a clipboard in the shade. She stopped and stared across the lawn at me and the man named Felix Ringo.

"You want something?" I asked him.

"I seen you somewhere before. You was a Ranger?" he said.

"What about it?"

"You guys did stuff at night, maybe killed some people that was fruit pickers crossing the river, that didn't have nothing to do with dope."

"You're full of shit, too, bud," I said, and walked toward the cab stand across the street.

I stepped off the curb and waited for a car to pass.

Then I heard her voice behind me.

"Hey, Billy Bob," she said.

"Yeah?"

She gave me the thumbs-up sign and smiled.

The next morning I drove along the fence line of my property to a section by the river where Lucas and Vernon Smothers were hoeing out the rows in a melon patch. I walked out into the field, into the heat bouncing off the ground, into Vernon's beaded stare under the brim of his straw hat.

"I want to borrow Lucas for a couple of hours," I said.

"What for?" he asked.

"Take a guess," I said.

He propped his forearm on his hoe handle and smelled himself. He looked out over the bluff and the milky green flatness of the river and the willows on the far side.

"I don't want to lose my melons to coons this year. I aim to put steel traps along that ditch yonder. That's where they're coming out of," he said.

"I need Lucas to help me with the case, Vernon. You're not putting any steel traps on my property, and you can forget about poisons, too."

"You ever see how a coon eats a melon? He punches a little hole, no bigger than a quarter. Then he sticks his paw in and cleans the

86

whole insides out. All he needs to do is get his paw in the hole and he don't leave nothing but an empty shell for anybody else."

His mouth was small and angry, down-turned on the corners, his stare jaundiced with second meaning.

"Let's go to the movies, Lucas," I said.

Lucas sat on the back steps and pulled off his boots.

"You don't have to do that," I said.

"I'll track your house."

We went into the library and I switched on the VCR that contained the videotape of Roseanne Hazlitt dancing. Lucas's face went gray when he realized what he was being shown.

"Mr. Holland, I ain't up to this," he said.

"Who are the other kids in that woods?"

"East End kids messin' around. I don't know them too good."

"I don't believe you."

"Why you talk to me like that?"

"Because none of this will go away of its own accord. You played in the band at Shorty's. You knew the same people Roseanne knew. But you don't give me any help."

He swallowed. His palms were cupped on his knees.

"I grew up in the West End. I don't like those kind of guys."

"Good. So give me the names of the other boys she went out with."

He fingered the denim on top of his thigh, his knees jiggling up and down, his eyes fixed on the floor.

"Anybody. When she was loaded. It didn't matter to her. Three or four guys at once. Same guys who'd write her name on the washroom wall," he said. He blinked and rubbed his forehead with the heel of his hand.

We drove into Deaf Smith and parked on the square and walked down a side street toward a brick church with a white steeple and a green lawn and a glassed-in sign announcing Sunday and Wednesday night services.

"Why we going to the Baptist church?" Lucas asked.

"We're not," I replied.

Next door to the church was the church's secondhand store. An alley ran along one wall of the store, and at the end of the alley was an overflowing donation bin. The pavement around it was littered with pieces of mattresses and mildewed clothing that had been run over by automobile tires. As soon as the store closed at night, street people sorted through the bin and the overflow like a collection of rag pickers.

Lucas's eyes fixed on a waxed, cherry-red chopped-down 1932 Ford with a white rolled leather interior and an exposed chromed engine parked in front of the store.

"You know the owner of that car?" I asked.

"It's Darl Vanzandt's."

"That's right," I said, and pointed through the glass.

Darl was sorting a box of donated books by pitching them one at a time onto a display table. When the box was empty, he opened the back door and flung it end over end into the alley.

"We need to have a talk with him," I said.

"What for? I ain't got no interest in Darl." The rims of his nostrils whitened as though the temperature had dropped seventy degrees.

"It'll just take a minute."

"Not me. No, sir."

He backed away from me, then turned and walked back to the car.

I got in beside him.

"What's the problem?" I asked.

"I don't fool with East Enders, that's all." He twisted at a callus on his palm.

"All of them, or just Darl?"

"You don't know how it is."

"I grew up here."

"They look down on you. Darl knows how to make people feel bad about themselves."

"Like how?"

"In metal shop, senior year, he was making Chinese stars in the foundry, these martial arts things you can sail at people and put out an eye with. Darl was hogging the sand molds, and this kid says, 'I got to pour my mailbox hangers or I won't get my grade,' and Darl goes, 'You got an S for snarf. Get out of the way.'

"The kid says, 'What's a snarf?'

"Darl says, 'You don't got a mirror at home?'

"After school Darl catches the kid out in front of everybody and says, 'Hey, a snarf is a guy who gets off sniffing girls' bicycle seats. But I had you made wrong. You don't get an S. You get an F for frump. That's a guy cuts farts in the bathtub and bites the bubbles.'"

Lucas's cheeks were blotched with color.

"Would Darl beat a girl with his fists, Lucas?"

"My father needs me back in the field," he answered.

That evening I opened up all the windows in the third floor of my house and let the breeze fill the rooms with the smells of alfalfa and distant rain and ozone and dust blowing out of the fields.

The house seemed to resonate with its own emptiness. I stood by the side of the hand-carved tester bed that had been my parents', my fingers resting on the phone, and looked out over the barn roof and windmill and the fields that led down to the clay bluffs over the river. Lightning with no sound quivered on a green hill in the west.

I punched in Mary Beth Sweeney's number.

"You mind my calling you?" I asked.

"I'm happy you did."

The line hummed in the silence.

"I know a Mexican restaurant that serves food you only expect in the Elysian Fields," I said.

"Let's talk about it tomorrow."

"Sure," I said.

"I'm sorry, I don't mean to be like this…That Mexican narc you were talking with? He's a bucket of shit. You watch your butt, cowboy."

Watch your own. You're working for the G, Mary Beth, I said to myself as I put down the receiver.

That night I heard the doors on the near end of the barn slamming in the wind. I rolled over and went back to sleep, then remembered I had closed the doors on the near end and had slipped the cross planks into place to hold them secure. I put on a pair of khakis and took a flashlight from the back porch and walked through the yard, the electric beam angling ahead of me.

One door fluttered and squealed on its hinges, then sucked loudly against the jamb. I started to push the other door into place, then I looked down the length of stalls, out in the railed lot on the far side, and saw my Morgan trotting in a circle, walleyed with fear, spooking at bits of paper blowing in the moonlight.

"What's wrong, Beau? Weather usually doesn't bother you," I said.

I got him into the barn and stroked his face, closed the door behind him, and unscrewed the cap on a jar of oats-and-molasses balls and poured a dozen into the trough at the head of his stall.

Then I saw the red, diagonal slash on his withers, as though he had been struck a downward blow by a metal-edged instrument.

His skin wrinkled and quivered under my hand when I placed it close to the wound.

"Who did this to you, Beau?" I said.

The electric lights in the barn were haloed with humidity, glowing with motes of dust in the silence.

At eight the next morning I drove to the edge of town, where Jack Vanzandt ran his business in a five-story building sheathed in black glass. His office was huge, the beige carpet as soft as a bear's fur, the furniture white and onyx black, the glass wall hung with air plants.

I sat in a stuffed leather chair, my legs crossed, the purpose of my visit like a piece of sharp tin in my throat.

"You want to buy some computer stock?" Jack asked, and grinned.

A door opened off to the side and Jack's wife walked out of a rest room. I rose from my chair.

"Hello, Emma, I didn't know you were here," I said.

"Good morning, sir. Where's your camera?" she said.

"Maybe I should come back later. I didn't mean to intrude upon y'all," I said.

"No, no, I'm delighted you came by. What's up?" Jack said.

"It's Darl."

"Unhuh?" Jack said.

"I can't represent him."

They looked at me quizzically.

"Can you tell me why?" Jack asked.

"I have a conflict of interest. I was retained earlier by Lucas Smothers. I think your son was at Shorty's the night Roseanne Hazlitt was attacked."

"Probably half the kids in Deaf Smith were," Jack said.

"Darl could end up as a witness at Lucas's trial," I said.

I could see the connections coming together in Jack's eyes, his good looks clouding.

"No, this goes beyond that, doesn't it?" He pointed one finger, bouncing it in the air. "You're making Darl a suspect to get Lucas off the hook."

"Nope."

"Well, I personally think you should be ashamed of yourself, Billy Bob," Emma said.

"I'm sorry," I said, rising from my chair. The room felt warm, the air astringent with the smell of chemical pellets in the hanging baskets.

Jack rose from his chair behind his desk. The balls of his fingers rested on the glass top. His lavender shirt with a white collar and rolled French cuffs and loose tie looked like a cosmetic joke on his powerful body.

"Do you want me to write a check right now, or does the bill come later for photographing my son so you can implicate him in a murder?" he asked.

"I didn't invent your son's history or his problems..." I shook my head. "I apologize for my remark. I'd better go now," I said.

93

"Jack, don't let this happen. We need to sit down and talk this out," Emma said.

"I might have some difficulty doing that. Get out of my office, Billy Bob," he said.

Outside, I could feel the blood stinging in my neck, my hands useless and thick at my sides.

CHAPTER

10

The next morning, when Lucas Smothers came to work with his father, he told me of the late-night visit he had received from people with whom he had gone to high school.

The cars cut their lights before they got to Lucas's house, but through his open window he could hear music on a radio and the voices of girls. The cars, five of them, were stopped in the center of the road, their engines throbbing softly against the pavement, their hand-rubbed body surfaces glowing dully under the moon like freshly poured plastic.

Then the lead car turned into Lucas's drive, followed by the others, and fishtailed across the damp lawn, scouring grass and sod into the air, crunching the sprinkler, ripping troughs out of the flower beds.

One girl jumped from a car, a metallic object in her hand, and bent down below the level of the bedroom window. He heard a hissing sound, then saw her raise up and look at him. No, that wasn't accurate. She never saw him, as though his possible presence was as insignificant as the worth of his home. Her face was beautiful and empty, her mouth like a pursed button.

"What are y'all doing?" he said, his voice phlegmy in his throat.

If she heard him, she didn't show it. Her skin seemed to flush with pleasure just before she turned and pranced like a deer into the waiting arms of her friends, who giggled and pulled her back inside the car.

By the time Lucas and his father got outside, the caravan was far down the road, the headlights dipping over a hill.

Lucas could see the girl's footprints by the water faucet under his window. The ground was soft and muddy here, and the footprints were small and sharp edged and narrow at the toe, and it was obvious the girl had tried to stand on a piece of cardboard to keep the mud off her shoes. Written in red, tilted, spray-painted letters below Lucas's screen was the solitary word LOSER.

That same day I drove out to the Green Parrot Motel, a pink cinder-block monstrosity painted with tropical birds and palm trees and advertising water beds and triple-X movies. The desk clerk told me Garland T. Moon was next door at the welding shop.

The tin shed had only one window, which was painted over and nailed shut, and the walls pinged with the sun's heat. Garland T. Moon was stripped to the waist, black goggles on his eyes, arc-welding the iron bucket off a ditching machine. The sparks dripped to his feet like liquid fire. He pushed his goggles up on his forehead with a dirty thumb and wiped his eyes on his forearm. His smile made me think of a clay sculpture that had been pushed violently out of shape.

"Were you out at my house two nights ago?" I asked.

"I got me a parttime job. I don't run around at night."

"I think either you or Jimmy Cole hurt my horse."

"I was out a couple of nights. The other side of them hills. There's all kind of lights in the clouds. You ever hear of the Lubbock Lights, them UFOs that was photographed? There's something weird going on hereabouts."

"I've rigged two shotguns on my property. I hope you don't find one of them."

"You don't have no guns. I made a whole study of you, Mr. Holland. I can touch that boy and I touch you. It's a sweet thought, but I ain't got the inclination right now."

"Jimmy Cole's dead, isn't he?" I said.

He pulled a soot-blackened glove from his hand one finger at a time.

"Why would a person think that?" he asked.

"You don't leave loose ends."

"If I was to come out to your place or that pup's with a serious mind, y'all wouldn't have no doubt about who visited you...You

96

cain't do nothing about me, Mr. Holland.
Don't nobody care what happens to crazy
people. I know. I majored in crazy. I know it
inside and out."

"Crazy people?"

"I heard the screw say it in the jail. You're
queer for a dead man. You're one seriously sick
motherfucker and don't know it."

He started laughing, hard, his flat chest
shaking, sweat rolling through the dirt rings
on his neck, the wisps of red hair on his scalp
flecked with bits of black ash.

I picked up Mary Beth Sweeney at her apartment that evening and we drove down the
old two-lane toward the county line. She
wore a pale organdy dress and white pumps
and earrings with blue stones in them, and I
could smell the baby powder she used to
cover the freckles on her shoulders and neck.

Twice she glanced at the road behind us.

"You having regrets?" I asked.

Her eyes moved over my face.

"I don't think your situation is compromised. The sheriff's corrupt, but he's not
Phi Beta Kappa material," I said.

"What are you talking about?"

"I think you work for the G," I said.

"The G? Like the government?"

"That's the way I'd read it."

"I'm starting to feel a little uncomfortable
about this, Billy Bob."

She gazed out the side window so I couldn't see her expression. We crossed the river and the planks on the bridge rattled under my tires.

"My great-grandfather's ranch ran for six miles right along that bank," I said. "He used to trail two thousand head at a time to the rail-head in Kansas, then he gave up guns and whiskey and became a saddle preacher. His only temptation in life after that was the Rose of Cimarron."

"I'm sorry. I wasn't listening," she said.

"My great-grandpa...He was a gunfighter turned preacher, but he had a love affair with an outlaw woman called the Rose of Cimarron. She was a member of the Dalton-Doolin gang. He wrote in his journal that his head got turned by the sweetest and most dangerous woman in Oklahoma Territory."

"I'm afraid you've lost me," she said.

I tried to laugh. "You're a fed. This county's got a long history of political corruption, Mary Beth. There're some violent people here."

"How about the prosecutor, Marvin Pomroy?"

"He's an honest man. As far as I know, anyway. Are you FBI?"

"Can we forget this conversation?" she said.

I didn't answer. We pulled into a Mexican restaurant built of logs and scrolled with neon. I walked around to the passenger side to open the door for her, but she was already standing outside.

The hills to the west were rimmed with a purple glow when I drove her back home. During the evening I had managed to say almost nothing that was not inept and awkward. I turned into her apartment building and parked by the brick wall that bordered the swimming pool.

"Maybe I should say good night here," I said.

"No, come in for a drink."

"I've made you uneasy. I don't want to compound it."

"You're patronizing me...I don't understand you, Billy Bob. You quit a career as a law officer and then as an assistant U.S. attorney to be a defense lawyer. You like putting dope mules back on the street?"

"I won't handle traffickers."

"Because you're a cop. You think like one."

I heard cars behind me on the road, the same two-lane that I could follow, if I were willing, into Val Verde County and beyond, across the river, into an arroyo where horses reared in the gunfire and a man in a pinstriped suit and ash gray Stetson and Mexican spurs grabbed at his breast and called out to the sky.

We were outside the car now. My ears were popping, as though I were on an airplane that suddenly had lost altitude.

I heard myself say something.

"I beg your pardon?" Mary Beth said, her mouth partly open.

My face felt cold, impervious to the wind, the skin pulled back against the bone. Like the penitent who refuses to accept the priest's absolution through the grilled window inside the confessional, I felt the words rise once more in my throat, as in a dream that knows no end.

"I killed my best friend. His name was L.Q. Navarro. He was a Texas Ranger," I said.

Her lips moved soundlessly, her eyes disjointed as though she were looking at a fractured image inside a child's kaleidoscope.

At noon the next day I walked from my office to the pawnshop down the street from the health club. The three-hundred-pound black woman who owned it, whose name was Ella Mae, wore glass beads in her hair and a white T-shirt that read: *I Don't Give a Fuck—Don't Leave Home Without American Express.*

On the wall behind the counter were scores of guns and musical instruments. I pointed at one.

"Can you give me a good deal, Ella Mae?" I said.

"Honey, if we was back in the old days, I'd pay to pick your cotton. That's the truth. Wouldn't put you on," she said.

But after she had rung up my purchase, her mood changed, as though she were stepping across a line she had drawn between herself and white people.

"The other day when you was here? You gone on to your car, but a man with red hair was watching you. He had a coat on without no shirt," she said.

"What about him?"

"The look in his face, honey. He started to come in here and I locked the door." She shook her head, as though she feared her words could make the image a reality.

That evening I drove to Lucas Smothers's house. Vernon was sitting on the steps, a bottle of strawberry soda beside him. His clothes were dirty from his work, his face lined with streaks of dried sweat. A wheelbarrow filled with compost and crisscrossed with rakes and a shovel stood in the front yard. Under Lucas's screen was a bright patch of white paint.

"Is Lucas home?" I asked.

"He took the truck to town."

"Did the sheriff do anything about those kids who tore up your lawn?"

"That tub of guts is doing good to get himself on and off the toilet seat."

"Is Lucas at the poolroom?"

"No, they're handing out free beer at the Baptist church tonight."

"It's always a pleasure, Vernon."

But Vernon had another side, one that wouldn't allow me the freedom to simply condemn and dismiss him. When I was almost out the drive, he rose from the steps and called my name and walked out to the road. He pulled a cloth cap from his back pocket and popped it open and flicked it against his thigh, as though he could not bring himself to admit the nature of his fear and love and his dependence upon others.

"What kind of chance has he got? Don't lie to me, either," he said.

"It doesn't look real good right now."

"It ain't right...I swear, if they send that boy to prison..." He breathed hard through his nose. "I killed people in Vietnam didn't do nothing to me."

"I'd get a lot of distance between me and those kinds of thoughts, Vernon."

"Damn, if you don't always have to get up on the high ground. Excuse me for asking, but who died and made you God?" he said, and went inside the house.

You didn't win with Vernon Smothers.

I drove downtown and parked in front of the poolroom, a gaunt, two-story building that was over a hundred years old. It had a wood colonnade and elevated sidewalk inset with iron hitching poles, a stamped tin ceiling, oak floors as thick as railroad ties, a railed bar with spittoons, card and domino tables, a wood-burning stove, and a toilet down a back hallway with the water tank high up on the wall.

Down the row of pool tables, I saw Lucas chalking a cue, sipping off of a long-neck beer. He wore a pair of gray slacks and loafers and a starched lavender shirt and he had put gel in his hair.

"Come on outside," I said.

"Now?" he asked.

"Half the people in here are my clients...I'd like to stay off the clock."

His face pinched with confusion. "What?" he asked.

It was cool outside, and down the street the live oaks on the courthouse lawn were gold and purple and freckled with birds in the sun's afterglow.

"You got a date?" I said.

"I'm supposed to talk with this guy about a job," he said.

"Have a seat in my car. I want to show you something."

As soon as he opened the passenger door he saw the twelve-string guitar propped up on the seat.

"Man, where'd you get that at?" he said.

"A client. I never could play one for diddly-squat, though. You want it?"

"*Do* I?"

"It's yours. I hate to use it for a fly swatter."

He corded the neck and ran his thumbnail across the strings.

"Wow, what a sound. Mr. Holland, I'll make this right with you."

"Don't worry about it. Look, those kids who tore up y'all's lawn?"

"My father and me fixed it. I don't care about kids like that."

"Listen to me. I don't know why anyone would..." I shook my head and started over. "Maybe they have too much money, maybe they're just mean, but it's important you understand what and who you are...Sometimes we look at the reflection in other people's eyes and that's who we think we are and the

103

truth is we're a whole lot better than that."

"You're a good guy, Mr. Holland. But I don't want to talk about this."

"Suit yourself. But you're an artist, the honest-to-God real article, Lucas. Some people will always envy and hate you for the talent you have."

He turned the guitar over in his hands and felt the polished mahogany and walnut belly and the spruce soundboard.

"It's funny, I seen one just like this in Ella Mae's pawnshop. She wanted three hundred dollars for it," he said.

"No kidding?"

His gaze wandered over my face, then he looked out the window at a man in cream-colored slacks and a tropical hat walking toward the poolroom.

"There's the guy I'm meeting," Lucas said.

"Felix Ringo? He's the guy talking to you about a job?"

"Yeah, I told you about him. He's got a furniture factory down in Piedras Negras."

"He's a Mexican drug agent."

"Yeah. He's got a furniture business, too."

"Wait here."

I got out of the Avalon and approached the man named Felix Ringo. His expression was flat, his eyes registering me with the valuative pause of a predator waking from sleep.

"I don't know why, but you're running a game on the kid in my car. It stops here," I said.

"You got some bad manners, man."

"I'll say it once. Stay away from him."

"I was at Fort Benning. The School of the Americas. I'm here with the permission of your government. I don't like to provoke nobody, but I don't got to take your shit."

"Don't bet on it."

"Hey, man, I got a good memory. I'm gonna remember where I seen your face. When I do, maybe you ain't gonna have a very good day."

I stepped off the sidewalk and got back in my car. He remained under the colonnade, staring at Lucas. Then he jerked his head at him, motioning him inside.

"He's dirty, Lucas. It's something you can smell on a bad cop. He'll take you down with him," I said.

"I cain't get on at any clubs. What am I gonna do, keep working for my dad the rest of my life?"

"It might beat chopping cotton with a gunbull standing over you," I said and started the car and drove down the street before he could get out.

"Why don't you treat me like I'm three years old?" he said, his face red with anger and embarrassment.

"I want the names of all Darl Vanzandt's friends," I said.

That night I sat at my library desk and read from Great-grandpa Sam's faded, water-stained journal that he had carried in a saddlebag through Oklahoma Territory.

L.Q. Navarro sat in a burgundy-colored

stuffed chair in the corner, fiddling with his revolver, an armadillo-shell lamp lighted behind his head. He spun the revolver on his finger and let the ivory handles snick back flatly in his palm. The blue-black of the steel was so deep in hue it looked almost liquid. He opened the loading gate with his thumb, pulled back the hammer on half-cock, and rotated the cylinder so that one loaded chamber at a time clicked past his examining eye.

"That Garland T. Moon? You can take it to him with fire tongs. That boy's not a listener," he said.

"I'm trying to read, L.Q.," I said.

"You going to find your answers in there? I don't hardly think so."

I rested my brow on my fingers so I wouldn't have to look at him.

I read from Great-grandpa Sam's journal:

In the Indian Nation, July 4, 1891
I always heard women in the Cherokee Strip was precious few in number and homely as a mud fence, but it was not held against them none. The Rose of Cimarron surely gives the lie to that old cowboy wisdom. She is probably part colored and part savage and perhaps even related to the Comanche halfbreed Quanah Parker. She is also the most fetching creature I have ever set eyes on. I would marry her in a minute and take her back to Texas, but I am sure I would not only be run out of the Baptist church but the state as well, provided she did not cut my throat first.

If the Lord made me for the cloth, why has my lust and this woman come together at such an inopportune time?

L.Q. stuffed his revolver in his holster and walked to the ceiling-high window and looked out at the hills. I could see the thick, brass cartridges in the leather loops on his gunbelt, and the Ranger badge clipped just in front of his holster.

"Your great-grandpa got rid of whiskey and guns in his life, but his propensities come out in a different way," he said.

"What's that mean?"

"Garland Moon, Jimmy Cole, that Mexican drug agent with the grease pencil mustache? You don't run them kind off with a legal writ, Billy Bob."

He took his revolver back out of his holster and hefted it from one palm to the other, the barrel and cylinder and moon-white grips slapping against his skin.

A pair of headlights turned into my drive, and through the library window I saw Mary Beth Sweeney pull her cruiser to the back of my house.

I stepped out on the back porch and opened the screen door. Her portable radio was clipped to her belt.

"You on duty?" I said.

"For another hour. I need to talk with you," she said. She stepped inside the porch and took off her campaign hat and shook out her hair.

107

"You can't just unload a bomb like that and walk off from someone."

"Last night?"

"Yeah, last night. I don't want somebody hanging his guilt on me like I'm some kind of dartboard."

"That wasn't my intention."

"Oh no? Like, 'Hey, I killed my best friend, and you remind me of it, so see you around and thanks for the great evening.'"

"Where do you get the in-your-face attitude?" I said.

"I knew it would be a mistake coming here."

"No, it wasn't," I said. I held my eyes on hers and realized what it was that drew me to her. The spray of pale freckles, the dark brown curls that had a silklike sheen in them, the obvious decency and courage in her behavior, these were all the characteristics that had probably defined her as a girl and had stayed with her into her maturity. But her eyes, which were bold and unrelenting, masked a level of past injury that she didn't easily share.

Her stare broke.

"Come in. I just baked a pecan pie," I said.

"I'd better not."

I put my hand under her forearm.

"You have to," I said.

She bit down on her bottom lip.

"I need help with this Mexican drug agent," I said.

"For just a minute." She walked ahead of me and sat at the kitchen table, with her hat crown-down in front of her.

"Felix Ringo told me he was at the School of the Americas at Fort Benning. Punch him up on the computer for me," I said.

"The federal computer, you're saying?"

"You got it."

"What's this School of the Americas?"

"It's supposed to be counterinsurgency training. But their graduates have a way of murdering liberation theologians and union organizers or anybody they don't approve of."

I placed a piece of pie and cup of coffee in front of her. She turned a tiny silver spoon in her cup, then put the spoon down and gazed out the window.

"I'm not saying I have access. But I'll do what I can," she said. Static, then a dispatcher's voice squawked on her portable. "I'll have to take a rain check on the pie."

She walked out onto the porch, both hands on the brim of her campaign hat.

I picked up one of her hands and traced my fingers down the inside of her arm and brushed her palm and touched her nails and the back of her wrist and folded her fingers across mine.

"You're really a nice lady," I said.

The wind filled the trees outside and blew through the screens, and a loose strand of her hair caught wetly in the side of her mouth. I removed it with my fingertips, then looked in her eyes and saw the consent that I knew she rarely gave, and I put my hands on her arms and kissed her on the mouth, then did it again, then slipped my arms around her and

109

touched her hair and the hard muscles in her back.

I felt a warm exhalation of her breath against my cheek, like that of a swimmer taking a self-disciplinary pause, then her palms pressing on my chest, and I was looking into her face again, the light brown freckles, the brightness of her eyes. She pursed her lips, then winked and was gone into the yard and the shadows and the moonlight and her cruiser, all that fast.

I stood in the drive and watched her back out into the road and pull away behind the row of poplar trees and myrtle bushes that bordered my front yard.

Down the road, I heard a second car engine start up, then a pair of headlights flared in the road and a sheriff's cruiser passed my driveway, with two men in it, headed in the same direction as Mary Beth. The man in the passenger's seat seemed to have his arm propped up on the sill so anyone watching from my house could not identify him.

I called 911 and told the dispatcher a drunk man with a gun was shooting at automobiles in front of my home.

CHAPTER

II

A half hour later I stood in the front yard and watched the last of five cruisers from the sheriff's department, including Mary Beth

Sweeney's, drive away. Temple Carrol had seen the emergency lights from her house down the road and had arrived only a few minutes ago. "Somebody shooting at cars? I didn't hear any gunfire," she said.

"I saw two guys in a cruiser follow that new deputy from my house, so I muddied up the water," I replied.

"Mary Beth Sweeney? What's she doing at your house?"

"I wanted her to run this Mexican drug agent for me."

"She had to come by your house to do it?" She looked across the road at my neighbor's cattle bunched in the field.

"She was in the neighborhood," I said.

"This broad always has a way of being in the neighborhood."

"You want a cup of coffee?"

She pulled a bandanna out of her jeans pocket and tied up her hair. "I can't sleep when I drink coffee. Or when I think your house is burning down," she said.

She walked toward her car.

"Temple?" I said.

She didn't answer.

I was rinsing the dishes after breakfast the next morning when Vernon Smothers tapped on my back door. He wore a broken straw hat and had a matchstick in the corner of his mouth.

"What is it?" I said, opening the door part way, without inviting him in.

He rolled his wedding ring on his index finger and looked at the palm of his hand.

"I made a mistake about something. I need your advice," he said. He blew air out of his nose, as though he had a cold, and looked away at the windmill behind the barn.

I widened the door for him. He sat down at the plank table on the porch. The heels of his cowboy boots were worn almost flat.

"Yesterday I hauled my car in to have the oil pan welded. To that shop next to the Green Parrot Motel?" he said.

He saw the recognition in my face.

"Yeah, that's right," he said. "The place where Garland Moon is working. Except I didn't know that and I didn't know what he looked like, either."

"Oh man," I said.

"He gets my car up on a jack and drains the oil and takes the pan off and welds it and sticks it back on, and I ask how much I owe him.

"'Hunnerd-twenty-five,' he says.

"I go, 'My ass. That job ain't worth one nickel more than seventy-five dollars.'

"He says, 'Then it looks like I got me a fishing car.'

"I give him eighty dollars cash and take out my MasterCard for the rest of it. He looks at the name and says, 'Vernon Smothers...Vernon Smothers...Is that little jailhouse bitch your son? Why, you're bird-dogging me, ain't you?'

"I told him I'd never laid eyes on him and didn't want to and didn't have no plan on seeing him again...He never said a word. He just smiled and wrote out my charge slip and handed it to me...I seen eyes like that on one other man in my life. He was a door gunner. If he caught them in a rice field or a hooch or coming out of a wedding party, it didn't make no difference."

"Forget it," I said.

"I think he's going to hurt my boy."

"We won't let that happen, Vernon."

He cupped his fingers over his mouth. His skin made a dry, rasping sound against his fingers.

The social circle of Darl Vanzandt wasn't a difficult one to track. They were rich and lived in the East End; they had flunked out of the University of Texas or they commuted to a community college or they held token jobs in the businesses they would inherit. But it was a strange solipsistic attitude toward others that truly defined them. They were animated and loud and unseeing in public, indifferent to the injury their words might cause anyone outside their perimeter. They drove too fast, running stop signs and caution lights, never making a connection between their recklessness and the jeopardy they arbitrarily brought into the lives of others.

Their accents were regional, but they had skied in Colorado and surfed in California, and they played golf and tennis at a country club where blacks and Mexicans picked up their litter from the greens and their sweaty towels from the court, as though that was the natural function of the poor. Their insensitivity was almost a form of innocence. Had they ever been brought to task for their behavior, they probably would not have understood the complaint against them.

But one member of this group was an exception. Bunny Vogel came from a family of shiftless mill workers whose front yard was always decorated with rusted washing machines and automobile parts. But Bunny'd had a talent. As a high school running back he had crashed holes through the enemy line like a tank through a hedge row. Then he had played two years on a no-cut athletic scholarship at Texas A&M, with every expectation of graduating and going to the pros. That was before he got caught paying off a grader and fellow athlete to change an exam score for a freshman named Darl Vanzandt.

After he was expelled, he turned his motorcycle on its side and ground a strip of metal, leather, and bone a hundred feet long on the highway to Austin.

I found him at his job out at the skeet club. He could have been a Visigoth, with his grained, ruddy face, his long bronze-colored hair tangled on his shoulders, a deep pink scar, with stitch holes, along one jaw. Bunny was deferential and soft-spoken, even likable, but I always felt that behind his smile a clock was ticking as he waited for that moment when he would be free of older people and the sanction and approval they could arbitrarily withdraw if he displeased them.

Shotguns popped in the warm breeze behind him, and beyond the row of oblong green traps, clay pigeons exploded in puffs of colored smoke against the sky.

"I'd like to hep you, Mr. Holland, but far as I know the only guy mixed up with Roseanne Hazlitt was ole Lucas. Sorry," he said.

"Were you out at Shorty's the night she was attacked?" I asked.

"I might have been. But I didn't see her...Seen Lucas...That ain't no hep, though, is it?" He smiled boyishly and brushed at the grass with one shoe.

"You think Lucas could rape and kill a girl?"

"Lucas?" He thought about it. "It's not like him. But a guy gets a snootful, who knows?"

"How you know he had a snootful, Bunny?"

He smiled with his eyes. "I never saw him out there when he didn't."

"See you around."

"Yeah, anytime, Mr. Holland. I hope it works out for Lucas." He bit the corner of his lip philosophically.

On the way to my car I saw Emma Vanzandt walking toward me from a pavilion. She wore a pair of tailored brown riding jeans and lizard boots and a maroon silk shirt that filled with the wind.

"You're not going to say hello?" she asked.

"How you doin', Emma?"

"You've been busy. All Darl's friends wonder what you might be up to."

"They haven't figured it out, huh?"

"*Billy Bob,*" she said, her voice climbing. "Be a little kind. Darl's not a bad boy."

"I didn't say he was."

She looked back at the pavilion. "Let's get in your car and I'll explain something...Darl suffers from—"

"Fetal alcohol syndrome. Jack told me about it."

"I'd never heard of it before. But our last psychiatrist took one look at him and seemed to know everything about him... They've all got the same face. The eyes are set far apart, the upper lip is too close to the nose." Then she looked at nothing and said, "What a club to belong to," and laughed, almost lewdly, as though giving vent to another person who lived inside her.

"His friends vandalized Lucas Smothers's house."

"Oh, I don't believe that."

"It's good to see you, Emma."

"He wet his bed until he was fifteen. He's not capable of raping anybody. I don't think he's learned how to masturbate yet," she said.

"Maybe he should start. He beat up a prostitute with his fists."

"You should have gotten married, Billy Bob. Then you wouldn't be such a stick in the mud."

"Really?"

She reached across the car seat and patted me on the wrist. "Jack's sorry for speaking harshly to you. Come by and see us. We'll work all this out."

"No, we won't," I said.

"Well, you're just a big pill. But one day you'll see we mean you well. Until then, you have a good life, sir," she said, and squeezed my hand.

She got out of my car, her long, Indian-black hair tucked behind her head with a silver comb. Then I saw Darl come to meet her, looking past her shoulder at me, his face oily and insentient with booze and tranquilizers, the glare in his eyes like yellow heat trapped under murky water.

The next day, in my office, Marvin Pomroy, the prosecutor, told me about the call that had come in to the rural fire station, his eyes moving across the rug as though he were clarifying the details to himself rather than to me.

No one would have seen the flames, but a shower broke in the predawn hours and a column of wet smoke rose from between two hills and hung in the sky like a long gray rope. At first the firemen thought they were simply putting out a pile of discarded automobile tires that had been heaped into a deep pit. Then they began to poke through the foam and pull apart the tires with their axes. The blackened figure at the bottom of the pyre looked atrophied, cemented at the joints, like an anatomically deformed manikin encased in a thick crust. Except for the white teeth, exposed by the skin that had stretched back on the skull in a death grin.

"You're sure it's Jimmy Cole?" I asked.

"Cole was missing two toes on his left foot. He cut them off with a hatchet to get out of the field in Sugarland," Marvin said. His eyes were bright, his gum snapping in his jaw. "The crime scene's clean, though. We can't tie it to Moon."

"You look like your circuits are burning," I said.

"The ME says Cole died somewhere else. His nose and mouth and ears were full of sediment and pig shit. The ME says he was probably buried in a hog lot, then dug up after rigor mortis set in." He glanced at my face. "*What?*" he said.

"I told Garland Moon I thought he'd killed Cole. He probably decided to move the body."

"What were you doing with Moon?"

"Either he or Cole was in my barn. I tried to warn him off."

"Don't try to 'front this guy on your own," he said. But I knew I was not the source of his agitation. He leaned forward in the chair, a heated sheen on his face. "Look, I've got a problem here that's eating my lunch. The fire was on the old Hart property. Nobody's lived there for thirty years. But I got the feeling most of those deputies had been there before. I also got the feeling the sheriff didn't want anybody hanging around there."

"Who owns the place now?"

"A California company that sells western real estate to people tired of shopping in malls where the Crips and the Bloods have firefights. But I don't see anything there worth hiding, a strip of ground between the hills, the kind of place where the hoot owls screw the jackrabbits."

"Why you telling me this?"

"That's the irony. I work in a county that's so corrupt I have to confide in a defense lawyer who rides his horse into barrooms. I grant you, it's a pitiful situation," he said.

"Thanks, Marvin. The ME thinks Jimmy Cole was suffocated in a hog lot?"

"Moon wouldn't do that to an old friend. He put an ice pick inside his head."

After work that day I took the rake and garden shears and a gunny sack out of the barn and walked to our family cemetery on the far side of the tank. It was bordered by sandstone fence posts drilled through the center to hold the cedar rails that my father had shaved and beveled and notched thirty-two years ago, the year before he had climbed down into a bellhole on a natural gas pipeline to mend a leak in a faulty weld.

Each year he faked his physicals or got someone else to take them for him, because, like many pipeline arc welders, his eyes were filled with tiny pinholes from weaving a circle of fire that was as white as the sun around a pipe joint. My mother said his vision had become so bad that clarity of sight came to him only when he struck the stringer-bead rod against the pipe's metal and saw again the flame that was as pure to him as the cathedral's bells were to the deaf bellringer Quasimodo.

My father never saw the apprentice with him pull a Zippo from his khakis and light a cigarette. The explosion blew the glass out of the welding truck like brittle candy.

My mother, who had been a librarian and an elementary school teacher, was buried next to him. After my father's death, she had purchased a common headstone for them both, inscribed with her name as well as his, with her birth date and a chiseled dash that left the date of death to another hand.

I raked their graves and Great-grandpa Sam's clean, and those of all the other Hollands buried there, trimmed the grass around the headstones, and weeded out the rose beds I had dug under the cedar fence rails. Then I picked wildflowers from the field and set them on my parents' graves, and cut a solitary yellow rose and laid it against Great-grandpa Sam's headstone.

The wind was warm blowing across the field, rippling the grass like new wheat, and I could smell the river and the water in the irrigation ditches and the day's heat baked into the scarred hardpan that had once been part of the Chisholm Trail. I didn't hear the footsteps behind me.

"I saw you from the back of the house," Mary Beth said. She wore tan slacks, with high pockets, and sandals and a magenta shirt, and she carried a picnic basket by the straw bail in her right hand.

"How you doin', slim?" I said.

"Slim? If you aren't a peach."

"You figure out who those guys in the cruiser were?"

"Take your choice."

"Maybe it's time your people pulled you out."

"Subject closed. You like fried chicken?"

"You bet."

We walked across the field to a grove of oaks on the bluff above the river. She spread a checkered cloth on the grass and set it with silverware, tiny salt and pepper shakers, turkey-and-cheese sandwiches, guacamole, taco chips, potato salad, and a thermos of lemonade. Her hair hung over her cheeks while she placed each item carefully on the paper plates.

"You're making me self-conscious," she said.

"You're a great-looking lady, Mary Beth."

Her eyes crinkled in the corners. I was standing by the edge of the checkered cloth now. When she rose to her feet her face was only inches away from mine. I touched her hair, then I put my mouth on hers. Her eyes were open, then they closed and she put her arms around my back and I felt her breasts against my chest and a moment later the heat of her cheek press against mine.

I was suddenly involved with the old male impossibility of making love with any degree of dignity while standing up. We sat on the grass, then I lay her back with her head on the edge of the checkered cloth and kissed her again. The wind was blowing from across the river, eddying through the grass above the bluff, and the clouds piled on the western horizon were purple and edged with fire. I looked down into her eyes.

Behind me I heard a horse's hooves moving through the dead oak leaves. I turned and saw Beau, my Morgan, coming through the shade, and a little boy with a haircut like a soft brush riding bareback atop him.

"Hi! What ch'all doin'?" he said, pushing a branch out of his face with his arm.

"Hey, Pete, what's goin' on?" I said, my voice coming back to me like a man bursting to the surface of a deep pool.

"We still going fishing?"

"Wouldn't miss it, bud. You want some chicken? This is Mary Beth."

He grinned at her. He was barefoot and in overalls and looked like a small clothespin on Beau's spine.

"I already eat," he said.

"We have some lemonade," she said. She was sitting up now, one arm propped behind her.

"That's all right. I'm butting in."

"I'd tell you, wouldn't I?" I said.

He grinned at nothing, flicking the reins across the back of his hand.

"I'm gonna take Beau back," he said.

"Billy Bob told me a lot about you, Pete. I'd like it if you'd join us," Mary Beth said.

His eyes shifted off her, his grin never fading, then he slipped off Beau's back onto the ground.

"This is the smartest little guy in Deaf Smith," I said.

"I knew you was gonna say that," he said.

That night I drove down the road to the convenience store to buy a carton of milk. The store was on the top of a rise, next to a cornfield, its bright white-and-red exterior and neon-scrolled windows and lighted gas pumps and wide cement parking area surrounded by rural darkness. It was also a hangout for East Enders dragging the main road through town.

Their cars were parked by the phone booth, their doors open to catch the breeze, the cement pad around their feet already littered with beer cans, dirty napkins, and the cigarette butts they had emptied from their ashtrays.

On the way back to my car Darl Vanzandt got up from the passenger seat of his cherry-red chopped-down 1932 Ford and came toward me, the pupils of his wide-set eyes like burnt cinders. He drank the foam out of a quart bottle of Pearl and flung it whistling into the darkness. When I tried to walk around him, he stepped into my path, his courage inflating now with the audience that had formed at his back.

"Whoa, there, bud," I said.

"You bothered all my friends. Now you're bothering my stepmother," he said.

"Wrong."

"You're setting me up to go to jail. All because of that little fart Lucas Smothers," he said.

"Good night," I said.

But he stepped in front of me again. He pushed me in the breastbone with his fingers, then he did it again, grinding his teeth slightly, thumping hard against the bone.

"Don't do this, Darl," I said.

The skin around his mouth was taut and gray, his nose tilted slightly upward, the fear and loathing in his eyes like a candle flame that didn't know which way to blow. I dropped my eyes, and a smile exposed his teeth.

He slapped the carton of milk from my hand. It exploded in a white star on the pavement.

I stepped backward, then walked in a wide circle toward my car.

I heard his feet running behind me. By the time I could turn he was almost upon me. I brought up my elbow and drove it into his nose.

He doubled over, his cupped hands smeared with blood as soon as they touched his face. Then Bunny Vogel was next to him, his arm around Darl's shoulders, holding a wadded T-shirt against Darl's nose.

"I'll get some ice, then we'll go home. It ain't broken. The blood's darker when it's broken," Bunny said.

"You tell his dad what happened, Bunny," I said.

"It ain't my job to tell on people."

"You're sure loyal to a kid who cost you a career in the pros. I wonder why that is," I said.

He led Darl back toward the parked cars of the East Enders. Then he glanced back at me, his eyes like those of a man who just realized his future will be no different from his past.

CHAPTER

12

The next morning I ate breakfast on the kitchen table and read from Great-grandpa Sam's journal.

July 7, 1891
Today I cane-fished in the river for perch and shovel-mouth with Jennie, which is the Christian name of the Rose of Cimarron. The hills was covered with Indian paintbrush and sunflowers and we cooked our fish in a brush arbor with a spring that stays wet through the summer months.

It is country that begs for a church house, but it is infested with a collection of halfwits and white trash that calls themselves the Dalton-Doolin gang. They live in mud caves along the river and consider it the high life. A Chinaman brings them opium and squaws give them the clap. They rob trains because the smell on them is such they would get run out of a town before they could ever make it to the bank.

A little twerp named Blackface Charley Bryant threw a temper tantrum and commenced firing a rifle into the sky and using profane language in Jennie's and my presence. He come by his nickname when his own revolver blew up in his hand and turned half his face into an eggplant. I informed him I did not want to forget my ordination and cause him injury, but I would probably do so should I put a third eye in the middle of his forehead.

I am tempted to wrap Jennie in fence wire and carry her out of here across my pommel. But Judge Isaac Parker has had over fifty federal lawmen shot to death in these parts, and I think he would as lief hang a woman outlaw as a man, since people tell me he has already hung a highwayman's horse.

Romancing that woman is like chasing cows in dry lightning. It's a whole lot easier getting into the saddle than out of it. Such is the nature of pagan ways.

When I walked out to my car Lucas Smothers pulled into the driveway in his skinned-up truck.

"My father says I got to tell you something. Even though it's just stuff I heard," he said.

"Go ahead."

He got out of the truck and leaned against the fender. The shadow of a poplar tree seemed to cut his face in half. He bit a hang-nail.

"About the firemen finding Jimmy Cole's body at the old Hart Ranch? Like, maybe Garland Moon killed him and tried to burn him up with some old tires? I mean, that's what the sheriff's thinking, ain't it?" he said.

"It's Moon's style."

"Darl Vanzandt and some others used to get fried on acid and angel dust out there. Roseanne went there with them once. She said Darl got crazy when he was on dust."

"What's Darl have to do with Jimmy Cole?"

"Six or seven months back, a hobo died in a fire by the railway tracks. The paper said he was heating a tar paper shack with a little tin stove and a can of kerosene. I heard maybe Darl and some others done it."

He looked at the expression on my face, then looked away.

"Why would he kill a hobo?" I asked.

"There's kids that's cruel here. They don't need no reason. Roseanne said maybe Darl's a Satanist."

"We're talking about murdering people."

"I seen stuff maybe older folks don't want to know about. That's the way this town's always been."

"Jimmy Cole wasn't killed on the Hart Ranch. His body was moved there."

"It wasn't Darl?"

"I doubt it."

He wiped his palms on his jeans. "I got to get to work...Mr. Holland?"

"Yes?"

He scraped at a piece of rust on the truck door with his thumbnail.

"You doing all this 'cause you figure you owe me?" he said.

"No."

He was silent while the question he couldn't ask burned in his face.

"Your mother and I were real close. If it had gone different, we might have gotten married. For that reason I've always felt mighty close to you. She was a fine person," I said.

His throat was prickled and red, as though he had been in a cold wind. He got in the truck, looking through the back window while he started the engine so I would not see the wet glimmering in his eyes.

But the lie that shamed, that I could not set straight, was mine, not his.

I parked my car around the corner from the bank and walked back toward the entrance to my office. Emma Vanzandt sat in a white Porsche convertible by the curb, two of her tires in the yellow zone. She wore dark glasses and her black hair was tied up with a white silk scarf. When I said hello, she looked at the tops of her nails. I stepped off the sidewalk and approached her car anyway.

"Is Jack inside?" I asked.

"Why don't you go see?"

"Your son attacked me, Emma."

The backs of her hands were wrinkled, like

the surface of bad milk, networked with thick blue veins. She spread her fingers on the steering wheel and studied them.

"If you think you can solve your problems at our expense, you don't know Jack *or* me," she said.

I went up the stairs and opened the frosted glass door into my outer office. My secretary was trying to busy herself with the mail, but the strain on her composure showed on her face like a fine crack across a china plate. Jack was staring at a picture on the wall, without seeing it, his hands on his hips. When he turned to face me, his vascular arms seemed pumped and swollen with energy, as though he had been curling a barbell.

"Come inside, Jack," I said.

"That's very thoughtful of you," he replied.

He closed the inner door behind him. He bit his bottom lip; his hands closed and opened at his sides.

"I can't describe what I'm feeling right now," he said.

"Your son's problem is dope and booze. Address the situation, Jack. Don't blame it on other people."

"I feel like taking off your head."

"Oh?"

"You put me in mind of a blind leper climbing into a public swimming pool."

"I get it. I'm the source of everyone's discontent but don't know it."

"You got this guy Moon stoked up, then you broke my boy's nose."

"Moon?"

"He wouldn't be around here if it wasn't for you."

"What do you care?"

"He hauled a dead man out to my property, what's his name, that character Jimmy Cole."

"Cole was found on the old Hart place."

"I have an eighth interest in it..." He seemed distracted and tried to regain his train of thought. "I want you to leave us alone. It's a simple request. You've fucked up your life and your career. But I'll be damned if you'll make my family your scapegoat."

I stepped closer to him. I could feel the blood rise in my head. In the corner of my eye I thought I saw L.Q. Navarro watching me, wagging a cautionary finger.

"You want to explain that, Jack?" I asked.

"I gave orders in Vietnam that cost other men their lives. It comes with the territory. That's what maturity is about. I'm embarrassed to be in your presence," he replied.

He went out the door, nodding to the secretary as he passed.

I sat alone in the steam room at the health club, the sting of his words like needles in my face. I pushed a towel into a bucket of water and squeezed it over my head and shoulders. L.Q. Navarro leaned against the tile wall, his dark suit bathed in steam, his face as cool and dry as if he stood on an ice floe.

"Don't let them kind get to you," he said.

"Which kind is that?"

"The kind with money. I don't know what that boy did in Vietnam, but down in Coahuila we went up against automatic weapons with handguns. We shot the shit out of those guys, too."

"I grant, they knew we'd been in town."

He took off his Stetson and spun it on his finger. His teeth shone when he smiled.

"That woman deputy, the tall one, Mary Beth's her name? She was good to the little boy. That's how you tell when it's the right woman," he said.

"You saved me from burning to death, L.Q. It was the bravest thing I ever saw anyone do."

He grinned again, then his face became somber and his eyes avoided mine.

"I got to leave you one day, bud," he said.

A fat man with a towel wrapped around his loins opened the steam room door and came inside. L.Q. fitted his hat on his head and walked toward the far wall, where the tiles melted into a horizontal vortex spinning with wet sand.

I showered and walked back to my locker in the dressing room, then caught myself glancing sideways at my reflection in the wall mirror, at the same reddish blond hair that Lucas had, the same six-foot-one frame, the puckered white scar on my upper right arm where a bullet had snapped the bone the night L.Q. died, the long stitched welt on top of my foot from the night he pulled me out of the grass fire and we thundered down the hills with tracers streaking over our heads in the darkness.

At age forty-one I had gained only ten pounds since I was a beat cop in Houston, and I could still bench two hundred pounds and do thirty push-ups with my feet elevated on a chair.

But I knew my self-congratulatory attitudes were all vanity. I was trying to reconstruct my pride like a schoolboy searching for a missing virtue in his reflection after he has been publicly humiliated.

I stuffed my soiled workout clothes in my gym bag and drove out to the old Hart Ranch.

It lay between two large hills, and the only access was down a rutted dirt road that wound through a woods with a thick canopy and layers of pine needles and dead leaves on the ground. The gate at the cattleguard was chain-locked and strung with yellow crime scene tape. I climbed through a barbed wire fence and walked a quarter of a mile into a wide glade that was green with new grass and dotted with wildflowers.

The main house, which had been built in the Victorian style of the 1880s, with a wide columned porch and stained glass in the windows, was now the color of cardboard, the roof destroyed by fire, the outbuildings and windmill wrapped with tumbleweeds.

I followed a creek along the bottom of the far hill, wandered back into a piney woods, crisscrossed the glade, then walked all the way to the river bluffs that bordered the opposite end of the ranch.

I found a small pioneer cemetery whose monuments were flat fieldstones scratched with dates from the 1850s; a steam tractor that had rusted apart in the creek bed; an impacted, overgrown trash dump probably left behind by loggers or CCC boys; a broken crosscut saw frozen in the trunk of a tree and sealed over by the bark; deer, coon, possum, and cougar tracks but not one human footprint except where the atrophied body of Jimmy Cole had been discovered among the stack of burning rubber tires.

It was a beautiful day, the sky blue, the trees on the hills in full leaf. I picked up a stone and sailed it clattering into the ruins of the abandoned house.

A hog burst out the back door and ran stumpily through the lot, past the windmill and the collapsed barn, into a stand of pine trees.

I followed him for five minutes, then came out into sunlight again and saw seven others in a slough, feral, rust-colored, layered with mud, their snouts glistening with gore.

In the center of the slough, her hind quarters pried apart, lay a disemboweled doe, a cloud of insects hanging like gauze above her head.

The slough was churned into soup, slick with patches of stagnant water, green with excrement. On the far bank, where the silt had dried in the sun, were at least three sets of human footprints.

The sheriff leaned over his spittoon and snipped the end off his cigar.

"Feral hogs, that means undomesticated?" he said.

"That's right," I said.

"Which kind is it that don't like rolling in slop?"

"I think Jimmy Cole was killed right there on the ranch," I said.

"Because you found pig shit in a slough and Jimmy Cole had it in his ears?"

"There was a dead campfire inside the house. I think he was hiding out there."

"And Darl Vanzandt and his pissant friends done it?"

"You tell me."

He leaned back in his chair and pulled on his nose.

"If you told me Darl Vanzandt was messing with sheep, I might believe it," he said. Then he stared at me for a long time, his face starting to crease, a private joke building like a windstorm inside his huge girth. "Is this how y'all done it in the Rangers, searching out pig shit in the woods? Damn, son, if you ain't a riot. Hold on, let me get my deputies in here. They got to hear this."

He laughed so hard tears coursed down his cheeks.

After supper that night, I stood at my library window and watched the sky turn black and lightning fork into the crest of the hills. I turned on my desk lamp and started a handwritten letter to Jack Vanzandt. Why? Maybe because I had always liked him. Also, it was hard to criticize a man because his love blinded him to the implications of his son's behavior.

But my words would not change the chemical or genetic aberration that was Darl Vanzandt, and after two paragraphs I tore my piece of stationery in half and dropped it in the wastebasket.

It rained hard, blowing in sheets across the fields and against the side of the house. I called Mary Beth's apartment and let the phone ring a dozen times. I had tried to reach her all day, but her answering machine was still off.

I replaced the receiver in the cradle, then glanced out the window into the driveway just as a tree of lightning split the sky and illuminated the face of Garland T. Moon.

He stood motionless in the driving rain, a thick hemp doormat held over his head, his blue serge suit and tropical shirt soaked through.

I turned on the porch light and stepped out the front door. He walked out of the shadows, his flat-soled prison shoes crunching on the gravel. Without invitation, he mounted the porch, his mouth grinning inanely, the raindrops on his face as viscous as glycerin.

"How did you get here?" I asked.

"Walked."

"From town?"

"They're holding old DWIs over my head so I cain't get a driver's license."

"You kill your buddy Jimmy Cole?"

The skin of his face seemed to flex, caught between mirth and caution, as though he were breathing with a sliver of ice on his tongue.

"I ain't had to. Somebody else done it," he said. "You sent them people after me?"

"Which people?"

"Ones come in my room with a baseball bat."

"Get off my property, Garland."

His eyes held on my face, unblinking, his mouth a dry slit.

"Then it's somebody figures I know something. But I ain't got no idea what it is," he said.

"I read the case file from LAPD. They say you were in that house for three hours. They say you killed them all one by one and made the survivors watch."

"Then why ain't I in jail?"

I walked close to him. I could smell the deodorant that had melted on his skin, his breath that was like chewing gum and snuff.

"You've got a free pass tonight. You won't get another one," I said.

His eyes, as blue and merry as a butane flame, danced on my face.

"The one with the bat? I caught him before he could get back to his truck. Check around the clinics. See if they ain't got a man won't be going out in public a lot," he said.

He stepped back into the rain and darkness and walked out to the road, the doormat above his head, his suit molded like a blowing cape against his body.

CHAPTER

13

The next afternoon Mary Beth answered her phone.

"Is anything wrong?" I asked.

"No. Why should there be?"

"Your machine's been off. I haven't seen you around."

"Can I call you back later?"

But she didn't. That evening I drove to her apartment. As I walked up the stairs, people were swimming laps in the pool, stroking through the electric columns of light that glowed smokily under the turquoise surface, and the air was tinged with the gaslike smell of chlorine, burning charcoal starter, and flowers heated by the colored flood lamps planted in their midst.

A heavyset man in a tie and business suit came out of Mary Beth's apartment and almost knocked me down. I stepped back from him and felt the place on my chest where he had hit me.

"Excuse me," I said.

He pushed his glasses straight on his nose and looked into my face, as though he recognized me. His hair was dark and neatly clipped, his part a pale, straight line in his scalp. His chin had a cleft in it and his cheeks were freshly shaved and his skin taut and scented with cologne.

"No problem," he said.

"No problem?"

"I said I was sorry, pal. I didn't see you."

"That's funny. I didn't hear you," I said.

He started to turn away, then his chest expanded and his stomach flattened, as though he were abandoning a useless protocol, and he faced me squarely with his left foot slightly forward, the right foot at an angle behind it.

"You have a reason for staring at me?" he asked quietly.

"Not in the least."

He glanced back at Mary Beth's closed door. "Have a good evening. Best way to do that, don't let it get complicated," he said. He raised his finger and eyebrows at the same time, then walked down the stairs.

She was in her uniform when she let me in. There were pools of color in her cheeks and her voice had a click in it when she spoke. She began straightening couch pillows and magazines that didn't need straightening, her back turned to me.

"I'm sorry to be in a rush. I have to be on duty in twenty minutes," she said.

"That guy's a fed."

"What, he threw a badge on you?"

"No, he's a self-important clerk who thinks arrogance and being a cop are the same thing."

"You don't like them much, do you?"

"He shouldn't be here. If I can make him, other people will, too."

"I have to go, Billy Bob." She removed her gunbelt from the closet shelf and began strapping it on her waist. She tucked her shirt inside the belt and kept her eyes on her fingers and the cloth as it tightened under the edge of the leather.

I waited until she raised her eyes again. "You have a personal relationship going with this guy?" I asked.

"I don't have to tell you these things." Then I saw her cheeks sink, as though she were disturbed by the severity of her own words.

"He's putting you in jeopardy. I don't like him. That offends you?" I said.

She picked up her purse from the counter that separated the kitchen from the living room. Her face was turned away from me. She pressed her fingers against her temple.

"I'm leaving and I don't have any more to say. Do you want to walk to the parking lot with me or stay here?"

"Somebody's trying to run Garland Moon out of town. Because of something he knows. But he doesn't know what it is."

She stared at me blankly, her freckled face like a young girl's, suddenly empty of all other concern.

Temple Carrol was sitting in a deerhide chair in my office when I arrived the next morning.

"I found our man," she said.

"How?"

"He told the guys in the emergency room he fell from a paint ladder through a glass window. They reported it as a knife wound."

"Why didn't they believe him?"

"Somebody had done a number on him earlier. A paramedic said he looked like he'd been drug by a rope." She propped her chin on her fingers and waited for the recognition to show in my eyes.

His name was Roy Devins, and he had been two times down in Huntsville and maybe once in Mexico under another name, and whatever had happened to him—an accident on a ladder, a knife beef in a bar—he had driven seventy miles down the highway without seeking help, or even accepting it when people at stoplights glanced into the cab of his pickup, then realized what they were looking at and remained sickened and numb and stationary at the light while he sped away from them.

He looked out of the bandages on his face with the attentiveness of a man who gives importance only to those who can harm him. Then the eyes registered and dismissed us and receded back into the ennui of looking at objects and listening to sounds that might satisfy a need or fulfill a desire—the possibility of cigarettes in my shirt pocket, the noise of a food cart in the hall, a film featuring Japanese gladiators in samurai combat on the television set.

"You remember me?" I said.

"Where's your horse?" he replied.

"You don't mind our being here, do you?"

"I don't give a shit what y'all do," he said.

"You can put Garland Moon down for the Bitch, Roy. Three-strikes-and-you're-out was made for this guy," I said.

There were thin white lines around his eyes, as if all sunlight and health had been siphoned out of his skin. The bandages on one side of his head were flat against the scalp and bone. When he turned his head on the pillow, a tic jumped in his throat, as though a fine fishbone were caught in his windpipe. I thought it was the pain.

"I'm going out to the Coast, get a new start. I'm through with all this running around. I fell off a ladder," he said. His eyes shifted off mine and looked at nothing.

"Listen up, Roy," Temple said. "They don't graft ears back on here. Medicaid doesn't pay for plastic surgery on slashed cheeks. How'd we know about you, anyway? He came out to Billy Bob's house and laughed about doing you."

His eyes filmed over and he turned his head on the pillow so that he faced the open door of his room and the sound of other people walking in the hall, rattling food trays, delivering flowers and fruit baskets, carrying with them all the beautiful portent that an ordinary day could offer.

"Think about it another way. The guys who got you to bust him up, have they been here to look in on you, pay your bills, tell you they're sorry it went south on you?" I said.

But our reasoning could not compete with the memory of Garland T. Moon and that moment when Roy Devins, dope mule and abuser of children, mainline con and fulltime loser, thought he could burst into a motel room with a baseball bat and inspire terror in a man he presumed was one of his own kind, no stronger or weaker or better or worse, unaware that all his experience with evil in county jails and state prisons was as worthless as every other precept that had betrayed him when he had believed himself on the edge of unlocking the magic doors to which everyone but he had always been granted access.

I sat on a bench in the side yard of the stucco church that Pete and I attended, and watched Pete and a group of boys his age play work-up softball out on the school diamond. The shade under the mimosa tree was flecked with tiny blades of sunlight, and Beau, my Morgan, was eating grass along the rain ditch that bordered the church yard. I opened the thick cover of Great-grandpa Sam's journal and turned the pages to my bookmark.

July 21, 1891

I think they aim to rob a train.

July 27, 1891
They rode out of here three days ago, headed due east into a red dawn that was hot enough to have come off the devil's forge. They was drunk when they come back in last night, stinking of rut and beer and tripe they was eating with their hands out of a leather poke. Whatever money they stole, they did not spend it on a bath house in Fort Smith. If you dipped them for ticks and lice, the water would be instantly black and probably have to be shoveled out of the vat and burned with kerosene.

I had thought I had put my violent ways behind me. But just as my loins yearn for the nocturnal caress of the Rose of Cimarron, my palm wishes to curve around the hardness of my Navy .36. I purely hate these men, God forgive me for my words, but they make me ashamed to be a member of the white race and give me dreams about the old life and the men whose faces I lighted with gunfire while people watched from the balconies of saloons and brothels.

Jennie and I have moved into a cabin up on the hillock overlooking the river. We have peach and apple trees in the yard and curtains in the windows she sewn from her old dresses. But I cannot pretend those outlaws are not down below in their mud caves, their squaws rolling opium in little balls for their pipes, the stolen dollars they almost lost in a river drying on clotheslines.

Maybe I hate them because the nature of their abode and of their fornication is the only difference between us. This question has troubled me sorely and I raised it to Jennie. She did not reply and went out to the woodstove in back and began frying meat for our breakfast. She was not hardly dressed and in the early light her young body looked like that of a savage. The sight of her filled me with a passion that I could not contain, that even in the cool air of our bedroom made my palms damp with my sweat.

I am fifty-six years old and fear I do not know who I am.

Pete walked hot and dusty and happy into the shade, his fielder's glove hooked on its strap through his belt.

"We still gonna get peach ice cream?" he said.

"I wouldn't go a day without it," I replied.

"You know them men out yonder, Billy Bob? They been around the block twice, like they was lost or something."

I looked over my shoulder, out on the hard-packed dirt street. Both the cars were dark and waxed, with tinted windows and radio antennas. I stood up and put on my Stetson and walked over to Beau and stroked his head and fed him a sugar cube with the flat of my hand. The cars pulled up along the edge of the rain ditch, and the passenger window in the front of the lead car rolled down on its electric motor.

The man from Mary Beth's apartment

looked at me from behind aviator's sunglasses.

"You already stomped the shit out of Roy Devins. Maybe it's time to leave his welfare to others," he said.

"You know how it is, a guy gets bored and starts to wonder why feds are running around in his county, making veiled threats, acting like heavy-handed pricks, that sort of thing," I said.

He laughed to himself.

"How about staying out of Dodge?" he said.

"I expect we're on the same side, aren't we?"

"You're a defense lawyer, pal. You get paid to keep the asswipes out of the gray-bar hotel chain." His gaze drifted to Pete, then back on me. "You really stick playing cards in the mouths of dead wets down in Coahuila?"

I stroked Beau once along his mane, then stepped across the rain ditch and leaned down into the open window of the lead car.

"I worked with a Ranger named L.Q. Navarro. We took down the mules and burned out the stash houses y'all didn't know how to find. You couldn't shine his boots, bud."

He took off his sunglasses and looked indolently into my face.

"You like the lady, don't make trouble for her. You're an intelligent man. You can work with this, I'm convinced of it," he said, and motioned to his driver.

Pete and I watched the two cars move slowly away, the windows sealed against the dust, the whitewall tires crunching delicately on the gravel as though the two drivers did not want to chip the gleaming finish on the cars' exteriors.

"You pretty mad, Billy Bob?" Pete said.

"No, not really."

"For a person that's been river baptized and converted to Catholic, too, you sure know how to tell a fib."

I rubbed the top of his soft, brushlike hair as the two cars turned down a dirt alley and their dust rolled across the wash hanging behind a row of clapboard shacks.

CHAPTER

14

The typical isolation unit in a prison is a surreal place of silence, bare stone, solid iron doors, and loss of all distinction between night and day. Its intention is to lock up the prisoner with the worst company possible, namely, his own thoughts.

But fear and guilt have corrosive effects in the free people's world as well.

Bunny Vogel passed my house twice, driving a customized maroon '55 Chevy, before he mustered the courage to turn in the driveway and walk out to the chicken run in back, where I was picking up eggs in an apple basket.

He wore an unbuttoned silk shirt and jeans and Roman sandals without socks, and his tangled bronze-colored hair seemed to glow on the tips against the late sun. With his classical profile and his abdominal muscles that were like oiled leather, he could have been a male model for the covers of romance novels, except for the sunken scar that curled like an inset pink worm along his jawbone.

"Pretty nice automobile," I said.

"What you said the night you busted Darl in the nose? About me being loyal to a guy who cost me a pro career?"

"I didn't mean to offend you, Bunny."

He let out a breath. "I think you're gonna pin the tail on any donkey you can. I ain't gonna be it, Mr. Holland," he said.

"You want to come inside?"

"No... The old black guy out at Shorty's told you Roseanne Hazlitt slapped somebody in the parking lot the night she was killed."

"How do you know that?"

"Darl heard the old guy'd been talking to you. So he kind of got in his face about it."

"He's quite a kid. I don't think I've ever known one exactly like him."

"It was me she slapped. I ain't gonna hide it no more."

I picked up a brown egg from behind a tractor tire and dropped it in the basket. I didn't look at him. I could hear him breathing in the silence.

"But that's when I left. I didn't see Roseanne or Darl or none of the others after that. I ain't part of nothing that happened later that night," he said.

"Who was?"

"God's truth, Mr. Holland, I don't know."

"You told me you weren't mixed up with Roseanne, Bunny."

He kneaded his fists at his sides and the veins in his forearms swelled with blood. Then his face colored and his eyes glazed with shame.

"Damn, I knew this was gonna be a sonofabitch," he said.

This is the story he told me.

He was a high school senior, on the varsity, with the kind of bone-breaking running power that left tacklers dazed and sometimes bloody in his wake, when he first noticed her watching him at practice from the empty stands.

He remembered the balmy gold afternoon that he walked over to her, his cleats crunching on the cinder-and-pea-gravel track, and tossed the football into her hands. He thought it was a clever thing to do, the kind of gesture that disarmed most girls, that made them feel vulnerable and a little foolish and gave them a chance to be coy and defenseless in his presence.

She flipped it back at him with both hands, so fast he had to duck to avoid being hit in the face. Then she opened her compact and put on lipstick as though he were not there.

"How old are you, anyway?" he asked.

"Fifteen. You got something against being fifteen?" She squeezed her knees together and wagged them back and forth.

He looked back over his shoulder at the practice field, at the second-string, whose attention was absorbed with thudding their pads against one another and running plays they would never be allowed to run in a game that counted.

"You want to go to a movie tonight?" he asked.

"The drive-in?"

"It don't have to be the drive-in."

"I'll think about it."

"You'll think about it?"

"I work at the Dairy Queen. I get off at six. I'll let you know then."

He watched her walk down the empty concrete aisle, then across the worn grass to the bus stop in front of the school, her hips swaying under her plaid skirt. He kept glancing back at the practice field, as though someone were watching him, and his own thoughts confused and angered him.

He was at the Dairy Queen at five-thirty.

They did it a week later, amid a drone of cicadas, in the back of his uncle's old Plymouth, on cushions that smelled of dust and nicotine, and he realized immediately she had lied and that she was a virgin and he was hurting her even more deeply than the gasp, the clutch of pain in her throat, indicated. But he couldn't stop, nor did he know how to be gentle, nor could he admit that most of his sexual experience had been with Mexican prostitutes in

San Antonio and the mill women his father brought home when he was drunk.

He was frightened when he saw how much she bled and he offered to drive her to a hospital in another county.

"You afraid to take me to one here?" she said.

"I don't want you in trouble with your folks, that's all," he lied.

"I don't need a doctor, anyhow. Did you like me?" she said.

"Yeah, sure."

"No, you didn't. But you will next time," she said, and kissed him on the cheek.

Her hand found his. The trees that had gone dark outside the car made him think of stone pillars wrapped with the tracings of fireflies, but he did not know why.

He saw her two days later in front of the shoe store downtown and bought her a lemon Coke at the small soda fountain in back of the Mexican grocery. He told her he would call her that evening but he didn't.

Two weeks passed before he realized it was not he who had avoided her; she had made no phone call to him, had not come out to the practice field as he had expected, had not told anything of their first date to anyone he knew.

He found himself watching her at her job at the Dairy Queen from his parked car across the street. Then one night at closing time he saw her go in back, in her uniform, and emerge moments later from a side door in suede

150

boots and tight jeans and hoop earrings and vinyl black jacket, her mouth bright with fresh lipstick, and mount the back of a motorcycle a Mexican kid who looked carved out of an oak stump sat splayed upon, his genitalia sculpted against his jeans.

A half hour later he found them both at the drive-in restaurant north of town.

"Get in my car, Roseanne," he said. Then to the Mexican boy, "Here's the drift, greaseball. You can ride your hog home and fuck your fist tonight. Or walk out of here on broken sticks."

"Oh yeah, she told me about you...Vogel, the running bohunk, right?" the Mexican replied. "I got news for you, spermbrain. She's jailbait. I hope you end up in the Walls and somebody jams a chain saw up your cheeks."

An hour later Bunny and Roseanne made love on a bare mattress in the darkened back of the filling station where he worked on weekends.

Through the rest of his senior year she was available whenever he wanted her. She rarely made demands or threw temper tantrums, and the fact that he didn't take her to the parties or places where his friends went seemed of no concern to her. But he would realize, again, belatedly, as had always been the case, he did not really understand the nature of the game. Just as he had worried that her age would diminish him in the eyes of his classmates (until he discovered that, as a West Ender, he was not expected to date anyone of significance, anyway), he also learned that Roseanne didn't care about his world or friends because she had brought him into hers.

Sophomore girls giggled when he walked by, and one time three of them hung a condom filled with milk on a string inside his hall locker. When they had slumber parties his father would be wakened by phone calls that made him wonder if his son had become a child molester.

Then Bunny began to wonder if there were not other men involved with Roseanne besides himself. She knew too much, controlled him too easily, discerned his moods and sexual weaknesses too easily, sitting on top of his thighs, pressing his face into her breasts, kissing his damp hair while he came inside her.

One night he forced the subject. "You making it with somebody else, Roseanne?" he said.

"You're such a silly fucko sometimes...Oh, I'm sorry, baby. Come here."

That same night they went to San Antonio and had small red hearts tattooed above their left nipples.

After graduation Bunny worked as a floorman on a drilling rig in Odessa. Then he reported for summer football camp at A&M and a strange phenomenon occurred in his life: he was no longer a West Ender.

He was invited to sorority mixers, into the

homes of the wealthy, taken to dinner at the country club by businessmen, treated as though a collective family of magically anointed people had decided to adopt him as their son.

He didn't return to Deaf Smith until Thanksgiving. He didn't call Roseanne Hazlitt, either.

He expected anger, recrimination, maybe even a trip on her part to College Station and a public scene that would be ruinous for him. But she surprised him again.

It was the last game of the season, a blue-gold late fall afternoon like the one the previous year when he had crunched across the track on his cleats and flipped the football into her palms. He got up from the bench and walked back to the Gatorade cooler and saw her standing by the rail in the box seats, next to a marine in his dress uniform. Bunny stared at her stupidly. She took a mum from the corsage on her coat, blew him a kiss, and bounced the mum off his face.

"Hey, you too stuck-up to say hello, you ole fucko?" she said.

His bare head felt cold and small in the wind, somehow shrunken inside the weight of his shoulder pads.

"Why'd she slap you in front of Shorty's, Bunny?" I asked.

He stuck the flats of his hands in his back pockets. He kicked at the dirt and didn't reply.

I looked beyond his shoulder at his customized maroon Chevy, with oversize white-walls and white leather interior.

"That's a great-looking car," I said.

The next day, after work, I lit a candle in front of the statue of Christ's mother at the stucco church. The church was empty, except for Pete, who waited for me in a pew at the back. I walked back down the aisle, dipped my fingers in the holy water font and made the sign of the cross, then winked at Pete and waited for him to join me out on the steps.

The western sky was ribbed with scarlet clouds, and the air smelled of pines and irrigation water in a field.

"You come here just to light a candle?" Pete asked.

"A friend of mine died on this date eleven years ago. Down in Mexico," I said.

"How old was he?"

"Just a mite older than me."

"That's young to die, ain't it?"

"I guess it is."

He nodded. Then his expression grew thoughtful, as though he were remembering a moment, a question, he had refused to face earlier. "Them men who was in the cars out there, the ones made you mad, that one man said something about you sticking a playing card in the mouth of a dead wetback? You ain't done anything like that, huh?"

"They weren't wetbacks, Pete. They were bad guys. They got what they asked for."

"That don't sound like you."

"I lost my friend down there."

"I didn't mean nothing."

"I know that. You're the best, Pete."

We walked Beau down the hard-packed dirt street, along the edge of the rain ditch, to the café and ate supper.

But I didn't tell Pete the rest of the story, nor have I ever told anyone all of it, at least not until now—the weeks of treatment in Uvalde and Houston for the wound in my right arm, the bone surgery, the morphine dreams that at first leave you with a vague sense of unremembered sexual pleasure, followed by a quickening of the heart, flashes of light on the edges of your vision, like gunfire in darkness, a feeling in the middle of the night that you are about to be violated by someone in the room whom you cannot see.

After the hospitals, I went back across the river, without a badge, into the arroyo where we were ambushed and the town south of it where three of our adversaries—psychotic meth addicts who would later be killed by *federales*—had celebrated L.Q.'s death in a whorehouse, then down into the interior, across dry lake beds and miles of twisted moonscape that looked like heaps of cinders and slag raked out of an ironworks, into mountains strung with clouds and finally a green valley that was glazed with rain and whose red-

155

dish brown soil was lined with rows of avocado trees.

I thought I had found the leader, the man L.Q. had taken the rifle from.

The owner of the only bar in the village thought for a moment about my offer, then picked up the fifty-dollar bill from the counter and folded it into his shirt pocket. He was a big man with a black beard, and part of his face was covered with leathery serrations like dried alligator hide.

"See, I was a migrant labor contractor in Arizona. That's where I first seen this guy. I think he was moving brown heroin on the *bracero* buses. Pretty slick, huh? Yeah, I don't owe that guy nothing. Come on back here, I'll show you something," he said.

The bar was a cool, dark building that smelled of beer and stone, and through the front door you could see horses tied to a tethering rail and the late sun through the long-leaf Australian pines that were planted along the road.

We went out the back door to a small cottage that was built of stacked fieldstones and covered with a roof of cedar logs and a blackened canvas tarp. The bartender pushed open the door, scraping it back on the stone floor.

"That was his bunk. Them stains on the floor, that's his blood. The guy don't got no name, but he got plenty of money. *Puta* too. A couple of them," the bartender said. "They told me they didn't like him, he talked about cruel things, made them do weird stuff, know what I mean?"

"No."

"He must have been in the army, maybe down in Guatemala, he done some things to the Indians...Here."

The bar owner picked up a bucket by the bail, walked outside with it, and shook it upside down. A broken knife blade and a spiral of bloody bandages tumbled out. He flipped the knife blade over with the point of his boot.

"That's what the doctor took out of him. Got to be a *macho* motherfucker to carry that and still have *puta* on the brain," he said.

"Where'd he go?" I could feel my heart beating with the question.

"A plane picked him up. Right out there in them fields...This guy killed somebody who was your friend?"

"Not exactly."

"Then I'd let it go, man. He told them two girls, his *puta*, he wired up people to electrical machines...You want your money back?"

"No."

"You don't look too good. I'll fix you a rum and something to eat."

"Why not?" I said, looking at the mist on the avocado orchards and a torn purple and yellow hole in the clouds through which the man without a face or name had perhaps disappeared forever.

157

CHAPTER

15

The next morning was Saturday, a blue-gray, misty, cool dawn that brought Mary Beth Sweeney to my back door at 6 A.M., still in uniform from the night shift, her thumbs hooked into the sides of her gunbelt.

I held open the screen. "Come in and join Pete and me for breakfast. We're fixing to go down to the river in a few minutes," I said.

She removed her hat, her eyes smiling into mine.

"I'm sorry for the other night," she said.

"You got to try some of Pete's fried eggs and pork chops. They run freight trains on this stuff, isn't that right, Pete?"

He grinned from behind his plate. "I always know when he's gonna say something like that," he said.

We rode down the dirt track in my car to the bluffs. The water in the river was high and slate green, tangled with mist, the current eddying around the dead cottonwood trees that had snagged in the clay.

Five feet under the surface was the top of an ancient car, now softly molded with silt and moss. In the winter of 1933 two members of the Karpis-Barker gang robbed the bank in Deaf Smith and tried to outrun a collection of Texas Rangers and sheriffs' deputies from three counties. Their car was raked with Thompson machine-gun bullets, the glass blown out, the fuel tank scissored almost in half. My father watched the car careen off the road, plow through the corn crib and hog lot, then ignite with a *whoosh* of heat and energy that set chickens on fire behind the barn.

The car rolled like a self-contained mobile inferno across the yellow grass in the fields, the two robbers like blackened pieces of stone inside. The ammunition in their stolen Browning Automatic Rifles was still exploding when the car dipped over the bluffs and slid into the river. It continued to burn, like a fallen star, under the water, boiling carp that were as thick as logs to the surface.

Today the car was a home to shovel-mouth catfish that could straighten a steel hook like a paper clip.

Mary Beth got out of the Avalon and stretched and hung her gunbelt over the corner of the open door. She watched Pete baiting his hook down on the bank, as though she were forming words in her mind.

"The man at my apartment, his name's Brian. I was involved with him. But not anymore. I mean, not personally," she said.

"Take this for what it's worth, Mary Beth. Most feds are good guys. That guy's not. He put you at risk, then he tried to lean on me."

"You?"

"I suspect y'all are DEA. The FBI doesn't send its people in by themselves."

"Brian leaned on you?"

"*Tried.* This guy's not first-team material."

Her eyes were hot, her back stiff with anger.

"I have to make a phone call," she said.

"Stay here, Mary Beth."

"I'll walk back."

I took her gunbelt off the corner of the door.

"Nine-Mike Beretta," I said.

"You want to shoot it?"

"No." I folded the belt across the holster and handed it to her. The nine-millimeter rounds inserted in the leather loops felt thick and smooth under my fingers. "I don't mess with guns anymore. Take my car back. Pete and I will walk."

Then she did something that neither Pete nor I expected. In fact, his face was beaming with surprise and glee as he looked up from the bank and she hooked one arm around my neck and kissed me hard on the mouth.

That afternoon the district attorney, Marvin Pomroy, rang me at home.

"We've got Garland Moon in the cage. He wants to see you," he said.

"What's he in for?"

"Trespassing, scaring the shit out of people. You coming down?"

"No."

"He's into something, it's got to do with the Vanzandt family. Anyway, we've got to kick him loose in another hour. So suit yourself."

160

The previous night, Garland T. Moon had showed up first at Shorty's, then at the drive-in restaurant north of town, dressed in plastic cowboy boots, white pleated slacks, a form-fitting sleeveless undershirt, costume jewelry on his hands and wrists and neck. He wandered among the cars in the parking lot, gregarious, avuncular, a paper shell of french fries in one hand, a frosted Coke in the other. He worked his way into groups of teenagers, as though he were an old friend, and told obscene jokes that made their faces go slack with disgust.

Then Bunny Vogel's '55 Chevy, with a girl in the front passenger seat, and Darl Vanzandt and another girl in back, cruised the lines of parked cars and backed into an empty space twenty feet from Moon.

He walked to their car, bent down grinning into the windows, his face lighted with familiarity.

"Who's that in there?" he said.

Inside the car, they looked at one another.

"How about we go for some beers? Maybe I score a little *muta?*" he said.

"We don't know you, man," Darl said.

"You kids got a look in your eyes tells me y'all don't care y'all end up in the gutter or not...I'm a student of people. I want to know where that look comes from. Let's make it scrambled eggs at my place."

"I just washed my car. Get your fucking armpits off the window," Bunny said.

A few minutes later every car in the drive-in had burned rubber out onto the highway and left Garland T. Moon standing alone, with his french fries and frosted Coke, amid the litter in the parking lot.

The next day Jack Vanzandt was among a foursome on the ninth green at the country club when a man in a cream-colored suit, a Hawaiian shirt printed with flowers that could have been shotgun wounds, and brand-new white Kmart tennis shoes with the word *JOX* emblazoned across the tops, strolled up from the edge of the water trap, his wisps of red hair oiled on his scalp, and said, "Excuse me, sir, I'd like to talk with you over at the Shake 'n' Dog about a mutual interest we got...Say, this is a right nice golf range, ain't it? I been thinking about getting a membership myself."

Garland T. Moon was in the holding cage on the first floor, by the elevator shaft that led up to the jail. He had stripped off his coat and shirt, and was standing bare chested in his slacks and JOX running shoes, his hands hooked like claws in the wire mesh.

"What kind of bullshit are you up to, Moon?" I said.

"I got 'em by the short hairs."

"Oh?"

"That little puke Darl Vanzandt done Jimmy Cole, thinks he's some kind of Satanist. I got news for y'all, there's people that's the real thing, that's made different in the womb, it's in the Bible and you can check it out. You getting my drift, boy?"

"Why'd you want to see me?"

"Tell his father I want a hunnerd-thousand dollars."

"Tell him yourself."

"Don't walk away from me...You gonna do what I tell you whether you like it or not. I can give testimony I heard Lucas Smothers confess to raping and killing that girl in the picnic ground."

"Have you been in a mental asylum?"

"Where I been is in this tub of nigger bathwater when I was fifteen years old." His mouth puckered into a peculiar grin, red and glistening, flanged with small teeth.

"It's the town, isn't it, not me or Lucas or some peckerwoods who worked you over with a cattle prod," I said.

"You know the old county prison north of the drive-in restaurant? Forty-one years ago two gunbulls put me over an oil drum every Sunday morning and took turns. Tore my insides out and laughed while they done it...Y'all gonna get rid of me the day you learn how to scrub the stink out of your own shit."

I turned and walked back toward the entrance.

"You won't pick up a gun 'cause you killed your best friend! I got the Indian sign on you, boy!" he called at my back.

Marvin Pomroy waited for me outside. He was a Little League coach, and because it was

Saturday he wore a pair of seersucker slacks and a washed-out golf shirt without a coat. But, as always, not a hair was out of place on his head, and his face had the serenity of a thoughtful Puritan who viewed the failure of the world through Plexiglas.

I told him what Moon had said.

"Why does he seem to have this ongoing obsession with you?" he asked.

"You got me."

"You never ran across him when you were a Ranger or prosecutor?"

"Not to my knowledge."

Down the street a construction crew was fitting a steel crossbeam into the shell of a building and a man in black goggles was tack-welding a joint in a fountain of liquid sparks.

"What kind of vocational training did Moon get inside?" I asked.

"He picked cotton. That's when he wasn't in lockdown... Why?"

"Moon's an arc welder. So was my father."

"Big reach."

"You got a better one?" I asked.

Late that evening the sheriff parked his new Ford pickup at his hunting camp above the river. He was proud of his camp. The log house on it was spacious and breezy, with cathedral ceilings, lacquered yellow pine woodwork, a fireplace built from river stones and inset with Indian tomahawks and spear points recovered from a burial mound, stuffed tarpon and the heads of deer and bobcats mounted on the walls and support beams, a green felt poker table cupped with plastic trays for the chips, a freezer stocked with venison and duck, ice-cold vodka and imported beer in the refrigerator, glass gun cases lined with scoped rifles.

He showered and dried off in the bathroom, then walked naked into the kitchen and opened a bottle of German beer, turned on the television set atop the bar, and punched in the number of an escort service in San Antonio on his cordless phone.

From the kitchen window he could see the sun's last fiery spark through the trees that rimmed the hills above the river, the gray boulders that protruded from the current, his dock and yellow-and-red speedboat snugged down with a tarp, the flagstone terrace where he barbecued a whole pig on a spit for state politicians who introduced him with pride to their northern friends as though he were a charismatic frontier reflection of themselves.

Not bad for a boy with a fourth-grade education who could have ended up road-ganging himself.

The sheriff had always said, "We all work for the white man. You can do it up in the saddle with a shotgun, or down in the row with the niggers. But there's no way you ain't gonna do it."

The woman who answered the number in San Antonio said his visitor would be there in two hours.

The sheriff drank the last of his beer and let the foam slide down his throat. His massive torso was ridged with hair, his back and buttocks pocked with scars from the naked screws on football shoes that had thundered over his body when he had played defensive lineman in a semipro league at age nineteen. He peeled the cellophane off a cigar, lit it, wet the match under the faucet, and dropped it into a plastic-lined wastebasket under the counter. Then he seemed to have turned from the sink, perhaps when a shadow fell across his neck and shoulders.

The ax was one he recognized. It had rested on a nail in the shed above his woodpile. He had honed it on a grinding stone until its edge looked like a sliver of ice.

The first blow was a diagonal one, delivered at a downward angle. The blade bit into the sheriff's face from below the left eye to the right corner of the mouth.

That was the first blow. The others were struck along a red trail from the kitchen to the gun case in the living room, where the sheriff gave it up forever and lay down among the stuffed heads that had always assured him he was intended to be the giver of death and never its recipient.

CHAPTER

16

Sunday morning, before the sun was above the hills, I watched from behind the crime scene tape while the paramedics rolled the sheriff's body on a gurney to the back of an ambulance. Marvin Pomroy nudged me on the arm, then walked with me toward my Avalon.

"You got any thoughts?" he asked.

"No."

"He was dead at least two hours before the hooker got there. The intruder could have cleaned the place out. But he didn't. So it's a revenge killing, right?"

"A lot of TDC graduates hated his guts," I said.

Marvin looked back at the log house. His face was dry and cool in the wind, but the skin jumped in one cheek, as though a string were pulling on it.

"Two Secret Service agents were in here earlier. What's their stake in a guy who spit Red Man on restaurant floors?" he said.

"Not DEA?"

"No."

"One of them was named Brian?"

"That's right, Brian Wilcox. A real charmer. You know him?"

"Maybe. You want to go to breakfast?"

"After looking at what's inside that house?"

"The sheriff was a violent man. He dealt the play a long time ago."

"Where the fuck do you get your ideas? Pardon my language. Violent man? That's your contribution? Thanks for coming out, Billy Bob. I don't think my morning would have been complete without it."

I drove up a sandy, red road that twisted and dipped through hardwoods and old log skids and pipeline right-of-ways that were now choked with second growth.

Up ahead, a dark, polished car with tinted windows and a radio antenna came out of an intersecting road and stopped in front of me.

The man whom Mary Beth called Brian got out first, followed by two others who also wore aviator's sunglasses and the same opaque expression. But one man, who had rolled down a back window part way, did not get out. Instead, Felix Ringo, the Mexican drug agent, lit a cigarette in a gold holder and let the smoke curl above the window's edge.

"Step out of your car," Brian said.

"I don't think so," I said.

The man next to him opened my door.

"Don't be shy," he said.

I turned off the ignition and stepped out among them. The air was motionless between the trees and smelled of pine and the rainwater in the road's depressions. Brian raised his finger in my face. It stayed there, uncertainly, as though he were on the brink of doing something much more serious and precipitous.

"I don't have the right words. Maybe it's

168

enough to simply say I don't like you," he said.

"You're over the line, bud," I said.

"You're not a police officer anymore, you're not an assistant U.S. attorney, you're a meddlesome civilian. That fact seems to elude you."

"You going to move your car now?"

"No." His finger was stiff, the nail thin and sharp and trembling below my eye. "Stay away from crime scenes that don't concern you, stay away from the lady... You got anything clever to say?"

"Not really. Except if you put your finger in my face again, I'm going to break your jaw. Now, get your fucking car out of my way."

I went back home and weeded the vegetable garden. I curried out Beau and cleaned his stall and set out catfish lines in the tank and shoveled out the chicken run and worked buckets of manure into my compost pile with a pitchfork, my calluses squeezing tighter and tighter on the smooth wood of the handle, until I finally gave it all up and flung the pitchfork into a hay bale and went inside.

The palms of my hands rang as though they had been stung by bees, as though they ached to close on an object that was hard and round and cool against the skin and flanged with a knurled hammer that cocked back with a loud snap under the thumb.

Moon had said some people are made different in the womb. Was he just describing himself, or did the group extend to people like me and Great-grandpa Sam?

Or Darl Vanzandt?

Through my open front windows I heard the deep, throaty rumble of the Hollywood mufflers on his '32 Ford, then a cacophony of straight pipes and overpowered engines and chopped-down Harleys behind him.

He turned into the drive, alone, the exposed chrome engine so fine-tuned a silver dollar would balance on the air cleaners. His friends pulled onto the shoulder of the road, on my grass, their tires crumpling the border of my flower beds. They cut their engines and lit cigarettes and lounged against their cars and trucks and vans and motorcycles, as though their physical connection to a public road gave them moral license to behave in any fashion they wished.

Darl swung a dead cat by its tail, whipping it faster and faster through the air, and thudded it against the screen door.

I went out on the porch with my cordless phone in my hand.

"I already put in a 911 on you, Darl. Time to head for the barn," I said.

"I'm gonna kick your ass. Don't believe me, you chickenshit lying motherfucker? Come out here and see what happens next," he said.

I walked toward him. His wide-set green eyes seemed to shift in and out of focus, as though different objects were approaching him at the same time. His upper lip was beaded with perspiration, his nostrils dilated and pale. The skin of his face drew back against the bone. I could smell beer and fried meat and onions on his breath.

"I mean you no harm. I never have. Neither does Lucas. Go on home," I said.

"You're in my face every day. You're spreading lies all over town."

"You and your friends killed somebody's cat? That's what y'all do to show everybody you're big shit?"

"I ain't afraid of you."

I stepped between him and the road, with my back to his friends, cutting off his view of them.

"Bunny Vogel's not here to bail you out. You're stoned and you're frightened. If you force me to, I'll show everyone here how frightened you are," I said.

"If I was scared, I wouldn't be here."

"You're afraid of what you are, Darl. Your folks know it. In their guts, those guys out there do, too. You elicit pity."

He opened his mouth to speak. It made a phlegmy, clicking sound but no words came out. His resolve, all the martial energy he had been able to muster while driving down the road with his Greek chorus surrounding him, seemed to fade in his eyes like snowflakes drifting onto a woodstove.

"Talk to your dad. Get some help. Don't do something like this again," I said.

"I been sick. I had flu all week. I don't

have to listen to anything you—" he said.

I cupped my hand around his upper arm. It felt flaccid, without tone or texture, as though the downers in his system had melted the muscle into warm tallow. I opened his car door for him, put him inside, and closed the door. His eyes were filled with water, his cheeks flushed with pale red arrowpoints.

"You want a cop to drive you home?" I asked.

He didn't answer. When I went back inside it was quiet for a long time, then I heard his engine start up and his tires crunch on the gravel and back out on the road. Some of the others followed, looking at one another, unsure, and some turned back toward town, all of them like people trying to create their own reality, from moment to moment, inside a vacuum.

The country club had been all-white since its inception in the early 1940s, first by the legal exclusivity the law allowed at the time, then by custom and defiance and contempt. It had remained an island of wealth and serenity in an era that had produced cities scrawled with graffiti and streets populated by the homeless and deranged.

The groundskeepers adjusted the amounts of water and liquid nitrogen fed into the grass to ensure the fairways were emerald green year-round, no matter how dry or cold the season. The swimming pool was constructed in the shape of a shamrock, and those who stepped down into its turquoise sun-bladed surface seem to glow with a health and radiance that perhaps validated the old literary saw that the very rich are very different from you and me.

The main building was an immaculate, blinding white, with a circular drive and a columned porch and a glassed-in restaurant with a terrace shaded by potted palm and banana trees that were moved into a solarium during the cold months. A hedge as impenetrable as a limestone wall protected the club on one side, the bluffs and the lazy green expanse of the river on the other. Recessions and wars might come and go, but Deaf Smith's country club would always be here, a refuge, its standards as unchanging as the European menu in its restaurant.

I had dressed for it, in my striped beige suit, polished cordovan boots, a soft blue shirt and candy-striped necktie. But dress alone did not always afford you a welcome at Post Oaks Country Club.

I stood by Jack and Emma Vanzandt's table, the maître d' standing nervously behind me, a menu in his hand. Jack and Emma were eating from big shrimp cocktail glasses that were deep-set in silver bowls of crushed ice.

"You want to go outside and talk?" I said to Jack.

He wiped his mouth with a napkin and looked through the French doors at several men putting on a practice green. "It's all right, André," he said to the maître d'.

Then he glanced at an empty chair across from him, which was the only invitation I received to sit down.

"Thanks, Jack," I said.

In the gold and silver light that seemed to anoint the room, Emma's Indian-black hair looked lustrous and thick on her bare shoulders, her ruby necklace like drops of blood on the delicate bones of her throat.

"Your boy was out at my place today. He's a sick kid. Do something about him," I said.

"You come to our dinner table to tell me something like this?" Jack said.

"Here's the street menu in Deaf Smith, Jack: purple hearts, black beauties, rainbows, screamers, yellow jackets, and China white if you want to get off crack. I hear Darl does it all. If you don't want to take a wake-up call, at least keep him away from my house."

He set his cocktail fork on the side of his plate and started to speak. But Emma placed her hand on his forearm.

"We're sorry he bothered you. Call either Jack or me if it happens again. Would you like to order something?" she said.

"Blow it off. I can't blame you. The sheriff did too. But now he's dead," I said.

They stared at each other.

"You didn't know?" I said.

"We just got back from Acapulco," Jack said.

"Somebody came up behind him with an ax," I said.

"That's terrible," Emma said.

"He had a lot of enemies. A lot," Jack said. But his eyes were fastened on thoughts that only he saw.

"I told the sheriff I think Darl killed Jimmy Cole. I don't know if there's a connection or not," I said.

Emma's eyes were shut. Her lashes were black and the lids were like paper, traced with tiny green veins, and they seemed to be shuddering, as though a harsh light were burning inside her.

"Leave our table, Billy Bob. Please, please, please leave our table," she said.

But later I was bothered by my own remarks to the Vanzandts. Darl connected with the sheriff's murder? It was unlikely. Darl and his friends didn't prey on people who had power. They sought out the halt and lame and socially ostracized, ultimately the people who were most like themselves.

The sheriff's widow was the daughter of a blacksmith, a square, muscular woman with recessed brooding eyes who wore her dark hair wrapped around her head like a turban. Whether she bore her husband's infidelities and vulgarity out of religious resignation or desire for his money was a mystery to the community, since she had virtually no friends or life of her own except for her weekly attendance at the Pentecostal church downtown, and the community had stopped thinking of her other than as a silent backdrop to her husband's career.

"The person done this was probably a lunatic got loose from some mental hospital," she said in her kitchen.

"Why's that?"

"'Cause it's what Davis Love always told me it'd be if it happened," she said. (Davis Love was her husband's first and last name and the only one she ever called him by.) "He said the man who killed him would probably be some crazy person, 'cause nobody he sent up to prison would ever want to see him again."

She let the undisguised heat in her eyes linger on my face so I would make no mistake about her meaning.

"He left his mark on them?" I said.

"They tended to move to other places."

I looked out the kitchen window at the rolling pasture behind her house, the neat red and white barn, an eight-acre tank stocked with big-mouth bass, the sheriff's prize Arabians that had the smooth gray contours of carved soap rock.

"I'm sorry for your loss," I said.

"They might bad-mouth him, but he worked hisself up from road guard to high sheriff, without no hep from nobody."

I nodded as her words turned over a vague

recollection in my mind about the sheriff's background.

"He was an extraordinary person," I said.

Her smile was attenuated, wan, a victorious recognition of the assent she had extracted from me. Then I saw it in her eyes. She had already revised him and placed him in the past, assigning him qualities he never had, as the roles of widow and proprietress melded together in her new life.

I had forgotten that the sheriff had started out his law enforcement career not as a cop but as a gunbull on a road gang, back in the days when the inmates from the old county prison were used to trench water and sewer lines and to spread tar on county roads. I remember seeing them as a boy, their backs arched with vertebrae, their skin sunbrowned the color of chewing tobacco, thudding their picks into a ditch while the road hacks stood over them with walking canes that were sheathed on the tips with cast-iron tubes.

Moon had been one of those inmates.

At age fifteen raped on a regular basis by two gunbulls in the county prison.

What were his words? *Tore my insides out and laughed while they done it... Y'all gonna get rid of me the day you learn how to scrub the stink out of your own shit.*

Was the splattered, red trail from the kitchen to the gun case in the sheriff's log house just the beginning of our odyssey with Garland T. Moon?

That night I called Mary Beth Sweeney and got her answering machine.

"It's Billy Bob. I'll buy you a late dinner—" I said, before she picked up the receiver.

"Hi," she said.

"Are you Secret Service?"

"No!"

"I had a run-in with this character Brian Wilcox this morning. Why are Treasury people interested in the sheriff's murder?"

"Ask Brian Wilcox."

"Come on, Mary Beth."

"I don't want to talk about him."

Through my library window I could see the moon rising over the hills.

"How about dinner?" I said.

"It's a possibility."

"I'll be by in a few minutes."

"No, I'll come there."

"What's wrong?"

"Brian watches my place sometimes. He's weird..." Then, before I could speak again, she said, "I'll take care of it. Don't get involved with this man...See you soon."

The breeze was cool that night, the clouds hammered with silver. It had been an unseasonably wet spring, and small raindrops had started to click on the roof and the elephant ears under my library windows. I walked out into the barn and the railed lot behind it and fed Beau molasses balls out of my hand. When he had finished one, he would bob his head and nose me in the shirt pocket and face until I gave him another, crunching it like a dry carrot between his teeth. I stroked his ears and mane and touched the dried edges of the wound someone had inflicted on his withers, and tried to think through all the complexities that had attached themselves to the defense of Lucas Smothers and had brought someone onto my property who would take his rage out on a horse.

I could hear the windmill's blades ginning in the dark and the bullfrogs starting up in the tank. My back was to the open barn doors and the wind blew across me and Beau as though we were standing in a tunnel. For no apparent reason his head pitched away from the molasses ball in my palm, one walleye staring at me, and then he backed toward the far side of the lot, his nostrils flaring.

I turned and just had time to raise one arm before a booted man in shapeless clothes swung a sawed-off pool cue at the side of my head. I heard the wood knock into bone, then the earth came up in my face, the breath burst from my chest, and I heard a snapping, disconnected sound in the inner ear, like things coming apart, like the sound of seawater at an intolerable depth.

I was on my elbows and knees when he

kicked me, hard, the round steel-toe of the boot biting upward into the stomach.

"You like roping people in bars? How's it feel, motherfucker?" he said.

Then a second man kicked me from the other side, stomped me once in the neck, lost his balance, and kicked me again.

My Stetson lay in the dirt by my head, the crown pushed sideways like a broken nose. I could hear Beau spooking against the rails, his hooves thudding on the mat of desiccated manure.

But a third man was in the lot too. He wore khakis and snakeskin boots, and hanging loosely from the fingers of his right hand was a curved knife, hooked at the end, the kind used to slice banana stalks. He dropped it in the dirt by the booted man's foot.

The booted man gathered it into his right hand and laced the fingers of his left into my hair and jerked my head erect.

"Just so you'll know what's going on, we're cutting off your ears," he said.

For just a second, through the water and blood and dirt in my eyes, I saw a flash of gold in the mouth of the man who had dropped the knife to the ground.

I brought my fist straight up between the thighs of the man who held me by the hair, sinking it into his scrotum. I saw his body buckle, the knees come together, the shoulders pitch forward as though his lower bowels had been touched with a hot iron.

Then headlights shone in my driveway,

bounced across the chicken run, and filled the barn and horse lot with shadows.

The three men were motionless, like stick figures caught under a pistol flare. I rolled sideways, stumbled and ran into the barn, my arms cupped over my head as one of them aimed and fired a pistol, a .22 perhaps, *pop, pop, pop,* in the darkness and I heard the rounds snap into wood like fat nails.

I thought I saw L.Q. Navarro, his tall silhouette and cocked ash-gray Stetson and gunbelt and holstered .45 double-action revolver superimposed against an eye-watering white brilliance.

Moments later Mary Beth Sweeney squatted next to me in Beau's stall, her nine-millimeter pushed down in the back of her blue jeans. My nose was filled with blood and I had to breathe through my mouth. She ran her hand through my hair and wiped the straw and dirt out of my eyes. My face jerked when she touched me.

"Oh Billy Bob," she said.

"Where are they?"

"They took off in a four-wheel-drive through the back of your property...Let's go inside. I'll call the dispatcher."

"No, call Marvin Pomroy."

I got to my feet, my hands inserted between the slats of the stall. The high beams of her car were still on, and the inside of the barn was sliced with electric light. She put her arm around my waist, and we walked together toward my back door as the wind twisted and bent the branches of the chinaberry tree over our heads.

CHAPTER

17

I stood shirtless in my bedroom on the third floor, the cordless phone held to one side of my head, a towel filled with ice held against the other. My shirt was on the floor, the collar flecked with blood. I could feel a burning in my lower back that I couldn't relieve, no matter which way I moved.

"You never saw them before?" Marvin said through the phone.

"No...I don't think."

"You're unsure?"

"The guy who watched, the one who dropped the knife on the ground...Maybe I'm imagining things."

"Where'd you see him?"

"It's like you remember people from dreams. I'm not feeling too well now, Marvin. Let me get back to you."

"I'll put a deputy on your house."

"No, you won't."

"No faith," he said.

"You're a good guy, Marvin. I don't care what people say."

I heard him laugh before he hung up.

I clicked off the phone and set it down on the table by the window where Mary Beth sat, her violet eyes close set with thought.

"You think you saw one of those guys before?" she said.

"L.Q. Navarro and I went up against this same mule down in Coahuila three or four times. I always saw him in the dark. Sometimes I see people at night who remind me of him, like you see people inside dreams. A therapist told me—"

"What?"

"That it was unexpiated guilt. It's the kind of thing therapists like to talk about."

"I worry about you."

"I'd better take a shower," I said.

"You should go to the hospital."

"I've wasted enough of the night on these guys. Why don't you get yourself something to eat in the kitchen?"

"Eat?"

"Yeah."

"Too much," she said.

After she went downstairs, I got into the shower stall and turned the hot water into my face and hair and propped my palms against the tile and let the blood and dirt and dried sweat boil out of my skin and sluice into the drain.

But when I closed my eyes I felt the bottom of the stall tilt under my feet and I saw streamers of colored light, like tracers in a night sky, behind my eyelids. I dried off and dressed in my underwear, one hand gripped on the bathroom door for balance. I saw the horizon dip outside the window and I heard a voice say *Just so you'll know what's going on, we're cutting off your ears,* and I toppled sideways across a chair onto the floor.

Then Mary Beth was beside me, her hands gripped under my arms, pulling me erect, helping me to the bed. I fell back on the pillow and dragged the sheet across my loins. She sat on the edge of the mattress, her eyes staring down into mine. Outside the window the sky was sealed with a flat layer of black clouds that pulsed with lightning.

"I'm all right," I said.

"You want me to go?"

I started to speak, but she saw the answer in my eyes and she leaned over me and brushed my forehead with her fingers and kissed me lightly on the mouth. The tips of her curls touched my cheeks, and I could smell her shampoo and the heat in her skin. I held her and kissed her again. She slipped off her shoes and lay beside me, her face inches from mine.

"I've seen your jacket. Your kind always gets hurt, Billy Bob," she said.

"You *are* a fed."

She didn't reply. Instead, she gathered her arms around me and pulled me against her, releasing her breath against my cheek, molding me against her, her ankle tucked inside mine.

I waited to sit up, to change my position, but I felt two bright tentacles of pain slip along my spine and wrap around the front of my thighs.

"Wait," she said. She stood up, unbuttoned her shirt and let it drop to the floor, then unsnapped her blue jeans and worked them off her hips and stepped out of them. Behind her, I could see clouds racing across the land, blooming with quicksilver, splintering the hills with electricity.

She turned away from me briefly, unhooked her bra and slipped off her panties, then sat on the edge of the mattress, pulled the sheet away from my body, and lay against me. I tried to turn on my shoulder so that I faced her, but again I felt a muscular spasm seize my lower back and send a pain through my thighs that made my mouth drop open.

"Don't move," she said, and spread her thighs and sat on top of me, her arms propped on each side of me. She smiled down into my face. The freckles on her shoulders and the tops of her breasts looked like tiny brown flowers. I traced my fingers around her nipples and took them in my mouth, then felt an unrelieved hardness and desire in my loins that I couldn't contain, that was like an envelope of heat glowing off of iron, that ached to enter her softness and the beauty and charity of her body, which gave satisfaction and sanctuary long before orgasm.

"I'll be here for you," she whispered, her lips against my cheek, her passion so genuine and pure that I knew secretly, as all men do, I was undeserving of it.

CHAPTER

18

Early the next morning, I put ice on the tubular swelling along the side of my head and went to a doctor for the muscle spasms in my lower back. He showed me a set of exercises that involved lying on the floor and raising the knees to the chest and sitting in a chair and touching the floor while I sucked in my stomach. I was amazed to find that a level of pain that had been so intense could drain out of my body like water, at least temporarily.

"Whenever you feel the pain, do the exercise. You'll be fine. Just avoid any sudden movement in your back," the doctor said. He took a ballpoint pen out of his shirt pocket. "You want a prescription?"

"No, thanks."

"It's light stuff."

"It always is."

"Tell me you're not still six-parts Baptist, Billy Bob."

Later, I went to the health club and sat in the steam room, then showered and walked to Marvin Pomroy's office in the courthouse.

"We put out a bulletin on the three guys but we didn't have much to go on," he said.

"Anybody question Moon about the sheriff's murder?" I asked.

"I don't see him as a strong suspect."

"Moon was in the old county prison when the sheriff was a roadbull," I said. Marvin was tilted back in his swivel chair. The connections didn't come together in his face. "Moon said a couple of guards sodomized him on an oil barrel. He said they did it to him every Sunday morning."

"You're saying the sheriff was a pervert?"

"I don't know anything he wasn't."

"If Moon's got a hard-on for the whole county, why does he wait forty years to come back and do a number on us? I think the sheriff was killed for other reasons," Marvin said.

"Some people might call an ax across the face an indicator of revenge."

But I could tell he was thinking of something else. He took off his glasses and polished the lenses with a piece of Kleenex. He fitted them back on his nose, his face blank, as though debating whether to expose the feelings he usually kept stored in a private box. His hair was so neat it looked like fine strands of metal on his head.

"I couldn't sleep last night," he said. "What those guys tried to do to you...I'd like to catch up with them on a personal basis."

"It's not your style, Marvin."

"You don't get it. I'm a law officer in a county that's probably run by the Dixie Mafia. I just can't prove it."

I walked back across the street to the office and took the mail out of the box in the first-floor foyer. The foyer was cool and made of stucco and tile and decorated with earthen jars

187

planted with hibiscus. Mixed in with the letters and circulars was a brown envelope with no postage, addressed to me in pencil.

For some reason—its soiled surfaces, the broken lettering, a smear of dried food where the seal had been licked—it felt almost obscene in my hand. I didn't open it until I was inside my office, as though my ignoring it would transform it into simply another piece of crank mail written by a dissatisfied client or a convict who thought his personal story was worth millions in movie rights. Then I cracked it across the top with my finger, the way you peel back a rotted bandage.

Inside was a Polaroid picture of Pete on the playground at the Catholic elementary school. The penciled page ripped out of a cheap notebook read: "This was took this morning. When we get finished carving on him, his parts will fit in your mailbox."

I called the principal at the school. She was a classic administrator; she did not want to hear about problems and viewed those who brought them to her as conspirators who manufactured situations to ruin her day.

"I just saw Pete. He's in the lunchroom," she said.

"I'll pick him up at three. Don't let him walk home," I said.

"What's wrong?"

"Some people might try to hurt him."

"What's going on here, Mr. Holland?"

"I'm not sure."

"I'm aware you pay his tuition and you're

concerned for his welfare, but we have other children here as well. This sounds like a personal matter of some kind."

"I'll call you back," I said. I hung up and punched in Temple Carrol's number.

"We need to throw a net over Roy Devins," I said.

"What happened?"

I told her about the visit of the three men to my house the previous night.

"They knew about my rope-dragging Devins out of the bar. Devins was in the sack with Pete's mother. She's a drunk and gets mixed up with bikers and dopers sometimes."

"You told this to Marvin?"

"What's he going to do? Half the cops in the county are on a pad. He's lucky he hasn't been assassinated."

"Look, don't handle that letter. If we can lift some prints, Marvin can run them through AFIS. I'll get back to you."

I closed the blinds and sat in the gloom and tried to think. These were the same men who thought they could terrorize Moon and run him out of town, except he turned the situation around on them and mutilated Roy Devins. But why put heat on Moon? Because he'd been out at the Hart Ranch? Who were they?

L.Q. Navarro sat in a swayback deerhide chair in the corner, one foot propped up on the wastebasket. He kept throwing his hat through the air onto the point of his boot, gathering it up, and throwing it again.

"Time to go to the bank," he said.
"I figured that's what you'd say."
"You just gonna study on it?"
"I gave it up, L.Q. It got you dead."
"Them that won't protect their home and family don't deserve neither one. That's what you used to tell me."
"Maybe I aim to cool them out. Maybe that's what's really on my mind."
"Come on, bud, that little boy cain't be hanging out in the breeze, not with some rat-bait writing letters about killing him. If it was me, I'd blow that fellow's liver out and drink an ice-cold Carta Blanca while I was at it...Sorry, my way of putting things probably ain't always well thought out."

I went downstairs to the bank, then into the vault where the safety deposit boxes were kept. I carried my rental box into a private enclosure and set it on a table and opened the hinged lid. Lying amidst my childhood coin collection and my father's Illinois pocket watch was L.Q.'s holstered double-action revolver. The steel had the soft sheen of licorice; the ivory handles seemed molded into the steel, rather than attached with screws, and age had given them a faint yellow cast, as though the layer of calluses on L.Q.'s palm had rubbed its color into them.
I pulled back the hammer to half-cock and opened the loading gate and rotated the cylinder so I could see the whorls of light in each

empty chamber. Then I holstered the pistol again and wrapped the belt and buckle around the holster and stuck it in a paper bag and walked back up to my office.

Temple Carrol had called back and left a message with my secretary—Roy Devins, whom Garland T. Moon had mutilated, had checked out of the hospital, all bills unpaid, and was thought to have taken a Greyhound bus out of town.

I took L.Q.'s revolver home that afternoon and placed it in my desk drawer in the library and read from Great-grandpa Sam's journal.

August 14, 1891

The Rose of Cimarron and me went to Denver last week on the Santa Fe Railroad and took a room as man and wife in the Brown Palace Hotel, a building which is a marvel even for these modern times. Jennie could not get over riding up ten floors on an elevator, and the truth is neither could I. The lobby was filled with potted ferns and red velvet chairs and settees that was brought from England and which Queen Victoria was said to have sat in. The dinner was prairie chicken stuffed with rice. They give us little bowls to wash our fingers in that Jennie thought was for soup. Later, we drank lemonade with mint leaves in it and ate oysters out of silver ice buckets and listened to the singer Lillie Langtry perform. Most of the guests seemed to be Republican business men. But they was a pretty good sort just the same.

Wyatt and Morgan Earp, Dallas Stoudenmire, Johnny Ringo, Joe Lefores, and the tubercular drunkard Doc Holliday have been here and have died or gone on to whatever places are left for their kind. The streets of Denver are lit with gas lamps, and gunmen and Indians and rowdy miners are not welcome. I don't think Jennie can see it though. Denver is not the future. It's the Cherokee Strip and her people and maybe even the likes of me that's the past.

I had a terrible lesson on the way back. A grass fire burned down the trestle over a gorge and we was stuck on the prairie for two days. We walked to a camp of Tonkawa Indians that stayed half-starved during the winter because the agents stole the money that was for their food. Jennie got a box of canning jars from the train and showed the squaws how to put up preserves. She looked right elegant in her long dress, boiling tomatoes on a stone oven and pouring the stew in glass jars with a spoon set inside so the glass didn't break from the heat. I thought maybe we might have an ordinary life after all, maybe up in Wyoming or Montana where nobody ever heard of the Doolin and Dalton gangs.

When we got back on the train I seen a dark smear on the floor by the woodstove, one that somebody had tried to scrub out of the grain with sand. I asked the conductor who had bled there. He said it was the wife of a railroad board member, and she had been shot to death when train robbers fired through the glass in the window three weeks ago.

Later Jennie asked me what I was studying on. I said, That collection of trash and lamebrains down the hillock from us has gone and killed an innocent woman.

She looked out the window, pouting, then said to me, The railroad stole the land from the Indians and I ain't a bit sorry for her.

If this was the Lord pulling the veil from my eyes, the light has fairly withered an old man's heart.

A motorcycle turned into my drive, the engine popping and misfiring. I turned on the porch light and stepped outside. Lucas Smothers sat astride an old, low-slung Indian motorcycle with dented, purple fenders, his T-shirt and jeans streaked with grease. He cut the engine and grinned.

"You ever see one like this?" he asked.

"Sure, they're collector's items."

"I'm gonna restore it. It's got a crack in the frame but I can braze it. The teacher at the high school body shop said I could use the equipment in the afternoon while they're still cleaning up."

"Where'd you get it?"

"Darl Vanzandt."

"Darl?"

Lucas's eyes went away from my face.

"He said he'd been going to church and trying to get right for the bad things he's done.

193

What was I supposed to say, 'I don't want to have nothing to do with you'?"

"I think he'll hurt you."

"By giving me an old bike?"

"Jimmy Cole *was* murdered on the Hart Ranch. You were probably right the first time. Darl and his friends found him hiding out there and killed him."

He pressed his palm on his forehead, smearing grease in his hair.

"Everything I do is fucked up. I feel worse every time I come over here," he said, his eyes glistening.

"Leave the bike here. I'll call his father and have it picked up."

"Yeah, 'cause the product of your broken rubber cain't take care of hisself. Thanks, anyway," he said.

He started the motorcycle, fed it the gas until the misfires became a dirty roar, then fishtailed off the gravel onto the county road, his hair whipping in the wind, his T-shirt pooling with air.

Way to go, Holland, I thought.

Mary Beth Sweeney called the next morning, just as I was about to leave for the office.

"Bunny Vogel got into it last night with a Mexican biker at Shorty's," she said.

"Which biker?"

"No name. He took off before I got there. But it looks like the fight had something to do with Roseanne Hazlitt."

"How do you know?"

"A couple of witnesses said the Mexican kid called Bunny 'spermbrain,' then 'Roseanne's pimp.' That's when they went at it. They tore up most of the side porch."

"Where's Bunny now?"

"I kept him downtown two hours, then kicked him loose. He's supposed to pay the owner half the damages."

"You're a good cop, Mary Beth."

"A good cop would take him to the Marine Corps recruiting station before he ends up in Huntsville. Have you ever been to California?"

"No, why?"

"These kids must go out there and take courses in how to screw up their lives."

Bunny lived on the west end of the county, not far from a train siding, a shut-down cannery, and a string of abandoned and overgrown wood cottages that had been used by migrant workers during the 1940s. His house was sheathed in ancient gray Montgomery Ward brick and elevated on cinder blocks, but the floor had settled through the center, so that the outside covering had cracked like a dried husk, exposing the tar paper underneath. Bunny's '55 maroon Chevy, with the rolled white leather interior, was parked in the dirt yard, as incongruous as a color cutout pasted on a gray stage set, its green-tinted windows filled with reflections of clouds.

Bunny stood in the backyard, in a sleeveless red sweatshirt and running shorts and half-top cleats, flinging footballs through a rubber tire that hung on a rope from the limb of a hackberry tree.

"I heard you got put in the bag last night," I said.

"Word gets around." He picked up another football from an orange crate and fired a bullet pass through the tire. It landed on a grassy knoll and rolled toward the train tracks.

"Who was the biker?"

"Just a greaseball who wants to take down a swinging dick in Shorty's. I ain't a swinging dick. But that's what the greaseball wants to think."

"He called you a spermbrain?"

"Yeah, I think that's what he said." He shook his hair back on his shoulders and flung another football at the tire. This time it caromed off the rim.

"He's the same guy who picked up Roseanne at the Dairy Queen, isn't he? The one you took her away from?"

"Maybe."

"Something bothers me, Bunny. Roseanne slapped you the night she was attacked. I think it was for something you're really ashamed of, maybe something related to her death."

"I guess I just ain't smart enough to figure all them things out, Mr. Holland."

"The Mexican kid called you a pimp?"

"If that's what somebody told you."

"That's when you swung on him?"

196

"Wouldn't you?" He cocked his arm to throw another football, then dropped it back into the orange crate. "I got to go to work. Anything else on your mind?"

"Yeah, what kind of game is Darl Vanzandt trying to run on Lucas Smothers?"

"What them two do ain't my business."

"What is?"

"Sir?"

"Cleaning up after a moral retard for the Vanzandt family?"

"People don't talk to me like that."

"I just did. Watch your back, Bunny. Before it's over, I think Darl will kick a two-by-four up your ass," I said, and walked back to my car.

I looked through the windshield at him before I backed out. His hands were propped on his hips, his mouth a tight seam, his disfigured profile pointed at the ground. Then he drove his cleated shoe into the slats of the orange crate and showered footballs over the yard.

CHAPTER

19

Pete's mother waited tables in a diner out by the slaughterhouse. Sometimes the men she met in bars beat her up, stole her money, and got her fired from her jobs. Last year she was found wandering behind a motel in her slip and was put in a detox center for three days. After she got out, a choleric judge who reeked of cigars and self-righteousness lectured her in front of morning court and sentenced her to pick up trash on the highways for six weekends with a group of high school delinquents.

I sat in her living room and explained why Pete needed to stay at Temple Carrol's house for a while. She listened without expression, in her waitress uniform, her knees close together, her hands folded in her lap, as though I held some legitimate legal power over her life. There were circles under her eyes, and her hair was lank and colorless on each side of her narrow face.

"Cain't y'all just go arrest the guy wrote you that letter?" she asked.

"There weren't any fingerprints on it. We don't know who sent it."

"The social worker wants him here when she makes her home call. Y'all ain't gonna keep him real long, are you? I cain't get in no more trouble with Social Services."

Late Friday afternoon I looked down from my office window and saw Darl Vanzandt's cherry-red '32 Ford turn into the square. The roof was "chopped"—vertical sections had been cut out of the body so that the top was lowered several inches and the windows looked like slits in a machine-gun bunker—and I had a hard time telling who sat in the passenger's seat, one gnarled arm hooked on the outside panel. Then the car turned out of the evening glare into the shade and I saw the profile of Garland T. Moon.

They parked off the square in front of the Mexican grocery and went inside. Then Moon came out alone, leaned against the car, and began eating ice cream with a plastic spoon from a paper cup.

I walked across the square through the shadows and stopped in front of him. He wore pleated, beltless khakis high up on his hips and a ribbed sleeveless undershirt that looked stitched to his skin.

"What are you doing with the kid?" I said.

He licked the ice cream off his spoon. A shaft of sunlight fell like a dagger across his face, and his receded eye watered in the glare.

"He likes Mexican girls. I introduced him to a lady friend of mine got a house across the border," he said.

"You ought to stick to your own kind. The Vanzandts are out of your league."

"Y'all all in my league, boy. Me and him got us an arrangement." He winked at me.

Inside the grocery, by the small soda fountain in back, I could see Darl talking to a group of kids three or fours years younger than he. The girls had earrings through their noses, even their eyebrows.

"You dealing, Moon?" I said.

"Me? I don't have nothing to do with drugs. I won't even go into a drugstore. That's a fact," he replied. He spooned the ice cream into his mouth. His lips dripped with whiteness when he smiled.

I drove over to Lucas Smothers's house and found him in the backyard, working on the Indian motorcycle. He had rolled the dents out of the fenders and repainted them and mounted a new sheepskin seat on the frame. The wind was still warm and I could smell the water that had just been released from the irrigation ditch into the vegetable rows beyond the barn.

"You know Darl's hanging with Garland Moon now?" I asked.

He set down a wrench on a rag that he had spread on the ground.

"With Moon?" he said.

"That's right."

He looked into space, then picked up the wrench and went back to work.

"Where can I find the Mexican biker Bunny Vogel got into it with?" I asked.

"Guy picked up Roseanne at work sometimes?"

"That's the one."

"He's supposed to be a Purple Heart. They used to be a Los Angeles gang. Some Mexicans in San Antone use their name now."

"Can you put me with this guy?"

"I never had nothing to do with gangs, Mr. Holland. I always went my own way. It didn't do no good, though."

"Why would he call Bunny a pimp?"

"That don't make sense to me. Bunny's stand-up."

"Stand-up? He does grunt work for the Vanzandts because he's afraid to start over again. What do you call that?"

"Everybody don't get to choose what they want to be," he said. Then he paused in his work and looked me directly in the face. "Or what last name they got, either."

That night Mary Beth and I went to a movie at the Rialto theater on the square. When we came back outside the air was warm and smelled of the few raindrops that tumbled out of an almost clear sky. The sidewalk was marbled with the green and pink neon on the marquee, and the tops of the live oaks on the courthouse lawn rustled in the wind and shaped and reshaped their silhouettes against the lighted clock tower.

The street was filled with the same long line of cars and motorcycles that filled it every Friday and Saturday night, radios blaring with rap music, an occasional beer bottle or can arching onto the courthouse lawn.

They weren't all bad kids, not even the East Enders, who were incapable of understanding a world where people lived from paycheck to paycheck and, in the last heat wave, even died because they couldn't adequately cool their houses.

Maybe what bothered me most about them was the way they feigned profligacy as almost a deliberate insult to the very fates that had blessed them.

For some reason I remembered a scene years ago with L.Q. Navarro. We had picked up a prisoner in Denver, leg-chained him through a D-ring on the back floor, and were headed back to Texas when L.Q. saw a faded wood sign by the roadside north of Trinidad.

"I want to stop here," he said.

"What is it?" I asked.

"I'll show you what guts was like back in 1914," he said.

We drove west down a dirt road flanked with piñon trees and hardpan, the mountains purple and edged with fire in the sunset, and stopped at a wire-enclosed monument erected by the United Mine Workers in memory of the striking miners and their families who were shot or asphyxiated to death by state militia and Rockefeller gun thugs during the Ludlow Massacre. There was no U.S. government or state memorial. The monument itself was a fairly simple one, a large block of inscribed stone adorned with statues next to a heavy trap door that opened on a flight of stairs and a basement with decayed plaster walls.

Inside that same enclosure eleven children and two women died when the tents above them were set on fire. The names on the monument were almost all those of Italian and Mexican immigrants.

"People who didn't have a sackful of beans took on John D. himself," L.Q. said. "Their strike got broke and Rockefeller come out here and danced with a miner's wife and made headlines."

"How you know so much about it?" I asked.

"That's my great-grandmother's name up there, bud."

Darl Vanzandt's '32 Ford passed us, its dual pipes throbbing against the asphalt. If he noticed Mary Beth and me, he didn't show it. Across the street, a girl in shorts sat astride the barrel of the Spanish-American War artillery piece, her hands clenched around the metal.

"What are you thinking about?" Mary Beth said.

"Nothing. It's a great country," I said.

"You worrying about Lucas?"

"On his worse day, I'll take that kid over this whole street."

She slipped her arm inside mine and squeezed it against her.

On Saturday afternoon Mary Beth and I took Pete to the rodeo at the county fair grounds. The parking lot was filled with pickup trucks and horse trailers, the viewing stands and midway packed, and a gentle brown haze lifted off the arena while a parade of mounted cowboys rode by the stands, American and state of Texas flags flying over their heads, and carnival rides reared and dipped in the sky.

We bought cotton candy and hot dogs and strolled past the chutes, where boys barely out of high school stood in clusters or perched up on the slats in skin-tight jeans, butterfly chaps, wide-brimmed black Stetsons, rayon shirts with outrageous mixes of the rainbow, and belt buckles polished like Cadillac bumpers.

They were West Enders and blue-collar kids from adjoining counties, their hair mowed into their scalps, their necks cuffed with sunburn. They postured and chewed Red Man and stuck wads of snuff between their lips and gums and tried to talk older than they were, but no one could deny the level of their courage.

The horses they rode sunfished out of the chutes while the rider tried to bring his spurs above the withers, one hand flung into the sky, his spine twisting like it was about to break loose from the tailbone.

Or they tied down their inverted palms on bulls that exploded between the legs when the chute opened, entering that breathless moment inside a vacuum before the bull's hooves touched the sod again, the cowbell clanged from its cinch, and the muscles in the bull's back seemed to wrench the rider's entrails out of his rectum.

They got pitched headlong into the dirt, trampled, stove in, flung against the boards, and sometimes hooked, the bull's horn piercing lung and kidney, tossing the rider in the air, trundling him across the arena like a cloth doll while clowns who wore football shoes tried to save the rider's life with a rubber barrel.

As L.Q. might say, you could find a worse bunch.

We were out on the midway when we saw

a country band assembled on a stage by a grassy area flanked with booths that sold Indian jewelry. In the back of the band was Lucas Smothers, his sunburst twelve-string guitar slung around his neck on a cloth strap beaded with flowers.

It was the first time, to my knowledge, he had played anywhere since his arrest. The band kicked it off with "The Orange Blossom Special" and "Bringing in the Georgia Mail," then bled right into Hank Snow's "Golden Rocket." Lucas stepped to the front of the group and held the sound hole of his guitar to a microphone on an abbreviated stand and went into an instrumental ride that was beautiful to hear and watch. His left hand corded up and down the frets, never pausing, never making a mistake, while the plectrum flashed across the strings over the sound hole, the double-strung octave notes resonating like both a bass guitar and a mandolin.

No one on the stage could approach his performance. But when he finished his solo, which also ended the song, the applause was broken, muted, like cellophane burning and then dying. I could see the emptiness in Lucas's face, his eyes blinking, one hand fiddling with his back pocket, as though he could hide his embarrassment there.

But the leader of the band, a decent man from Austin who well knew his audience, was not one to let a wrong go unchecked. He picked up the microphone and said, "That boy can do it, cain't he? That was gooder than my mama's grits..." He extended his arm back toward the band. "Lucas Smothers, ladies and gentlemen, Deaf Smith's own! How about giving him and the whole band a big hand?"

One of those loudest in his applause was Darl Vanzandt, who stood at the back of the crowd, a smear of cotton candy on his mouth. Three girls, slightly younger than he, were with him. When the band took a break, he touched one of the girls on the shoulder, and she and her two friends went to the stage and began talking excitedly to Lucas.

"What cha studying on?" Pete said.

"Oh, not much," I said, and ran my palm over the soft top of his crewcut.

"Turn loose of it, Billy Bob. He'll be all right," Mary Beth said.

"No, he won't," I said.

She looked at my face, then followed my eyes to Garland T. Moon, who sat on top of a loading chute to the left of the stage, eating a snow cone, crunching the ice to the top by squeezing his fist tighter and tighter along the cone. Darl Vanzandt gave him the thumbs-up sign.

Later, I looked down from the stands and saw Moon wandering along the main aisle, smiling, staring up at the crowd with friendly approval, as though he were one of us, a member of the community enjoying a fine day. He bought a fresh strawberry snow cone from a vendor and bit into it like he was a starving man and it was wet fruit. He touched the pigtails on a little girl's head and brushed his loins against a woman, then stepped back with an elaborate apology on his face.

"I'll be back," I said.

"Billy Bob?" Mary Beth said.

Moon went out the side exit of the stands to a long, flat cement building that served as a public shower and men's room during Indian powwows and rodeos and county fairs. A few kids stood at the urinals but no Garland T. Moon.

I walked along the duckboards, past the row of toilet stalls, until I saw a pair of plastic cowboy boots under a door and heard a man coughing deep in his throat. Next to the boots was a strawberry snow cone that had splattered on the duckboards.

I already saw the next moments in my mind's eye—the door of the stall flying back in his face, my fist nailing him across the bridge of the nose, my boots coming down on his head when he hit the floor.

But that wasn't the way it played out.

When I shoved the door open, I watched a man imploding inside, his head and chest bent over the toilet bowl, his hands wedged against the walls, while he tried to expel a stream of dark blood from his mouth and keep from strangling on it at the same time.

"Hold on, Moon. I'll get here with the medics," I said.

I found the ambulance by the entrance to the arena and walked along beside it to the cement building and watched two paramedics load Moon on a gurney and wheel him back outside. A white towel was wrapped around his throat and chin. Each time he coughed the towel speckled with blood.

"You know this man?" one of the medics asked me.

"Not really," I said.

"Yeah, he does. You might say I'm an old friend of the family," Moon said.

"You're not a clever man, Moon," I said.

The muscles in his face contorted; his hand came off the gurney and locked around my wrist like links in an iron chain.

"This don't change nothing. One day I'm gonna tell you something that'll turn you into a dog trying to pass broken glass," he said.

CHAPTER

20

I talked to Marvin Pomroy on the telephone Monday morning. Across the street, the trees on the courthouse lawn were a hard green in the sunlight, and I could see an inmate in jailhouse whites smoking a cigarette behind a barred window on the top floor of the building.

"The doctor says Moon's insides looked like they'd been chewed by rats. Did you know somebody poured a can of Drano down his mouth when he was a kid in Sugarland?" Marvin said.

"Moon was a snitch?"

"I doubt it. It was probably because he wouldn't come across. That's not what's causing his problems today, though. He's got cancer of the stomach."

"That's why he's back, isn't it? This is his last show," I said. "I should have put it together."

"I'm not with you."

"He told me he didn't drink. Then he told me he had some old DWIs hanging over his head."

"Next time leave him in the toilet stall."

I don't know to what degree Garland T. Moon helped coordinate the events of the next night. The pettiness of mind, the vindictiveness, the level of cruelty involved were all part of his mark. But so were they characteristic of Darl Vanzandt. They had found each other, and I suspected neither of them doubted for a moment the intentions and designs of the other, in the same way the psychologically mal- formed in a prison population stare into hun- dreds of other faces and immediately recognize those whose eyes are like their own, window holes that give onto the Abyss.

I heard the story from the outside and the inside, from Mary Beth, whose cruiser was the first to arrive on the 911 at the country club, from Vernon Smothers, and from Bunny Vogel. It was the kind of account, as Great- grandpa Sam had said, that made you ashamed

to be a member of the white race. Darl Vanzandt and Moon were aberrations. But how
about the others who, with foreknowledge
and joy of heart, went along with their scheme?

Lucas had worked with his father in the
fields that day and had told him he was going
to play with the band that evening before a
baseball game out at the old Cardinals training
camp. Vernon Smothers did not believe him,
but he had long ago come to believe his son
would never tell him the truth about anything,
that lack of trust was the only permanent
reality in their relationship, and so he said
nothing at four o'clock when Lucas walked hot
and dusty from the field, stripped to his shorts
by the barn, and picked the wood ticks off his
body in a sluice of water from the windmill.

Lucas went inside and showered and dressed
in a new pair of slacks and shined yellow
boots and a form-fitting western-cut sports coat.
When he came out on the porch the wind
was fresh and cool in his face, the late afternoon filled with promise. He sat on the steps
with his twelve-string guitar and waited for
Bunny Vogel to pick him up. Lucas's father
was still hoeing in the field, his body like a piece
of scorched tin silhouetted against the sun, his
back knotted with anger, perhaps, or just the
demands of his work.

There were girls in Bunny's car, girls Vernon
Smothers hadn't seen before. They wore tiny
gold rings threaded through their eyebrows
and the rims of their nostrils; they were thin
and immature and not sexually appealing but

dressed and behaved as though they were, wearing no bras, their shirts partially unbuttoned, their voices urgent and wired, as though they were in the midst of a party that had no walls.

Vernon didn't understand them. But how could he, he thought, when he couldn't even define what was wrong in his own life. Maybe it was the whole country, he told himself. Everything had gone to hell back in the 1960s. It was that damn war and the people who didn't have to fight it.

For a few minutes, that thought seemed to bring him solace. He watched from the window as Bunny's car drove away with his son.

Bunny, Lucas, and the girls went first to a bar and restaurant owned by Bunny's cousin on top of a hill that overlooked a long green valley. They ate barbecue sandwiches on a roofed porch in back and drank vodka collins that were filled with shaved ice and cherries and orange slices. The day had cooled, and the meadows on the hillside were bright with flowers and spring grass. The cousin gave them double shots for the price of one, and Lucas began to feel a closeness to Bunny and the girls that made him see them all in a new light, as though they had always been fast friends, more alike than he had ever thought, and the perfection of the evening was an affirmation that the world was indeed a fine place.

"You were great at A&M, Bunny," Lucas

said. "I mean, you could still make it in the pros, I bet."

"Yesterday's ink, kid," Bunny said.

"He's not a kid. He's a...He's a...I don't know what he is," one of the girls said, and giggled. She took a drink from her collins glass, and her mouth looked red and cold, like a dark cherry that waits to burst on the teeth. "You're the best musician in the county, Lucas. You should have gone to East High. My father knows Clint Black and George Strait." Her eyes blinked, as though the effort of organizing her thoughts had left her breathless.

"He owns the studio where Clint Black started out," another girl said.

"No kidding?" Lucas said.

"He did 'til a bunch of Jews took it over," the first girl said. Her eyes were blue, her head covered with blonde curls, and the alcoholic flush on her face made her look vulnerable and beautiful in spite of the harshness of her words.

"Clint Black is good as they get. So is George Strait," Lucas said.

Bunny looked off at the hills, his coppery hair glinting against the late red sun. He seemed lost in his own thoughts now. The girls were silent, as though waiting for something, and for just a moment Lucas knew they didn't care about the names of country musicians and that he bored the girls by wanting to talk about them. But then why did they bring up the subject?

"Ain't we supposed to go to the country club now?" he asked.

212

"We've got time," the girl whose father had owned a recording studio said. She held up her glass to a Mexican waiter and handed it and a credit card pressed under her thumb to him. She didn't speak, and upon his return with the drinks, she signed the charge slip and let him pick it and the pen off the table without ever speaking to him.

Lucas kept staring at the clock on the wall, one with green neon tubing around the outside of the face. The hands said a quarter to seven; then, when he looked again, he was sure only moments later, the hands said 7:25. He went to the men's room and washed and dried his face and looked in the mirror. His eyes were clear, his skin slightly red from the day in the fields. He wet his comb and ran it through his hair and walked back through the bar area, his boots solid on the stone floor.

Outside, Bunny looked at his watch. "I guess we ought to haul ass," he said.

Lucas picked up the fresh collins in front of him and drank half of it. It was as sweet as lemonade, the vodka subtle and cold and unthreatening. The girls watched him while he drank.

"What's going on?" he asked.

They smiled at one another.

"We were saying you're cute," the third girl said.

"I'm fixing to boogie. Y'all coming or not?" Bunny said.

"Darl *can* throw a shitfit if you keep him waiting," the blonde girl said.

"Darl?" Lucas said.

"We're gonna meet him at the drive-in. If he's not too wiped out," she replied.

"Y'all didn't say nothing about Darl," Lucas said.

"He wants to come. What's the law against that?" the blonde girl said. She stood up. Her face seemed angry now, vexed. "People can go where they want. He can't help it if he's rich."

"I didn't say that he...," Lucas began. He rose from his chair and felt a rush, like a hit of high-grade speed, a white needle that probed places in his mind he had never seen before. "I just meant..."

But he didn't know what he meant, and he followed Bunny through the bar and out into the parking lot, the gravel crunching under his boots now, the wind hot for some unexplainable reason, tinged with the smell of alkali.

Later, they backed into an empty slot at the drive-in restaurant, next to Darl's softly buffed '32 Ford, and ordered a round of long-neck Lone Stars. Lucas could see the back of Darl's neck, thick and oily, pocked with acne scars. Three other boys were in the car with him, their caps on backward, their upper bodies swollen from steroid injections and pumping iron. One of them flipped a cigarette at the waitress's butt when she walked by.

Lucas drank down the beer. It felt cold and bright in his throat. But he was sweating now, his heart beating faster than it should.

"I got to get out," he said from the backseat.

"What's wrong?" Bunny said.

"I don't know. I got to get out. I cain't breathe good. It's hot in here."

He opened the back door and stood in the breeze. The hills were flushed with a dark purple haze now, the strings of lights over the parking lot humming with a hot buzz like nests of electrified insects.

He walked to the men's room, but the door, which was metal and fire engine-red, was bolted from the inside. He stared at the rows of parked cars, at the Mexican and black cooks through the kitchen window, the waitresses who carried metal trays loaded with food and frosted mugs of root beer. They all seemed to function with an orderly purpose from which he was excluded, that he witnessed as a clown staring through a glass wall. His face tingled and simultaneously felt dead to the touch. He hadn't felt this drunk, no, train-wrecked, since the night Roseanne Hazlitt was attacked. That thought made him break into a fresh sweat.

He gave up waiting for the person to come out of the locked rest room and walked back to Bunny's car, his eyes avoiding Darl and his friends. The engines in both the Chevy and Ford were idling, the Hollywood mufflers throbbing above the asphalt like a dull headache.

"Hey, what's happenin', man?" Darl said.

"Hi, Darl," Lucas said.

"You want to ride out with us?"

"Bunny's taking me. Thanks, anyway."

"Good-looking threads, man. They're gonna dig it," Darl said. Somebody in the backseat laughed, then dropped his unfinished fish sandwich out the chopped-down slit of a window.

Darl grinned at Lucas as he drove the Ford out of the parking lot onto the highway, his boxed haircut and one-dimensional profile rippled with the glow of the overhead beer sign. When he gave the Ford the gas the rear end rocked back on the springs and wisps of smoke spun off the back tires.

Lucas started to open the back door of the Chevy. Bunny's head was twisted around in the window, looking at him, the corner of his lip pinched down between his teeth.

"Kid, you ain't got to do this. Most of those country club people are dickheads. Maybe we ought to say fuck it," Bunny said.

The girls sat expressionless, their gaze fastened on their cigarettes, waiting, as though caught between Bunny and a predesigned plan that was about to go astray.

"I'm all right. I'm gonna get some coffee out there. It's not a late gig, it's just one or two sets, anyway," he said. He sat down on the rolled white leather and tried to wash a taste like pennies out of his mouth with the last swallows in a bottle of Lone Star that one of the girls handed him.

Bunny didn't seem to move for a long time, biting a piece of skin off the ball of his thumb. Then he shifted the Chevy into gear and turned out of the lighted parking lot into the darkness of the highway.

By the time they reached the country club, Lucas's hair was mushy with his own sweat; his tongue felt too large for his mouth; his hands had the coordination of skillets.

He saw the columned front porch of the country club go by the back window of Bunny's Chevy, then the swimming pool that was built in the shape of a shamrock. The voices around him were like cacophony in a cave. Up ahead, Darl Vanzandt's Ford and two other cars with kids inside them were parked in the shadows, under live-oak trees, just outside the flood lamps that lighted the terrace where people in formal dress were dancing to orchestra music. Bunny slowed the Chevy and turned in the seat and looked at Lucas.

"You gonna be sick?" he said.

But Lucas couldn't answer.

Bunny hit the steering wheel with the flat of his fist. "Oh man, how'd I get in this?" he said.

Then Darl was at the window, his friends behind him. Their cigarettes sparked like fireflies in the darkness. One of them carried a lidded bucket by the bail.

"How much acid you give him?" the boy with the bucket said.

"I didn't give him nothing," Bunny said.

"Pull him out," Darl said.

"Let it slide, Darl. He's really fried," Bunny said.

"Smothers is a geek. So he gets what geeks got coming," Darl said.

"Come on, think about it. Your old man's gonna shit a bowling ball," Bunny said.

"Here's twenty dollars. Go down to San Antone and get a blow job. You'll feel better," Darl said. He was leaning on the window jamb now. He touched the stiffened edges of two ten-dollar bills against Bunny's jawbone.

Bunny pushed his hand away.

"I ain't gonna do this," he said.

"Pretty fucking late, Bunny," the boy with the bucket said. Then he dropped his voice into a deep range and said, "I ain't gonna do this. I got my fucking standards."

"You know what it's like to pull a two-by-four out of your ass?" Bunny said.

"So you don't have to help. Pop the trunk," Darl said.

Two of Darl's friends lifted Lucas by his arms out of the backseat and held him between them like a crucified man. Bunny breathed loudly through his nose, then pulled a latch under the dash. Darl reached into the trunk, took out Lucas's twelve-string guitar and case by the handle, and slammed the lid.

"Thanks for hauling the freight. No hard feelings. You got no beef with him. I do," Darl said.

Bunny started his car and began backing off the grass toward the drive. He had cut his headlights, but in silhouette he could see Darl and his friends pulling off Lucas's clothes, like medieval grave robbers stripping a corpse. The girl in the front seat with Bunny clicked on the radio, increased the volume, and began putting on fresh makeup.

"He buys you blow jobs? That's disgusting," she said.

"Act like your brain stem ain't a stump," he said, then in his frustration clenched the steering wheel so tightly his palms burned.

"Let's go back to the drive-in. I got to pee," a girl in the backseat said.

Bunny wanted to floor the Chevy across the grass and hedges and flower beds onto the drive, but he stared dumbly at the scene taking place in front of him, wondering even then how he would deal with this later, wondering, perhaps, even who or what he was.

Lucas was shirtless, sitting on his buttocks now, his trousers pulled down around his feet, encircled by Darl and the three boys from the drive-in and the others who had gotten out of their cars. But Bunny's attention was diverted by another figure, an older man, one whose pale skin seemed to glisten with a dull sheen like glycerin. On the edge of the circle, his face softly shadowed by the branches of a long-leaf pine, was Garland T. Moon, a cigarette cupped in his hand, like a soldier smoking furtively on guard duty. The corner of his mouth was wrinkled in a smile.

Two boys with their caps on backward hiked Lucas up from the ground. Darl draped the guitar from its cloth strap around Lucas's

219

neck while another boy tightened Lucas's belt around his ankles. Then they stretched wide the elastic on his Jockey undershorts and poured mud and straw and liquid excrement from a feeder lot down his buttocks and genitals and dragged him to the edge of the terrace.

Then the two boys holding Lucas stopped, unsure, wavering in the roar of brass and saxophones.

"No, no, it's show time, babies," Darl said.

His words, his cynicism, his vague and encompassing contempt, seemed to animate the two boys, who for just a moment had probably themselves felt like moths hovering outside the radius of a flame. They carried Lucas into the space between the orchestra and dance area, his feet dragging on the flagstones, his head lolling on his shoulder, a befouled, bone-white man who looked as though his neurological system had melted.

When they dropped him and ran, he tried to push himself to his feet. But he tripped and fell, his guitar clattering on the stone. His skin was beaded with sweat and dirt and aura-ed with humidity in the glare of the flood lamps; his mouth was a stupefied slit across a roll of bread dough. He propped himself on his elbows and stared out at the dancers.

But the membership and management at Post Oaks Country Club were not made up of people who let the world intrude easily upon them. The band never faltered; the eyes of the dancers registered Lucas's presence for no more than a few seconds; and a security guard and waiter wrapped a tablecloth around him and removed him as they would a sack of garbage a prankster had thrown over the wall.

But later, inside the aluminum shed where Lucas sat on a bench among the club's garden tools, throwing up in a sack that had once contained weed killer, he got to see the less public side of the club's management. The manager was a thick-bodied bald man who wore dark trousers and a wine-colored sports jacket, and he was flanked on each side by a security guard.

"You're telling me Jack Vanzandt's son did this?" he said.

"Yes, sir, that's right. It was Darl set it up."

The manager pointed his finger into Lucas's face. "You listen to me, you nasty thing, you tell these lies to anybody else, I'll have you put in jail," he said. "Now, when the sheriff's car gets here, you go home, you never mention this to anyone, and don't you ever come near here again."

"It was Darl. I'll say it to anybody I want. It was Darl, Darl, Darl. How you like that, sir?" Lucas's eyes went in and out of focus, and a vile-tasting fluid welled up in his throat.

"Get him out of here. And wash off that bench, too," the manager said.

It was noon the next day, and I stood in Bunny's backyard and listened to the last of his account. He buffed the hood of his car while he talked, his triceps flexing, his voice flat and distant, as though somehow he were only a witness to events rather than a participant.

He finished talking. He rubbed the rag back and forth in the thin horsetails of dried wax on the hood. Finally he looked at me over his shoulder, his hair bunched in a thick S on his cheek.

"You ain't gonna say nothing?" he asked.

"He told me you were stand-up. I thought you might want to know that."

"Who said that?"

"The kid you delivered up like a trussed hog."

The color flared in his cheeks. I turned to walk away.

"Maybe I'm a Judas goat, but there's a question you didn't ask," he said at my back.

"What might that be, sir?"

"How come he went out there to begin with. It's 'cause Darl got the girls to tell him you were gonna be there. So maybe I ain't the only one hepped pour cow shit on that boy."

CHAPTER

21

I drove from Bunny's house to Jack Vanzandt's office. His secretary said he had already gone for the day. She went back to her work, concentrating her gaze on a computer printout as though I had already left.

"Where did he go?" I asked.

"To one of the lakes, I think."

"The yacht basin?"

"I'm not sure."

"Do you know if Darl is with him?" I asked.

She stared thoughtfully into space. "I don't think he mentioned it," she said.

"I'd really like to have a talk with them. Both of them. Would you get Jack on his cell phone?"

She removed her glasses, which were attached to a blue velvet cord around her neck.

"Please, Mr. Holland. I'm just the secretary," she said, her face softening to an entreaty.

"Sorry," I said.

She smiled at me with her eyes.

The lake where Jack usually kept his sailboat was in a cup of wooded hills that sloped down to cliffs above the water's edge. The western cliffs were in shadow now, the stone dark with lichen, but out in the sunlight a solitary boat with enormous red sails was tacking in the wind, the hard-blue chop breaking like crystal needles across its bow.

Jack Vanzandt stood bare chested behind the wheel, his skin golden with tan, his white slacks tight across his hips and the ridges of muscle in his abdomen.

I waited for him at the boat slip, where a black man was grilling steaks by a plank table under a shed. If Jack was uncomfortable with my presence, he didn't show it. In fact, he seemed to take little notice of me. He was talking to his two guests, who sat in chairs by the cabin with tropical drinks in their hands—the Mexican drug agent, Felix Ringo, and a man from Houston by the name of Sammy Mace.

Jack stepped off his boat, laced a rope around a cleat, and walked toward me. His eyes were flat, but they took my full measure and watched my hands and expression.

"You going to lose it here?" he asked.

"Can't ever tell," I said.

"Don't."

"Your kid's a coward and a sadist. But you probably already know that. I just wanted to tell you he's hooked up with Garland T. Moon now."

"You want to eat, or insult me some more?"

Felix Ringo and the man named Sammy Mace were at the end of the dock, watching a yellow pontoon plane come in low over the hills and skim across the water.

"Sammy Mace is mobbed-up, Jack," I said.

"Then why isn't he in Huntsville? Look, I don't feel good about some things Darl has done. So I've tried to help out."

"Oh?"

"Felix Ringo is an old friend I knew at Benning. He's got a lot of ties in the Hispanic community. He found a kid who might clear Lucas."

I didn't reply. I looked into his eyes.

"Eat with us. Let's end all this foolishness," he said.

"Found which kid?" I asked.

"A biker. Belongs to a gang called the Purple Hearts. He's had a couple of beefs with Bunny Vogel."

Then Felix Ringo and Sammy Mace were under the shed, smiling, nodding, while the black man ladled steaks onto metal plates. Out on the boat, Emma Vanzandt stepped out of the cabin with sunglasses on and shook out her hair.

Sammy Mace was in his fifties now, his hair silver and combed straight back on his head, his face distinguished, almost intellectual with the square, rimless glasses he wore. Except for his eyes, which did not match his smile. They studied me, then flexed at the corners with recognition.

"You were a uniform in Houston? A Texas Ranger got in some trouble later?" he said.

"Good memory, Sammy," I said.

"You remember me?"

"You bet. You killed a Houston cop."

"Hey," he said playfully, raising a finger on each hand, as though he were warding off bees. "I shot a guy coming through my bedroom window without no shield in his hand, in the middle of the night, in a neighborhood with cannibals mugging old people down at the church."

"What's with this guy?" Felix Ringo said.

"Nothing. Billy Bob's all right. He's just trying to work some things out," Jack said.

"You take it easy, Jack," I said.

I walked back down the dock toward my car. The wind was warm on my back, the water sliding through pebbles and sand onto the grass. I heard Jack's leather sandals behind me.

"That kid's going to come to your office. His name's Virgil Morales," he said.

"Why are you doing this?" I asked.

"Because you keep laying off your problem on Darl. Don't make it hard. Take the favor."

"Does Sammy Mace come with it?"

"He's got the biggest chain of computer outlets in south Texas. I lit up villages in Vietnam; you killed people in Mexico. Why don't you get your nose out of the air?"

When I drove away I saw Felix Ringo screw a cigarette into a gold holder, then stop what he was doing and rise from his chair when Emma Vanzandt joined their table. The black cook took a bottle of chilled wine from an ice bucket, wrapped it in a towel, and poured into the goblets on the table. The diners cut into their steaks and ate with the poise of people on the cover of *Southern Living*.

I wanted to take Jack Vanzandt off at the neck.

After dinner I took out my mother's old family photo album and began leafing through the stiffened pages of forty years ago. At the top of the page my mother, always the librarian, had written the year each group of pictures was taken. On the pages marked *1956* were five black-and-white photos of my father at work or at a company picnic. One shot showed him out on the pipeline, smiling, his welder's hood pushed up on his head, a teenage boy in pinstripe overalls standing behind him with

226

an electrical brush in his hands to clean the weld on the pipe joint. In another photo, my father sat at a picnic table filled with lean-faced blue-collar men and their wives. In the midst of the adults was the same teenage boy, burr-headed, jug-eared, his face an incongruous tin pie plate among those grinning at the camera.

I went to Marvin Pomroy's office in the morning and got him to pull Garland T. Moon's jacket. The first of many mug shots was paper-clipped to the second page. I pulled it loose and dropped it and the two photos from my mother's album on Marvin's desk.

"This mug shot was taken when Moon was seventeen. Look at the kid in the pictures of my father," I said.

Marvin propped his elbows on the blotter and peered down through his glasses at the photos, his fingers on his temples.

"You called it. He knew your old man. But I don't know what difference it makes," he said.

"I think he's got some kind of obsession with my father."

"So what? Jack the Ripper was probably a surgeon or a Mason or the queen's grandson. The bottom line is he eviscerated hookers."

"You're really a breath of fresh air, Marvin. You ought to get a Roman collar and start counseling people," I said.

"This isn't Mexico. You stay away from Moon, Billy Bob."

"You want to spell that out?"

"We don't have free-fire zones in Deaf

Smith. You get into any of that Ranger-danger dogshit here, you're going to be in front of a grand jury yourself."

I picked up the photos of my father from his desk blotter and put them in my shirt pocket.

"Sammy Mace is in town. Hanging with Jack Vanzandt and this Felix Ringo character. I'd give it my attention," I said, and didn't bother to close the door when I left.

That afternoon I was staring down from my office window into the street, wondering if I would ever extricate Lucas from the legal process that was about to eat him alive, when a Mexican kid on a Harley pulled to the curb and walked into the archway on the first floor. A minute later my secretary buzzed me and I opened the door of my inner office.

"You're Virgil Morales?" I said.

He was tall, his bare arms clean of jailhouse or biker art, his Indian-black hair curly on the back of his neck. His face could have been that of a male model, except for one eye that had a lazy drift in it.

"How'd you know?" he asked.

"Oh, you hear things." I grinned. "Why'd you decide to come see me?"

He looked at the glass-encased guns of my great-grandfather on the wall.

"I want to do the right thing," he replied.

"Good for the conscience, I guess."

"They re-filed some old charges against

228

me in San Antone. Mr. Ringo says he can square it."

"What charges?"

"Holding some reefer and a few whites. I'm on probation, see, and my PO can stick me back in county. I might get consecutive time, too."

"It all makes sense," I said.

"They get you in the system, they jam you up. It's like they only got so many names in the computer and these are the guys they keep jamming up."

"What have you got for me, Virgil?"

He wore a sleeveless purple T-shirt and jeans and shined, half-topped leather boots. He sat down and rubbed his hands up and down his forearms.

"The night Roseanne got killed? I stopped in that picnic ground," he said. "Lucas was passed out drunk in his truck. Roseanne wanted me to drive her home. I wish I had. But there ain't no way Lucas killed her."

"Anybody else see this?"

"Yeah, some college girl from Austin. She was on my bike. That's why I couldn't give Roseanne a ride. Maybe you can find her."

I nodded while he talked. His eyes wandered around the office; occasionally he squeezed the inside of his thigh, high up by his scrotum. I had the feeling he could eat a hot cigarette and not miss a beat.

"Why didn't you tell someone this earlier?" I asked.

"I was in county."

"You got into Bunny Vogel's face the other night. You weren't in county then."

"I just got out. You don't want the information, I'll boogie. Where'd those old guns come from?"

"Out at Shorty's you called Bunny a pimp. Why would you do that?"

"I don't remember saying that."

"Other people do."

He shook his head profoundly. "It don't come to mind. Maybe I was just hot. Bunny and me had some trouble over Roseanne once."

"He took her away from you?"

Virgil shrugged. "Yeah, that about says it. I still liked her, though. She was a good girl. Too good for all them rich kids."

I tried to read his face, his voice, the apparent genuine sentiment in his last statement.

"How old are you, Virgil?"

"Twenty-one."

"I think you got a lot of mileage."

"You gonna tell Mr. Ringo I hepped out?"

I pushed a yellow legal pad and a pencil across the desk to him.

"Write this stuff down for me, will you?" I said.

After he was gone, I walked to the window and watched him start his Harley and roar off the square, his exhaust echoing between the buildings. When I turned around, L.Q. Navarro was sitting in the deerhide chair, throwing cards from his Ranger deck into the crown of his hat.

"*You believe him?*" he asked.

"He can bust Marvin's case."

"That boy's jailwise, bud."

"Right. So why would he trade off a chick-enshit possession charge against perjury in a homicide trial?"

"Picking up the soap in a county bag ain't no more fun than it is in Huntsville."

"L.Q., you could have out-debated Daniel Webster."

He cut his head and grinned, as he always did when he had decided to desist, and with two fingers flipped the joker into the hat.

Through my library window the sun was red and molten over the hills, the willows on the edge of the tank puffing in the wind. Mary Beth and Pete had been making dinner sandwiches in the kitchen. I didn't hear her behind me.

She saw L.Q.'s revolver, the belt wrapped around the holster, on top of my desk, next to Great-grandpa Sam's open journal. I had removed the old cartridges from the leather loops and inserted fresh ones from a box of Remingtons. Then I had taken apart the revolver and cleaned and oiled the springs and mechanisms in it and run a bore brush through the barrel until a silver luster had returned to the rifling.

"I didn't think you kept any guns in your house," she said.

"It belonged to L.Q. Navarro," I said.

"I see."

"I had it in a safe deposit box. I was afraid

it might rust." I put it and the box of Remingtons and the bore brush and the can of oil
inside the desk drawer and closed the drawer.

She went to the window and looked at the
sunset.

"Is it for Moon?" she said.

"Sometimes a guy keeps a blank space in his
mind."

"Not a good answer."

She walked back into the kitchen.

We went down to the tank and spread a
checkered cloth on the grass and set out our
sandwiches and deviled eggs on paper plates.
Pete scooped night crawlers out of a coffee can
and baited the hooks on three cane poles and
swung the bobbers out on the flooded reeds.
The sun dipped over the hills, and the dusk
felt moist and heated from the water and
dense with insects.

"You need to back off," she said.

"From a guy like Moon?" I asked.

"From all of it. You're straying too deep into
federal territory."

She kept her gaze on the tank and never
looked at me. She hooked her thumbs in the
pockets of her riding pants.

I put my hand on her back. I could feel the
heat in her skin through her shirt.

"These guys threatened Pete; they were
going to take me down in pieces," I said.

"You think that's lost on me?"

"We're seeing each other and I don't even
know who you are," I said.

She didn't reply.

"Mary Beth?" I said.

"Maybe you don't know who you are your-self, Billy Bob," she said. She turned and looked me full in the face. Her throat was bladed with color. "I know what y'all did in Mexico. The man you idolize was a self-appointed executioner. Is that what you want to be?"

"He was a brave man, Mary Beth. You shouldn't speak of him like that."

She opened the top of the wicker basket and took out the tin cups for lemonade and started to fill them. Then she stopped and brushed a long curl out of her eye.

"I apologize for remarking on your friend. Say good night to Pete for me," she said, and walked toward the house and her car.

I went to the health club at six-thirty the next morning and lay on the tile stoop at the rear of the steam room and began the series of exercises the doctor had recommended for my back. The room was empty, billowing with vapor, the temperature set at 130 degrees.

Then the door opened and closed and Sammy Mace and Felix Ringo entered and sat down naked on the stoop. They paid no attention to me. Felix Ringo was telling a story, pumping his hands as though he were rotating the inverted pedals on a bicycle.

"You get it going real fast, man. The wires are already clipped on the guy, and the guy starts jerking around and jittering and his words are popping on his lips like sparks. The faster you pump it, the faster his mouth is working," Ringo said, giggling. "This was the same guy says he ain't never going to give nobody up, spitting on people, acting like he don't care when we walk him into the basement. They got it coming, man, you seen some of the stuff they done."

He continued his story, tilting forward on his arms, looking at Sammy Mace's profile for reaction. Sammy placed two fingers on Ringo's arm and looked in my direction. Then he wrapped his loins in a towel and moved down the stoop and sat next to me. His face was flushed, slick with sweat, heated by the room and the animus that drove his thoughts, like that of a man to whom lust, anger, and vindictiveness were interchangeable passions. His eyes took my inventory, dropped briefly to my genitalia, settled on my mouth, then my eyes.

"You a lawyer here now, huh?" he said.

"You got it."

"I like it here. It's clean. That biker kid Felix found help you out?"

"Too soon to tell, Sammy."

His eyes were so dark they were almost black, the eyebrows silver. His stare held on mine, trying to read what I wanted, what lie did my words conceal.

"Jack Vanzandt was a pathfinder, a war hero. He ought to be governor of Texas. Why you trying to hurt his family?" Sammy said.

"It's a nice day. I think I'm going to get back in it," I said, and started to rise.

"I'm talking to you," he said, touching me

in the sternum with the balls of his fingers. "You brought up that cop-killer stuff in front of my friends. I let it go. But that don't mean I forgot."

"You still live in River Oaks?"

"So what?"

"It's probably the richest neighborhood in the United States. That cop had a wife and four kids. You providing for them, Sammy?"

I walked past him, out the door and into the shower. I turned on the hot water in my face and let it fountain over my head and shoulders. But my encounter with Felix Ringo and Sammy Mace was not over. They were at the far end of the shower, lathering under the nozzles, soap roiling off their swimming-pool tans, men who knew that youth might fade but money and power did not.

I didn't want to look at or engage them again, but an image registered in the corner of my eye, one that connected somehow with memory and dreams and the voice of L.Q. Navarro. On Felix Ringo's right side, low in the back, was a six-inch scar, as thick as a night crawler, welted, perforated with stitch holes along the edges.

I walked into the dressing area and opened my locker. Felix Ringo followed me, drying his head with a wadded towel, his body hair glowing against a bank of lighted mirrors behind him. He rubbed a stick of deodorant under his arm.

"I hear your PI is checking out the kid I sent you," he said.

235

"Maybe."

"That kid's a good witness. You a guy who sees plots all the time. Don't fuck it up."

"Who carved on your kidney?" I said.

The glare in his eyes made me think of a phosphorous match burning inside brown glass.

CHAPTER

22

Friday afternoon Temple Carrol asked me to walk across the square with her to the Mexican grocery store. The wind was warm, even in the shade of the trees on the courthouse lawn, and we sat in the back of the grocery, under the fans by the old soda fountain, and ordered tacos and iced tea. She read from the notebook opened by her elbow while she ate.

"Virgil Morales is everything he says he is," she said. "Hangs with some biker pukes called the Purple Hearts, in and out of juvie since he was thirteen, a couple of times down in county for dope and barroom bullshit. He's also had three paternity suits filed against him. In other words, your average Mexican gangbanger who operates on two brain cells and believes his Hollywood career is right around the corner."

The overhead fan blew a strand of hair in her face.

"How do you think he'd do on a lie detector?" I asked.

"A kid who'd probably roll a joint during the Apocalypse? You tell me."

"How about the girl he says was with him?"

"She lives in Austin, all right, but she's no college student. Not unless you count being a barmaid in a rathskeller next to the campus. Anyway, she's been in detox once, has butterflies tattooed on her shoulders, and gets off on bikers. You might think about hiring a speech coach for her."

"Why's that?"

"Every third word in her vocabulary rhymes with *duck*."

"She gives the same account as Virgil?"

"She says Lucas was passed out in his truck and Roseanne Hazlitt was throwing up in the bushes. She said they tried to wake him up and couldn't do it."

"Lucas was passed out when the first cruiser got to the murder scene," I said. "Drunks don't wake up from stupors and kill other people and go to sleep again. You did a great job, Temple."

She didn't reply. She looked at the front screen door, her eyes as empty as glass.

"What's wrong?" I said.

"There's a smell to this. It found us too easy."

"They both tell the same story. Why would the girl commit perjury for Lucas?"

She shook her head. "You're personally involved with this one, Billy Bob. You're not seeing things like you should...How do I say it?"

"Come on, Temple. Don't be that way."

"How about that Sweeney broad? You know she's an undercover operative of some kind. When the feds or whoever they are get finished with whatever they're doing around here, she'll take off and you and me and Pete and Lucas will still be chopping in the same cotton patch. Except one of us never knew who his real friends were."

"That's not true. You know the respect I have for you."

"The word the girl in Austin uses all the time? It's *fuck*. Yeah, that's it, *fuck*. As in *fuck it*."

I picked up the bill and paid it at the register in front. When I came back to the table, Temple had gone.

I couldn't sleep that night. I went downstairs in my robe and turned on the desk lamp in the library and, with heat lightning veining the sky outside, read from Great-grandpa Sam's journal.

August 26, 1891
I convinced myself the Rose of Cimarron should not be blamed for the crimes committed by her kinfolks. She was reared among people that's hardly human and it is only through God's grace she has survived as unsoiled as she is. But that don't mean I have to abide the likes of Blackface Charley Bryant and them others who think holding unarmed people at gunpoint somehow adds several inches to

what I suspect is their pitiful excuse for a pecker.

This collection of homicidal pissants not only steals from each other, they pass their diseases back and forth through their squaws. Their defenders might say they was victims of the railroads or carpetbag government. But I was with boys of the Fourth Texas at Gettysburg who went up those hills into federal cannon with their uniforms in rags and without no shoes on their feet. In camp you could hang your gold watch on a tree branch overnight and come morning it'd be glinting in the sunlight when you opened your eyes.

It is thoughts like these that has been building in me like steam in a tea kettle with a cork in the snout.

The stink on this bunch has run off all the game, and in the meantime they won't keep their hogs penned and have let them turn feral. So now when they can't rustle cows they have taken to shooting wild horses for meat. In the late evening they lay up on the bluff with an old Sharp's buffalo rifle that has an elevator sight on it and kill them as they come down to drink from the Cimarron. It is a heart-wrenching and sickening spectacle for anyone who loves horses to witness.

What finally tore it was I looked out the back window of our cabin and there was the biggest shithog I ever seen, an ax-handle thick across the shoulders, rooting out every one of our potatoes and trampling our tomato vines into green string. I put a rope on him and walked him behind my horse down to Blackface Charley's cave and told him and three others they owed me a season's worth of canned produce and they'd better pick it out of their own gardens and not steal it, either.

Charley said since I fed the hog, it was now mine and we was square. The skin where he was burned by his own revolver blowing up in his face crinkles like dried snake skin when he smiles.

Last evening about eight of them headed for Pearl Younger's cathouse in Fort Smith. I kept looking at them caves and the garbage on the banks and the squaws peeling strips of jerky off a skinned horse, and finally I holstered on my Navy .36s and walked on down to the bluffs with a five-gallon can of coal oil. One of the Doolin boys thought he had a case to make, so I did have to gun-whip him a mite and haul him by the seat of his britches down the slope and fling him in the river, although that had not been my intention. In the meantime the squaws sat down and watched and thought it was all big fun. In ten minutes I had four of them caves blooming with black smoke, long columns of it that fed way up into the sky. The burlap and blankets and straw give it heat, and you could hear ammunition popping like firecrackers and whiskey jugs and preserve jars blowing apart inside. Jennie stood up on the hillock in a deerskin dress and watched me like I had lost my mind.

When I come back up the slope she was

nowhere in sight. I figured it was not easy for her to see me burn out her kinfolk. I was fixing to tell her I didn't bust nary a cap from my Navy .36s, which was not the way it would have gone before my ordination. Then I seen her bareback on her horse out in a field of sunflowers, wearing that old deerskin dress without no underclothes. In the twilight her skin had the glow of a new rose, and she was smiling at me, and I knew she was truly the most beautiful woman a man was ever graced with.

Maybe I got rid of the worst part of my violent nature. But damn if I've banked the fires of my love and desire for the Rose of Cimarron.

Oh well. I reckon the story of us all is an ongoing one.

While I was reading from my great-grandfather's journal, a retired school janitor and his wife were parking their car in front of their home in Deaf Smith's black district. It was a Honda, one they had bought used three years ago through a finance company and had just made the final payment on the previous week.

The thieves who boosted it that night slim-jimmed the door, broke the steering wheel lock, and wired the ignition in less than three minutes. By the time the retired janitor, who heard the snapping sound of the wheel lock through the window of his second-story bathroom, could get down the stairs to the front door, his Honda was speeding through the inter-section at the end of the block, followed by what he described as a "hot rod car got a shine like a red candy apple."

The thieves parked the stolen car in the grass by the four-lane divided highway out-side of town, then squirted a can of lighter fluid over the upholstery and tossed a burning truck flare through the open window. The flames rippled along the fabric like strips of warm color from a chemical rainbow, then the wind swirled the fire in a vortex that flat-tened against the headliner and curled out over the roof, consuming the seats, popping the front windows into Coke bottle glass on the hood.

The thieves waited on the pedestrian over-pass, drinking from quart bottles of beer, passing a joint back and forth while the Honda burned a hundred yards north of them. One of them took time to urinate against the abut-ment that supported the chain-link archway overhead, one that the thieves sliced open with bolt cutters by the north rail so the peeled-back wire could not be seen by a car approaching from the south.

Mary Beth patrolled this same section of high-way around 11 P.M. every night she was on duty. She usually cruised through the drive-in restaurant just outside the city limits, the parking lot at Shorty's, the picnic area by the river where Roseanne Hazlitt was attacked, then made a U-turn through the center ground at the county line, just north of the overpass.

The retired janitor called in the report on

his Honda at 10:26. The report of a burning automobile by the side of the highway was called in anonymously at 10:49. Two minutes later Mary Beth had hit her siren and emergency flasher and was headed full-bore for the overpass.

As she approached from the south, she saw three males in silhouette inside the chain-link archway, possibly kids who had climbed the overpass to better see the fire that had spread from the stolen car into an adjacent field.

She saw the three figures turn and run to the far side of the overpass, her blue, white, and red flasher whip off the support walls on each side of her, then an object that came from above, out of the darkness, that seemed to have no source or context.

The thieves had probably taken the seventy-pound block of concrete from the site of a demolished building. It was rectangular in shape, jagged on each end, spiked with twisted steel rods that protruded from the concrete like handles.

It exploded through the center of the front window, gutting the dashboard, raking the twelve-gauge pump shotgun out of its locked holder, blowing glass and electrical dials and radio parts into the backseat, embedding in the wire-mesh screen behind the front seat like a cannonball.

The cruiser spun sideways, its tires scorching black lines across the asphalt, an ambulance behind it swerving out of control into the center ground to avoid a collision.

A paramedic was the first person to the cruiser. When he opened the door, Mary Beth's campaign hat rolled out on the grass, the crown marbled with blood.

CHAPTER

23

The next morning I got off the hospital elevator on the fifth floor and started through the waiting area toward the nurses' station. Brian Wilcox and two other federal agents came around the corner at the same time.

"I don't believe it. Like a fly climbing out of shit every place I go," he said.

"I don't want to 'front you today, Brian."

"What makes you think you can call me by my first name?"

He wore a blue suit and tie and white shirt. His hair had the dull sheen of gunmetal, with silver threads in the part. He stood flat-footed in front of me, heavy, solid, his shoulders too large for his suit. The cleft chin, the cologned, cleanly shaved jaws, the neatness that he wore like a uniform, did not go with the expression in his eyes.

"Let me by, please," I said.

"She's in that room because those kids went through her to get to you."

"If they did, Garland T. Moon put them up to it."

"Same problem. You can't stay out of his face. But other people end up in the barrel."

"Moon wandered into something out at the old Hart Ranch. He's just not sure what it is. But you probably know all this. Run your game on somebody else."

I started past him, but he grabbed my arm. I flung it away and felt my fingers accidentally hit his chest. His face flared and he grabbed at me again, with both hands, his chin raised, his teeth bared. I shoved him away and stepped back, raising my arm in front of my face, then the other two agents were on him, splaying their hands against his chest.

"Get going," one of them said over his shoulder.

"The problem's not mine."

"Don't fool yourself, ace," he replied.

Mary Beth was sitting up, with a pillow behind her back, when I entered her room. Her right arm was bandaged, the skin purple and red between the strips of tape, swollen tight and hard against the dressing like a wasp sting. Her hair was tied on top of her head with a bandanna to keep it off the dressing where a steel rod had incised the scalp almost to the bone.

"You look good," I said.

"Sure I do."

"When can you go home?"

"Today. There's no big damage done."

She wore no makeup, and in the slatted

sunlight through the window her face looked opaque, as though it hid thoughts she herself had not dealt with.

"Did you sleep last night?" I asked.

"Yeah, some."

"When I was shot, I couldn't close my eyes without seeing gun flashes again. That's the way it is for a while."

Her gaze roved over my face and seemed to go inside my eyes.

"What is it?" I asked.

"The other day you said you didn't know who I was," she said. "My father was a motorcycle cop in Oklahoma and a high sheriff in Kentucky. He was a good man, but he had a special hatred for sex predators. He killed two of them after they were in custody."

"They weren't trying to escape?"

"What are the odds of a cop having to shoot an escapee on two occasions?"

"Seems like old history, Mary Beth."

"He hated those men because a degenerate got in our back window when I was three years old."

My eyes shifted off her face.

"He died going in a house after a serial rapist. At night, without backup, with a 'throw-down' taped to his ankle. You figure out what the plan was," she said.

"You blame yourself?"

She thought about it. "No," she said. "But you're not going to use me to take down Garland Moon or Darl Vanzandt or whoever it is you're thinking about."

"I just ran into Brian Wilcox. If that guy's the cavalry, I think we're all going to be wearing Arrow shirts."

She smiled in spite of herself. I sat on the edge of her bed and picked up her hand. I touched the freckles on her face. "Pete and I'll take you home today, then bring supper over," I said.

She rested her head on the pillow and squeezed the top of my arm.

The man who had replaced the murdered sheriff was named Hugo Roberts. If you asked him how he had made his living the last thirty years, he would answer, "I ain't spent a whole lot of time in the private sector." He'd been a county road hack, a deputy sheriff, a city patrolman, a bailiff, a jailer, and some said a volunteer on a firing squad in Utah. He was shaped like a lean pear and smoked constantly, even though he had already lost one lung and wheezed like a leaking inner tube when he talked.

He sat at the corner of the old sheriff's desk, flipping ashes into the spittoon, his narrow shoulders hunched into the cigarette smoke that swirled about his head.

"Did I lock up Darl Vanzandt? Do bears shit in the woods? Does my wife read the Bible all night and tell me I'm the reason our kids are ugly?" he said. "Hell, yes. What else you want to know, Billy Bob?"

"Where's Darl now?"

"I had the little fucker shot."

"Give it a break, Hugo."

"All we got on him is some roofies. Far as I know, they're not even illegal."

"Roofies?"

"Rohypnol. Ten times stronger than Valium. It's made overseas for insomnia. It tends to show up in date rape cases. How long you been gone from law enforcement?"

"Is he upstairs?"

"Get real, Billy Bob. His old man was down here with his lawyer at six this morning. I cain't charge him. The black man owned the stolen vehicle didn't get a license number and never saw a face...Look, I ain't sure myself it was Darl. There's a mess of customized cars hereabouts that same shade of red."

"How many of them are owned by people like Darl Vanzandt?"

He spit, then wiped his mouth on his palm.

"*Know* and *prove* ain't a difference I should have to explain to a lawyer," he said.

"I think the county found the right man for the job, Hugo."

"The air-conditioning unit in here does about as much good as an ice cube on a wood-stove. Make sure you close the door snug on your way out," he said.

It was noon and the sun was white and straight up in the sky when I got home. I went into the library and took L.Q.'s revolver out of the desk drawer. I opened the loading gate, clicked back the hammer to half-cock, and rotated the cylinder until the empty sixth chamber came back under the hammer again.

Great-grandpa Sam carried his Navy .36s down to the bluffs on the Cimarron when he burned out the Dalton-Doolin gang and never had to pop a cap, I told myself.

"Wrong way to think, bud," L.Q. Navarro said behind me.

"All right, I'll bite," I answered.

"You don't tote it as a fashion statement. The other guy's got to know you cain't wait to use it. Elsewise, it's got the value of tits on a boar hog."

I eased the hammer down, locking the cylinder, and slipped the barrel back into the holster.

"You know what's really fretting you?" he said.

"Why don't you tell me, L.Q.?"

"It ain't that I got shot accidentally. It's because you believe it wouldn't have happened if we hadn't been down in Coahuila vigilanting them dope mules."

I kept my back to him. The sky outside was hot and bright, and dust was blowing in gray clouds out of the fields.

"Hey, the blood lust wasn't yours, bud; it was mine. I loved flushing them out of the poppies and blowing feathers when they ran. It could have been you instead of me," he said.

"The new sheriff's corrupt."

"That's like going to the whorehouse and saying the place is full of whores."

"Everything was straight lines in Coahuila.

249

It was us against them, and at sunrise we added up the score," I said.

L.Q. didn't answer. I turned and looked at him. He stood with one arm propped against the bookshelves, staring at his foot, the brim of his Stetson shielding his face.

"You don't usually lack for words," I said, my throat burning at what I knew was coming next.

"We mortgaged tomorrow for today, bud. Even for me, that thought is about like swallowing a piece of barbed wire," he replied.

He walked toward the doorway, his back to me, his hands on his hips, splaying his coat out. I raised my hand to speak, then he was gone into the hallway and I heard the wind fling open the front door and fill the house with a creaking of boards and wallpaper.

I parked my Avalon behind the tin shed where Garland T. Moon worked as a welder and entered through the back door. The heat inside was numbing. A propane-fed foundry roared in one corner, a cauldron of melted aluminum wedged in the flames. Moon wore sandals without socks and a pair of flesh-colored gym shorts that were molded against his loins. He was bent over a machinist's vise, cutting a chunk of angle iron in half with an acetylene torch, his back spiderwebbed with rivulets of sweat.

He heard me behind him, screwed down the feed on the torch, and pulled off his black goggles with his thumb. Dirty strings of soot floated down on his head and shoulders. His eyes dropped to my belt. He pulled at his nose.

"You come here to gun me?" he said.

"What's your hold on these kids?"

"It ain't no mystery. Cooze and dope. The high school clinic already gives them the rubbers. I just introduce them to what you might call more mature Mexican women."

"You're a genuinely evil man, sir."

"You got to stick a gun down in your britches to tell me that?" He laughed to himself and wiped his hands with an oil rag. The muscles in his stomach looked as hard as corrugated metal. "You got your ovaries stoked up 'cause them boys poured cow shit on your son?"

"They almost killed a deputy sheriff last night."

He picked up a can of warm soda from the workbench and drank, his throat working smoothly, his gaze focused indifferently out the door on the river.

"The doctors said I was supposed to be dead eight years ago. Said I was plumb eat up with cancer. I smell death in my sleep. It comes to somebody else first, better them than me," he said. He wiped his armpits with the rag and threw it on the floor.

I looked at his softly muted profile, his recessed, liquid blue eye, the ridged brow that was like a vestige of an earlier ancestor. My forearm rested on the butt of L.Q. Navarro's revolver. I lifted the revolver from my belt, my palm folded across the cylinder, and laid it on the workbench.

"Pick it up," I said.

He lit a cigarette, picked a particle of tobacco off his lip and dropped it from between his fingers.

"I cain't be hurt, boy. I live in here," he said, and pointed to the side of his head. "I learned it when a three-hundred-pound nigger stuffed a sock in my mouth and taught me about love."

I pulled a photograph from my shirt pocket and held it up in front of him.

"Is the boy in overalls you?" I asked.

He lifted it out of my hand and smiled while he studied it. He tossed it on top of the revolver and smoked his cigarette, a merry light in one eye.

"My father taught you how to weld, didn't he?" I said.

"He wasn't bad at it. I'm better, though."

"I think a man like you must come out of a furnace."

"That's the first thing you said today made any sense."

I took a six-inch bone-handled game knife out of my pocket and pried open the single blade. Two days ago I had ground it on an emery wheel in the barn and stropped it on an old saddle flap, and the buffed ripples along the edge looked like the undulations in a stiletto.

I lay the photograph down on his work-bench and sliced it in half.

"My father was a fine man. You're a piece of shit, Moon. You don't belong in his past anymore than you do in our present," I said.

I pulled loose the severed image of the child who had become the man standing before me and dropped it into the foundry. It curled immediately into a film of ash and rose into the air like a black butterfly.

Then I hit him across the mouth with the back of my hand, my ring breaking his lip against his teeth.

Moon grinned and spit blood onto the molten rim of the foundry. He blotted his mouth with his palm before he spoke. "A man got that much hate in him is a whole lot more like me than he thinks," he said.

CHAPTER

24

Virgil Morales, the San Antonio Purple Heart who liked to call other people "spermbrain," sat in my office with his girlfriend from Austin, looking at his watch and waiting for me to get off the phone. The girlfriend was named Jamie Lake and she had winged dragons tattooed on both her sun-browned shoulders. She also smelled as if she had been smoking reefer inside a closed automobile.

Temple Carrol leaned against a table behind them, her arms folded, looking at Jamie Lake as though Jamie had swum through a hole in the dimension.

I finished talking to my friend whom I had paid to run polygraphs on both of them.

"He says all indications are you're telling the truth," I said to Virgil.

"So that's supposed to make me feel good?" he replied.

"The tests aren't always conclusive. Yours is," I said.

"Glad to hear it. When you want us back?"

"We empanel the jury in ten days."

"I been this route before. No disrespect, but I don't want to come up here every morning at seven-thirty and sit on a bench in a hallway and play with my Johnson till somebody remembers I'm a friend of the court," he said.

"How about I send somebody for you? Will that be okay?" I asked.

He stretched out one leg and rubbed the inside of his thigh. "Yeah, that's probably the best way to do it. Call first, though, okay?"

Jamie Lake chewed gum with her mouth open. Her hair was long and dark blonde and her face narrow, with a pinched light in it. "Why do I get the feeling I'm anybody's fuck here?" she asked.

"My friend, the man who ran the polygraph on you, says he couldn't make a determination. It happens sometimes," I said.

"Yeah? Well, I don't believe you. I think your friend was trying to see down my tank top," she said.

"Maybe he was."

"So get fucko back on the phone. I told him the truth. I didn't come all this way for y'all's bullshit."

In the background, Temple cocked her head and looked at me.

"My friend thinks you might have had contact with a few pharmaceuticals before the test," I said.

"You had us both UA-ed. You tell that asshole I have an IQ of one-sixty and I remember everything I see, like in a camera. Also tell him I think he's probably a needle dick."

"I'll try to pass it on," I replied.

"Do we get some expense money for gas and meals?" Virgil said.

"You bet. The secretary's got it. Y'all have been real helpful," I said. I didn't look at Jamie Lake.

"Kiss my ass," she said.

Just then, my secretary buzzed me on the intercom.

"Billy Bob, it's Lucas Smothers," she said, and before I could respond, Lucas opened the inner office door and walked inside.

"I'm sorry. I didn't know you was in here with anybody," he said.

"It's all right," I said.

Jamie Lake's eyes seemed to peel Lucas's clothes off his skin. Then she turned her glare on me.

"Ask him what other time he had that shirt on," she said.

"Excuse me?" I said.

"The night we saw him in the picnic ground. That's all he had on. His pants were around his knees and he was passed out, and he had that blue-white check shirt on, with the little gold horns on the shoulders. He was passed out, with his underwear down on his moon, and she was puking in the bushes," she said.

Lucas's face turned dark red.

"Yeah, she's right. But I don't understand what's going on," he said.

Temple walked from behind Jamie's chair and put one hand on Jamie's shoulder, her fingers stroking the tattoo of a winged dragon.

"Let's talk about long-sleeve blouses, kiddo. What do you wear, like a medium or a ten?" she said.

After Jamie and Virgil had gone, Lucas sat down in front of my desk.

"It's my dad. He don't usually drink. But last night he sat out on the windmill tank and drunk durn near a pint of whiskey," he said.

"This has been hard on him," I said.

"That ain't it." He turned around and looked at Temple.

"Go ahead. It won't leave this office," I said.

"He wouldn't come in. He slept out there on the ground. This morning he showered and ate some aspirins and I fixed him some breakfast, and he sat there eating it like it was cardboard."

I waited. Lucas pulled at his shirtsleeve and snuffed down in his nose, as though the room were too cold.

"He was talking about getting even with Vanzandt. I go, 'You mean Darl, 'cause of what he done at the country club?'

"He says, 'Darl does them things 'cause his father lets him. His father gets away with it 'cause he's rich. That's the way this county works.'

"I said, 'It's Darl. There's something wrong with him. It ain't his daddy's fault.'

"He goes, 'You're a good boy, son. You make me proud. Jack Vanzandt's fixing to have his day.'

"My father ain't ever talked like that before, Mr. Holland. His pistol, the one he brung home from the army, I looked and it ain't in his drawer."

"I don't think your dad would kill anyone, Lucas."

He looked around behind him again.

"You want me to leave?" Temple said.

I raised my hand. "Go ahead, Lucas," I said.

"He done it in the war. A lieutenant kept getting people killed. My dad threw a grenade in his tent."

"Where is your dad now?"

"Getting a haircut down the street."

I winked at him.

But my confidence was cosmetic. Neither I nor anyone I knew in Deaf Smith had any influence over Vernon Smothers. He believed intransigence was a virtue, a laconic and mean-spirited demeanor was strength, reason was the tool the rich used to keep the poor satisfied with their lot, and education amounted to reading books full of lies written by history's victors.

I was almost relieved when I asked in the barbershop and was told Vernon had already gone. Then the barber added, "Right next door in the beer joint. Tell him to stay there, too, will you?"

The inside of the tavern was dark and cool, filled with the sounds of midday pool shooters, and at the end of the long wood bar Vernon Smothers sat hunched over a plate, peeling a hardboiled egg, a cup of coffee by his wrist.

I had rather seen him drunk. Under the brim of a white straw hat, his face had the deceptive serenity of a man who was probably threading his way in and out of a nervous breakdown, his eyes predisposed and resolute with private conclusions that no one would alter.

I waved the bartender away and remained standing.

"We found a couple of witnesses, Vernon. I think Lucas is going to walk."

"You want an egg?"

"Jack Vanzandt doesn't have any power in that courtroom."

"The hell he don't."

"You won't trust me?"

"I trusted the people sent me to Vietnam. I come home on a troop ship under the Golden Gate. People up on the bridge dropped Baggies full of shit on us."

"To tell you the truth, Vernon, I don't think you'd have had it any other way," I

258

said, and walked back down the polished length of the bar into the sunlight.

It was a cheap remark to make, one that I would regret.

I crossed the street to the courthouse and opened Marvin Pomroy's office door. He was talking to his secretary.

"Got time for some early disclosure?" I asked.

"No more deals. You've got all the slack you're getting," he said.

"I'm filing a motion to dismiss."

"I've got to hear this. I haven't had a laugh all day," he replied.

I followed him into the inner office.

"I've got two witnesses who saw Lucas passed out at the murder scene when Roseanne Hazlitt was still alive," I said.

"Winos?"

"A Mexican biker from San Antone who just passed a polygraph, and a gal who puts me in mind of a chain saw going across a knee joint. By the way, I wonder what percentage of our jury is going to be Hispanic?"

Marvin leaned back in his swivel chair and pulled at his red suspenders with his thumbs.

"You feeling pretty good about yourself, huh?" he said.

"It's reasonable doubt. A kid who's so drunk three people can't wake him up doesn't suddenly revive himself and rape and beat someone to death."

"Who says?" But he was looking into space now, and the conviction had dissipated in his voice.

"Why not cut your losses?" I asked.

"Because 'the people' are the advocate of the victim, Billy Bob, in this case a dead girl who doesn't have a voice. I represent *them* and her. I don't cut *my* losses."

"Lucas Smothers is a victim, too."

"No, he's your son. And that's been the problem since the get-go. He lied through his teeth about how well he knew her. What makes you think he's telling the truth now? Go look again at the morgue pictures. You think she did that to herself?" Then his face colored and he rubbed a finger in the middle of his forehead.

"You're going to lose," I said.

"So? For me it's a way of life. Say, what kind of rap sheet does your Mexican biker have? Or does he just use his hog to go to and from Mass?"

Pete and two of his friends had come over to ride Beau that evening. I saw the three of them, mounted in a row on his back, turn Beau up the embankment on the rim of the tank, then disappear through the pasture where it sloped down toward the river. A half hour later I heard Beau's hooves by the windmill, then on the wood floor of the barn. I walked out into the yard.

"Y'all didn't want to stay out longer?" I asked.

"There's a man fishing by that sunk car. He's standing in the water in a suit," Pete said.

A boy and girl Pete's age sat behind him on Beau's spine. They both kept looking back over their shoulders, through the open doors behind them.

"What color hair does he have, bud?" I asked.

Pete pulled his leg over Beau's withers and dropped to the ground and walked toward me, his expression hidden from the others. He kept walking until we were on the grass in the yard, out of earshot of his friends.

"It's red. We was letting Beau drink. Juanita was up on the bank, pulling flowers. This man standing in the water says, 'That your girl-friend?' I say, 'I ain't got no girlfriend.'

"He says, 'She's a right trim little thing. You don't get it first, somebody else will.'

"I said I didn't know what he meant and I didn't want to, either. I told him I was going back to my house. He says, 'Old enough to bleed, old enough to butcher.'

"It was the look on his face. He kept watching Juanita. I ain't never seen a grown person look at a kid like that."

I put my hand on the back of Pete's head.

"Y'all go inside and fix yourself some peach ice cream," I said.

I drove the Avalon down the dirt track, past the tank, and through the field to the bluffs over the river, the grass *thropping* under the bumper. Five feet out from the bank, submerged to his hips, in his blue serge suit with no shirt

261

under his coat, was Garland T. Moon. He flung his bait with a cheap rod out into the current.

I got out of the Avalon and looked down at him from the bluff. Against the late sun his skin looked bathed in iodine.

"This waterway is public property. State of Texas law," he said. A brown, triangular scab had formed on his bottom lip where I had hit him.

"I'm going to have you picked up anyway."

He had to lick the scab on his lip before he spoke. "Thought you might want to know I got me an ACLU civil rights lawyer from Dallas."

"You know who Sammy Mace is?" I said.

"A greaseball out of Houston?"

"He's in town. I think you've stumbled into his business interests. Maybe I'm wrong."

He retrieved his bait out of the water and flipped it in an arc back into the current.

"'Fore you hit me, you said your daddy was a fine man. That 'fine' man run me off the job. Sixteen years old, carried me out on the highway, told me to get out of his truck. Without no home, food, people, nothing."

"If he ran you off, you probably stole from him or did worse. I suspect it was 'worse.'"

He was quiet a long time, smiling at nothing. Then he said, "You ever asked yourself why your daddy hepped out a jailhouse kid like me?"

"He was kind to animals and white trash. That was his way, Moon."

"My hair is darker red than yours, but maybe that's 'cause my mama was a redhead.

Think about it, boy. Your daddy ever pipeline around Waco fifteen years or so before you was born?"

I got in the Avalon and drove back to the house and called 911, a wave of nausea surging into the bottom of my throat.

By the time a deputy in a cruiser got to the house and I went back down to the river with him, Moon had disappeared.

"What's wrong, Billy Bob?" Pete said later in the kitchen.

"Nothing, bud. Everything's solid."

Don't let Moon wound you, I told myself. That's his power over people. He makes them hate themselves.

"You want some ice cream?" Pete asked.

"Not tonight."

He continued to stare at me with a puzzled look, then I heard Temple's car in the drive and a moment later Pete going out the screen door for his ride back to her house.

It's the moment every decent cop dreads. It comes unexpectedly, out of nowhere, like a freight train through a wall. Later, when you play the tape over and over again, seeking justification, wondering if there were alternatives, you're left invariably with the last frame on the spool, the only one that counts, and it tells you daily what your true potential is.

Mary Beth went back on duty after only two days' rest.

The 911 call reporting a trespasser and

disturbing-the-peace incident at the skeet club should have required little more than the dispatch of a cruiser, perhaps a mediation, perhaps escorting someone off the property or even putting him in jail for twenty-four hours.

Vernon Smothers started looking for Jack Vanzandt at his office, then his home and the yacht basin and the country club. It was late afternoon when he found his way to the skeet club and parked by the pavilion in front of the row of traps that sailed clay pigeons toward a distant treeline.

Bunny Vogel saw him first, saw the energy in his face that was like both anger and fear at the same time, and walked from the pavilion to intercept him.

"You a guest here this evening, Mr. Smothers?" Bunny asked.

Vernon's khakis and denim shirt were pressed and clean, his white straw hat tilted on the back of his head, his eyes wide, unblinking. A heated, dry odor seemed to envelop his skin and his clothes.

"You got to be a member or a guest, Mr. Smothers. You can go over to the clubhouse there and see about a membership..."

"I see Emma Vanzandt there. Where's her husband at?" Vernon said.

"Sir, I don't think this is a good idea. I'm sorry for what happened to Lucas. I mean, I'm sorry for my part in it..." He gestured in the air, then his voice trailed off.

Jack Vanzandt, Sammy Mace, and a middle-aged man with a ponytail and thick lips and glasses that magnified his eyes walked out of the squat, green building that served as a clubhouse and approached the pavilion. Jack had the breech of a double-barrel shotgun cracked open on his forearm.

Vernon put one hand on Bunny's shoulder and moved him aside, as he would push open a door.

"I ain't up to no traveling shit storms today, Mr. Smothers. I got orders about—" Bunny began.

But Vernon was already walking away from him as though he were not there.

Jack and Sammy Mace and the man with the ponytail sat down at a plank table with Emma Vanzandt. None of them paid attention to Vernon Smothers until he was three feet from their table.

"How you doin', Vernon?" Jack said.

"Your boy and his friends vandalized my house and humiliated my son," Vernon said.

"I don't think that's true," Jack said.

"Go ask Bunny Vogel. He's the little Judas Iscariot hepped Darl do it."

Jack blew out his breath.

"This isn't the place for it. Come to my office," he said.

"I know you for the type man you are, Jack Vanzandt. That man next to you is a goddamn criminal," Vernon said.

"Hey! This is a private club here. You watch your language," Sammy Mace said.

"Get up, Jack," Vernon said.

The man with the ponytail put his hand

on top of Jack's forearm. "It's all right. I'll walk this guy to his truck. Is that your truck there, big man?" he said.

"No," Jack said. "Listen, Vernon. Kids get into trouble. It doesn't make it any better if the parents fight. Now—"

Vernon reached out and, with the flat of his hand, popped Jack on one cheek.

"You ain't no war hero. You just a rich man bought all the right people," he said.

"Jack, put an end to this," Emma said.

But Bunny Vogel had already called the sheriff's department, and Mary Beth's cruiser had been only two hundred yards from the skeet club when the dispatcher's voice came over her radio.

She turned off the highway and drove onto the grass almost to the pavilion, got out of her cruiser and slipped her baton through the ring on her belt.

She went straight for the source of the problem, Vernon Smothers.

"You're trespassing, sir...No, there won't be any debate about it. You get in your truck and drive back on the highway," she said.

"Hey, we got the marines here," Sammy Mace said.

"You shut up," Mary Beth said.

"*What?*" Sammy said.

"In your truck, Mr. Smothers," Mary Beth said.

"Hey, what'd you just say to me?" Sammy Mace asked.

"I said you stay out of this unless you want to go to jail," she replied.

Sammy opened his hands and made a shocked expression to the man in the ponytail.

"You believe this broad?" he asked.

"Last chance," Mary Beth said.

"You got no right to be impolite. We're not the offending parties here," the man in the ponytail said.

"We're out of here, Jack. Right now," Emma said.

Mary Beth cupped her hand around Vernon's arm.

"Walk with me, sir," she said.

But she knew it was unraveling now, in the way that dreams take you in high-speed cars over the edges of canyons and cliffs.

Sammy Mace walked up behind her and punched her with one finger between the shoulder blades.

"No cunt talks to me like that. Hey, did you hear me? I'm talking here. Turn around and look at me," Sammy said, and punched her again with his finger.

She slipped her baton from its ring and whipped it across Sammy's left arm. Even from ten yards away, Bunny Vogel said he heard the bone break.

Sammy's face went white with pain and shock. He cradled his arm against his chest, his mouth trembling. Then he extended his right hand, like an inverted claw, toward the man in the ponytail.

"Give it to me!" he said.

Mary Beth pushed Vernon Smothers away from her.

"Down on the ground, on your face! Do it, both of you, now!" she said to Sammy and the man in the ponytail.

Then she saw Sammy lunge toward his friend and try to pull a .25-caliber automatic from a small holster inside the friend's coat. She swung the baton again, this time across the side of Sammy's face, and shattered his jaw. It hung locked in place, lopsided, blood that was absolutely scarlet issuing off his tongue. His glasses lay broken on the grass.

Sammy collapsed to his knees, then grabbed at her legs and at the nine-millimeter on her hip, while the man in the ponytail at first pushed her, then watched stupidly as his .25 automatic fell from its holster into Sammy's lap.

The man in the ponytail tried to disentangle himself and back away while Sammy pulled the trigger impotently on the automatic and fought to get the safety off.

Mary Beth gripped her nine-millimeter with both hands but fired high with the first shot at Sammy Mace and hit the man in the ponytail in the groin. He stumbled away, his face rearing into the sky, his hands clutched to the wound as though he wanted to relieve himself.

Her second round entered Sammy's eye socket and blew the back of his head out on the grass.

Suddenly there was no sound in the skeet

club except the wind fluttering an American flag on top of the pavilion.

CHAPTER

25

It was hot that night, and still hot at false dawn, as though the air had been baked, then released again on the new day. I got a handful of molasses balls from the tack room and fed them to Beau in the lot, then turned him out and walked down to the river and watched the darkness go out of the sky. The current was dark green and swirling with froth from dead cottonwood trees that were snagged along the shore, and I could hear bream popping the surface where the riffle channeled under the tree trunks.

I tried to think clearly but I couldn't. I had stayed with Mary Beth until eleven last night. The man with the ponytail had lived three hours and died on the operating table. His name was Sixto Dominque, and his sheet showed only one felony conviction, for extortion in Florida, for which he had received a gubernatorial pardon. His wallet contained a permit for the .25-caliber automatic.

"They thought they were in Dog Patch. They got what they deserved," I told her.

"I should have hooked up Vernon Smothers and taken him to the cruiser and called for backup," she said.

"Listen, Mary Beth, you're an officer of the law. When a lowlife puts his hand on your person during the performance of your duty, you bounce him off the hardest object in his environment."

"I blew it."

I offered to stay with her.

"Thanks, anyway. I've got to spend some serious time on the phone tonight," she said. In the electric lighting of her apartment the color seemed washed out of her face, her freckles unnatural, as though they were painted on her skin.

"Don't drink booze or coffee. Don't pay attention to the thoughts you have in the middle of the night," I said.

"Was it this way with you?"

"Yeah, the first time it was."

"The *first* time?" she said.

My stare broke, and I tried not to let her see me swallow.

Now, the next day, I squatted on my boot heels in the grass and tossed pebbles down into the water on top of the submerged car that had once contained the bodies of two members of the Karpis-Barker gang, nameless now, buried somewhere in a potter's field, men who thought they'd write their names into memory with a blowtorch.

What was it that really bothered me, that hid just around a corner in my mind?

The answer was not one I easily accepted.

I had made a career of living a half life. I had

been a street cop, a Texas Ranger, a federal prosecutor, and now I was a small-town defense lawyer who didn't defend drug traffickers, as though somehow that self-imposed restriction gave a nobility to my practice that other attorneys didn't possess. I was neither father nor husband, and had grown to accept endings in my life in the way others anticipated beginnings, and I now knew, without being told, that another one was at hand.

The sun broke above the horizon and was warm on my back as I walked toward the house. Then my gaze steadied on the barn, the backyard, the drive, the porte cochere, and two black sedans that shouldn't have been there.

I walked through the back porch and kitchen into the main part of the house, which Brian Wilcox and five other Treasury people were tearing apart.

"What the hell do you think you're doing?" I asked.

Wilcox stood in the middle of my library. Splayed books were scattered across the floor.

"Give him the warrant," he said to a second man, who threw the document at me, bouncing it off my chest.

"I don't care if you have a warrant or not. You have no legitimate cause to be here," I said.

"Shut up and stay out of the way," the second man said. He wore shades and a military haircut, and his work had formed a thin sheen of perspiration on his face.

"Come on, Wilcox. You're a pro. You guys pride yourselves on blending into the wallpaper," I said.

"You're interfering with a federal investigation," Wilcox said.

"I'm what?"

"I think you've been running a parallel investigation to our own. That means there's probable cause for us to believe you possess evidence of a crime. Hence, the warrant. You don't like it, fuck you," he said.

I used the Rolodex on my desk and punched a number into the telephone.

"I hope you're calling the judge. He's part Indian. His nickname is Big Whiskey John. He's in a great mood this time of day," Wilcox said.

"This is Billy Bob Holland. I've got six Treasury agents ransacking my home," I said into the receiver. "The agent in charge is Brian Wilcox. He just told me to fuck myself. Excuse me, I have to go. I just heard glass breaking upstairs."

The agent in shades picked up my great-grandfather's journal from a chair, flipped through it, and tossed it to me. "Looks like a historical document there. Hang on to it," he said, and raked a shelf of books onto the floor.

"That was the newspaper," I said to Wilcox. "It's owned by an eighty-year-old hornet who thinks fluoridation is a violation of the Constitution. Does the G still have its own clipping service?"

"You think you're getting a bad deal, huh?

You cost us eight months' work. That's right, we were about to flip Sammy Mace, then you showed up. Plus your gal just got pulled out by her people."

He looked at the reaction in my face, and a smile broke at the corner of his mouth.

"Her people?" I said numbly.

"Call her apartment. She's gone, bro. She got picked up in a plane at four this morning. She wouldn't survive an IA investigation," he said.

I started to pick books off the floor and stack them on my desk, as though I were in a trance.

"You were a cop," Wilcox said. "You don't use a baton to bring a suspect into submission. You never deliver a blow with it above the shoulders. They'd crucify her and drag her people into it with her."

"I can't stop what you're doing here. But somewhere I'm going to square this down the line," I said.

"Yeah, that's going to be a big worry of ours," Wilcox said.

The man in shades began rifling my desk. He removed L.Q. Navarro's holstered .45 revolver and flipped open the loading gate on the brass bottom of a cartridge.

I fitted my hand around his wrist.

"That belonged to a friend of mine. He's dead now. You don't mind not handling it, do you?" I said, and squeezed his wrist until I saw his lips part on his teeth and a look come into his eyes that his shades couldn't hide.

"We're done here," Wilcox said, raising his palm pacifically. "Don't misunderstand the gesture, Holland. Touch a federal agent again and I'll put a freight train up your ass."

I waited for her call, but it didn't come.

I worked late at the office that day. Through the blinds I could see the sun, like a burning flare, behind the courthouse and the tops of the oak trees. At just after seven Temple Carrol came by.

"I'll buy you a beer," she said.

"I still have some work to do."

"I bet." She sat with one leg on the corner of my desk. She lifted her chestnut hair off her neck. "It's been a hot one."

"Yeah, it's warming up."

"She blew Dodge, huh?"

"I don't know, Temple. Not everybody reports in to me."

"You want to talk business, or should I get lost?"

I pushed aside a deposition I was reading and waited.

"I took Jamie Lake shopping for some clothes that make her look half human," she said. "At first she's looking at these see-through things and I tell her, 'Jamie, it might be the nature of prejudice and all that jazz, but tattoos just don't float well with juries.'

"'Oh I get it,' she says. 'Upscale people

tell the truth. Trailer court people lie. Wow! Tell me, which kind was that needle-dick polygraph nerd who was trying to scope my jugs?'

"I say, 'We do what works, kiddo.'

"She goes, 'There's nothing like being sweet, is there? I once told a narc, "Gee, officer, I wouldn't have smoked it if I had known it was harmful to my health." He was such a gentleman after that. He took it out of his pants all by himself.'

"Billy Bob, this gal is major off the wall."

"Most of our clientele is. That's why they're in trouble all the time," I said.

"Here's the rest of it. She had her nose really bent out of joint by this time. So she takes out her MasterCard and buys four hundred dollars' worth of clothes I couldn't afford."

"It doesn't mean she's dirty."

"Yeah, and Jack Vanzandt and this greaseball Felix Ringo brought her to us out of goodwill."

I rubbed my forehead and looked at the soft orange glow of the sunset over the trees. Mockingbirds glided by the clock tower on the courthouse.

"Yeah, this guy Ringo doesn't fit. He's a friend of Jack, he was hanging around Sammy Mace, and he's hooked up with the G at the same time," I said.

I felt the fatigue of the day catch up with me. I tried to think straight but I couldn't. I felt her eyes on my face.

"Go to supper with me," she said.

"I'm going to put Darl Vanzandt on the stand," I said.

That night there was still no call from Mary Beth. In the morning I drove to the office, then walked to the thrift store operated by the Baptist church, where Emma Vanzandt was a volunteer worker.

She was in back, sorting donated clothes on a long wood table. She wore tailored jeans and red pumps and a white silk blouse with red beads. She didn't bother to look up when I approached her.

"Jack and Felix Ringo gave me some witnesses that are almost too good to be true," I said.

"Oh, how grand," she said.

"I think Jack may have done it to get me off your son's back."

She looked me in the face and silently formed the word *stepson* with her mouth.

"Excuse me, your stepson, Darl."

"Why tell me, good sir?"

"Because Darl's going on the stand just the same."

"Would you kindly take the okra out of your mouth and explain what you're talking about."

"Darl was at Shorty's the night Roseanne Hazlitt was attacked. He's mentally defective and has a violent history. He's beaten women with his fists. He goes into rages with little provocation. You figure it out, Emma."

"Ah, our conscience feels better now, doesn't it? You take Jack's favor, but to prove your integrity, you subpoena a walking basket case and fuck him cross-eyed in front of a jury of nigras and Mexicans."

A woman paying for her purchase at the counter turned around with her mouth open.

"Tell Jack what I said."

I walked back out the front door. Then I heard her behind me. In the sunlight her makeup looked like a white and pink mask stretched on her face, her black hair pulled tightly back on her forehead, her eyes aglitter with anger or uppers or whatever energy it was that drove her.

"You're a fool," she said.

"Why?"

Her mouth was thick with lipstick, slightly opened, her eyes fastened on mine, as though she were on the edge of saying something that would forever make me party to a secret that she imparted to no one.

"Bunny Vogel," she said.

"What?"

Then the moment went out of her eyes.

"I wish I were a man. I'd beat the shit out of you. I truly hate you, Billy Bob Holland," she said.

My father was both a tack and hot-pass welder on pipelines for thirty years, but all his jobs came from the same company, one that contracted statewide out of Houston. I called their office and asked the lady in charge of payroll if their records would indicate whether my father ever worked around Waco in the late 1930s or early 1940s.

"My heavens, that's a long time ago," she said.

"It's really important," I said.

"A lot of our old records are on the computer now, but employees' names of fifty years ago, that's another matter—"

"I don't understand."

"The company has to know where all its pipe is. But back during the Depression a lot of men were hired by the day and paid in cash. WPA boys, drifters off the highway, they came and they went."

And the company didn't have to pay union wages or into the Social Security fund, either, I thought.

"Can you just determine if y'all lay any lines around Waco about 1940 or so?" I asked.

"That's a whole lot easier. Can I call you back when I have more time?" she said.

I gave her my office number and went home for lunch. The light on my telephone answering machine was flashing in the library. I pushed the "play" button, trying not to be controlled by the expectation in my chest.

"It's me, Billy Bob. I'm sorry I left the way I did. I'm not even supposed to call you. I'll try to get back to you later," Mary Beth's voice said.

The tape announced the time. I had missed her call by fifteen minutes.

I fixed a sandwich and some potato salad

and a glass of iced tea and sat down to eat on the back porch. The fields were marbled with shadow and the breeze was warm and flecked with rain and I could smell cows watering at my neighbor's windmill. On the other side of the tank, beyond the line of willows that puffed with wind, was the network of baked wagon ruts and hoofprints where the Chisholm Trail had traversed my family's property. Sometimes I believed Great-grandpa Sam was still out there, in chaps and floppy hat, a bandanna tied across his face against the dust, trying to turn his cows away from the bluffs when dry lightning caused them to rumble across the prairie louder than the thunder itself.

I wished I had lived back in his time, when men like Garland T. Moon were bounced off cottonwood trees and federal agents didn't make you fall in love with them and then leave on airplanes at four in the morning with no explanation.

It was a self-pitying way to think, but I didn't care. I went into the library and got out Sam's journal and read it while I finished lunch.

August 28, 1891
Maybe burning out them four caves wasn't such a good idea. The gang has come back from Pearl Younger's whorehouse and now the Dalton brothers seem to think their leadership is on the line. To make matters worse, Emmett Dalton, the only one of them who probably has half a brain, told me my name has been put

on a warrant by the U.S. court up in Wichita, because I am now considered a known associate of train robbers and murderers.

I understand the judge who done this is the same one who told the Colorado cannibal Albert Packer there was only seven good Democrats in the mountains where Packer got froze in for the winter and Packer had went and ate five of them. I now wish Packer had carried his knife and fork into the court and made it six.

The Cimarron is naught but ribbons of muddy water now and carrion birds perch on the ribs of the wild horses the Dalton-Doolins have shot and butchered down on the banks. The hills are orange and sear with drought all the way to Kansas, and dust and chickweed blows up in flumes that will sand the skin off your bones.

The poppy husks in the fields have hardened and dried and they rattle and hiss like snakes when I ride down to the river to draw water for our garden. When I see the fireflies in the trees and hear the cicadas in the evening, I wonder how I have strayed so far from the smell of rain and flowers on the Texas Gulf. It is the feeling I always had as a child, that everything was ending, that the world's sins was fixing to turn the sky to flames. I never could account for the notions I had as a child. But it is feelings like this that always made the word whiskey want to break like a bubble on the back of my tongue.

I know if I stay on the Cimarron, I will be gunned down for sure or forced once again to kill other men. Jennie woke me last night when she heard sounds by the outhouse. It was only hogs, but she commenced crying and said she has heard her relatives talking and she fears for my life. I have not knowed her to cry before.

It is cowardly to run, though, particularly from the likes of them down in the mud caves. We never done it when we marched alongside Granny Lee and I'll be damned if I'll do it now.

These are prideful thoughts, all. God forgive me for them. I feel desolate and lost and would ride into the worst storm on earth for just a drop of rain.

I didn't hear from Mary Beth again that day. That night I dreamed of a picnic ground filled with children. A green river curled through cottonwoods behind them, and a rainbow arched through the sky over their heads. In their midst was a goat-footed satyr, his vascular arms as white as milk, a clutch of balloons strung from one fist. At first I couldn't see his face, then he rotated his head toward me, his mouth grinning, the scab on his lip as shiny as plastic. The children ran toward the balloons and swirled about his thighs like disembodied figures in a maelstrom.

CHAPTER

26

In the morning I drove to Bunny Vogel's house. His father came out on the porch, barefoot and without a shirt. He was an inept tank of a man, whose doughlike hand dwarfed his cigarette.

"You the lawyer been coming around?" he said.

"That's right."

"He went swimming. At the beach, up the river," he said. "You going up there?"

"I expect."

"Tell him he went off without cleaning the grease trap. Now there's some black gunk overflowing out of the sink. Whole house smells like an elephant backed up and farted in it."

I drove to the small stretch of sandy beach built by the county at the curve of the river. Bunny's maroon '55 Chevy was parked back in the trees, the waxed finish and green-tinted windows sprinkled with pine needles. A heavy-set Mexican girl in a black bathing suit sat at a picnic table, watching Bunny do push-ups, his toes on the table, his arms propped on a bench. He wore only a pair of lavender running shorts, and his triceps and back muscles ridged like rolls of metal washers.

When he saw me, his face reddened, and he sat on the bench and dusted the sand off his feet and began fitting on his flip-flops. His long,

bronze-colored hair hung down over his disfigured jawline.

"Your name keeps coming up in my trial
preparation," I said.

"I ain't interested," he said.

I looked at the girl and waited for him to
introduce me. When he didn't, I realized the
redness in his face was not because I had
caught him impressing a girl with his strength.

"I'm Billy Bob Holland. How do you do?"
I said to her.

"It's nice to meet you," she said. A gold tooth
shone in the back of her mouth.

"Yeah, excuse me, this is Naomi. We was
taking a swim," he said, and his hand gestured
at nothing, as though he needed to offer an
explanation.

"So that's what I'm gonna do," she said, and
picked up her towel.

"You ain't got to go, Naomi," Bunny said.

She smiled and walked into the water, the
backs of her thighs wrinkling below the rim
of her bathing suit. She leaned over and
cupped water on her shoulders and spread it
on her arms. Bunny watched her, his jaws
slack, his eyes trying to take him out into the
sunlight, away from the conversation he was
about to have.

"I'm calling you as a witness at Lucas's
trial," I said.

"Oh man, don't tell me that."

"You'll have a lot of company—Darl Vanzandt, Virgil Morales, a biker girl named

Jamie Lake, an elderly black man who saw Roseanne Hazlitt slap you."

"Morales? That pepper bel...that kid from the Purple Hearts? What's he got to do with this?"

"Why'd Roseanne hit you? Why'd Morales call you a pimp, Bunny?"

Bunny put the tips of his fingers on his temples.

"You don't know what you're doing. You're setting my life on fire, Mr. Holland."

"*Your* life? How about the girl who's in the cemetery? How about Lucas Smothers's life?"

Above his left nipple was the tattoo of a small heart.

"I didn't want none of this to happen. People don't plan for stuff like this to happen," he said.

"Emma Vanzandt called me a fool yesterday. When I asked her why, she used your name. Like you were a key I didn't know how to fit on the ring."

"Emma done that?" He twisted around on the bench and stared at me, his eyes burning. "That bitch done that?"

"That doesn't sound like you, Bunny."

"Yeah, what does? Human dildo?"

He waited for me to comprehend his meaning. I kept my expression flat.

"Rich woman catches her husband milking through the fence, how does she stick it to him? She gets a young guy to put the wood to her."

"You and Emma?"

"It was a one-time deal. She drove a hundred

284

miles to a motel that was between two oil rigs. The walls was vibrating off the foundation. I think she was whacked out on speed. She wanted to call him up on the phone during a certain moment. I had to talk her out of it."

He stared out at the river and at the Mexican girl whose body was bladed with the sun's reflection off the water. After a while he said, "She's a nice girl. Naomi, I mean. She don't know about none of this. She thinks I'm hot shit 'cause I played football at A&M."

"Maybe you're a better guy than you think," I said.

"No, I know what I am. I blame my trouble on the Vanzandts, but they knew the kind of person they was looking for."

"You're still a young man. You haven't done anything that can't be undone." When he didn't answer, I said, "Have you?"

He looked down at the tops of his feet. His fingers were pressed into his bronze hair like white snakes. When I walked to the car I realized I had forgotten to deliver his father's message, but I felt Bunny didn't need another reminder that day of who or what he was.

I almost didn't recognize her when she got out of a taxi cab in my drive at noon the same day. She wore a powder-blue suit, heels, a white blouse, and a beige shoulder bag. But for some reason, in my mind's eye, I still saw the tall, naturally elegant woman in tan uniform and campaign hat. I opened the side door and stepped out under the porte cochere.

"Wow," I said.

"Wow, yourself."

"You sure look different."

"That's the welcome?"

"Come in." I opened the screen.

She hesitated. "I don't want to interrupt your day."

We seemed to be looking at each other like people who might have just met at a bus stop.

"I don't know what to say, Mary Beth. I got one phone message. My only source of information about you has been Brian Wilcox."

"Brian?"

"He got a warrant and tossed my house."

She looked away, her face full of thought.

"I'm not supposed to be here. My people are cutting a deal with the new sheriff," she said.

"Your people?"

"Yes."

The wind blew the curls on the back of her neck. I could hear the tin roof on the barn pinging with heat, like wires breaking.

"The locals are trying to jam you up on the shooting?" I said.

"It's their out. I handed it to them on a shovel."

"Sammy Mace was a cop killer. He got what he had coming," I said.

"Can we go inside, Billy Bob? We were in Denver this morning. I overdressed."

She sat down at the kitchen table. I poured her a glass of iced tea. I ran cold water over my hands and dried them, not knowing why

I did. Outside, the barn roof shimmered like a heliograph under the sun.

"My office is taking the weight for me. I screwed up, but they're taking the weight, anyway," she said.

"A stand-up bunch. We're talking about the DEA?" I said.

Her back straightened under her coat. Her hand was crimped on a paper napkin, her gaze pointed out the window.

"I thought coming here was the right thing to do. But I'm all out of words, Billy Bob."

"Can't we have dinner? Can't we spend some time together without talking about obligations to a government agency? You think you owe guys like Brian Wilcox?"

"This is pointless. Because you hung up your own career doesn't mean other—" She didn't finish. She put both her hands in her lap, then a moment later placed one hand on top of her shoulder bag.

I opened the refrigerator door to take out the iced tea pitcher again. Then closed it and stood stupidly in the center of the room, all of the wrong words already forming in my throat.

"An English writer, what's his name, E. M. Forster, once said if he had to choose between his country and his friend, he hoped he'd have the courage to choose his friend," I said.

"I guess I missed that in my English lit survey course," she said, rising from her chair. "Can I use your phone to call a cab? I should have asked him to wait."

"I apologize. Don't leave like this."

She shook her head, then walked into the library and used the telephone. I stood in her way when she tried to walk down the hall to the front door.

"You see yourself as a failure. You put yourself through law school. You were a Texas Ranger and an AUSA. You can be a law-man again, anytime you want," she said.

"Then stay. I'll cancel the cab."

I put my hand on her arm. I saw the pause in her eyes, the antithetical thoughts she couldn't resolve, the pulse in her neck.

"I'd better go. I'll call later," she said.

"Mary Beth—"

Then she was out the door, her cheeks glazed with color, her hand feeling behind her for the door handle so she would not have to look back at my face.

But by Monday morning there was no call. Instead, a dinged gas-guzzler stopped out front of my office and a woman in a plat-inum wig and shades and a flowered sun-dress got out and looked in both directions, as though by habit, then entered the downstairs foyer.

A minute later my secretary buzzed me.

"A Ms. Florence LaVey. No appointment," she said.

"Who is she?"

"She said you'd know who she was."

"Nope. But send her in."

288

The inner door opened and the woman in the platinum wig stood framed in the doorway, her shades dripping from her fingers, her face expectant, as though at any moment I would recognize her relationship to my life.

"Can I help you?" I asked. Then I noticed that one of her eyes was brown, the other blue.

"The name doesn't turn on your burner, huh? San Antonio? The White Camellia Bar?"

"Maybe I'm a little slow this morning."

"I know what you mean. I always get boiled on Sunday nights myself. I think it has something to do with being raised Pentecostal...Let me try again...A nasty little fuck by the name of Darl Vanzandt?"

"You're the lady he beat up. You're a waitress?"

"A hostess, honey." She winked and sat down and crossed her legs. She opened a compact and looked at herself. "I'd like to slip some pieces of bamboo deep under his fingernails."

"His father says you and a pimp tried to roll him."

She wet the ball of one finger and wiped at something on her chin and clicked the compact shut.

"His old man paid me ten thousand dollars so he and his son could tell whatever lies they wanted to. You interested in what really happened?"

"It's not of much value if you took money to drop the charges."

"I'm not talking about what that little shit did to me. I read about that girl in the paper when she got beaten to death. But I didn't make any connections. Then last night him and this ex-convict named Moon come to this new bar I'm working in. Fart Breath starts talking about a trial, about this girl got gang-raped and her head bashed in, about how some lawyer is trying to make him take somebody else's fall. I'm standing behind the bar. I keep waiting for him to catch on who I am. Forget it."

"Yes?"

"Get the girl dug up. See if she wasn't stoned-out on roofies."

"We're talking about Ro—"

"You got it. Rohypnol. That's what the Vanzandt kid uses. He picks up a girl and dumps it in her drink so he can do anything he wants with her." She fitted her glasses on, then removed them again. "I wish I'd sent him to the Ellis Unit at Huntsville. The colored boys always appreciate new Ivory soap when they come out of the field."

"I've seen the autopsy. She was full of booze but no dope."

She brushed a long red thumbnail back and forth across a callus. "He sat on my chest and spit in my face. He broke both my lips. I told this to his old man. He goes, 'Ten thousand is my limit.'"

"The Vanzandts have their own way of doing things," I said, my attention starting to wander.

She got up to leave.

"Forget about the dope. Either that kid did her, or y'all got real bad luck."

"What do you mean?"

"Two like him in one town? This might be a shithole, honey, but it doesn't deserve that," she said.

Just before lunch, the lady in charge of payroll at my father's old pipeline company called from Houston.

"We didn't contract any jobs around Waco during the late Depression or the war years. But of course that doesn't mean in itself your father wasn't there," she said.

"Well, what you've found is still helpful," I said.

"Wait a minute. I did some other checking. I don't know if it will be useful to you or not."

"Yeah, please, go ahead."

"Your father worked steadily for us in east Texas from 1939 to 1942. Then evidently he was drafted into the army. I don't know how it would have been possible for him to have worked for another company around Waco at the same time. Does this help you out?"

"I can't tell you how much." I thanked her again and was just about to hang up. Then I said, "Just out of curiosity, would the 'search' key on your computer kick up the name of a man named Garland T. Moon?"

"Hold on. I'll see. When did he work for us?"

"During the mid-1950s."

I heard her fingers clicking on the keyboard of a computer, then she scraped the phone up off the table.

"Yes, we have a record of a G. T. Moon. But not during the 1950s. He was a hot-pass welder on a natural gas line down at Matagorda Bay in 1965. Is that the same man?...Hello?"

I don't remember if I answered her or not. I recall replacing the receiver in the cradle, the residue of moisture and oil that my palm print left on the plastic, the skin tightening in my face.

My father had been blown out of a bellhole while mending a leak on a pipe joint at Matagorda Bay in 1965.

CHAPTER

27

I walked across the street to the one-story sandstone building, which was now the office of the new sheriff, Hugo Roberts. He sat with one half-topped boot propped on his desk, the air around him layered with cigarette smoke.

"You want Garland T. Moon's file? Marvin Pomroy don't have it?" he asked.

"It's gone back into Records."

"What d' you want it for?"

"Idle curiosity. Since he probably killed your predecessor with an ax, I thought you might be interested in it, too."

He dropped his foot to the floor.

"Damn, Billy Bob, every time I talk with you I feel like a bird dog sticking his nose down a porcupine hole." He picked up his phone and punched an extension. "Tell Cleo to stop playing with hisself and to bring Garland Moon's sheet to my office," he said. He put the phone back down and smiled. "Hang on, I got to take a whiz."

He went into a small rest room and urinated into the bowl with the door open.

"You got Moon made for the sheriff's murder, huh?" he said.

"That'd be my bet."

He washed his hands, combed his hair in the mirror, and came back out. "Since nobody else has figured that out, what gives you this special insight?" he said.

"Because you're not worried about who did it."

"Beg your pardon?"

"The sheriff was on a pad. In this county the pad is passed on with the office. If the sheriff was murdered by the guys he was taking juice from, you'd be walking on eggshells, Hugo. You're not."

A deputy opened the front door and stuck his head in. "You wanted the file on Moon?" he said.

"Give it to the counselor here," Hugo said. "Billy Bob, you don't mind reading it outside, do you? There's a nice table under the trees. Then carry it on back to Cleo."

I took the manila folder from the deputy and

started to follow him outside. Hugo lit a cigarette from a match folder with cupped hands. "Read the weather warning, son. This is the last time you track your shit in my office," he said.

I sat under an oak tree filled with mockingbirds and went over the long and dreary history of Garland T. Moon. In Texas alone, he had been jailing for five decades. His career stretched back into the tail end of a prison farm system that had held the gunfighter John Wesley Hardin, Buck and Clyde Barrow, and the twelve-string guitarist Huddie Ledbetter. Hollywood films had always portrayed the Georgia chain gang as the most severe form of penal servitude in the United States. But among old-time recidivists, the benchmark was Arkansas, where convicts were worked long hours, fed the most meager of rations, and beaten with the Black Betty, a razor strop attached to a wood handle. Among these same recidivists, Texas always came in a close second.

At Huntsville Moon had been written up repeatedly for "shirking work quota" and "weighing in with dirt clods."

In the old days a convict at Huntsville had to pick a certain quota of cotton each day. If he didn't, or if he was caught weighting his bag with dirt from the field, he was separated out from the other inmates, taken hot and dirty to a lockdown unit, not allowed to shower or eat, and forced to stand with two others on top of an oil drum until the next morning. If he fell off the drum, he had to deal with the gunbull in the cage.

Moon had been hospitalized twice for head lacerations and broken foot bones. No cause for the injury was given. Each hospitalization took place after an escape attempt. His stomach had been seared by liquid Drano, his back held against a hot radiator, his calves branded with heated coat hangers. Everything in his record indicated he was as friendless and hated among the prison population as he was among the personnel.

But what good did it do to dwell upon the cruelty that had been inculcated in Garland T. Moon or that he had cultivated and nourished in himself and injected systemically into the lives of others? The day you understood a man like Moon was the day you crossed a line and became like him.

I needed to know what had happened between him and my father around the year 1956. Moon had said my father had put him in his truck and dropped him on the highway without food or money or destination. My father was a good-hearted and decent man, slow to anger and generous to a fault. If Moon's account was true, Moon had either committed a crime so heinous or represented a threat so grave to others my father had felt no reservation in abandoning an ignorant, sexually abused boy to his fate.

I went back to the first entries in Moon's file.

He had been released from the county prison, at age sixteen, in February of 1956. His record remained clean until August 17 of that same year. The words "suspicion of abduction" were typed out neatly by the date without explanation.

I walked across the square to the newspaper and asked permission to use the paper's morgue. The issues from 1956 had never been put on microfilm and were still bound in a heavy green cardboard cover that had turned gray with age around the borders. I turned to the August issues and found a four-inch back-page story about a missing ten-year-old Negro girl who was later discovered hiding in a cave. She told officers a white man had come into her yard and had led her into the woods behind her home. She refused to tell anyone what had happened to her between the time she left home and the time she had been found by sheriff's deputies.

Four days later there was a follow-up story about a juvenile who had been brought in for questioning about the girl's abduction. The story did not give his name but stated he had been working on a pipeline nearby the girl's home.

The juvenile was released from custody when the parents refused to bring charges.

The date on the newspaper follow-up story was August 18, the day after the date on Garland T. Moon's rap sheet.

I walked back across the street and threw Moon's file on the sheriff's desk.

"Sorry, I couldn't find Cleo," I said. "By the way, some exculpatory evidence disappeared from the Roseanne Hazlitt homicide investigation. I'm talking about some bottles and beer cans taken from the murder scene by your deputies. You mind going on the stand about that, Hugo?"

Pete's mother was waiting for me when I got back to the office. She wore a pink waitress uniform, her lank, colorless hair tied behind her head. She kept twisting the black plastic watchband on her wrist.

"The social worker says she's got to certify. If Pete ain't living at home no more, she cain't certify." She sat bent forward, her eyes fastened on the tops of her hands.

"I'll talk to her," I said.

"It won't do no good."

"It's dangerous for him, Wilma."

"They ain't done nothing but write that note. They sent it to you. They didn't send it to us." The resentment in her voice was like a child's, muted, turned inward, resonant with fear.

"I'll ask Temple to bring his stuff home after school," I said.

"You been good to Pete and all but..." She didn't finish. Her eyes looked receded, empty. "I'm gonna move away. This town ain't ever been any good for us."

"I don't think that's the answer."

Then I saw the anger bloom in her face, past

the fearful restraint that normally governed her life.

"Yeah? Well, why don't you just raise your own son and leave mine alone for a while?" she said.

At six that evening Mary Beth called from Denver.

"Am I going to see you again?" I asked. My throat was dry, my tone vainly ironic and preemptive, the receiver held too tightly against my ear.

"I can't come back there for a while."

"I can get a flight to Denver...Mary Beth? Are you there?"

"Yes...I mean, yes, I'm here."

"Did you hear what I said?" But I already knew the answer, and I could feel a weakness, a failing in my heart as though weevil worms had passed through it.

"Some people here are still upset about the way things went in Deaf Smith," she said.

"With you and me?"

"That's part of it."

"I think the problem is Brian Wilcox. Not you, not me, not the shooting of Sammy Mace and his bodyguard. I think Wilcox is poisoning the well everywhere he goes and your people are overlooking it to save the investigation."

"Maybe that's true. But I can't do anything about it."

I could hear her breathing in the silence.

"Can you give me a telephone number?" I said.

"We're leaving tonight for a meeting in Virginia."

"Well, I hope it works out for you," I said.

"What? What did you say?"

"Nothing. I never did well inside organizations. I hope you do. That's all I meant."

In the silence I could hear her breath against the receiver.

"Mary Beth?"

"Yes?"

"I'll need you to testify at Lucas's trial. About the cans and bottles those other deputies lost or destroyed."

"It's a bad time to bring that up."

"Bad time? That's what's on your mind? It's a bad time?"

"Good-bye, Billy Bob."

After I hung up the receiver, I stared at the telephone in the fading light through the window, as though I could will it to ring again. Then I walked outside, under an empty dome of yellow sky, into a sand-bitten wind that shredded leaves from the chinaberry tree. I got into my Avalon, the wind buffeting the windows, and drove to Pete's house.

"You're by yourself?" I asked.

He stood on the porch in a pair of pin-striped overalls and a Clorox-stained purple T-shirt.

"My mother don't get off from work till nine," he replied.

"Did you eat yet?"

"Some."

"Like what?"

"Viennas and saltines."

"I think we'd better get us a couple of those chicken-fried steaks at the café."

"I knew you was gonna say that."

It was dusk when we got to the café. We sat under a big electric fan by the window and ordered. Down the street, the sun was red behind the pines in the church yard. Pete had wet his hair and brushed it up on the sides so that it was as flat as a landing field.

"You have to be careful, bud. Don't talk to strangers, don't let some no-count fellow tell you he's a friend of your mom," I said.

"Temple done told me all that."

"Then you won't mind hearing it again."

"That ain't all she told me."

"Oh?"

"She said for a river-baptized person you been doing something you ain't supposed to. What'd she mean by that?"

"Search me."

"It's got to do with that lady from the sheriff's department. That's my take on it, anyway." He bit off a bread stick and crunched it in his jaw.

"Really?"

"Temple talks about you all the time. She said she feels like going upside your head with a two-by-four."

"How about clicking it off, bud?"

"You gonna come to my ball game this weekend?"

"What do you think?"

He chewed the bread stick and grinned at the same time.

In a candid moment most longtime cops and prison personnel will tell you there are some criminals whom they secretly respect. Charles Arthur Floyd was known for his scrupulousness in paying for the food he was given by Oklahoma farmers when he hid out on the Canadian River. Clyde Barrow finished a jolt on a Texas prison farm, then went back and broke his friends out. Men who have invested their entire lives in dishonesty do max time rather than lie about or snitch-off another con. Murderers go to their deaths without complaint, their shoulders erect, their fears sealed behind their eyes. The appellation "stand-up" in a prison population is never used lightly.

But the above instances are the exceptions. The average sociopath is driven by one engine, namely, the self. He has no bottom, and his crimes, large or small, are as morally interchangeable to him as watching TV with his family or walking back to a witness at a convenience store robbery and popping a .22 round through the center of her forehead.

Darl Vanzandt pulled his '32 Ford into my drive the next evening, then saw me currying Beau in the lot and drove his car to the edge of the barn and got out and stood in the wind, his face twitching from the dust that swirled out of the fields or the chemicals that swam in his brain.

He approached the fence and lay his forearm on the top rail, studying me, his unbuttoned shirt flapping on his chest. I hadn't noticed before how truncated his body was. The legs were too short for his torso, the shoulders too wide for the hips, the hands as round and thick as clubs.

"Say it and leave," I said.

"Bunny Vogel quit his job at the skeet club. My mother got him that job. He walks in yesterday and tells the manager he's finished bagging trash and cleaning toilets. Big fucking superstar. He's gonna dime me, that's what he's doing."

"Who cares?"

"It's Bunny who started it all. I'm talking about Roseanne. You listening? Bunny pretends he's a victim or something. Believe me, 'cause he's got a messed-up face doesn't mean he's a victim."

"Not interested."

He made an unintelligible sound and his face seemed to wrinkle with disbelief.

"I can give you Bunny, man," he said.

"I'm not interested, because you're a liar, Darl. Your information is worthless," I said.

He inched farther down the fence rail, as though somehow he were getting closer to me.

"You want Garland Moon? I can do that too.

302

I got stuff on that geek can make you throw up," he said.

"Nope."

"What's with you?"

I pulled Beau's left front hoof up between my legs and pried a rock out of his shoe with my pocketknife. I could hear Darl's shirt puffing and flapping in the wind.

"You and Marvin Pomroy got to work some kind of deal," he said. "The judge said I fart in the street, I'm going to the Walls. I'm still a kid."

I put down Beau's left hoof and stooped under his neck and picked up his other front hoof. The wind blew my hat across the lot into the barn.

"My old man," Darl said.

"What?"

"That's who you're really after. You want him, I can give him to you."

I stood erect and stared at him. No shame, no expression except one of expectancy showed in his face. I folded my pocketknife blade in my palm and walked toward him and placed my hand on the smoothness of the fence rail next to his. His skin was sunburned inside the peach fuzz on his cheeks; there was a small clot of mucus in the corner of his mouth.

"I don't want anything you can give," I said.

"Wha—"

"I'm going to take it from you on the stand," I said.

I turned away from him and stroked Beau's face and took a sugar cube from my shirt pocket and let him gum it out of the flat of my hand. A moment later I heard Darl's car engine roar, then the dual exhausts echo off the side of the house and fade away in the wind.

CHAPTER

28

The evening before opening statements I drove to Lucas Smothers's house and took a new brown suit, white shirt, and tie off the clothes hook in the back of the Avalon and knocked on the door. Lucas appeared at the screen with a wooden spoon in one hand and a shot glass in the other.

"You got your hair cut," I said.

"Yeah, just like you told me."

"What are you doing with a whiskey glass?"

"Oh, that," he said, and smiled. "I'm baking a cake for my father's birthday. I use it for measuring. Come on in."

I followed him into the kitchen, the plastic suit bag rattling over my shoulder.

"What's that?" he asked.

"It's your new suit. Wear it tomorrow."

"I got a suit."

"Yeah, you've got this one. Tomorrow, you sit erect in the chair. You don't chew gum, you don't grin at anything the prosecutor or a witness says. If you want to tell me something, you write it on a pad, you never whisper. You do nothing that makes the jury think you're a wiseass. There's nothing a jury hates worse than a wiseass. Are we connecting here?"

"Why don't you carve it on my chest?"

"You know how many defendants flush themselves down the commode because they think the court is an amusement park?"

"You're more strung out about this than I am."

Because I know what you'll face if we lose, I thought. But I didn't say it.

He stood tall and barefoot at the drainboard, measuring vanilla extract into the shot glass. Outside the screen window, the windmill was silhouetted against a bank of yellow and purple clouds.

I watched him pour the vanilla extract into the cake bowl, his long fingers pinched lightly on the sides of the shot glass.

"Why you looking at me like that?" he asked.

"The first time I interviewed you at the jail, you told me you and Roseanne were 'knocking back shots,'" I said.

"Yeah, Beam, with a draft beer on the side."

"But you were working with the band that night. You had on that blue-check shirt with the gold trumpets sewn on the shoulders, the shirt you bought to play in the band."

"Yeah, like that Jamie Lake gal said."

"Why'd you start doing boilermakers while you were working?"

"We were on the break. I just had two. My stomach must have been empty or something. I remember Roseanne was mad 'cause of something Bunny said. She wanted to get a six-pack and go down the road and drink it. I wouldn't have done it, but I was jackhammered by then."

"Did she drink as much as you did?"

"Yeah, I guess."

"But you passed out and she didn't."

"I just ain't following you, Mr. Holland."

"Where was Darl Vanzandt when you decided to smash down a couple of boiler-makers?"

"He was at the bar. Darl never gets far from the juice man when he's inside Shorty's...What's wrong?"

"I never saw it. I kept thinking about the autopsy report on Roseanne. I was thinking about the wrong person."

"What per—"

"A hooker from San Antone told me Darl probably doped Roseanne with roofies. But he didn't. He doped you."

Lucas set the shot glass down on the drain-board and looked at it numbly.

"They laced me with downers twice? I reckon that makes me pretty dumb, don't it?" he said.

"I'll pick you up in the morning," I said.

"Mr. Holland, Darl didn't have no reason to kill Roseanne."

"He doesn't need one. He enjoys it."

My motion to dismiss was denied by Judge Judy Bonham, known as Stonewall Judy for her malleability and sense of humor. She was perhaps forty years old, had a complexion that seemed never to have been exposed to sunshine, and black hair that looked waved permanently in place. Four times a week she lifted free-weights at the health club in a pair of sweatpants and a heavy, long-sleeve jersey. When she did stomach stretches on the bench, her hips and buttocks flattened and seized against her sweats like metal plate.

The court had never been air-conditioned and depended for cooling on a cross breeze through the open windows and the oscillating electric fans affixed high up on the walls. The courthouse lawn was still in early-morning shadow, the sprinklers slapping against the tree trunks, when Marvin Pomroy began his opening statement.

It was eloquent, filled with a subdued outrage at the brutality of the crime, the degradation visited upon the victim before she died, her betrayal by a young man "whom she had trusted, whom she had probably loved, perhaps hoped to marry, until in a drunken rage he ripped the young life out of her body."

As always, Marvin called upon his greatest talent, namely, his ability to convey to a jury that, regardless of what the evidence did or did not indicate, he himself was absolutely convinced of the defendant's guilt. Over half the jury was black and Hispanic. It didn't matter. Marvin became the hard-shell southern Baptist who did not apologize for what he was and instead made you feel you shared the same sense of decency and tragic loss as he. The rectitude in his eye, the bloom on his cheeks, the knot in his words when he mentioned the blows that had rained down on the victim's face, were such that the listener heard the voice of principle, the preacher in his own church, the moral instruction of his mother and father.

On his left hand, Marvin wore a silver ring with a gold cross embossed on it. During his opening statement, that hand would clench the rim of the jury box several times.

In fact, his opening statement was too convincing. The doubts I had seen in him during our last meeting were gone. Which meant something had happened since that day I had told him I had found two witnesses who would testify Lucas was passed out in his truck when Roseanne was still alive.

I walked toward the jury box.

"The prosecutor has told you about the level of injury and the humiliating death visited upon the victim, Roseanne Hazlitt," I said. "He will come back to those images again and again. The implication is that someone must be punished for what was done to this young woman. And that's the problem: the prosecutor is telling you *someone* must be punished, even if it's the wrong person.

"Two people have been victimized by this

crime. The second victim is Lucas Smothers, a nineteen-year-old boy who never hurt anyone in his life. From the time of his arrest at the crime scene, when he was virtually unconscious, incapable of attacking anyone, the sheriff's department has not made one attempt to investigate the very real probability someone else was responsible for Roseanne Hazlitt's death.

"Instead, a boy who has never been arrested except for a traffic violation was put in a lockup unit with two psychopaths, written off as guilty by the prosecutor's office without even a preliminary investigation, and brought to trial after the prosecutor knew, *knew,* we had found witnesses who could prove Lucas Smothers could not have committed this crime.

"You'll hear from these witnesses, just as you'll hear about sheriff's deputies who either lost or destroyed crime scene evidence that may have told us who the real assailant was.

"The prosecutor, Mr. Pomroy, once told me our legal system exists to give voice to those who have none. He's right. But it also exists to protect the innocent and to punish the guilty and to ensure they do not commit their crimes again. In this case, not only has an innocent young man been charged and brought to trial, the real assailant has been allowed to remain free, in our community, free perhaps, in the words of the prosecutor, to rip the life from the body of another woman."

I talked about reasonable doubt, the lack of

motive, the fact that some of Roseanne's friends who came from wealthy families (and I meant Darl Vanzandt) had never been questioned during the investigation. But at the moment when I mentioned the element of wealth, a strange division took place in the jury box. The eyes of the black and Mexican jurors remained fixed on my face, unperturbed at my words, while the gaze of four white, upper-income jurors shifted into neutral space, click, just that fast.

When we recessed, Marvin Pomroy passed the defense table and said, "You stepped in the bubble gum on that last one, counselor."

I rubbed my temple and looked at his back.

"What'd he mean?" Lucas asked.

"Don't tell a Republican the system that protects his money is corrupt."

Marvin's first witness was Roseanne Hazlitt's aunt. She walked with a cane to the stand, her back bent at the spine. She seemed even more frail than when I had interviewed her at her house. Her hand quivered on the curve of her cane; deep lines fanned out from her mouth like those in a mummy; her eyes jittered with the rheumy death light of the mortally ill.

But her animosity toward Lucas flared in her words, stripped the obstruction from her throat, reached out like knots in a whip.

"Did your niece tell you she thought she might be pregnant?" Marvin asked.

"Objection. Irrelevant," I said.

"Goes to motive," Marvin said.

"Overruled," the judge said.

"Yes, she did," the aunt said.

"Pregnant by whom?" Marvin asked.

"Your honor, the victim was not pregnant. The prosecution is trying to introduce a nonexistent situation into the trial," I said.

"Then bring that out in cross-examination. In the meantime, sit down and shut up, Mr. Holland," the judge said.

"She thought that 'un yonder made her pregnant," the aunt said.

"You're indicating Lucas Smothers?" Marvin said.

"I'm pointing at the one right there beat her to death and y'all didn't have guts enough to prosecute in the first degree," the aunt said.

"Objection," I said.

"Sustained. Jury will disregard the witness's last remark," the judge said.

But the pointed finger of accusation, the anger that seemed to indicate an unspoken knowledge about Lucas's guilt would not leave the jury's memory because of a judge's admonition. After Marvin sat back down, I rose and approached within five feet of the stand.

"Ms. Hazlitt, I interviewed you right after your niece's death, correct?" I said.

"You come out to the house, if that's what you mean."

"I asked you about someone she had slapped at Shorty's the night she was attacked, correct?"

"I told you she never hurt nobody in her life, too."

"You surely did. Then you told me some-thing like, 'It was them hurt her.' Isn't that correct?"

"I don't recall that."

"Then I asked you who 'them' was, who *were* those other people who had harmed her in the past. Isn't that correct?"

"Objection, counsel's testifying, Your Honor. The witness already stated she didn't remember," Marvin said.

"Where are you going with this, Mr. Hol-land?" the judge said.

"The witness obviously has hostile feel-ings toward the defendant. However, in a previous conversation she indicated her niece had been injured in some fashion by people other than Lucas Smothers."

"There's no evidence of this conversation. Mr. Holland is putting words in the witness's mouth and then questioning her about them. It's bizarre," Marvin said.

"I'll give you a short piece of rope, Mr. Holland," the judge said.

"Ms. Hazlitt, did you tell me people other than Lucas Smothers had harmed your niece?"

"Objection, your honor. He's doing it again," Marvin said.

"Sustained. Last warning, counselor," the judge said.

"I apologize, your honor. I'll rephrase the question. Ms. Hazlitt, did you indicate some-one other than Lucas had harmed Roseanne in the past?" I said.

"I don't recall that," the aunt replied.

"You didn't refer to her male friends as people who had 'gotten the scent of it,' or as 'dogs sniffing around a brooder house'?"

Marvin was on his feet again, but the judge spoke before he could.

"That's it. Both of you approach the bench," she said. She leaned forward and covered the microphone with her palm. "You two guys are starting to piss me off, particularly you, Mr. Holland. This isn't the trial of the century. You got problems with each other, settle them outside. And you, Mr. Holland, either you join the Screen Actors Guild or put an end to these diddle-doo theatrics. Are we clear on this?"

At lunchtime Lucas, Temple, and I walked across the square to the Mexican grocery store and ordered takeout from the small café in back, then carried it back to my office. Vernon Smothers caught up with us on the sidewalk. He had put on a tie and coat and white shirt, and his face was sweating in the sun.

"What's going on? When you gonna put on them damn deputies destroyed evidence?" he said.

"I'll talk with you about it later, Vernon," I said.

"That's my son. I'm supposed to figure out his trial by watching the evening news?"

I glanced at Temple. She touched Lucas on the arm and walked with him into the foyer and up the stairs of my building.

313

"I can't call the deputy I need. Why? I don't even know where she is. Why? She shot two guys out at the skeet club. You want me to go on?" I said.

I expected his face to tighten with anger, as it always did when Vernon heard something he didn't like. But he surprised me. He closed his eyes and rubbed his fingers hard in the middle of his brow.

"I screwed up again, didn't I? I should have listened to you and left things alone. I just ain't good at hearing what people tell me sometimes," he said.

"You were doing what you thought was right. It's not your fault, Vernon."

He looked back at me uncertainly, as though I had spoken to him in a foreign tongue.

Upstairs, I stood at the window and looked at the courthouse square, the dust on the trees and the heat waves bouncing off the sidewalks. Lucas was eating at the side of my desk in his shirtsleeves, his cuffs rolled back over his forearms.

"Ms. Hazlitt's testimony presents a little problem for us," I said to him.

"You mean when she said Roseanne thought it was me made her pregnant?"

"Yeah, that's part of it."

"But the autopsy showed she wasn't pregnant," he said.

"The jury just heard a story about a homicide victim who was sexually involved with only

314

one individual—you. Five members of that jury are over sixty years old. Older people tend to listen to other older people. Are you with me?"

He set down the taco he was eating. The glare through the slats in the blinds made his eyes water. "I ain't sure. I mean, if she wasn't pregnant—"

"It is also easier for the jury to identify with the victim when they believe the victim to be an innocent person, totally undeserving of such a brutal end," I said. "Then the jury gets mad and wants to bash the betrayer, the sexual exploiter, the predator in our midst. Marvin Pomroy is going to talk about Roseanne's innocence and your guilt, her vulnerability...her trusting attitude...and your depravity."

Lucas nodded his head as though he understood. But his eyes were as clear as glass, and he had no comprehension of what a good prosecutor like Marvin Pomroy could do to him.

"We need to show the jury the videotape of Roseanne smoking a joint and taking off her clothes. They'll also see the kind of kids she hung around with," I said.

He pushed his plate away with the heel of his hand, his eyes blinking.

"The tape simply shows the world she lived in, Lucas," Temple said. "Dope and booze and getting it on with lots of guys. We're not knocking her. That's just the way it was."

"She might have done all them things you say, but that don't mean she wasn't a good girl," he said.

"That's true. But somebody else killed her, Lucas. Maybe his face is on that tape," I said.

His right hand was clenched on the back of his left wrist. His throat was splotched with color.

"I ain't going along with this," he said.

"Excuse me?" I said.

"I was sleeping with Roseanne and told you I didn't hardly know her. That makes me a liar and a coward. I ain't gonna get myself off by seeing her tore down in front of all them people."

"You really want to go to prison? Is that what you're telling me?" I said.

"Maybe I deserve to be there."

"What?" I said.

"You say Darl doped me. Maybe I was just drunk. I'll never know the truth about what I done that night."

He was bent over in the chair, his head hung forward. The glare through the blinds made strips of light on his back.

"Lucas, we need to clear something up here. There's only one person in this room running your defense," Temple said.

But I motioned at her with two fingers. She looked at me with a puzzled expression, then chewed on the corner of her lip and stared silently out the window.

That evening I took off my shirt and hung it on a fence rail and raked out the chicken run and horse lot and dumped a load of manure and decayed straw in the compost pile, then filled a bucket with water from the windmill pipe and began digging a line of postholes so I could reset the rail fence and enlarge the lot for Beau. It was a lovely evening. The sun had dipped below the hills, its last rays breaking into pink wagon spokes against the sky. The wind was blowing in the trees and I could smell wildflowers in the fields and bream spawning under the lily pads out in the tank. I almost didn't hear Brian Wilcox's car crunching up my drive.

He got out of the car and walked through both sets of barn doors into the lot. Behind him, I could see the Mexican drug agent, Felix Ringo, sitting in the passenger seat of the car, the window down to catch the breeze, his tropical hat on the back of his head.

Wilcox's mouth was painted with an ironic smile.

"You hang a revolver on a fence post while you work?" he said.

"Some guys blindsided me out here one night. I hate repeat situations," I said.

"You know what quid pro quo is, right, one thing for another?...I'm doing you a big one, Holland, but I want something in return."

"Go fuck yourself."

"That's kind of what I expected from you, but here it is, anyway. Mary Beth is coming back to give you the testimony you need, but you'd better not drag your shit into our investigation again."

"Meaning?"

"Our sun-darkened friend out there in the car is a valuable man. He doesn't get compromised."

I pulled the handles of the posthole digger out of the hole and knocked the dirt free from the blades, then tipped more water from the bucket into the hole.

"Nothing to say?" Wilcox asked.

"Yeah, that guy was at the School of the Americas at Fort Benning. Their graduates have a funny way of showing up in death squads and torture chambers."

"So maybe I don't like putting my fingers in bean dip. But the object is to make the case, right? All you've got to worry about is leaving us out of your trial."

Behind him, I saw Felix Ringo get out of the car and walk toward us.

"When's Mary Beth coming?" I asked.

"I thought I'd get your attention this time...Tonight, probably."

"I don't think you arranged this at all. I think she's coming on her own."

He pinched a breath mint out of a roll and slipped it in his mouth.

"You're quite a guy," he said.

Temple Carrol's car came up the drive and pulled around Wilcox's, disappeared beyond the side of the barn, then stopped by the windmill.

Felix Ringo walked up to Wilcox, ignoring me. He smoked a cigarette in a gold holder without removing it from his lips. "You finished talking here? I got to shower and meet a lady for dinner," he said.

I heard Beau's hooves thudding behind me. I turned and saw him spooking back against the fence rails, walleyed, his head tossing.

I stared at Felix Ringo. "He knows you," I said.

Ringo curved his fingertips into his sternum.

"Your horse knows me?" he said, his mustache winking.

"Beau never forgets children or a bad person. You've been here before, haven't you?" I said.

"I been here before? The horse knows I'm a bad guy or something, 'cause he's got this kind of computer memory?" Ringo's fingers gestured impotently in the air.

"You were one of the guys who attacked me. I thought the guy had a gold tooth. But it was your gold cigarette holder I saw."

Ringo removed his tropical hat, with the green plastic window in the brim, and wiped out the inside with a handkerchief.

"I'll be in the car," he said to Wilcox. "This guy here, he's got a disease in his thinking, like clap or something. I don't want to be hearing it no more."

He walked back through the open barn doors, the wind billowing his loosely buttoned shirt. The butt of a black automatic was pushed down in the back of his trousers.

"You got the wrong man. Felix works for us," Wilcox said.

"That's the problem," I said.

I thudded the blades of the posthole digger

into the hole and expanded the handles and turned them in a circle, the grain of the wood twisting against my calluses. I could feel the sweat in my eyebrows, my heart beating in my chest.

Brian Wilcox continued to stare at me, his mouth still painted with that ironic smile.

"So maybe this is the last time I see you," Wilcox said.

He's going to do it, I thought.

I lifted the posthole digger free and rinsed the blades in the bucket of water. The wind popped in my ears, as though it were filled with distant pistol reports. I opened and closed my mouth and pressed with one thumb under my right ear.

"You all right?" he asked, and cupped his hand on my bare shoulder. I could feel the heat and oil in his skin, as though he were rubbing a layer of fouled air into my pores.

Don't let it happen, I told myself.

"Sorry we tossed your house," he said.

"Forget it."

"About Mary Beth..."

"Yes?"

"She'll come for you a second time, but you have to stay on top. There's something about the missionary position with her. She just can't get over the crest when she's sitting on you."

I caught him right below the bottom lip, saw his teeth bare and his mouth go out of shape with the blow; then I drove my fist into his eye socket, hooked him with my left in the nose and hit him again in the mouth. His knees buckled and his head bounced off a fence rail. I felt him try to grab my waist as he went down, his eyes wide with fear, like those of a man who realizes he has slipped forever off a precipice, and I knew the old enemy had once more had its way and something terrible was happening in me that I couldn't stop.

He was at my feet now, his face strung with blood, his tie twisted backward on his neck, his chest laboring for breath.

Then among the thud of Beau's hooves, I saw Felix Ringo running at me through the tunnel of light inside the barn, simultaneously pulling back the slide on his nine-millimeter, his hat blowing off his head.

"You wasn't born, *gringo*. You was picked out of your mother's shit. This is for them people you killed down in Coahuila," he said.

My hands felt swollen and useless at my sides, my chest running with sweat in the wind, the spilled water bucket ballooning in the dust by my feet. I could hear the blades on the windmill clattering like a playing card clipped inside whirling bicycle spokes. Felix Ringo extended the nine-millimeter in front of him with both hands, crouched in a shooter's position, as though he were on a practice range, and flipped off the butterfly safety with his thumb.

Temple Carrol stooped under the top fence rail, ripped L.Q. Navarro's revolver from the holster I had hung on a fence post, and screwed the barrel right behind Ringo's ear. She cocked the hammer, locking the cylinder in place.

"How your pud hanging, greaseball? You want to wear your brain pan on your shirt?" she asked.

CHAPTER

29

There was no false dawn the next morning. The sky was a black lid above the velvet green crest of the hills, the clouds veined with lightning. I opened all the windows and let the smell of ozone and wind and distant rain fill the house. Mary Beth called while I was fixing breakfast.

"Where are you?" I asked.

"At the hotel downtown."

"When did you get in?"

"Late. I went right to bed."

"I could have picked you up."

"You mean if I'd called?"

"No, I meant—"

"My schedule's not too predictable these days."

"I just didn't know when you were coming. That's what I meant."

"I heard about you tearing up Brian. What started it?"

"The conversation got out of hand."

"He won't file charges. His career's unraveling on him. He's one step from Fargo, North Dakota, already."

I felt my palm squeeze involuntarily on the telephone receiver.

"Can you take a cab out to the house? We can drive back into town together," I said.

"I have a bunch of incoming calls," she said.

"I see."

"Some people in my office weren't comfortable with me coming back here."

"Yeah...I understand. I appreciate your doing it."

I felt foolish and stupid, a mendicant holding a telephone to his ear as though it were a black tumor.

"When do I testify?" she asked.

"Probably this afternoon. Mary Beth, is it the career? Or am I just the wrong man for you?"

"I don't know how to say it, Billy Bob."

The house seemed to fill with the sounds of wind and silence.

"You always think of yourself as an extension of your past," she said. "So every new day of your life you're condemned to revisiting what you can't change."

"I'll be at the office directly if you have a chance to drop by," I said.

After I replaced the receiver I walked to the library window and looked at the darkness over the hills. The pages of my great-grandfather's journal fluttered whitely in the rush of wind through the screen. The silence in my head was so great I thought I heard the tinkling of L.Q. Navarro's roweled spurs.

An hour later Mary Beth walked from the hotel to my office. She wore a pink suit and white blouse with a purple brooch and looked absolutely beautiful. But if I had expected to mend my relationship with her at that moment, the prospect went out the window when Temple Carrol came through the door thirty seconds later.

The three of us were standing in a circle, like people who had met inconveniently at a cocktail party.

"Y'all know each other, of course," I said.

"Sure, the lady who pops in and out of uniform," Temple said.

"Excuse me?" Mary Beth said.

"Billy Bob kicked the ass of a federal agent. Has he told you about it?" Temple asked.

"No. Why don't you?" Mary Beth said.

"I don't remember the details very well. I was more worried about the Mexican dirtbag, what's his name, Felix Ringo, the greaseball who fronts points for y'all, he tried to use the situation to cap Billy Bob. A great guy to have on a federal pad," Temple said.

Mary Beth turned toward me. "I didn't know that," she said.

I pulled up the blinds loudly on a sky that swirled with storm clouds. The wind gusted under the trees on the courthouse lawn and blew leaves high in the air. "Let's talk about our agenda today," I said.

But *agenda* was the wrong word. The prosecution's case was not a complex one. Lucas Smothers was found passed out thirty feet from the homicide victim. He was sexually involved with her. He feared she carried his child. His semen, no one else's, was inside the victim's vagina. The pathologist would testify the damage to the genitalia indicated the assailant was probably driven by sexual rage. Lucas himself had told the arresting officers he had no memory of his actions after he had taken off his trousers in the pickup truck. Finally, Lucas had lied and denied even knowing Roseanne Hazlitt's last name.

But my problem was not with any evidence or possible testimony I had learned about in discovery. Instead, I had the brooding sense the loaded gun, the one pointed at Lucas's heart, was in my hand, not Marvin Pomroy's. But I didn't know what to do about it.

That afternoon Marvin rested his case, and while the rain drummed on the trees outside the window, I called Hugo Roberts to the stand.

His sheriff's uniform was freshly pressed, his brass name tag full of light on his pocket, an American flag sewn on the sleeve, but an odor of cigarettes and hair tonic and antiperspirant radiated from him as though it were sealed in his skin. He looked at the jury and spectators and at Marvin Pomroy and at the rain clicking on the windowsills, at virtually everything around him except me, as though I were of little consequence in his day.

"Your unit was the first one to arrive at the crime scene, sheriff?" I said.

"Yeah, I patrolled that area for the last couple of years. While I was a deputy, I mean."

"Have you run a lot of kids out of there?"

"Yeah, after dark, when they don't have no business being there."

I picked up a vinyl bag from the exhibit table and removed five Lone Star beer cans and two dirt-impacted wine bottles from it.

"Are these the cans and bottles you recovered at the crime scene, sir?" I asked.

"Yeah, that looks like them."

"They are or they aren't?"

"Yeah, that's them."

I introduced the cans and bottles into evidence, then walked back toward the stand.

"These were all you found?" I asked.

"That's what the report says. Five cans and two bottles." He laughed to himself, as though he were tolerating the ritual of a fool.

"Since those bottles were probably there for years, I won't ask you about them. Whose fingerprints were on the beer cans?"

"Lucas Smothers's and the victim's."

"Nobody else's?"

"No, sir."

"Do teenage kids drink and smoke dope out there with some regularity?" I asked.

"I guess some do."

"But you found no cans or bottles that would indicate anybody else had used that picnic ground recently besides Lucas Smothers and Roseanne Hazlitt?"

"I cain't find what ain't there. Street people pick up gunny sacks of that stuff. Maybe I should have stuck some used rubbers in there."

Spectators and some of the jury laughed before the judge tapped her gavel. "Lose the attitude in a hurry, sheriff," she said.

"Sheriff, why do you think the prosecution didn't introduce the evidence you put in that vinyl bag?" I said.

"Objection, calls for speculation," Marvin said.

"Overruled. Answer the question, Sheriff Roberts," the judge said.

"How the hell should I know?" he replied.

After a ten-minute recess, I called Mary Beth to the stand. The windows were raised halfway; rain dripped from the trees out on the lawn and a fine mist floated through the window screens. Mary Beth wore little makeup and sat erect in the witness chair, her hands folded.

"You were the second deputy to arrive at the picnic ground?" I asked.

"Yes, that's correct."

"You saw Hugo Roberts pick up a number of bottles and cans from the area around Lucas Smothers's truck?"

"Yes, sir."

"How many cans and bottles would you say he recovered?"

"Maybe a couple of dozen," Mary Beth replied.

"Objection, relevance, your honor. This

beer can stuff is a red herring. A thousand fingerprints on other cans or bottles doesn't put anybody else at the crime scene when the assault was committed," Marvin said.

"I was trying to point out that Hugo Roberts and others either lost or deliberately destroyed exculpatory evidence," I said.

"Approach," the judge said. She leaned forward on her forearms, her hand covering the microphone. "What's going on here, Mr. Pomroy?"

"Nothing, your honor. That's the point. Mr. Holland is trying to distract and confuse the jury."

"Destroyed evidence, whether or not of probative value, still indicates conspiracy, your honor," I said.

"What's your explanation, Mr. Pomroy?" she said.

"Incompetence has never precluded membership in the sheriff's department," he replied.

"That's not adequate, sir. You're too good a prosecutor to let some redneck bozos jerk you around. You'd better get your act together. Don't be mistaken, either. This isn't over. I'll see you later in chambers...Step back," she said.

Flowers for Stonewall Judy, I thought.

Then Marvin began his cross-examination of Mary Beth.

"Who's your employer, Ms. Sweeney?" he asked.

"The Drug Enforcement Administration."

"The DEA?"

"Yes."

"Were you employed by the DEA while you were working as a deputy sheriff in this county?"

"Yes."

"Did you tell anyone that?"

"No."

"Did you lie about your background when you went to work for the department?"

"Technically, yes."

"Technically? In other words, you came here as a spy, a federal informer of some kind, and lied about what you were doing. But you're not lying to us now? Is that correct?" Marvin said.

"Your honor," I said.

"Mr. Pomroy," she said.

"I have nothing else for this witness," he said.

Temple Carrol handed me a note over the spectator rail. It read, *Garland Moon's at your office and won't leave. You want him picked up?*

Stonewall Judy granted a twenty-minute recess, and I put a raincoat over my head and walked across the street and up the stairs of my building. Moon sat in the outer office, wearing a gray, wide-necked weight lifter's shirt, with palm trees and VENICE BEACH, CALIFORNIA ironed on the front, and tennis shoes and gray running pants with crimson stripes down the legs. His face knotted with self-satisfied humor when he saw me.

"Got you away from your pup. I 'spect you study a lot more on me than you admit," he said.

"Go inside my office," I said.

He picked himself up lazily from the chair, arching a crick out of his neck, flexing his shoulders. When he went through the doorway into the inner office, he casually scratched a match on the wooden jamb and lit a cigarette with it.

"Billy Bob, I hope someone kills that man," Kate, my secretary, said.

I went into the inner office and closed the door behind me. Moon stood at the window, one finger pulling the blinds into a V, staring down at the wet street, at the people who moved along on it, oblivious to the pair of blue eyes that followed them.

"A rich person made me a deal. Kind of work a man like me can handle," he said.

"Get to it, Moon."

"Money ain't no good to me. I want the place should have been mine. At least part of it."

"You want what?"

"Ten acres, on the back of your property, along the river there. I'll build my own house, one of them log jobs. With a truck patch and some poultry, I'll make out fine."

"What do I get?"

"I'll fuck whoever you want with a wood rasp. I done things to folks you couldn't even guess at."

"I think your benefactor will use you for a golf tee, Moon."

330

I saw the heat climb from his throat into his face.

"There's a kid hereabouts thinks he's a swinging dick 'cause he can throw a football—" Then Moon caught himself, his mouth drawn back on his teeth.

"You molested a little Negro girl when you were sixteen. That's why my father fired you off the line," I said.

He walked to my desk and mashed out his cigarette. His arms were still damp from the rain and his muscles knotted and glistened like white rubber.

"The little girl lied. It was her uncle done it," he said.

"You were at Matagorda Bay when my father was killed in 1965."

His eyes lighted and crinkled at the corners.

"You're hooked, ain't you?" he said.

"Nope, it's just time for you to find another wallow. Deal with that wet rat that's eating out your insides."

He sucked his teeth, then scraped a thumbnail inside one nostril, his expression hidden. "You got a mean streak, boy, but I know how to put the stone bruise down in the bone," he said.

He strolled through the outer office into the hallway, dragging one finger across the secretary's desk.

I opened the windows, heedless of the rain that blew in on the rug, then told the secretary to call the police if Moon came back again.

When I walked down the stairs into the foyer, he was waiting for me. The rain danced on the street and sidewalk and gusted inside the archway.

"Your mama probably told you your daddy died a brave man," he said. "He was rolling around in the dirt, squealing like a charbroiled hog, praying and begging folks to take him to a hospital, his pecker hanging out his pants like a white worm. I went behind the toolshed and laughed till I couldn't hardly breathe."

I took a yellowed free newspaper from a mailbox that had no cover. I unfolded it and popped the wrinkles out. I walked to within six inches of Moon's face, saw the skin under his recessed eye twitch involuntarily.

"Here, Garland, put this over your head so you don't get wet. That's a real frog-stringer out there," I said, and crossed the street through the afternoon traffic.

CHAPTER

30

Virgil Morales, the San Antonio Purple Heart, was my next witness. He wore knife-creased white slacks, tasseled loafers, a purple suede belt, and a short-sleeve shirt scrolled with green and purple flowers. His freshly combed hair looked like wet duck feathers on the back of his neck. His walk was loose and relaxed, his eye contact with the jury deferential and respectful; in fact, he had transformed from bad-ass biker into the image of an innocuous, slightly vain, blue-collar kid who simply wanted to cooperate with the legal system. I couldn't have wished for a better witness.

"You're sure the defendant was unconscious while Roseanne Hazlitt was alive?" I said.

"The guy was a bag of concrete. You could look in his eyes and nobody was home. I was worried about him," Virgil replied.

"Worried?"

"I thought he might be dead."

Then the judge asked Marvin if he wished to cross-examine, and I knew I had a problem.

"No questions at this time, your honor. But I'd like to reserve the right to recall the witness later," he said.

It was 4:25 when Jamie Lake took the stand, which meant she would be the last witness of the day, and it was her testimony that would be the most clear and influential in the jury's memory overnight. I couldn't believe her appearance. She had showed up in sandals, hoop earrings, faded jeans that barely clung to her hips, and a tie-dye beach shirt that exposed the dragons tattooed on her shoulders. She had peroxided her hair in streaks and pinned it up on her head like a World War II factory worker. She popped her gum on the way to the stand, her hips undulating, and let her eyes rove across the jury box as though she were looking at chickens perched in a henhouse.

This time Marvin didn't pass on cross-examination.

"Did you think the defendant was dead?" he asked.

"No," she answered.

"Why not?"

"Because he was breathing. Dead people don't breathe."

"Thank you for telling us that. Did anybody pay you to come here today?" he asked.

"No," she replied.

"Did anybody pay your friend Virgil Morales to come here today?"

She chewed her gum and turned her right hand in the air, looking at the rings on her fingers.

"Did you understand the question?" Marvin said.

"Yeah, I'm thinking. How come you question me and not him? Like, I'm dumb and he's smart, or I'm smart and Virgil's a beaner can't understand big words?" she replied.

"Have you been using any narcotics today, Ms. Lake?"

"Yeah, I just scored some crystal from the bailiff. Where'd they get you?"

Then Marvin introduced into evidence the subpoenaed bank records of both Jamie Lake's and Virgil Morales's checking accounts.

"You and Virgil both made deposits of five thousand dollars on the same day three weeks ago, Ms. Lake. How'd y'all come by this good fortune?" Marvin said.

"I didn't make a deposit. It just showed up on my statement," she said.

"It has nothing to do with your testimony today? Just coincidence?"

"I was UA-ed and I took a polygraph."

"What you took is money."

"What's-his-face over there, Lucas, looked like a corpse that fell out of an icebox. You don't like what I tell you, go play with your suspenders. Excuse me, I take that back. Go fuck yourself, you little twit."

Set up and sandbagged, and I had walked right into it.

An hour later I drove Mary Beth to our small airport. The windows of my car were beaded with water, and lightning forked without sound into the hills.

"Don't feel bad," she said.

"It was a slick ruse. Those two kids were telling the truth, but somebody gave them money and turned them into witnesses for the prosecution."

"Felix Ringo and Jack Vanzandt sent them to you?"

"Let's talk about something else."

"Sorry."

There was nothing for it. Everything I said to her was wrong. We stood under a dripping shed and watched a two-engine plane taxi toward us, its propellers blowing water off the airstrip. I felt a sense of ending that I couldn't give words to.

"I didn't do you much good, did I?" she said.

"Sure you did."

"I have to think over some things. I'll be better about calling this time," she said.

Then a strange thing happened, as though I were an adolescent boy caught up in his sexual fantasies. I hugged her lightly around the shoulders, my cheek barely touching hers, but in my mind's eye I saw her undressed, smelled the heat in her skin, the perfume that rose from her breasts, felt her bare stomach press against my loins. It wasn't lust. It was an unrequited desire, like a flame sealed inside my skin, one that would not be relieved and that told me I was completely alone. For just a moment I understood why people drank and did violent things.

"So long," she said.

"Good-bye, Mary Beth."

"Watch your butt."

"You bet."

I watched her plane take off in the rain, its wings lifting steadily toward a patch of blue in the west. I got in my car and drove back to town. The hills were sodden and green under clouds that churned like curds from burning oil tanks.

L.Q. Navarro was waiting for me when I got home. He leaned his hands on the windowsill in the library and looked out at a cold band of light on the western horizon.

"It's been a mighty wet spring," he said.

"I might have blown the trial today, L.Q."

"You know what you got on your side? It's that boy's character. He's got sand. You know why?"

"Tell me."

"He's your son."

"You always looked after me, L.Q."

"Know how I'd run it? Put that boy on the stand and let the jury see what he's made of."

I still had my hat on. I sat in the stuffed leather chair in the corner and pulled my hat brim down over my eyes. I could hear L.Q.'s spurs tinkling on the rug.

"That DEA woman got you down?" he asked.

"Remember the time we went to that beer garden in Monterrey? The mariachi bands were playing, and you flamenco danced with that lady who played the castanets. It was cool every night and we could see fires out in the hills when the sun went down. Life was real good to us then, wasn't it?" I said.

"What's her name, Mary Beth, I still think she's a right good gal. Sometimes you got to let a mare have her head."

"Hope you won't take offense, L.Q., but how about shutting up? I said.

"Read your great-grandpa's journal. All good things come to the righteous and the just."

I fell asleep amid the sounds of distant thunder. When I woke up a half hour later, L.Q. was gone and Bunny Vogel was banging on my door.

He sat at my kitchen table with a cup of coffee in his hand, his bronze hair splayed damply on his neck.

337

"Start over again," I said.

"The old man was in the sack with this woman works at the mill. He said he'd latched the screen. He figures Moon slipped a match cover in it and popped the hook up. It was the gal, Geraldine's her name, who saw him first. She goes, 'Herbert, there's a man in the doorway. He's watching us,' and she rolls the old man off her and tries to pull the sheet over herself.

"Moon was leaning against the doorway, smoking a cigarette, tipping his ashes in his hand. The old man says, 'You get the fuck out of here.'

"Moon says, 'I wouldn't let that in my bed unless I painted it with turpentine and run castor oil through it first.'

"The old man says, 'I got a gun in my drawer.' Moon laughs and goes, 'A fat old fart like you would have to Vaseline his finger to get it through the trigger guard.'

"Then he picks up Geraldine's dress and tosses it at her and says, 'Go 'head on, woman. I ain't interested in what you got.'

"The old man tried to get up, and Moon pushed him back down with three fingers. A big fat naked guy, wheezing on cigarettes, trying to get off the mattress while another guy kept shoving him down."

"What did Moon tell him?"

"He says, 'Sorry I missed Bunny. I hear he ripped some Longhorn ass up at A&M. I like that.'"

"Nothing else?"

Bunny stared at the door of the icebox, widening his eyes, flexing his jawbone, as though he were watching a moving picture on the unblemished whiteness of the door. Then his throat made a muted sound and he started over and said, "He put my old man's nose between his fingers and squeezed and twisted it. He kept smiling down at him while he done it."

The whites of Bunny's eyes had turned pink and glistened with an unnatural shine, like the surface of a peeled hard-boiled egg that's been tainted with dye. He stared down into his coffee cup.

"There's something else, isn't there?" I said.

He shook his head.

"What is it, Bunny?

"The old man had me drop him at the bus depot. He said he was gonna visit my grandma in Corpus. He said I ought to do the same."

"Don't be too hard on him," I said.

Then Bunny began to weep.

"What are you hiding, kid? What makes you so ashamed?" I asked.

But he didn't reply.

I couldn't sleep. I went to the café by the church to eat a late dinner, but it was closed. So I drove to the drive-in restaurant north of town, that neon-lighted square of neutral territory that was dominated by East Enders during the week because of the amount of money they had to spend and their freedom from jobs and responsibility. Or maybe it was the only place where they could take their secret need and see it in the faces of others and for a short time not be bothered by its presence in themselves.

I sat in a red vinyl booth by the window and looked through the rain at the line of parked cars under the canvas awning that had been pulled out on guy wires. The windows of the cars were steamed from the inside, some of the engines running, the tailpipes wisping tongues of smoke in the rain. Occasionally, a cigarette would drop sparking from a wind vane, or a shoulder, a clutch of hair, would press against the glass. But no one, at least not I, knew what went on inside each of those hand-buffed, lacquered, chopped and channeled cars whose surfaces seemed to ignite like colored flame when touched by neon.

It was a week night, so the kids inside those cars were not the kind to worry about school. Did they neck with the innocent, dry lust of a previous generation? Or drink beer with a sense of discovery and wonder, as though the spring season and their own physical yearning and the brassy cold glow in the backs of their throats held a portent for them that was like an endless song? Was the greenness of their lives like a bursting flower scattering pollen from their open palms?

Or were they already bitten with ennui and hatred of one another, joyless in their couplings, insatiable in their disdain for difference without knowing why? Darl Vanzandt's '32 Ford was backed into the middle of the row under the canvas awning. Its cherry-red finish gleamed with the wet, hard luster of a tunnel wound. The passenger's window was rolled down, and Darl's bare arm was curled on the sill, the bicep pumped like a small, white grapefruit. A girl sat on his lap, combing his hair, shaping and reshaping it as though she were creating a sculpture. He turned his face toward the restaurant window and his expression was as morally empty, his eyes as sightless, as a perforated sack of skin stuffed with chemical jelly.

The waitress brought me a steak, with two fried eggs on top of it, and an order of refried beans and tortillas. I broke the egg yolks on the steak, sliced the meat in strips and rolled the strips with beans inside a tortilla. When I looked up, the girl from Darl's car was running through the rain for the restaurant. She came through the door, shaking water out of her hair, and dropped a quarter into the payphone by my booth, glancing back through the window, her slippered foot tapping on the floor.

"Mr. Vanzandt?...Yeah, it's Holly. Look, Darl's not exactly in good driving shape," she said. "Yeah, well, I'd drive him home and all that, but he just told me to take my diaphragm and get the fuck out of his life, so I think I'm just gonna say nighty-nighty and let somebody else clean up his shit. Bye, now."

After she hung up she looked at the phone and said, "Fuckhead," and went out the door.

While I was paying my check at the cash register, I saw Jack Vanzandt's Cadillac drive into the parking area with a black man behind the wheel and Jack get out in a pair of jeans and tennis shoes and a polo shirt and walk to his son's car. Darl still sat in the passenger's seat, but now with his head on his chest. Jack tipped Darl's head back and tried to wake him, but Darl's face was bloodless, his eyes closed, his skin glowing with the tallowy shine of melted wax.

By the time I started my Avalon, Jack had gotten behind the wheel of Darl's car and had driven the two of them to the highway's entrance. Jack was waiting for a line of traffic to pass so he could turn left, while I was about to turn right and go back to the West End. Then I had one of those moments that nullify all easy definitions about human behavior and the nature of love.

A pair of truck high beams flooded the interior of the chopped-down Ford with a naked white brilliance, and I saw Darl's head on his father's shoulder, his eyes still closed. Then Jack brushed something away from his boy's eye, a food crumb, perhaps, and kissed him on the forehead, his face filled with an undisguised grief.

It was still raining and dark at sunrise the next morning. I read from Great-grandpa Sam's journal at the breakfast table.

August 30, 1891

The preacher who ordained me had been branded in the face with burning horse shoes. He said all good things come to the righteous and the just. His words rose like snow flakes from the heat that had been seared into his skin. But today those words ring hollow on my ears. I have proved unworthy of my ordination. It is a folly for me to pretend otherwise.

Them in the mud caves are drunk tonight. They brought in two white prostitutes and killed a wild pig and cooked it in a brush fire on the river bank and danced around the flames to fiddle music. I have thought of heading south for the Red River and Texas, but federal marshals have been stationed along the tick-fever line to keep sick herds from trailing up to the railheads in Kansas and I will be served with a federal warrant and locked in manacles for sure.

My oil lamp has burned low and our little house is filled with shadows as I write these lines. The dirt in our garden is dry and cracked and swarming with insects, and Jennie is trying to swat the deer mice out of the melons and pumpkins with a burlap bag. It won't do no good, but I will not try to tell her that.

It is hard for me to think of myself as a fugitive from the law. The idea of it makes the insides of my hands sting as though bitten by sweatbees. Them from the mud caves are dipping whiskey out of the busted head of a barrel now, framed in the firelight like painted Indians. At Little Round Top I watched soldiers, boys, really, die in the V of my musket sight. Those memories cause me grave regret, even though it was war. But now I see rocks high on the hill above the Cimarron, a sharpshooter's den made for a Henry repeater or Winchester rifle. Down below, the Doolins and Daltons tip their cups in the firelight. I have to wipe the sweat off my palms onto my britches and not think the thoughts I am thinking.

I tell myself, Better to slake thirst with whiskey than blood. But if I have come to this, I know my life as a drunkard is about to begin again. Tomorrow I'm going to ride north to the court in Wichita and leave the Rose of Cimarron behind. I have great trepidation about my treatment in a Yankee court and do not know if I will ever see her or Texas again. I hear tell a Scottish slaver wrote the beautiful hymn "Amazing Grace." I never thought much on the words "a wretch like me" until this moment.

I'll ride through the camp below the mud caves in the morning, just so the Daltons and Doolins can never say they didn't have a chance at my back. Emmett can usually control the others, but if he ain't around, maybe my stay on the Cimarron won't end so bad after all.

CHAPTER

31

The next day Marvin Pomroy recalled Virgil Morales to the stand and tore him up. After Marvin sat back down, I looked over at his table. His coat hung on the back of his chair, and his white shirt looked as bright as new snow against his fire-engine-red suspenders. He saw me looking at him and raised his eyebrows and shrugged. Marvin didn't take prisoners.

During a midmorning recess Emma Vanzandt rose from a bench in the corridor outside the courtroom and stopped me and Temple Carrol. Darl remained seated behind her, dressed like a fraternity boy, in gray slacks and a blue sports coat, a gold chain and tiny gold football strung outside the collar of his shirt.

"Got a minute?" she said. Her face was heavily made up, and threadlike lines spread from her eyes and the sides of her mouth when she feigned a smile for passersby.

"Sorry," I said. Down the corridor I saw Jack Vanzandt buying a cigar at the concession counter.

Emma's thumb and index finger circled my wrist.

"Don't do this," she said.

"What?"

"Blame the girl's death on Darl."

"He's not a defendant."

"Don't insult me, Billy Bob."

"Your boy's never been made accountable. Why don't y'all let him stand on his own for once?"

"Jack's made arrangements to send him to a treatment center in California. It's a one-year in-patient program. For God's sakes, give us a chance to correct our problem."

"Darl came out to my house. He offered to give up his father," I said.

"He offered to—" Her face had the startled, still quality of someone caught in a photographer's strobe.

"You've got a monster in your house, Emma. Whatever happens in this courthouse won't change that," I said.

Temple and I left her standing in the middle of the corridor, her mouth moving soundlessly while her stepson snipped his fingernails on the bench behind her.

Temple and I went up to the second floor of the courthouse and bought cold drinks from the machine and drank them by a tall, arched window at the end of the hall. It had stopped raining temporarily, but the streets were flooded and the wake from passing automobiles slid up onto the courthouse lawn.

"You bothered about what you said to Emma?" Temple asked.

"Not really."

"If you're worried about hanging it on Darl Vanzandt—"

"The jury won't see motive in Darl. We can make him an adverb but not a noun."

She was silent. I heard her set her aluminum soda can on top of the radiator.

"You want to spell it out?" she asked.

"Bunny Vogel's going to have a bad day," I said.

"Wrong kid for it."

"Damn, I wish I could adjust like that. 'Wrong kid for it.' That's great."

I walked back down the hall to the stairs, my boots echoing off the wood floor.

She caught me halfway down, stepped in front of me on the landing, her arms pumped. A strand of her chestnut hair was curved on her chin. "There's one person only, *one*, who has always been on your side. Sorry I never let you fuck me a few times so I could leave town without even a phone call. You only get that kind of loyalty with federal grade," she said.

She walked down the rest of the stairs alone, the anger in her eyes her only defense against tears. I stood in the silence, wondering what the final cost of Lucas's trial would be.

After Darl Vanzandt took the oath he sat at an angle in the witness chair, lowered his eyes coyly, as though the world's attention were upon him, played with his class ring, suppressed a smile when he looked at his friends.

"Bunny Vogel used to go out with Roseanne Hazlitt, didn't he?" I asked.

"Everybody knows that."

"Is Bunny your friend?"

"He used to be."

"He looked out for you at Texas A&M, didn't he?"

"We were from the same town, so we hung out."

"He paid off a grader to change an exam score for you, didn't he?"

Darl's green eyes looked at nothing, then clouded and focused on me for the first time, as though the words he heard had to translate into a different language before they became thoughts in his mind. He rubbed the peach fuzz on his jawline. "Yeah, we both got expelled," he said.

"Did your stepmother get him a job at the skeet club?"

"Yeah."

"You double-dated and you hung out at the drive-in restaurant together?"

"Sometimes."

"I'd say y'all were pretty tight, right?"

"That was then, not now."

"You let people get in your face, Darl?"

"What d' you mean?"

"Dis you, push you around, act like you're a woosh?"

"No, I don't take that stuff."

"What happened to the Mexican kid who scratched up your car with a nail?"

"I kicked his ass, that's what."

"Because people don't get in your face and

abuse your property, right? You stomp their ass?"

"Yeah, that's right."

"You ever beat up a woman, a prostitute in San Antonio by the name of Florence LaVey?"

"No, I didn't. I protected myself from people who were rolling me."

"What happens when people hit your friends, Darl? You kick their ass, too."

"You goddamn right." He looked at his friends and grinned.

"Did you see Roseanne Hazlitt slap Bunny Vogel the night she was attacked?"

He pushed at his nose with the flats of his fingers. His eyes were threaded with veins, fixed on mine.

"Yeah. At Shorty's. It wasn't a big deal. She always had her head up her hole about something," he said.

"It made you mad to see your friend get hit, didn't it?"

"No. I bought her and Lucas a drink. I wasn't mad at anybody."

"Is that when you put roofies—downers—in Lucas's drink?" I asked.

"Objection, your honor. He's badgering and leading his own witness," Marvin said.

"Withdrawn," I said. "Darl, why'd Roseanne slap Bunny Vogel?"

"She said she was getting baptized. She wanted him to take her to this holy-roller church that's on TV."

"Baptized?"

"I told you, she had boards in her head. She goes, 'Do something decent for a change. Take me to my baptism. Maybe it'll wash off on you.' So Bunny says, 'Let's take a drive. I'll roll down the windows so you can air the reefer out of your head.'

"She goes, 'I'm going down to the Lakewood Church in Houston. I done talked to the preacher already.'

"Bunny says, 'Shorty's is a funny kind of church house to show folks you been saved.' She goes, 'I'm here to meet Lucas Smothers. At least he don't treat his old friends like yesterday's fuck.' Another guy goes, 'That's 'cause you're Lucas's reg'lar fuck now.'

"Bunny put his hand on her arm and said he'd take her home. That's when she slapped him. She walked on inside and shot him the bone."

Darl's eyes smiled at his friends.

"Did Roseanne once work in the same church store you do, Darl?"

I saw a thought, like a yellow-green insect, catch in his eye. Then I realized his distraction had nothing to do with my question. He was staring at a spectator in the back of the courtroom. The spectator, Felix Ringo, sat by the aisle with his tropical hat on his knee, one elbow propped on the chair arm, three fingers resting across his mouth.

"What's that got to do with anything?" Darl asked.

"Answer the question," the judge said.

"Yeah, she worked there," Darl said.

"Who got her the job?" I asked.

350

"My parents did. They felt sorry for her 'cause she had a crummy life."

"How'd your parents know Roseanne Hazlitt, Darl?"

"Bunny brought her over. You saying I was mixed up with her? I wouldn't touch her. It was probably like the Houston Ship Channel down there."

He leaned forward mischievously, his eyes bright under his blond brows, as though in leaning closer to his friends, whose faces were lit with the same mocking grin as his, he shut out the rest of the courtroom.

"Did you and your friends dope Lucas Smothers and strip off his clothes and pour a bucket of feces on him at the country club? Did you vandalize his house? Did you try to threaten me at my home? Did you murder an indigent man, Darl?"

"Mr. Holland, you're way beyond anything I'll allow," the judge said.

"Withdrawn," I said.

Darl got down from the stand, his face stupefied, his mouth round and wordless, his teeth exposed like those of a hungry fish.

At noon Marvin Pomroy caught me in the corridor and asked me into his office. He sat down behind his desk, took his glasses off, and rubbed one eyebrow with the back of his wrist.

"I'm not comfortable with some stuff that's going on here," he said.

"Gee, Marvin, sorry to hear that," I said.

"I checked into this threat Moon supposedly made against Bunny Vogel and his father. But there's no handle on it...He walked into their house without knocking."

"So why tell me about it?"

He picked up a sheet of pink carbon paper from his desk blotter.

"That gal down the road from you, Wilma Flores, the mother of the little boy who's always fishing in your tank?" he said.

"Pete's mother."

"Yeah, that his name, Pete. She made a 911 at five this morning. She was showering to go to work. She went to wipe off the bathroom window to see if it was still raining outside. Six inches from her face is a guy with tufts of red hair slicked down on his head and blue eyes like she's never seen in a human being before."

I felt a tingling, a deadness, in my hands that made me open and close my palms.

"The deputy put it down as a Peeping Tom incident. Nothing would have come of it, except I heard him talking about it when I was in the bullpen this morning. I made him go back out to the house with mug shots of Garland Moon and five other of our graduates. The deputy said she took one look at Moon's photo and wouldn't even touch it with her finger when she identified him," Marvin said.

"Where's Pete now?"

"At school. I'll put a deputy at their house this afternoon."

"Your deputies are worthless. Did you pick up Moon?"

"He has two witnesses who say he was eating breakfast in a diner at five A.M."

"You believe them?"

"It's a Peeping Tom complaint. Even if we could charge him, he'd be out on bond in an hour."

Then his defensiveness, his frustration with me and his job went out of his face.

"I called the lady and offered to keep Pete at our house for a while. She said I was helping Social Services take her little boy from her...Where you going?" he said.

Stonewall Judy granted a recess until the following morning.

I drove home and went into the barn, unlocked the tack room and sorted through the garden hoes and rakes and mauls and picks and axes that were stacked inside an old Mayflower moving drum. The edges of the tools were flecked with bits of dried mud and tangles of dead weeds from cleaning the vegetable garden and flower beds in the early spring, or strung with resinous wisps of pine from the cords of wood I had split last fall. But I knew the tool I was looking for.

It was a mattock whose heavy, oblong iron head had already worn loose from the helve. I clamped a pair of vise grips on the wedge that held the handle fast inside the mattock head, twisted it out of the wood, and slipped the handle free. It was made from ash, thick across the top to support the weight of the iron head, the grain worn smooth at the grip. I propped it on the passenger seat in the Avalon and headed down the road to town just as a curtain of rain moved in a steady line across the clumped-up herd of red Angus in my neighbor's draw.

I parked behind the tin shed where Moon worked. The rain pattered on my slicker and the brim of my Stetson as I pulled open the back door of the shed. A black man in a bikini swimsuit with a yellow rag tied around his head was grinding a metal bracket on an emery wheel.

"Hep you?" he asked.

"Is this your shop?"

"What you want?"

"Garland Moon."

His eyes went over my person. "That a chunk of wood under your raincoat?"

"It's been that kind of day."

He nodded. "He gone down to Snooker's Big Eight."

"You going to use the telephone on me?"

"Rather y'all do it there than here…Tell you something, a man like that is looking for somebody to click off his switch. You don't do it, he'll find the right man sooner or later."

I drove a half mile down the road to a bluff above the river and a long wood building that was ventilated with window fans and set in a grove of oak trees that had been the site of a beer garden during the 1940s. The parking lot was full of pickup trucks and motorcycles, and rain was blowing through the trees and streaking on the front windows, which glowed with purple and red neon.

I walked the length of the building, stepping across puddles, looking through the spinning blades of fans at the felt tables, pinball machines that swam with light, bikers drinking beer at the bar, an enormous Confederate flag ruffling against the far wall. Then I looked through a screen door and saw him bent over a cue, sighting on the diamond-shaped nine-ball rack, the triceps of his poised right arm knotted with green veins. He drove the cue ball into the rack like a spear.

He raised up, his mouth smiling at the perfection of the break, his fingers reaching for the chalk. Then he heard the screen open and close behind him and he turned toward me just as I whipped the mattock handle, edge outward, across his jaw.

His knees buckled slightly, and a choked sound, a grunt, came out of his throat. He pressed his hand against his cheek as though he had a toothache, his eyes glazing with shock and surprise, and I hit him again, this time whipping the helve across his mouth.

His pool cue had clattered to the floor. He looked at it rolling away from him, his mouth draining blood on the apron of the table, and I hit him again, in the ribs, and again in the head, the neck, across the ear; then Moon was stumbling out the back screen door, through the trees, along the edge of the bluff. Down below, the river was covered with rain rings.

I swung the mattock handle with both hands across his spine. I seemed to slip out of time and place, as though I had been absorbed into a red-black square of film that was like the color of fire inside oil smoke. Then, like a man awakening from a dream, I realized the mattock handle was no longer in my grasp, that I was on one knee beside him, his head lolling against a tree trunk, my fist driving into his face.

"That's enough, motherfucker," a voice said behind me.

I turned and looked up into the disjointed, heated eyes of a booted man in a leather vest whose body glowed with odor.

"Private conversation," I said. But my words sounded outside my skin, as though they had been spoken by someone else and I heard them through the rain. The back of my right fist was flecked with Moon's blood.

A biker next to him studied my face and extended his arm across his friend's chest.

"His name's Holland. Sonofabitch is crazy. Leave him alone. Snooker done already called the Man," he said.

They and those who had followed them walked away, their boots splashing in puddles, as though water had no effect on their clothes and bodies, their hair blowing in the wind like dirty string.

I looked again at Moon, his face, the tree he lay against, the grass stains on his elbows, the skinned lesions around his eyes, the rain dripping out of the overhead branches, all of it coming into focus now, my breath quieting in my throat, as though a bird with blood in its beak had flown out of my chest.

"You think you're conwise, but somebody's laughing at you, Moon, just like those gunbulls did when they draped you over a barrel and made a girl out of you," I said.

He pushed his back up against the tree, wincing slightly, grinning at me. He started to speak, then cleared his mouth and spit in the grass and started over.

"This don't mean nothing. I done something to you won't ever change," he said.

"The people who hired you are the same people who tried to run you out of town earlier."

He grinned again and wiped his nose on his sleeve, but I saw my words catch in the corner of his eye.

"You and Jimmy Cole wandered into something you shouldn't out at the Hart Ranch. Then some guys tried to take you down with a baseball bat at your motel. The same guys jumped me behind my barn. One of them was a dude named Felix Ringo."

He looked out into the rain, his brow knurled, his recessed eye bright, brimming with water.

"A Mexican narc works out of San Antone?" he asked.

"Guy's got a nasty record, Moon. He likes to hurt people. But unlike you, he's got juice with the government."

"That don't change nothing between me and you."

"The Big C has its own clock."

"You still ain't caught on, have you? How come that pipe joint blowed out on your old man? 'Cause some kid lit a cigarette down in the bellhole?"

I stood up and straightened my back. I felt two long ribbons of pain slip down my spine and wrap around my thighs.

"Come on, boy. Ask me," he said. His legs forked out straight in front of him, like sticks inserted inside his trousers. His flat-soled prison work shoes glistened with mud.

I picked up my hat and slapped the dirt off it on my coat. "You come near Pete or his mother again, I'll shoot you through the lungs. It's a promise, Moon," I said, and started to walk away.

"I went back into the pump station and turned on the gas. That pipe was loaded when his arc bit into it. You ever watch a cat chewing on an electric cord? You ought to seen his face when it went," Moon said.

He began to laugh, holding his ribs because they hurt him, his face convulsing like a pixie's. He pushed the mattock handle at me with one shoe, trying to say something, shaking his head impotently at the level of mirth bursting from his chest.

Moon had to reach into the past to injure me, but across town, at that moment, Darl Vanzandt was buying a length of steel cable and a set of U-bolts, perhaps to prove that no matter what happened to Garland T. Moon, his legacy would be passed on to another generation in Deaf Smith.

CHAPTER

32

You followed Darl from the courthouse?" I said to Temple.

We sat on my back screen porch. Pete was in the house, watching television, and the yard was full of pools with islands of leaves floating in them.

"You rubbed his face in it, in front of his friends. A kid like that doesn't pray for his enemies," she said.

"I'm sorry for the stupid remark I made to you yesterday."

"I already forgot about it." She picked up her coffee spoon from her napkin and set it in her saucer.

I waited, but her eyes were deliberately empty, the balls of her fingers motionless on the table, and I said, "What's he want with a pair of U-bolts and twenty feet of steel cable?"

She shook her head, then said, "For some reason, those words and the name of Darl Vanzandt make my stomach crawl...You really gonna strike a match on Bunny's soul?"

"It's going to get even worse later."

She looked at me and then looked through the screen. Her face was quiet, full of the thoughts and connections that she seldom shared. Her shirt had pulled out of her jeans and her baby fat creased on her hips. "You want to have dinner with me and Pete?" she asked.

Pete's mother had consented to let him return to Temple's house for the next few days. That night we ate at a cafeteria, then I dropped them off and parked my car in back, turned on the flood lamps in the yard, poured some oats in Beau's stall, and walked all the way around the outside of the house with L.Q.'s .45 revolver under my raincoat.

Then I fell asleep on the third floor, with Great-grandpa Sam's journal open in my lap, an illogical image of torn steel cable and roaring car engines threading in and out of my dreams.

Bunny Vogel was dressed in a brown suit and sandals and a wash-faded pink golf shirt when he took the stand. He kept scratching his face with four fingers, as though an insect had burrowed into his cheek, and staring out into the courtroom, as though looking for someone who should have been there but wasn't.

I walked toward the jury box so Bunny would either have to face them when he answered my questions, or avert his eyes or drop his head. It wasn't a kind thing to do.

"Did you sleep with Roseanne Hazlitt, Bunny?" I asked.

"We went out in high school."

"Did you sleep with her?"

"Yes, sir."

"Would you say you loved her?"

"Yeah, I reckon. I mean, the way kids do."

"You were a senior and she was only fifteen when y'all met, is that right?"

"Yes, sir."

"Was she a virgin?"

"She told me she wasn't."

"You found out different, though, didn't you?"

He knitted his fingers together, glanced out at the courtroom, at the Vanzandts, the boys he had played football with, the Mexican girl he dated now, at the few empty seats in back where maybe his father would come in late and sit down.

"Bunny?"

"Yes, sir, I found out I was the first," he said.

"You hurt her, didn't you? You thought you should take her to a hospital?"

"Yes, sir."

"But not in the county where people might know you?"

He turned his head away from the jury and cleared his throat. "That's right," he said.

"The witness will speak up," the judge said.

"I was afraid. She was underage," Bunny said. He pushed himself up in the chair and rubbed his hand on the back of his neck.

"Then you went to A&M and dumped her?" I said.

"She didn't lack for boyfriends. She found some a whole lot better than me."

"Did you punch out Virgil Morales at Shorty's?"

"Yeah, we got a bad history."

"He called you a pimp?"

Bunny's right hand squeezed on his thigh. He ran his tongue over his lips. "Yeah, that's what he did," he said.

"How did Roseanne Hazlitt come to know Mr. and Mrs. Jack Vanzandt, Bunny?"

"I took her out to their house once. I intro—"

"Introduced her to whom?"

"Just what I said. I took her to their house."

His words were binding in his throat now, the scar along his jaw turning as dark as blood against his tan.

"Did you have sexual intercourse with Mrs. Vanzandt?" I asked.

"Relevance, your honor," Marvin said.

"I'll allow it," the judge said. "The witness will answer the question."

"I did it once. It was 'cause she was mad over something, I mean with her husband. She was like that," Bunny said.

"Did Roseanne ever slap you before that night at Shorty's?"

"No, sir."

"Roseanne said her baptism might wash off on you. Why was she so angry at you, Bunny? Why did she feel so betrayed?"

"'Cause she didn't have no friends left.

362

Except Lucas. He's the only one done right by her."

"But she wanted you to take her to her baptism? Because you owed her in a big way, didn't you?"

"I guess that's what she thought."

"Why did you owe her, Bunny? Why did she say her baptism might wash off on you?"

He kneaded his hands between his thighs, the balls of his feet tapping neurotically on the stand, his head pulled down on his chest. His long hair fell down around his throat like a girl's. "Answer the question, please," I said, but I had lowered my voice now, the way you do when you hope your own capacity for cruelty will be forgiven.

"I drove her to Dallas to meet Mr. Vanzandt. He rented three rooms at the Four Seasons, like there wasn't nothing unusual about him being with a couple of young people. But we all knew why we was there. I took her down to his room the first night, for drinks out on the balcony and all, but I left by myself," he said.

He rested his forehead on his fingers, staring numbly at the floor. Then he added, as though his own behavior had been explained to him by someone else, "That's what I done, all right."

Emma Vanzandt rose from her chair and walked down the aisle and out of the courtroom, her face like parchment about to wrinkle in a flame.

"How many times did you do this?" I asked.

"Whenever he wanted her. At least up until she thought she was pregnant and he told her to get it cut out of her, 'cause he wasn't gonna have no woods colt with his name on it..."

The only sound in the courtroom was the hum of the fans and the rain clicking on the windowsills. No one looked at Jack Vanzandt, except his son, who studied his father as though a strange and new creature whom he didn't recognize had just swum into his ken.

Fifteen minutes later a power failure darkened the building for three hours, and Temple and Lucas and I drove to a barbecue restaurant on a hill that overlooked the river outside of town. It had stopped raining, and the sky in the west was blue and you could see the shadows of clouds on the hillsides.

Lucas couldn't eat. I reached over and picked a piece of blood-dried tissue paper off his cheek where he had cut himself shaving.

"There's nothing to it. Just be who you are," I said.

"Be who I am?" he said.

Temple was watching my face.

"You heard me. Tell the truth, no matter what it is. When you go on that stand, you just be Lucas. Don't try to hide anything, don't try to manipulate the jury, don't back away from a question," I said.

"What are you gonna ask me?"

"I don't know."

He looked seasick.

"Do what Billy Bob tells you," Temple said.

He pressed his napkin to his mouth, then got up from the table and walked quickly to the men's room.

"You're gonna take him apart, huh?" Temple said.

We waited in my office until the power went back on in the courthouse, then a bailiff phoned me and we went downstairs and across the street and met Marvin Pomroy coming down the courthouse walk.

"I need to talk to you," he said to me.

"What's up?"

He looked at Temple and Lucas.

"I bet it's earth-shaking stuff, like prosecuting parking offenders in the most corrupt shithole in Texas," Temple said, and went up the walk with Lucas.

Marvin looked at her back, his eyes involuntarily dropping to her hips.

"You think she'd work for me?" he asked.

"How about getting to it, Marvin?"

"Getting to it? You stoked up Garland Moon and aimed him at this Mexican drug agent, didn't you?"

The air smelled of wet leaves and sewer mains swollen with rainwater and pavement drying in the sunlight. A sheriff's deputy led five black inmates in jailhouse whites past us on a wrist chain.

"Look at me!" Marvin said.

"Take it easy, Marvin."

"Felix Ringo's got a fuck pad at the Conquistador. He says a guy he swears is Garland Moon tried to get through the bathroom window. He says the guy was carrying one of these small chain saws, the kind you cut up cordwood with."

"That's bad news, isn't it?"

"Are you out of your mind? You bust up a psychopath with an ax handle, then screw down his dials and turn him loose on a policeman. You're supposed to be an officer of the court."

"How do you know I sent him after Ringo?"

"Because you're still a vigilante. Because you still think this is the O.K. Corral."

"Thanks for sharing, Marvin. I really appreciate it."

"Sharing? Moon trashed Ringo's place down in San Antone. Get this. He defecated on the upholstery. What's all this tell you?"

"He's terminal and knows it."

"Yeah, well, here's the surprise. Felix Ringo's getting a Mexican warrant on Moon for scoring some dope across the border. Moon might do time in a Mexican slam. The centipedes come free with the rice and beans."

"For some reason, you don't look all broken up."

"You're still not hearing me. When Moon gets word of this, and he will, who's he going to come after?"

"Well, you never know what's down at the bottom of the Cracker Jack box, Marvin."

He shook his head and walked away, trying to smooth the wrinkles out of the seersucker coat he held in his right hand, a good man who would forever serve causes that were not his own.

Lucas took the oath just after one o'clock. He sat very still in the witness chair, his hands splayed on his thighs, his face damp in the humidity. His throat was already streaked with color, as though it had been rouged.

"When you were first arrested, you said you hardly knew Roseanne Hazlitt. You said you didn't even know her last name. That was a lie, wasn't it?" I said.

"Yes, sir."

"Why would you lie like that?"

"'Cause she told me she was pregnant. 'Cause y'all would think it was me hurt her if y'all knew it was my baby..." He took a breath. "I lied 'cause I didn't have no guts."

"How'd you feel about Roseanne?"

"She was a good person. She couldn't hep the things she done, I mean, with drinking and that kind of stuff."

"Did she tell you who might have made her pregnant?"

"Objection, hearsay," Marvin said.

"I'll allow it," the judge said.

"Some older guy she was seeing in town. I didn't ask. It didn't make me feel too good."

"You thought the baby could be yours, didn't you?"

"Yes, sir."

"Why?"

"Sir?"

"Why did you think it could be yours?"

"'Cause we was making love."

"That's not what I'm asking you, Lucas. Did you use a condom?"

He rubbed his palms on his trousers and looked at the judge.

"Answer the question, please," she said.

"No, sir, we didn't use none," Lucas said.

"That sounds dumb to me. Why not?"

"Objection, your honor. He's badgering and cross-examining his own client," Marvin Pomroy said.

"Approach," the judge said. She took off her black-framed glasses and pushed aside the microphone. "What are you doing, Mr. Holland?" she said.

"I'm going to prove my client is psychologically incapable of having committed the crime," I replied.

"Psychologically incapable? Wonderful. Your honor, he's not only appointed himself the repository of Freudian thought, he's psychoanalyzing someone who was drunk," Marvin said.

"Mr. Holland?" the judge said.

"My client has taken the stand of his own volition, your honor. The rest of his life is at stake here. How can justice possibly be harmed by the questions I've asked?"

"Mr. Pomroy?" she said.

"I think he's turning this trial into a snake-oil show."

"I caution you, sir," she said.

"Mr. Holland says he means no harm. Neither does a skunk wandering into a church house," Marvin said.

"Your objection is noted and overruled. Mr. Holland, I'm giving you some unusual latitude here, but don't abuse it. Step back."

"Your honor—" Marvin said.

"Take a seat, Mr. Pomroy, and stay in it for a while, please," she said.

I walked to the right of the witness stand, so the jury would look into Lucas's face when he spoke.

"Let's forget that stuff about condoms, Lucas. What would you have done if Roseanne had been carrying your child?" I said.

"I wouldn't have done nothing."

"Would you have asked her to get an abortion?"

"No, sir."

"Why not?"

"'Cause it would have been our baby."

"A baby with no father? You'd just let her rear it on her own?"

"That's not what I meant."

"What did you mean?"

"I figured we'd get married," he said.

"You have a flop in the hay, then suddenly you want to be a father and a married man? Who you kidding, Lucas?"

"I told you the truth," Lucas said.

"I don't believe you."

"I wouldn't let no kid of mine grow up without a last name. I don't care what you believe."

"Why all this moral righteousness about fatherhood? It's a little hard for me to swallow."

"Your honor—" Marvin said.

But the judge made a placating gesture with her hand and didn't take her eyes off my face.

"'Cause I know what it's like," Lucas said.

"To be like what? You're not making sense."

"Not to have a father." His breath was coming hard in his throat now, his cheeks blooming with color.

"Vernon Smothers is not your father?"

Lucas's shoulders were bent, his head tilted sideways, his eyes pink with broken veins, glimmering with water, riveted on mine.

"My real father never give me his damn name. You know what I'm talking about, too," he said.

"Your honor, I object," Marvin said.

"Mr. Holland—" the judge said.

"Who is your father?"

"I ain't got one."

"Say his name."

"You are! Except you'd never admit it! 'Cause you slept with my mother and let somebody pick up after you. That's what you done. You think I'd do that to my own kid?"

Then he started to cry, his face in his hands, his back shaking.

Judge Judy Bonham leaned her chin on her hand and let out her breath.

"Take your client down from the stand, Mr. Holland, then report to my chambers," she said.

Marvin leaned back in his chair, flipped a pencil in the air, and watched it roll off the table onto the floor.

CHAPTER

33

It went to the jury late that afternoon. I stood at my office window and looked out at the square, at the trusties from the jail scraping mud out of the gutters, the scrolled neon on the Rialto theater, the trees puffing with wind on the courthouse lawn, all in their proper place, the presummer golden light of the late sun on the clock's face, as though the events of the last few days had no significance and had ended with a whisper.

Then Darl Vanzandt came out of a side street on a chopped-down chromed Harley motorcycle, wearing shades and bat-wing chaps, his truncated body stretching back on his arms each time he gunned a dirty blast of air through his exhaust pipe.

He drove around and around the square, mindlessly, with no apparent purpose, causing pedestrians to step back on the curb, his metal-sheathed heel scotching the pavement when he cornered his bike, his straight exhaust echoing off the buildings like an insult.

Then he turned into the shade of a narrow street and opened up the throttle, his tan shoulders swelling with blood and power, blowing newspapers and a cluster of Mexican children out of his path.

The phone rang on my desk.

"We'll probably fly in there this weekend. You going to be around?" the voice said.

"Mary Beth?"

"I'm in Houston with a task force. Brian is out of the picture. We're about to pull the string on some individuals in your area."

"Let me know what I can do."

"I don't think you quite understand, Billy Bob. The greaseball drug agent, Felix Ringo? He's gone apeshit. We get the impression you put some glass in Garland Moon's breakfast food."

"So what?"

"So Ringo is part of a bigger story than the town of Deaf Smith."

"Bad guy to break bread with."

"Yeah? Well, as FDR once said of Somoza, 'He might be a sonofabitch, but he's *our* sonofabitch.'"

"I never found a lot of humor in that story."

"No, you wouldn't."

I waited for her to say something else but she didn't. "Why'd you call?" I asked.

"I don't know, Billy Bob. I really don't."

I heard her lower the receiver into the cradle. I took the phone away from my ear and then put it to my ear again, the dial tone buzzing against my skin, as though somehow that would restore the connection. I stared at the shadows on the courthouse tower; they had the deep purple hue of a stone bruise, the kind that goes through the muscle into the bone.

I went home and cooked a steak in the backyard. I ate on the back porch, then sat at my desk in the library with Great-grandpa Sam's journal opened under the desk lamp and tried to read. L.Q. Navarro sat in the burgundy chair in the corner, twirling his gold pocket watch on its chain.

"Don't think too harsh of her. Working for the G and falling in love with a guy like you probably ain't a good combo," he said.

"Not tonight, L.Q."

"Stonewall Judy might have give you the riot act, but you could tell she admired what you done. I like when she said, 'Get your star back, Billy Bob, or stay out of my court.' That's the kind of female I can relate to."

"I'm trying to concentrate."

"You got to turn loose of what's fretting you. You and I both know what that is, too."

"I mean it, L.Q. Stop it."

"You cain't be sure that Mexican is the right fellow."

"I see his face in the gun flashes. You broke your knife blade off in his kidney."

"So you gonna bust a cap on him and always wonder if you killed the right man? Ain't you had enough grief over that stuff down in Coahuila?"

I picked up Sam's journal and turned on the light in the kitchen and read at the breakfast table. I heard L.Q.'s spurs tinkling behind me, then it was quiet a moment and their sound disappeared down the front hall into a gust of wind that pushed open the screen door and let it fall back against the jamb.

September 3, 1891

I washed my jeans, my blue cotton shirt, my socks and underwear in a big cook pot and dried them on a warm rock the evening before I was to ride out. Then I packed my saddle bags with my Bible, spectacles, word dictionary, almanac, razor, soap, and a box of Winchester rounds, and rolled a blanket inside my slicker. The Rose of Cimarron seen all this but said nary a word. I don't know as she was hurt or if she did not give a damn. Tell me if there's a louder silence than that of a woman.

I lay down in the dark and thought she would come to my side. But she walked down the hillock with a pout on her face to the mud caves, to join in the drunken frolic of her relatives I reckoned, and I knew I had commenced the most lonely night of my life. Outside the window I could see trees of lightning busting all over the sky. In my sleep I thought I heard thousands of cows lowing at the smell of rain, then going from hell to breakfast over a bluff that didn't have no bottom.

The morning broke cold and mean out of

the north. You could see hail bouncing on the hardpan and big clouds swirling and getting darker all the time, like a twister was kicking up dust and fanning it out across a black sky. Jennie had not come back from the mud caves. I cooked my breakfast on the woodstove and fried some salted pork and put it and three smoked prairie chickens in my saddle bags. I put on my slouch hat, my vest and cotton shirt, my chaps that has turned black from animal grease and wood smoke, and hung my Navy revolvers from my pommel and pulled my Winchester '73 from its scabbard and rode down the hillock through the dead campfires and litter and venison racks of the subhumans that calls themselves the Dalton-Doolin gang.

The burlap sacks that was hung across the cave entrances was weighted down with rocks to keep the wind out. My horse clattered across some tin plates and tipped over a cook's tripod and iron kettle and pushed over a table loaded with preserve jars. But not a soul stirred up in the caves where my Jennie slept. I looped my lariat and tossed it over a venison rack and drug it through the firepit and kicked down a lean-to with a drunk man in it and dropped the gate on the hog pen and stove out the bottom of a boat that was tied in the bulrushes.

But it was for naught. Jennie did not come out of the caves. Instead, one of the Doolin party did, this fellow with a beard like black grease paint and a head the shape of a watermelon. He was barefoot and in long red underdrawers with a bottle of whiskey in one hand and a pepperbox pistol in the other. I laid one across his cheek with my Winchester barrel and left him sitting in the mud like a man just discovered he had mumps.

But my behavior was that of a child. My Jennie was gone, just like my reckless youth.

I forded the Cimarron and rode north in the storm. I was a drover and meat hunter on the high plains after the War, but I never saw the like of this storm. The tumble brush was like the Lord's crown of thorns dashed in the face. I could actually hear the dust clouds grinding across the hardpan, the way a locomotive sounds when the wheels screech on the grade. Up ahead the sleet was white all the way across the crest of the hills, and I knew me and my poor horse was in for a mighty hard day.

I didn't turn in the saddle when I heard hooves coming behind me, supposing it was just hail beating on my hat. Then I seen her pouring it on her buckskin, bent low over the withers the way a savage rides so he can shoot under the horse's neck, her dress hitched plumb over her thighs.

I don't know how to explain it, but whenever I saw that woman ride a horse a banjo seemed to start ringing in my lower parts.

Hailstones and wind and flying brush could not diminish the beauty of the Cimarron Rose. Her smile was as beautiful as a flower opening in the morning and my heart fairly soared in my breast. Tied to her pommel was the fattest carpet bag you ever seen.

Are you looking for company? she asked.

I surely am, I said.

Then I would dearly like to ride along with you.

You was all packed and never told me? That's a mean trick to play on me, Jennie.

This bag here? No, this here is money that's twice stole. They ain't coming for it, though. I turned their horses out.

I beg your pardon? I said.

My relatives has robbed Pearl Younger's whorehouse and the Chinaman's opium den in Fort Smith. You reckon this is enough to build a church?

Good Lord, woman, you don't build church houses with money from a robbery.

I could see I had hurt her feelings again.

I can't preach nowhere cause I got a warrant on me, anyway, I said.

They say there ain't no God or law west of the Pecos.

We rode on like that, the wind plumb near blowing us out of the saddle. We stopped in a brush arbor, just like the one I got ordained in, and I put my slicker on Jennie and tied my hat down on my head with a scarf and built us a fire.

I bet there ain't no preacher like you on the Pecos, she said.

Just gunmen and drunkards, Jennie.

My mother says under the skin of every drunkard there's a good Baptist hiding somewhere.

Now, what do you answer to a statement like that?

Then she says, I bet the devil don't hate nothing worse than seeing his own money used against him.

I unrolled my blanket and covered our heads with it and put my arms inside her slicker, her face rubbing like a child's on my chest. I could feel her joined to me the way married folks is supposed to be and I knowed I didn't have to fight no more with all the voices and angry men that has lived inside me, and I saw the hailstones dancing in the fire and they was whiter than any snow, more pure than any words, and I heard the voice say Forgiven and I did not have to ask Who had spoken it.

The bailiff called from the courthouse. The jury was back in.

CHAPTER

34

It wasn't a dramatic moment. It was a Friday night and the jury had asked the judge they be allowed to deliberate that evening, which meant they had no plans to return Saturday or Monday morning. The courtroom was almost deserted, the shadows of the oscillating fans shifting back and forth across the empty seats, the sounds of the late spring filtering through the high windows, as though the theater in our lives had already moved on and made spectators of us again.

Except for Lucas when the jury foreman read the verdict of not guilty. He shook hands with the jurors, the judge, with me and Vernon and Temple, with the bailiff, with the custodian mopping the hallway, with a soldier smoking a cigarette on the courthouse steps.

"That's it? There ain't no way it can be refiled, huh?" he said.

"That's it, bud," I said.

His face was pink in the waving shadows of the trees. I could see words in his eyes, almost hear them in his throat. But Vernon stood next to him and whatever he wanted to say stayed caught in his face, like thoughts that wanted to eat their way out of his skin.

"Good night," I said, and walked with Temple toward my car.

"Hold on. How much is the bill on all this?" Vernon said.

"There isn't one."

"I ain't gonna take charity."

"Well, I won't have you unhappy, Vernon. I'll send you the biggest bill I can."

"Somebody's making obscene phone calls in the middle of the night. I think it's that little shit Darl Vanzandt."

"Don't you or Lucas go near that kid."

"What's Lucas supposed to do, live in a plastic bubble?...Hold on. I ain't finished. What you said when Lucas was on the stand, I mean, what you done to yourself to get him off, well...I guess it speaks for itself."

His face looked flat, his hands awkward at his sides.

"Good night, Vernon."

"Good night," he said.

Pete came by early the next morning to go fishing in the tank. He was barefoot and wore a straw hat with a big St. Louis Cardinals pin on it and a pair of faded jeans with dark blue iron-on patches on the knees.

"The water's pretty high after all that rain," I said.

"What's a fish care long as you drop the worm in front of him?"

"You surely are smart."

"I always know when you're gonna say something like that, Billy Bob. It don't do you no good." He grinned at me, then looked out confidently at the world.

We picked up our cane poles in the barn and walked past the windmill down to the tank. The sun was soft and yellow on the horizon and patches of fog still hung on the water's surface. A bass flopped inside the flooded willows on the far bank, and a solitary moccasin swam across the center of the tank, its body coiling and uncoiling behind its triangular head. Pete trapped a grasshopper under his hat and threaded it on his hook, then swung his line and bobber out past the lily pads.

"There's a lady knocking on your back door, Billy Bob," he said.

I turned and looked toward the house. She wore a white skirt and blouse and a wide hat with flowers on it, and even at a distance I could almost feel the electricity in her movements, the anger in her balled fist as she continued, unrelentingly, to knock on the screen door.

"Is it that government lady who used to come out?" Pete asked.

"No, I'm afraid it's a walking neurosis by the name of Emma Vanzandt."

He mouthed the words *walking neurosis* to himself.

Then Emma saw me and got in her car and drove around the barn and out to the tank. She stepped out of the car and stood at the bottom of the levee, her ankles and knees close together, her face strangely composed, like that of a person who lives with ferocious energies that she can call upon whenever necessary.

"I wanted to say something to you at your home, so you'd know my words weren't spoken to you as a result of a chance encounter," she said.

"I've never underestimated your sense of purpose, Emma."

"You've ruined my marriage and destroyed our family. I don't blame you for wanting to get your son off, but at heart you're a voyeur with the instincts of a garbage rat. The fact that we've had you in our home fills me with a level of disgust that's hard to express."

"How about the dues other people have paid for you, Emma? Lucas and Roseanne Hazlitt and Bunny Vogel? Don't their lives mean anything?"

"Bunny Vogel is an overall-and-denim gigolo. I never met your son. And I gave

Roseanne Hazlitt a job in our church's store. Does that answer your question?"

"Jack was in business with Sammy Mace. Y'all are friends of Felix Ringo. Why don't you check out this guy's record? I heard him tell a story about wiring up somebody to a telephone crank."

"I have nothing else to say to you, sir. You're an ill-bred, disingenuous, violent man. You live in the West End where you can pretend you're otherwise. I just feel sorry for those who are taken in by you."

Her eyes lingered on Pete with a look of both pity and disdain.

Then she got in her car and realized she had removed the keys from the ignition and had placed them either on the seat or the dashboard. She stuck her fingers down the cracks in the seat, searched along the back floor, felt over the top of the dashboard, stirred through the coins and litter inside the pocket of the console. Her fingers started to tremble and lines appeared in the caked makeup on her brow like string in wet clay and her breath speckled her lips with saliva.

I picked up the keys off the ground and handed them to her through the window.

"Garland Moon's off his chain. If y'all sicked him on Bunny or me through Felix Ringo, you'd better hire some private security," I said.

She was hunched over the wheel, twisting the key in the ignition, her eyes manic with rage and humiliation.

"I'm going to have the skin peeled off your body in strips," she said.

She dropped the car in reverse, knocked me aside with the open door, and gouged a huge divot out of the levee with the back bumper. Then she corrected the front wheels and pressed the accelerator to the floor and scoured mud and shredded grass into a green balloon behind her car.

I walked down the levee with my pole and stood above a cluster of lily pads and bounced a worm up and down on the bottom, my scalp tightening with the tangle of thoughts in my head.

"That lady didn't have the right to say them kind of things to you," Pete said.

"When you're a cop, or sometimes a lawyer, you serve up people's lives on a dung fork, Pete. They usually deserve it, but it's never a good moment."

"I wouldn't pay that lady no mind. You're the best friend I ever had, Billy Bob."

"That man who came by y'all's house and looked in your mom's window?"

The expression went out of his face, as though he had remembered a bad dream that should not have been part of the waking day.

"I gave him a beating, then turned him loose on somebody else. Maybe on that woman who just left," I said.

Pete looked at me, then averted his eyes. His mouth was parted, his cheeks gray.

"You done that?" he said.

The Conquistador Apartments were built of white stucco and blue tile on the highway that led to San Antonio. The gardens around the pool and the outside wall were overlaid with gravel and planted with Spanish daggers, cactus, crown of thorn bushes, and mimosa trees, which gave it a hot, arid appearance out of context with the surroundings. It was built during the oil boom of the 1970s, and the people who stayed there seemed to have no geographical origins. They wore lizard-skin boots, vinyl vests, turquoise jewelry, hand-tooled belts, and cowboy hats with a feather in the band, as though they had stopped at a roadside souvenir shop outside Phoenix and taken on a new identity. They could have been drug traffickers or owners of fast-food chains. The swimming pool was always iridescent with a residue of suntan lotion and hair gel.

I used the building directory to find Felix Ringo's apartment, which was located off an arched flagstone walkway. No one answered the bell and I could hear no movement inside. I slipped a screwdriver in the jamb, pried the bolt out of the wood, pushing it back into the lock's mechanism, then threw my shoulder into the door and snapped it free.

The apartment was furnished with heavy, hand-carved oak chairs and tables and cabinets, the windows covered with blue velvet drapes, the thermostat set below sixty degrees. Even when I turned on the lights the rooms seemed dark, the cracks around the curtains as bright as tin. An acrylic painting of a picador with his lance embedded in the pack of muscle behind a bull's neck hung over the water bed. In the drawer of the nightstand were a .25-caliber automatic, four boxes of condoms, a velvet rope, a jar of Vaseline, and a spring-loaded, leather-encased blackjack that was shaped like a darning sock.

I told myself I had broken into a man's apartment to see justice done, perhaps even to see Felix Ringo in custody so he would not become the victim of Garland T. Moon. But that was not the reason. Even inside the refrigerated gloom of the apartment, I could still see the muzzle flashes of guns blooming in the darkness down in Coahuila, hear the labored breathing of L.Q. Navarro's wounded horse, see L.Q. stirrup-dragged across the rocks and cactus.

Men like Felix Ringo did the jobs for the forces of Empire that no government ever acknowledged. They went to special schools and carried badges and were endowed with marginal respectability, but their real credentials lay in their bottomless cruelty. And no matter what explanations they offered others for their behavior, each of them daily fed his perversity like a gardener tending a hothouse filled with poisonous flowers.

Political assassins always kept journals; sadists kept trophies, and they never strayed far from them.

I found the box at the bottom of a desk

drawer. It was made of sandalwood, fitted with gold hinges and hasps, fastened with a soft bungee cord. A wood tray divided into compartments was inset in the top of the box. It contained military decorations, a sergeant's chevrons, gold teeth, polished finger bones, empty shell casings, a switchblade knife with a green serpent inlaid in the handle, a long strip of black hair wrapped inside a plastic bag.

Under the wood tray was a thick pack of pornographic photos held together with a rubber band. They were yellow with age, mounted on cardboard, and featured Orientals involved in every possible sexual act and position. But it was not these that shocked or sickened the sensibilities. The bottom of the box was layered with Polaroid color photos that made the eye film, the hand vaguely soiled at the touch: a freshly dug pit in front of which four peasant men and a woman stood bound and blindfolded; a man on his knees with his thumbs tied behind him, a disembodied arm pointing a pistol behind his ear; a man with a pesticide sack over his head, hung by his arms between two stone walls; grinning enlisted men posing at the end of a dirt street littered with bodies that had started to bloat; a woman strapped in a chair, her face and shirtless upper torso streaked with blood.

At the bottom of all these photos was a playing card emblazoned with the badge of the Texas Rangers. Written in felt pen across the badge was the word *Muerto* and the date I accidentally killed L.Q. Navarro.

When I got back home Lucas Smothers was sitting on the steps of my front porch, twisting the tuning pegs on a mandolin, *tinking* each string with a plectrum. He wore a pair of starched khakis and cowboy boots and a short-sleeve denim shirt rolled above his triceps. His reddish blond hair was combed into faint ducktails on the back of his head. It was cool where he sat in the shade, and he drank out of a soda can and smiled at me.

"I got a bluegrass gig at a club over in Llano County. My dad didn't say nothing about it, either," he said.

"Go to college," I said.

"So I can be like them rich pukes out in East End?"

"Come in the house. I have to use the phone."

Inside the library, he looked at the titles of books on my shelves while I punched in Marvin Pomroy's home number on the phone.

"Marvin?" I said.

"Oh gee," he said when he recognized my voice.

"Felix Ringo isn't taking Moon down on a Mexican warrant. He's taking him off the board," I said.

"What gives you this special insight?"

"Does it figure Ringo's going to bust a guy who can testify against him?"

"Ringo's a cop. Moon's a nut case."

"I just creeped Ringo's place at the Conquistador. He was a dope mule down in Coahuila."

"Say again? You did what?"

"My partner and I capped some of those guys, Marvin. His name was L.Q. Navarro. He put a playing card in the mouth of every dead mule we left down there. Ringo has one of those cards in a sandalwood box filled with his trophies. He wrote the date of my friend's death on it."

"You're telling *me,* the district attorney, you broke into a policeman's apartment?"

"Ask Ringo to show you his Polaroid collection of life down in the tropics."

"Let this go, Billy Bob."

"Moon killed my father."

He repeated my statement back to me incredulously. When I didn't reply, he said, "Do you realize what you just told me? If this guy shows up dead..."

"Get a life, Marvin," I said, and eased the phone receiver down in the cradle.

Lucas stood at the bookshelves, Great-grandpa Sam's journal spread in his hands, his mouth open.

"What's up, bud?" I said.

He blinked, then closed the journal.

"Moon killed your dad?" he asked.

"Yeah, I guess he did."

"What are you gonna do about it?"

"That journal was kept by my great-grandfather. He was a drunkard and a gunfighter who became a saddle preacher on the Chisholm Trail. It took him a long time, but he learned how to put aside his violent ways."

"What happens when the other guy don't put aside his?"

"You talking about Moon or Darl Van-zandt?"

"I seen Darl out at the drive-in this morning. He was melting screamers in dago red. He said I was yellow. He said he's gonna pop me in the face every time he sees me."

"He'll crash and burn, Lucas. He's a pitiful person."

"You told Marvin Pomroy you capped some dope mules."

"So I'm a bad example."

"No, you ain't. You're a good man. And that's why I come here, just to tell you that. I'm proud we're...Well, I'm proud, that's all. I'll see you, Billy Bob."

He went down the front hall and out the door to his pickup. Through the screen I could see shadows on the hillside and wildflowers rippling and bending and straightening in the wind, like colored confetti flickering in a world that had almost gone gray.

CHAPTER

35

That afternoon I drove to the welding shop where Moon worked. It was padlocked, and the owner of the motel next door, where Moon kept a room, said he had not seen him in two days.

I went home and worked in the yard and tried to think my way out of an impossible situation.

Great-grandpa Sam, at age fifty-six, had prevailed against the Dalton-Doolin gang but had kept faith with his ordination and had not taken human life. *I* had manipulated a psychopath, perhaps putting the Vanzandts at risk as well as Felix Ringo. Intellectually I regretted what I had done, but secretly I still lusted for revenge and my wrists swelled with blood and my calluses rasped against the grain of the mattock when I thudded it into the roots of a willow that had threaded themselves into my water well.

I sat in the grass on the riverbank and watched the current riffle across the top of a submerged cottonwood. Directly below me, lost in the murk and high water, was the sunken automobile where two members of the Karpis-Barker gang had died. Garland T. Moon had waded through this water and fished here, wearing a suit, flinging a hook full of bloody melt into the current that flowed through the car's empty windows.

Why this particular spot, I wondered. Did he know the sunken car was there, that it was a nest for shovel-mouth catfish, that bass hung under the bluffs and fed on the insects that fell from the grove of trees upstream?

My father probably took him fishing here, walked these same banks with him as he did with me in later years, a sack of bread-and-butter sandwiches swinging from his big hand.

Moon had tried to extort ten acres from me on the back of my property. What were his words? *I want the place should have been mine.*

At least part of it. Was that it, I thought. Maybe I had been wrong, he hadn't returned to Deaf Smith simply for revenge. Somehow he had convinced himself he was owed part of my father's estate. He had also gone to Jack Vanzandt, perhaps a surrogate for my father, walking into the middle of his golf game, as though somehow the door to wealth and acceptance in Deaf Smith society would open for him if he could only turn the right handle.

Now he had disappeared. Where would a man dying of cancer, beaten with a maul handle, and hunted by a sadist go in a county that had been the origin of his travail and the denier of what he believed was his inheritance?

What places was he even familiar with? Perhaps just the motel room with water bed and X-rated cable he lived in, the old county prison where he had been sodomized by two roadbulls, the tin welding shed that was like stepping into the devil's forge, the wide, green sweep of the river below the bluffs at the back of my property.

And the Hart Ranch, where he had seen lights in the clouds he associated with UFOs.

I went back to the house, wrapped the belt around L.Q.'s holstered .45 revolver, and set it on the seat next to me in the Avalon.

But I didn't get far. Bunny Vogel pulled his '55 Chevy into my drive and got out with a sheet of lined notebook paper gripped in his hand. His Mexican girlfriend sat in the passenger's seat.

"What's wrong, Bunny?" I said.

391

"I went to Lucas's house. To tell him I'm sorry for my part in that cow-flop stuff out at the country club. There wasn't nobody home. That Indian motorcycle was gone, too. I found this note wadded up on the porch."

I smoothed it out on Bunny's hood. The handwriting, in pencil, was like a child's.

Lucas,
We got a new name for you. Its Baby Shit. In case you dont know, baby shit is yellow. You got everybody to feel sorry for you at the trial because you dont have parents. You know what the truth is? You dont have parents because nobody ever wanted you. Baby shit gets wiped off. It doesnt get raised.

I gave you my collectors bike and you snitched me off. I thought you could hang out with us but you couldnt cut the initiation at the country club. You got one way out of your problem, Baby Shit. Maybe you can prove your not a spineless cunt. Bring my bike out to the Rim Rocks at 6. Ill be there by myself because I dont have to run to my old man to square a beef.

You thought Roseanne was a good girl? She was good, all right. Down past the part you couldnt get to.

It was unsigned.
"The Rim Rocks?" I said.
"There's a dirt road in the woods at the top of the cliffs, about two miles upriver from the Hart Ranch," Bunny said.

"The steel cable," I said.

"The what?" he asked, his head tilted peculiarly in the wind, as though the air held a secret that had eluded him.

I pulled into the drive of the Vanzandts' home. Bunny and his girlfriend parked by the curb and did not get out of their car. The sun had dipped behind the house, and the pine trees in the front yard were edged with fire, the trunks deep in shadow. Far up the slope, sitting in deck chairs on their wide, breezy front porch, were Jack and Emma, a drink tray set between them.

So that's how they would handle it, I thought. With booze and pills and assignment of blame to others. Why not? They lived in a world where use was a way of life and money and morality were synonymous. Perhaps they believed the burden of their son's errant ways absolved them of their own sins, or that indeed they had been made the scapegoats of the slothful and inept whose plight it was to loathe and envy the rich.

Jack rose from his chair as I approached the porch. He wore a canary-yellow sports shirt and white slacks and a western belt and polished cowboy boots, and his face looked as composed as that of a defeated warrior to whom victory was denied by only chance and accident.

"I'd invite you for a drink, Billy Bob, but I suspect you're here for other reasons," he said.

393

Emma lit a cigarette with a gold lighter and smoked it as though I were not there, her red nails clicking slowly on the arm of the chair.

"Is Darl around?" I asked.

"No, he went to a show with friends," Jack said.

"This morning he was melting screamers in red wine. But tonight he's eating popcorn at the theater?" I said.

"What in God's name are you talking about now?" Emma said.

"Screamers, leapers, uppers, black beauties, whatever you want to call them. They tie serious knots in people's brains," I said.

"Maybe you'd better leave," Jack said.

I handed him the note Darl had left on Lucas's porch. He straightened it between his hands and read, his feet spread slightly, pointed outward, like a man on a ship.

"This isn't even signed," he said. But his voice faltered.

"Why would your boy buy twenty feet of steel cable at a building supply, Jack?" I asked.

"Cable?" he said.

"With U-bolts," I said.

He kneaded the sheet of paper with one hand into a ball and dropped it on the drink table. It bounced and rolled onto the floor.

"I'll be back," he said to his wife.

"Jack...," she said. Then she said it again, to his back, as he walked around the side of his house to his four-wheel-drive Cherokee.

I bent over and picked up Darl's note and put it in my pocket. I thought Emma would say something else. But she didn't. She simply propped her elbow on the arm of the chair and rested her forehead on her fingers, the smoke from her cigarette curling out of the ashtray into her hair.

I walked back down the drive in the cooling shadows to Bunny's car. At the end of the block, the taillights of Jack's Cherokee turned the corner and disappeared up a winding street whose high-banked, blue-green lawns hissed with sprinkler systems.

"Can you take me to the Rim Rocks?" I said to Bunny through his window.

He didn't reply. Instead, he was looking at something through the front windshield. He opened the door and stepped out on the pavement.

"I think that boy done growed up on us," he said.

Lucas and Vernon Smothers slowed their pickup truck to the curb. They were both eating fried chicken out of a plastic bucket. They got out and walked to the back of the truck. Lucas dropped the tailgate and slid a plank down to the pavement to offload the Indian motorcycle, which was held erect in the truck bed with four crisscrossed lengths of bungee cord. He kept looking at us, waiting for one of us to speak.

"Hi, what cha y'all doing *here?*" he said.

What follows is put together from accounts given me by Marvin Pomroy, a sheriff's deputy, and a seventeen-year-old West End girl who had not guessed that a late-spring evening high above a lazy river could prove to be the worst memory of her life.

The wind was cool on the outcrop of rocks above the gorge, the evening star bright in the west, the air scented with pine needles, wood smoke from the campfire, the cold odor of water flowing over stone at the base of the cliffs.

Earlier, the others had been worried about Darl. Speed took his metabolism to strange places. His face had popped a sweat for no reason, then it had run like string out of his hair while he sucked air through his mouth as though his tongue had been burned. He peeled off his shirt and sat on a rock, his hand pressed to his heart, a blue-collar girl from the West End named Sandy mopping his skin dry.

He toked on a joint sprinkled with China white and held the hit in his lungs, one time, twice, three, four times, until his eyes blinked clear and the angle iron twisting in his rib cage seemed to dissolve like licorice on a stove.

He snapped the cap off a beer and drank it in front of the fire, bare chested, the leggings of his butterfly chaps molded against his thighs like black tallow.

His face was serene now. His mouth seemed to taste the wind, the blue-black density of the sky, the moon that rose out of the trees.

"This is the way it's supposed to be, ain't it? We're up here and everybody else is down there. It's like a poem I read. About Greeks who lived above the clouds," he said. "Know what I mean?"

The others, who sat on motorcycles or logs or on the ground, stoned-out, euphoric in the firelight, their skin singing with the heat of the day and the alcohol and dope in their veins, toked and huffed on joints and nodded and smiled and let the foam from their beer bottles slide down their throats.

"What about you, Sandy? You read that poem?" he said to the West End girl, who sat on an inverted bucket by his foot.

"I wasn't too good in English," she said, and raised the corner of her lip in a way that was meant to be both self-deprecating and coy.

He twitched his metal-sheathed boot sideways, so it tapped hard into her bare ankle.

"Then you should read this poem. Because it's a great fucking poem," he said.

"Yeah, sure, Darl."

"What makes you think you got to agree with me? You haven't even read it. That's an insult. It's like you're saying..." He paused, as though on the edge of a profound thought. "It's like you're saying I need you to agree with me, or otherwise I'm gonna be all broken up 'cause my ideas are a pile of shit or something."

"I didn't mean that, Darl."

Her eyes looked into the dark. He stepped closer to her so his chaps intruded on the edge of her vision. His beer bottle hung loosely from his hand. The orange hair on his wrist glowed against the fire.

"What *did* you mean, Sandy?" he asked.

"Nothing. It's just real neat out here. The wind's getting cool, though." She hugged herself, feigning a shiver.

"You ever pull a train, Sandy?" he asked.

The blood went out of her face.

"Don't worry. I was just seeing if you were paying attention," he said, then leaned over and carefully spit on the top of her head.

Jack Vanzandt had found the access road to the Rim Rocks at the bottom of the hill. He shifted down and ground his way up the slope, through woods that yielded no moon or starlight, bouncing through potholes that exploded with rainwater, shattering dead tree limbs against his oil pan. Gray clouds of gnats and mosquitoes hung in his headlights. In the distance he thought he heard the flat, dirty whine of a trail bike, then the roar of a Harley. But he couldn't tell. The camping equipment in his Cherokee caromed off the walls; the glove box popped open and rattled the contents out on the floor; a rotten tree stump in the middle of the road burst like cork against his grill.

Then he reached a fork, with a sawhorse set in his path. He stopped the Cherokee and moved the sawhorse to the other side of the fork and went on. He looked in the rearview mirror at the divide in the road and at the reflection of his taillights on the barrier and was disturbed in a way he couldn't quite explain, like cobweb clinging briefly to the side of the face.

Then the trees began to thin and the road came out on the hill's rim, and he could see the moonlight on the river below and the piled wood burning on a sandy shelf of rock, one that protruded out into nothingness, and Darl's silhouette against the flames and the gleaming chrome and waxed surfaces of his friends' motorcycles.

Jack strained his eyes through the mud and water streaked on his windshield and the shadows his brights threw on the clearing. He did not see Lucas Smothers among the faces that looked like they had been caught in a searchlight, and he let out his breath and felt the tension go out of his palms and he wiped them one at a time on the legs of his slacks.

Then he realized they did not know who he was.

"If you're dirty, kitties, now's the time to lose it," he heard his son yell.

Bags of reefer and pills showered out into the darkness, sprinkling the water far below.

Darl Vanzandt swung his leg over his Harley, started the engine, his face shuttering with a familiar ecstasy as he twisted the gas feed forward and the engine's power climbed through his thighs and loins.

He cornered his bike on the far side of the fire, his boot biting into the dirt, then righted the bike's frame and roared down the road that Jack had just emerged from, his face turned into the shadows to avoid recognition.

His tire tracks showed he never hesitated when he hit the fork in the road, leaping potholes, occasionally touching the soft earth with his boot, his path marked by the strip of starry sky overhead, the province of gods who lived above the clouds, rather than the narrow, eroded track sweltering with heat and filmed with gnats between the trees.

The night had gone down bad, but he didn't doubt the wisdom of the plan he had conceived that morning, when he drank wine laced with speed out of a stone beer mug, nor did he doubt his partial execution of it. It was still a good plan, one he could pull off later, when that punk Lucas Smothers mustered enough guts to run a chicken race along the unbarricaded road that led back to the cliff's edge. Just let Lucas get in the lead and take the road that was open while he, Darl, swerved around the barricade and found his way to the bottom of the hill, safe and removed from whatever might happen when Lucas Smothers discovered the cost of jerking on the wrong guy's stick.

Or maybe he thought none of these things. Maybe he was simply intrigued with the frenetic bouncing of his headlight on the pines, the latent sexual power girded between his chaps, the way reefer wrapped a soft gauze around the uppers surging in his veins, as though his skin was a border between his universe and the one other people lived in.

Darl swerved around the barrier his father had moved, opened up the Harley, the back

400

wheel ripping a trench through the earth, and plowed into the steel cable that was stretched neck-high between two pine trunks.

His bike spun away into the trees, the engine roaring impotently against the ground.

The cable was thinner in diameter than a pencil, and Darl had tightened each end until the steel loops had bitten so deeply into the pine bark that the cable looked like it grew horizontally out of the trunks.

He died on his back, the headlight of his Harley shining across his face. His mouth was open, as though he wanted to speak, but the cable's incision had cut his windpipe as well as his jugular. When his father found him, three misshapen, emaciated dogs with spots like hyenas were licking Darl's chest, and Jack had to drive them from his son's body with a stick. The medical examiner later said the dogs were rabid. He refused to answer when a reporter asked if the dogs had found Darl before the time of death.

CHAPTER

36

But when I drove down the rutted road to the Hart Ranch that same night I knew of none of the events I just described.

The gate that gave onto the ranch was open, the padlocked chain snapped by bolt cutters. I turned off my headlights and drove the

Avalon across the cattle guard, parked in a grove of mesquite, and slipped L.Q.'s revolver from its holster. Then I pulled six extra rounds from the leather cartridge loops on the belt and dropped them in my pocket and stepped out into the darkness. The revolver felt heavy and cold and strange in my hand.

The moon was above the hills, and I could see deer grazing in the glade between the woods and the river, and in the distance the roofless Victorian home that had been gutted by fire and the log and slat outbuildings and rusted windmill in back, wrapped with tumbleweed.

The edges of the house were silhouetted by a white light that glowed in the backyard. I moved along the perimeter of the woods, spooking coveys of quail into the darkness. The grass was almost waist high from the rain, and a set of car tracks stretched through the glade and ended where a 1970s gas-guzzler was parked in the shadows. A second set of car tracks, fresher ones, the grass pressed flat and pale-sided into the wet sod, led past the parked car to the back of the house.

I walked between the woods and parked car and looked through the car window. In the moonlight I could see the ignition wires hanging below the dashboard. From behind the house I heard a metallic, screeching sound like a board with rusted nails in it being pried loose from a joist.

I walked to the right of the house, through a side yard that was strewn with plaster and broken laths that looked like they had been ripped from the interior walls and thrown outside. A Coleman lantern as bright as a phosphorous flare hissed on the ground in the center of the backyard. Farther on, a blue van was parked by a barn with a tractor shed built onto one side, and through a dirty window in the shed a second lantern burned inside and the shadows of at least two men moved back and forth across it.

I crossed the yard, outside the perimeter of light. My foot went out into a pool of shadow, where there should have been level ground, but instead I stepped into a hole at least a foot deep, my ankle twisting sideways inside my boot, a pain as bright as the sting of a jellyfish wrapping around the tendons in my lower back.

The shadows beyond the window froze against the light.

Then I thought I heard L.Q. Navarro's voice say, *"The dice are out of the cup. Make 'em religious, bud."*

I limped forward and flung the door back on its hinges and pointed L.Q.'s revolver into the room.

Felix Ringo and a second man stood just beyond a worktable where Garland T. Moon was wrapped fast against the wood planks with chains that were clamped and boomed down on his chest and thighs. Moon's face was turned away from me, as though he were napping. The clothes of Ringo and the second man were streaked with soot and bits of hay and dried horse manure. Behind them, the flooring in the barn had been ripped up, the plaster board gouged out of a bunk area, a rusty hot water tank split open with an ax.

The room was hotter than it should have been, filled with a hot smell that at first I thought came from the lantern.

"You don't look too good, man," Ringo said.

I could feel the muscles constrict across my back, just like someone had taken pliers to my spine. I propped one arm against the doorjamb and held the pistol level with the other. The second man clutched a plastic bag full of credit cards in his hand. He had the scarred eyebrows of a prizefighter and small ears and hair so blond it was almost white.

"Both you boys put your hands behind your head and get down on your knees," I said.

The second man studied my face, his tongue moving across his bottom lip. "Fuck you, buddy," he said, and bolted into the barn, crashing out the door into the yard.

But I didn't fire. Instead, I kept the .45 pointed at Ringo's face, my other hand holding on to the doorjamb for balance. When I took a step forward, the pain caused my jaw to drop open. I heard the van start up outside and drive out of the yard.

"You want to go to a hospital? I can do that for you, man," Ringo said.

I eased my hand onto the worktable, inches from the JOX running shoe on Moon's foot, stiffening my arm for support. An odor like the smell of burned scrapings from a butchered hog rose into my face.

"Last chance, Ringo. Get on the floor," I said.

"You're all mixed up. This is DEA. You don't got no business here."

I pulled back the hammer on the revolver.

"Okay, man. My friend gonna come back with some local law. They gonna jam you up, man," Ringo said, and knelt on the floor and laced his fingers behind his neck. He crinkled his nose, his mustache wiggling on his lip, as though he were about to sneeze.

I worked my way around the other side of the table. Moon's eyes were staring at nothing. The skin of his face looked shrunken on the bone, puckered and red like a rubber Halloween mask. The cloth of his flowered shirt was crisscrossed with scorch marks, and inside the scorch marks were lesions that looked like they had been cut into the skin with a laser.

The blowtorch was turned on its side by the far wall.

"I'll take a guess. Crystal coming in, counterfeit credit cards going out," I said.

"Hey, the *guapa* you was in the sack with? Ask her. This is a federal operation, man. She gonna fuck you again, except this time you ain't gonna enjoy it."

"If y'all were looking for some of your stash, you tortured the wrong guy. It was probably Darl Vanzandt and his friends who ripped you off."

"You want to take me in? That's good,

man. 'Cause I'm gonna be on a plane back to Mexico City tomorrow morning. So let's go do that, man."

"I don't think so."

His eyes studied my shirt front.

"What's that you got in your pocket?" he asked.

"This? It's funny you ask. A friend of mine dropped it down in Coahuila."

A dark and fearful recognition grew in his face, like smoke rising in a glass jar.

I moved toward him, my hand sliding along the table for support. Inches away from my forearm, a viscous tear was glued in the corner of Moon's receded blue eye.

"I bet ole Moon spit in your face," I said.

Felix Ringo rose to his feet and began running toward the back of the barn, his head twisted back toward me. He grabbed onto a stall door and pulled an automatic from an ankle holster and fired three times, the rounds slapping into the front wall, then he began running again. He passed a tack room and flung the plywood door open in his wake, his arms waving almost simultaneously, as though hornets were about to torment his flesh.

I held on to a wood post by a stall and fired one round after another, the powder flashes splintering from the cylinder and the barrel. The explosions were deafening, the recoil knocking my wrist high in the air. Each round blew divots out of the tack room door that yawned open in the passageway, tore even larger holes in the outside door, whined away into the woods with a sound like piano wire snapping.

Dust and lint and smoke drifted in the light from the Coleman lantern. My right ear was numb, as though frigid water had been poured inside it. I put the hammer on half-cock and shucked out the empty shell casings on the floor and rotated the cylinder and inserted six fresh rounds in the loading gate, then lowered the hammer again and locked the cylinder into place.

I limped slowly past the stalls and closed the splintered door of the tack room. Felix Ringo lay on the floor, the slide on his automatic jammed open by a partially ejected shell casing. Blood welled from a wound that looked like a crushed purple rose inserted inside the torn cloth on his hip.

"My friend L.Q. Navarro used to say ankle hideaways are mighty cool, but the problem is they only work for midgets," I said, and sat down heavily on a hay bale that puffed dust and lint into the air.

"I got to have a doctor," Ringo said.

I felt weak all over. Gray threadworms floated in front of my eyes. I touched my upper chest and my hand came away coated with something that was warm and damp and sticky.

"Looks like we both got a problem here, Felix." I breathed slowly and wiped the sweat out of my eyes. From my shirt pocket I pulled the playing card emblazoned with the badge of the Texas Rangers and marked with the date of L.Q.'s death. "You remember the rules down in Coahuila. When you lose, you get one of these stuck in your mouth."

"I'm hurt bad. Look, man, I die here, I gotta have a priest."

"You killed Roseanne Hazlitt, didn't you?"

"Yeah, okay, we done that." He breathed hard through his nose.

"And set up Lucas Smothers?"

"Yeah, that, too."

"All that grief, just to protect Jack Vanzandt."

"There was a lot at stake, things you don't know about, man. Ask the *guapa*, the DEA woman, it's like a war, man, there's casualties. Hey, man, I work for your fucking government. That's what you ain't hearing."

He stared at me for a long time, waiting, his eyes lustrous with hate and apprehension.

"What you gonna do, man?" he said, his voice climbing into a higher register.

"I guess you're just up shit's creek, bud," I replied.

His face was gray from loss of blood, beaded with sweat. He closed his eyes, his mouth trembling.

"No, you got it all wrong, Felix," I said. "L.Q. Navarro used to own this card. I wouldn't soil it by putting it on your body. But you parked one in my chest. So the medics won't be coming for either one of us tonight."

I winked at him and grinned.

Or thought I did. The passageway was slatted with moonlight, redolent with dust and the musky smell of field mice and moldy hay and fresh deer droppings in the barnyard and wind and flowers in the glade and wet fern and creek water coursing over stone. I felt myself slip in and out of time, then the darkness bled out of the sky and a pink light glowed through the holes in the barn's walls and out in the fields I saw a group of federal agents in blue hats and vests walking through the mist, their weapons at port arms, like the emissaries of Empire, a statuesque woman with brown freckles in the lead whose fingers would be as cool and bloodless as alabaster when they touched my brow.

EPILOGUE

Felix Ringo was DOA at the county hospital. I had the feeling the DEA considered his passing his greatest public service. To my knowledge, no investigation into his background was ever made. I tried to tell newspapers in Dallas and Houston about Felix Ringo, then the wire services, and finally anyone who would listen. But the time came when I accepted the fact that societal hearing and sight are a matter of collective consent, and I desisted from trying to undo the cynicism and cruelty of governments and learned to walk away when people spoke of the world as a serious place.

Jack Vanzandt plea-bargained down to

three years in a federal facility. It seemed like a light sentence, at least for a man who had trafficked in crystal meth and counterfeit credit cards and indirectly caused the death of a young woman, until the morning I read in the paper that Jack had taken poison in the psychiatric unit of a federal hospital and had suffered a brain seizure that cost him his eyesight.

Emma divorced him after their home and their assets were confiscated by the government. I heard her stepson's ashes were left behind in an urn on the mantelpiece and she never tried to recover them. Today she runs her parents' mail-order wedding cake business in Shreveport and sometimes appears on a televangelical cable program and denounces drug use among teenagers. I never saw Mary Beth again, at least not when I was fully conscious. After the surgery that removed the .25-caliber round from my chest, I floated for days through a warm pool of morphine and was sure I saw her in the room with L.Q. Navarro. But one morning I woke to sunlight and the realities of physical recovery and spoke both their names repeatedly, my hands as useless as blocks of wood, my face tingling with thousands of needles, until a black male nurse pushed me back on the bed and held me there, his eyes lighted with pity.

On a Friday evening in late summer Temple Carrol and I went to watch Pete play in a ball game at the Catholic elementary school. I had let him ride Beau to the game by himself, and later we walked from the diamond to the café down the street and ate buffalo burgers and blackberry milkshakes. Outside the window, Beau pulled his tether loose and walked into the grove of pines by the stucco church and began grazing in the grass. The attic fan in the café drew the air through the open door and windows, and I could smell the evening coming to its own completion, the dusk gathering in the streets, the water that ebbed out of the irrigation ditch into the grass, the pine boughs etched against the late sun, the hot sap cooling on the bark of the trees.

"That's good about Lucas going to A&M this fall, ain't it?" Pete said.

"It's a fine school," I said.

"Can I ride Beau back by myself tonight?"

"You're the best, Pete," I said.

"He's a mighty good little boy, that's what he is," Temple said, and hugged him against her.

"I'm gonna ride Beau out on the hardpan, where that Chisholm Trail is at," Pete said, and grinned as though he had already begun an extravagant adventure.

Temple's eyes settled on mine, and I looked at the redness of her mouth and wanted to touch her hands.

Outside, I heard Beau's hooves thumping on the earth and I dipped a strip of buffalo steak in catsup that was as thick as blood and for just a moment, in my mind's eye, I saw dust clouds filled with hail swirling across the high plains, and I thought of Comanche Indians and sad-

411

dle preachers and trail drovers and outlaws and was sure that somewhere beyond the rim of the world Great-grandpa Sam and the Rose of Cimarron turned briefly in their saddles and held up their hands in farewell.

If you have enjoyed reading this large print book and you would like more information on how to order a Wheeler Large Print Book, please write to:

 Wheeler Publishing, Inc.
P.O. Box 531
Accord, MA 02018-0531